THE BOOK OF WEBSTER'S

J.N. WILLIAMSON

LONGMEADOW
PRESS

Chapter 12 of this novel originally appeared,
in different form,
as a short story entitled
"The Book of Webster's" in *Night Cry* magazine,
Spring 1986
(TZ Publications, Montcalm Publishing Corporation).

Published by Longmeadow Press,
201 High Ridge Road,
Stamford, CT 06904.

Cover design by Kelvin P. Oden
Interior design by Donna Miller

Library of Congress Cataloging-in-Publication Data

Williamson, J. N. (Jerry N.)
   The book of Webster's / by J.N. Williamson. — 1st ed.
      p.   cm.
   ISBN 0-681-41598-3
   I. Title.
PS3573.I456277B6   1993
813'.54—dc20   92-46747
                                                       CIP

Printed in United States of America
First Edition
0 9 8 7 6 5 4 3 2 1

Dedications can be matters of habit or protocol. A few of mine have been so, yet each has begun by thanking my wife, Mary, so they've all started on a note of sincerity. There's nothing of habit, protocol, or propaganda in the case of *The Book of Webster's*. I dedicate it with my whole heart, soul, and thanks to Mary; John and Joyce Maclay; Joseph Welhoelter, Mary and Scott Hays, John and Debra Williamson, my sister Marylynn, and all their kids; James Kisner; Kay and Kirby McCauley; Lin; Burke; and Ed Gorman; Tom Millstead; the writers I know mostly as Mort, Gary, Lee, Rex, Rick, Matt, Bill, Joe, Ray, Tracy, Alan, and Paul; the editors who kept saying they wanted to buy this book, and Pam, the editor who did. Dedications aren't supposed to run this long. I really don't care. The people I listed I care about with everything that best defines me. God bless.

The novels of J. N. Williamson:

Don't Take Away the Light
The Longest Night
The Black School
Ghost
Playmates
Monastery
The Book of Webster's

Life is driving through traffic.
—John Maclay

Part I

A REAL TRIP

C H A P T E R

1

(A period of time long enough ago for a teenage boy to have matured physically, and for all his early warped beliefs about reality to have hardened into a yen for violence—and a need for truth and guidance.)

It was a juvenile detention center in a metropolitan city, and neither the center nor the city was different enough from others of its kind to be worth specifying. The apprehensive glance that arriving teenagers got of the building's exterior showed them for

the most part little more than a bigger, more institutional version of their own drab homes; it tended
to be only the brighter, imaginative boys and girls
who noticed the steel mesh on the windows. For
some of them, the concrete indication of captivity
was just a materialized rendition of what they had
known all their lives.

Inside the juvenile center, beyond the main hall
that struck some visitors as looking like the lobby
and check-in desk of some cheap hotel in a 1940s
private-eye film, was a network of seemingly count-
less short hallways. Each one appeared to lead
somewhere important, but most of them merely led
to tiny offices that looked exactly alike, or to other,
crossing hallways. The center was too deficient in
imposing bureaucratic-type employees and generally too innocent of intention to seem Kafkaesque to
most callers, but it did the job on most of the first
offenders (who didn't know Kafka from Kaiser
Wilhelm).

The principle reason why most of the newcomers wound up feeling ample apprehension was because of the bolted-door cell area, cosmetically
constructed at the back of the building on the long,
ill-lit second floor. It was one thing to talk tough on
the streets, something else to see the doors locking
behind you—and to accept the fact, at last, that you
wouldn't be departing the center until time pre-
scribed by the first-floor juvenile court finally
passed. Mean-spirited rumors some newcomers
heard shortly after arrival, that workers at the center
used speed and often went mad, were similarly

successful in concentrating the attention of a kid with a tote bag containing only the homely necessities—not that the rumor mongers had anything altruistic in mind.

But there were exceptions. Many of the repeat offenders were eager—oddly enough—to convey the most desirable fact to the new kids: no one could legally be kept there once they turned eighteen. And while it was true that they would become subject to adult laws after that, each boy and girl craved liberty so much that not even the center's more unforgiving social workers could blame them for rejoicing at the facts of their confinement: nothing really terrible was apt to happen if they did their time halfway peaceably, and when their sentence was over, they'd be released to go back and resume whatever they had been doing before society got fed up with it—and them—and sent them to juvenile court to begin with.

The small, dowdy and brilliantly read psychiatrist Dr. Lenora Middel was almost painfully aware of the juvenile situation, knew it was largely the case for offenders under the age of eighteen everywhere in the nation. Seated in her uncannily undifferent postage-stamp office with her number (not her name) stenciled on the door, Lenora was burdened by an array of facts no shrink at the center liked to dwell upon. It was her obligation to interview each young offender before he or she was allowed to leave, but leave they would when their time was served—unless, Dr. Middel supposed, she could catch them before they departed in the act of trying to set fire to her nose. Always, there was a fresh supply of juvenile offenders ready (if not eager) to take their place and the majority of the youngsters she interviewed would make it clear in various ways that nothing they'd experienced during their detention had scared them into improving their attitudes toward society or their own lives. A percentage would probably run into enough minor opportunities, through acquaintances, to be dissuaded from pursuing an active life of crime, but another, sizable percentage—male and female—would become lifewastrels who'd spend half their numerous last days harming neither themselves nor others but still being sent to institutions not appreciably different from this one. This would occur when they succumbed to some ill-fated blow of outrage or simply could not cope with undirected liberty any longer. One or two might turn into really noteworthy citizens, but probably not—and a couple of boys, plus roughly .08 percent of the girls, would exhibit to Dr. Lenora Middel the capacity for becoming lawbreakers whom half of society would, given their druthers, prefer to have exterminated.

Lenora swung those little feet, which never reached the floor regardless of what chair she was occupying, opened her desk drawer, found her favorite ballpoint pen. She stuck it between her lips, munched. She was not a dwarf or midget, in spite of the conclusions she suspected a lot of strangers drew about her. She wasn't for the simple reason that she failed each of the dictionary and clinical definitions of *dwarf* and *midget*. She rather enjoyed believing that her head was much larger than those of most human beings—it was not—because then it made sense to her that she possessed a giant brain, which was nature's compensation for being both remarkably small and remarkably unpretty. On days such as this, when she thought her vocation kept her as confined to the appalling old building as any of the juvenile offenders, her talents fundamentally untested, unexplored, and cruelly wasted, she avoided mirrors as assiduously as any vampire and told herself that the ballpoint pen she liked to masticate was slowly poisoning her (its possible Freudian symbolism was too depressing and commonplace to consider).

Dr. Middel's fingers—so small they seemed knuckleless—toyed with the file folder atop the stack on her desk. She read the name typed on its bland and inoffensive surface with nothing registering except the fact that it was a male name. There was a lot more data she found irksome and dreary without even looking into a folder. All those confined at the center came to know that so long as they were under eighteen years of age, they were society's sweethearts and could get by with damned near anything. Lenora found that unpalatable both because she herself hadn't acquired that information when she was fifteen—half her life ago—and because there hadn't been much of anything antisocial it had occurred to her to do. She might have come up with something if she had known society gave her the license to *try*.

The situation and the regs also annoyed her

professionally and frequently gave her reason to pause because the psychology stank. People of any age, class, or intellect might or might not be deterred from committing ultimate acts of violence by living with the knowledge that they'd get the chair for it. The same people might well decide to do anything at all if they understood that the worst they'd get was three squares a day in a center that could be likened to a Catholic retreat. That was merely how people *are.* She'd spent too many years of virtually insufferable boredom reading textbooks no one alive should be expected to endure not to be certain of something like *that.* Locking youngsters up in an institution during their last formative stages where the one lesson they couldn't miss learning was that some people had rights and others didn't have—reinforcing their desperate belief that they were *special*—was an act so incredibly stupid that it amounted to diametric opposition to everything psychology had learned.

Lenora Middel turned the pen in her mouth, sucked in on the poison, peered up at the trite institutional clock above the door. One more special darling with a telltale acne-streaked face to be let loose again on a society with which he shared a mutual detestation, then home again, jig-a-jig. There had been a time when she executed her duties of the final interview with time's-up departing juvies with a real attempt to discern which kind of youth she was cutting loose on humankind— the full-time petty hoodlum, the eventual short-order cook-*cum*-welfare case, the woeful and even

told himself, were dirt dumb. So if you were pretty sure they had some magic to 'em, you just had to *take* it off 'em. He'd figured that much out himself from the way Mom stole the men's good juices, got them to pay her some money for gettin' sex from a *lot* of johns, then made them leave—or, when she liked a guy, get him to sit around and hear her read bad news about his future!

But Mom, well, she got herself purely sick after a while—she'd confided that to Dell once when she was drunk enough on cheap gin to loosen her tongue—which meant that no matter how far away any of the men she called "johns" went, they couldn't ever get so far that Mom's predictions about their futures wouldn't catch up with 'em! That, Dell thought, was *real* magic!

It was also how he'd wound up at juvie, though—by finding out one of Mom's men appeared to have magic, because (to Dell's astonishment) the fella'd come back a second time. Dell had almost killed the man, trying to make him reveal his secrets of immortality.

Pushing eighteen now, Dell understood with ruefulness what had been going on and that the fella had not possessed one iota of magic. In fact, Dell heard that the man *was* dead, now. Mom had made him disappear right along with the others. So that didn't mean nobody at all had magic, including the ugly dwarf-shrink across the desk from him. He just wondered how hard he'd have to work to make her give it to him, if she had any.

"Your record," Middel said softly, "indicates a

great deal of violence." She had a tinny voice, like a recording or a record made from another recording and all the equipment sucked.

"Yes, ma'am," Dell agreed with a nod. "Trying t'kill thet man is why they took me here." It wasn't a very magical thing the dwarf had said. "Everbuddy knows it."

"But I wasn't merely referring to that particular act of brutality." She stared at Dell to see how he'd take such directness.

Dell wondered if Middel was trying to see his crotch better. Then he saw she was just staring at his big, hairless hands. "See, I can't dope out why bustin' his butt got me in trouble when I know for a fack, now, nobuddy likes whores *or* johns."

"Nobody?" Middel asked pointedly. She looked into his strange eyes. "Dell . . . how do you feel about your mother?"

He kept her gaze and grinned. "I hope to kill her, someday."

"I see," Middel answered. *Not much of a stall, Lenora,* she told herself. "By that I take it that you mean you hate her—possibly . . . disapprove . . . of your mom?"

"Yew go right ahead, if yew wants t'think that, ma'am," Dell said.

There was nothing arrogant to it, Middel saw; the boy was being generous. Tolerant!

"You were frequently suspended from class, eventually expelled," Middel tried afresh, taking a different tack. "Was it always over something violent?"

He leaned back as if needing to ponder that question. Yet he was nodding already, too. "A lot of folks, they don't see things my way. Not right off, leastwise."

She risked meeting his gaze again. "Is that how it should be, Dell? Other 'folks' should usually see things your way—or, perhaps, *always* do so?"

Dell shifted in the leather chair, though more as if desiring plain comfort than that the psychiatrist's questions were troubling to him. He was a tidy, clean boy; give him that. And there was an un-rushed air to him, which, combined with the way he appeared eager to ask questions himself, was dis-turbingly adult. What was there about him, about the way he thought, that gave him such unruffled confidence?

"Well, Doctor," he answered, "'less they *say* why their ideas is better, I don't see why mine aren't as good as theirs."

"You feel that way about your instructors, too? Authority figures in general, including those here at the center?"

After she asked her question Lenora became conscious of a noise hanging in the air between them, an odd sound that seemed for a moment like buzzing. Then she realized that the lanky boy with the big hands was uttering a part-humming, part-muttering noise from his closed and smiling lips like a ventriloquilist. When he finally replied none of his muscles appeared to tense, yet he gave off a tension that was almost palpable. It was as though another entity inside him was trying to communicate.

"Y'know, Doctor, I've wondered who the real aw-thorities in my life are and jest how they *got* to be over me." He had a festering pimple on one cheek and it seemed to Middel like his last symbol of boyhood. "Most of the time I don't wonder *out loud*. I ain't no fool. I seen people hold real tight to any aw-thority they got 'cause it's as close as they ever gets t'magic." He grinned with a methodical deliberation that halted just short of challenge. "What I seed is thet them folks is all *older* than me. So I keep track of jest about *how* old they is and I figger when I'm the same age, well, I reckon they won't have no right t'be *my* aw-thorities no more."

Despite herself, Lenora smiled. Slightly relaxed, she looked down to read more of this peculiar boy's file record, then peered up again. "The tests you've taken indicate you're slightly brighter than normal. Not much—not a great deal—but marginally. Why do I have the impression that you may not have done the best you could on your scholastic tests, that you held back on them?"

His reaction startled her. "Yew have some magic!" Dell said, brows rising. "Honest t'Gawd, yew *do*! Nobuddy ever seen thet. Yew're *real* smart!" A quality in the teenager's eyes—one of them drooping badly, focusing off to Middel's side somewhere, as though searching for things she couldn't see (*or wouldn't want to*)—heightened Dell's sudden approval of her. His regard was oddly chilling.

Lenora also noticed that he hadn't answered her question, but she chose not to pursue it. Another entry in his record caught her attention; immediately, she was far more interested in it. Point of fact, Middel's heartbeat began to accelerate. That second, getting her old pen out of her desk drawer and easing it between her waiting lips was something she very much needed to do. She didn't dare, not yet.

"Dell," she began with caution, "there's evidence here that you are—well, a persistent thumbsucker." That could be viewed as a comment of considerable scorn. The tiny office felt close, claustrophobic, and she braced herself for his violent reaction.

"Oh, I might be." He'd answered her equably and seemed quite unoffended by it. A wavery smile on his wide mouth momentarily turned him into the boy he should have been. "I s'pose folks have seed me doin' it while I'm asleep, huh? Well, ma'am, I imagine I do a lot of things I don't know about when I'm sleepin'. I sure do hope I ain't gonna be blamed for *alla* thet."

"As a fetus in your mother your lips were your first external organs." She spoke softly as she always did, but each of them, doctor and patient, heard the tightness, the tension, in her voice. "Psychology knows that . . . sucking . . . is a source of pleasure for people. Though it tends to be sublimated after two years of life." She paused before dipping a toe in uncharted waters. "Do you know . . . Dell . . . what 'libido' is?"

"No, I purely do not," he said honestly, his gaze on Middel now as if he intended it to stay there forever. "But if *yew* tell me, I'll allus remember. I'll remember *anythin'* yew say now."

Her breath was quickly drawn. "Libido is the sexual urge. In psychology, it has a psychic element, too. The libido has three stages, the oral—thumb-sucking, nail-biting, even breast-feeding—being the first stage."

"Thet part is okay," Dell said. He went on smiling, the beam undimmed.

The office seemed to grow smaller for Lenora. "The other two stages—healthy people advance to these—are anal, pertaining to an interest in feces and in collecting, hoarding, which tends to become the urge to collect money as an adult. Then, the third, genital."

"I reckon shit don't int'rest me much," Dell commented. "The genital part, now—"

"But there's a *reason* why the anal doesn't register with you, and why, in my professional opinion, you are retarded in the area of genital development. *Look at your nails!*" To Dell's astonishment, the little psychiatrist rose, flung out her arms and grasped his hands, turned them so that the two of them could clearly see his thumbnails. *"Just look at those thumbs!"*

Startled, Dell did what he was told. But because it wasn't as if he hadn't seen them before, he realized he was more interested in discovering that Lenora Middel's touch was indisputably feminine, not in the least unpleasant. "Well, there they are, right there. One thumb on each hand."

"Don't you dare be insolent!" Unexpectedly,

Lenora released the large hands but, in the process, raked the top of his right thumb with her own nails. "You *used* those massive thumbs on the man who was with your mother, *didn't you*? You attempted to strangle him with *those thumbs*!"

"Well, Doctor, I reckon I did," Dell confessed. He stared at the brief, red line where she had scratched him. He wondered if she'd noticed what she did; probably she didn't care. He wouldn't have. "T'tell the truth, I purely did not know what else to strangle him with."

She glanced up to see if he meant to be insolent again. Drawing in a breath, she tugged her desk drawer open as if to get something out of it. Then she slammed it shut, sat down again, perspiration glistening on her forehead. "I was making the point that those people who are normal, according to social definition, advance from stage to stage. It's clear to me that your advancement has been retarded, stalled."

"Should I try t'like shit better?" Dell inquired, putting his wounded thumb in his mouth.

"No!" She found the familiar drab office reeling and focused her gaze first on the clock—nearly four P.M.—and then on the teenager's file folder, which she gripped firmly between her small hands. "Young man, I am embarked on a new boulevard of thought that may well prove to be the most important new step in psychology—preventive psychology—in decades."

"I s'pose thet's real good." He wasn't sure he'd spoken clearly around his thumb. "*Real* good."

"Anthropologists see the thumb as the ruler of what's termed the 'palmar kingdom,'" she continued. "In evolution, its development marked a vital, tremendous step toward everything human beings have become." She remembered Dell trying to kill a man with his thumbs and wondered if his attentiveness was genuine or if he possessed the intuitive understanding to know *she* would be—as a person—receptive to any kind of nurturing. She still saw no reason not to share her views with someone who was going nowhere in life. "Your fingers are immaculate for a teenage male's. Without knowing it, Dell, you *serve* those thumbs—make *love* to them, in a way of speaking—base many unconscious choices on them. Partly it's because you've witnessed your mother—at whose breast you fed—sharing herself with strange men, I believe!"

"I suck 'em at night as a rule." He removed his thumb, part way. "I'm jest doin' it now 'cause you made me bleed."

"But *night* is when your unconscious mind is fully given its head!" Suddenly she needed the tall, lanky boy—however warped he probably was—to understand her amazing theory. "Try to follow me, Dell. Can you imagine the potential for internal motivation toward antisocial behavior when your personality is stalled in the first libidinal stage?"

"Well, I don't recall Mom breast-feedin' me. I think I'd remember a thing like that. 'Less she was even uglier when I was a tiny baby, which ain't impossible." He was cautious about what he said because he was passionately eager to grasp her ideas, even if some of them were beginning to sound like bullshit. "I'm bad 'cause I suck my thumb whilst I have dreams of hurtin' people 'stead of playin' in my shit or something?"

"That isn't quite it, but it's close." This raw-boned youth was not without charm. "You are the first to have even an inkling of my theory." She thought of his record, filled with senseless acts of violence, and sighed. "It's a shame you yourself are a living example of my conclusions."

He leaned toward her, careful to keep his hands in his lap. "Kin yew tell me what yore conclusions are?"

Lenora did not answer at once. Her mind was spinning anew with the details of her historic discovery and the way another person had grasped part of its significance. She attempted to answer him circuitously. "Thumbs, clearly, have an *enormous* phallic importance. And big ones like yours denote strength, power, and determination; little ones indicate weakness. A lack of force. Why, even the Chinese conducted a study into thumbs." Peering carefully at him, she was reminded of the inquisitive streak that lay at the teenage boy's roots. "One must not forget that, in the days of ancient Roman gladiatorial combat, the upraised thumb—which obviously referred, representationally, to an erect phallus—was the very signatory of life."

"Yew're startin' t'give me magic, ma'am," Dell blurted with gratitude and narrowly refrained from groping for her tiny hand across the desk that separated them. "I allus *knew* they was magic!" He swallowed. "Now I got to have more, to *learn*. A *lot* more."

"Magic, indeed!" Dr. Middel snapped, beginning to pull herself together. "I've confided in you only my knowledge, a portion of my present thinking—though to the pre-anal personality, rare insights may *appear* magical. There are studies of backward tribes which—"

"*Doc.*" Dell remained seated but everything inside him appeared to crane toward the tiny authority figure, nearly keening. "I gots t'learn how to . . . to *be*. Whether yew call it magic or not, yew just got to give me some more. Yew *got* to 'cause yew *can*."

Lenora Middel inhaled to steady herself, then considered his odd request before answering. This Dell was courteous, interested in her views. What could it hurt to share with him her most guarded and noteworthy discovery? "I'll confide this much to you, young man." Her voice dropped so low that it was more a hiss than a whisper. "Dell, I have learned that—like you—the Tower Killer, Charles Whitman . . . Richard Speck, who slaughtered several nurses . . . Charles Manson, and *probably* Adolf Hitler . . . were all—thumb-suckers!" With a furiously abrupt movement, Middel got her ballpoint pen from the drawer of her desk and began to chew on it. "There's also some intriguing but partly confirmed evidence that Attila the Hun, Roman Polanski, Senator Joseph McCarthy, Alfred Hitchcock, and Ed Sullivan were thumb-suckers, too—but it's

premature to cite them publicly with any measure of scientific confidence."

"I'll be damned," Dell said.

"And," Dr. Middel went on, scarcely intelligible with the pen between her lips, "that awful man Starkweather—he ran around with a perfect *bitch* of a girl, doing dreadful things to innocent people—he was almost *cer*tainly one of your kind!"

"I heard about him," Dell said reflectively. His boyish face gaped at Lenora in awe; he felt magic wash over him as if he were being anointed. "Okay, where do I git a girl t'travel with me? How do I start puttin' all thet to *use*?"

"To use?" she retorted, confounded. She chewed harder. "Dell, the long, lonely road to mental health begins deep within each of of us."

"But, ain't thet where the first magic shows up?"

Lenora tapped the edge of his file folder on her desk. "Let me be frank with you, Dell. Young males with the sort of history, the kind of stalled libidinal progress you have, are likely to find themselves on one or more of four life paths. To a visionary level, at which you believe yourself to be more all-knowing than anybody else. To a hedonistic attitude, wherein you place your pleasures ahead of those of any other person. To an outlook of mission-orientation, in which one's difficulties can be explicated solely by setting out to right the wrongs in society. Or toward a power-and-control level, which should be self-explanatory."

"I don't think it is, though," Dell said candidly.

He was sweating now, too, avid to learn all he could about his own possibilities in life.

"The power-and-control freak—sorry; that isn't the clinical term—can only enjoy peace of mind passingly, by assuming the right to powers that aren't his. Controlling other human beings so he can see in them what he wants, fantasizes, to see."

What the boy said then stopped Dr. Middel in her tracks. "Did yew say I could be more than *one* a them?" he asked with enormous earnestness. "'Cause I'd have t'say—not braggin' or nothin'— that they's *all* how I am." Both his good and bad eyes shone.

For the first time Middel fully realized that this Dell wasn't the ordinary kind of boy she met in the center and was, in all likelihood, the hideous, pro- spective mass murderer she had hypothesized but had not interviewed. He understood the things he had done and the things he hinted he'd like to do, and their consequences—he was shockingly *honest* in his way, and open! But he simply didn't care. He was actually flattered by her definition of the worst sort of criminality. For one awful moment Lenora tried to recall, even repudiate, the finer points of analysis she had just confided to someone who was little more intellectually than a childishly vicious thumb-sucker!

"Ma'am, will you please see me again before I'm released?"

Lenora regarded the cockeyed, sincere, inexpli- cably sycophantic male face suddenly bobbing like a balloon on the opposite side of her desk with a

degree of confusion quite close to terror. Her nerve was failing her, she saw that she was no longer the clear-headed professional totally in control, who utilized her knowledge to redefine her patients' outlooks, who believed absolutely in Freudian tenets and derived the deepest pleasure from knowing that she had the authority to restructure the unacceptable fancies of others. Dell frightened her, made her see in a way she had not experienced since her own psychoanalysis that there were other desires, views, even strengths, that could shred her bastion of tissue-thin perceived infallibility. The only good thing she could take from their discussion—aside from the condemnatory notes she would definitely leave in the boy's file—was that Dell could not conceivably have grasped enough of what she had said to use it in any sinister or antisocial fashion.

"There's no time for another meeting. Your release date is set for a week from now." The pure psychiatrist in her was surfacing again, thank heaven. "I don't know any way to detain you past that date. You're going to be free again." She could not keep the taint of bitterness from creeping into her last words.

But Dell jumped so abruptly to his feet—appeared to become so menacingly tall—it was as if he'd announced his intention to charge at her. Flinching, Lenora completely forgot the fail-safe buzzer on her desk, and only allowing the ballpoint pen to fall from her mouth kept her from choking on it.

"*No!*" Dell shouted, and there was rage in it

along with a note of pleading. Although he hadn't screamed loudly enough to bring anybody from outside the office, there was an intensity—a command—in his voice Middel hadn't heard from anybody before and it froze her in place, all but horizontal with the desk. She was conscious of appearing so small, with nothing except her button eyes in view, that she had virtually disappeared. "Guwdammit, don't send me away till I knows how to *be* out there!" Dell's voice broke, became higher. "The only way I know how t'be happy now is by bein' like you said I am. That'd be fine—but it put me in *here*!"

His hysteria imbued Lenora with the courage to regain control of the situation. "Pursuing happiness is not the business of psychology," she said, and drew herself erect in her chair. The pen she liked to chew lay on the floor where it had fallen. It would have to be washed thoroughly in hot water now. "Happiness—and magical solutions—have no real place in science. Psychology and science are functions."

Dell's weepy eye blinked down at her from his side of the desk. His wide, bony shoulders were slumped but not, she intuited, with complete despair. "Well, tell me then where they *do* belong?" he demanded. "Where do I *git* 'em?"

Lenora had no answer, but she thought about his question often in the following seven days. She did so with diminishing interest, however; other offenders came for their final interviews and a few provided her with potential insights into her com-

bined study of libidinal and anatomical p
None was as intriguing as Dell, who wa
sociopathic but nonetheless had shown h
for her views. Lenora did not expect t
again; it was sufficient to add a brief but p
cautionary appraisal of him to his person

She arrived home one night with new
nation to coin a suitable name for her
theory. Psychology and other realms o
were no longer free of the need for catc
remembered names. *An acronym that forn
word might work*, Lenora was thinking as
locked her front door, entered the dark ho
discovered she had an uninvited caller.

Dell, relaxed as Jesus where he sat ir
front room chair, offered her his inquisiti
boy's smile. He wore a tank top, frayed jear
tegrating tennies, and gloves with all the fin
off except for the thumbs. It was not cold
thought, though there was a distinct nip in

He greeted her mildly. "Dr. Middel," he r
exactly as if they'd run into each other at th
store.

"How did you f-find out my address
asked. To combat the surge of fear, she res
briefcase on its usual place on a table just ins
living room, exhibiting as much aplomb as sl
able to muster; then she went to hang her
weight jacket in the closet and returned to th
room. No desk with a buzzer to summon assi
was anywhere in her little condo. It occur
Lenora—it positively *flamed* in her—to run fi

life, but that was scarcely a professional response when the boy had made no kind of threatening move. Besides, she imagined Dell to be far too intelligent, too prepared, not to have planned a way to reach her before she got to the door. The popular view of sociopaths, even in this boy's budding stage, held that they possessed brilliant animal cunning, and her professional self did not have a sizable enough sampling to argue the point.

"Well," Dell said reasonably enough, "I found yew in the phone book." His young face was as relaxed and free of malice as it had been in her office, and she detected no threat in his face or in how he had carelessly folded himself into her favorite chair. Since he'd shown such interest in her theories she could almost have welcomed him, except that he had broken in.

"They let me go. I jest wanted t'see yew."

"Very well, you have; we're both here," Middel said evenly. She sat nonchalantly on the sofa, near him, smoothing her skirt round her knees. Then came the inevitable wish that her feet would at least touch the floor; this time it was accompanied by an awareness of how much bigger he was than she. "You must know that breaking and entering could put you right back into the center."

He regarded her with such pleasantness! He was like an out-of-town son who had just dropped by. "But yew ain't gone t'tell 'em I'm here, are yew?"

Was that a threat? Or his confidence in their relationship? "If I recall our interview accurately,

you . . . wished more *magic* from me. Is that correct?"

He nodded. The lower part of his jaw went on forever. "Yes'm." His weepy eye was troubling him and he sopped at it with his knuckles like a sleepy overgrown child. He appeared to have almost no beard whatsoever. He wasn't jerky, spastic, yet it was hard to focus on the indisputable fact that he was in her home without her permission—and that the assessment she had entered in his juvenile record was that he would probably prove to be exceedingly dangerous as time passed. He had a quality of . . . commonplaceness . . . at the same second he revealed thought patterns so askew and dark that, Lenora realized, he would probably prove to be that rare creature, a sociopath with periodic psychotic tendencies. "I tole somebuddy in yore office I wanted t'see yew. I even left a note."

Dr. Middel twisted on her sofa. His presence in her chair made her the stranger in her own front room. "There's never any time at the center, Dell—it *is* Dell?" She waited for the short nod he gave her. She realized then that his feelings had been hurt. "I suppose it's conceivable that I *could* help you . . . over a period of time. However—"

"I don't rightly think so," he said

It was a wholly unexpected rejection. She knew she should be surprised, but she wasn't, because she sensed it was her fault. She realized now that she was in the greatest peril of her life.

"Yew never really wanted t'give me any help or magic," Dell said easily. "And I think yew don't know what magic you got to give." This was quiet accusation, Lenora thought. Though his inflections had not changed and he had not raised his voice, there was no doubt in her mind that he was purposefully saying more than his words suggested. He himself might not know yet that he was threatening her, but she knew it. "Everything you said about thumbs was right. Thet's *part* of yore magic."

"But it's cursory, incomplete," she said, trying to amend it and leaning forward toward him just enough to do something she ordinarily never did: display her own, slight feminine charm and her slight feminine cleavage. "If we could work *together*, if I got more *deeply* into analyzing your problems—"

"Yew said I'm a retard," Dell announced, and it was the flattest statement of fact Lenora Middel had ever heard. She began to try to deny it but the brow above his healthy eye ascended warningly and so did the palm of one huge hand. "I'm not sayin yew're wrong, but like I tole you, I'll *allus* remember what yew said." He bobbed his head, recalling with shocking clarity the sense of what she'd said in her office. "My lee-bydo is like a retard and stuck in the o-ral stage."

"But it doesn't have to be *permanent*." She spoke quickly. Now her front room, her entire house, was closing in, temperatures soaring. "With our work, together—"

His raising one massive thumb halted her. "Yew also said I got thumbs with 'strength, power and determination,' and thet's nice. Then, yew told me about the anal part; baby shit; makin' money. After thet came the third lee-bydo part." Both his eyes burned into hers. "Thet's about my . . . privates."

"Not yours *personally*," Middel corrected him, quickly. "You remember, even the genital stage was simply part of the connective phase of my *theory*—"

"What's thet?"

Lenora had no idea what he was referring to but turned her head around instantly, wildly, striving to determine what had broken his track of thought and hoping to return it to anything but her own evaluation. She realized at length he was staring at an inexpensive piece of statuary she had bought for a decorative touch a few years ago. It sat on a low bookcase within arm's reach of the chair he was sitting in. "It's a phoenix," she explained, overflowing with relief at his sudden interest in something different. "A mythical bird, Egyptian in origin I think."

"Egyptian and not from Arizona?" he murmured. "I wondered since I never heard of a lot of weird birds flyin' around Phoenix."

"The phoenix is supposed to be immortal, I think, able to return to life after—"

"About thet last lee-bydo stage," Dell said, standing and fumbling with the buckle of his belt. The sight stunned Lenora, froze even her mind into inaction. "Yew got to help me find out if I don't have that part yet either." His jeans fell to the ground, revealing both Jockey shorts and a state of readiness Middel certainly had not anticipated. "I'm like Speck, Charlie Manson, Whitman—even Hitler—

yew said. Okay. But I don't want t'go to jail a long while or git kilt. So yew see, I got t'git me to a diff'rent stage." He kicked the jeans away to free his legs for movement and headed straight for her. "And I *got* t'take yore magic."

Her tiny feet hit the floor and she took a single short step toward the front door.

He put his arms out like the wings of a great, descending bird and they engulfed her. The press of his long body and long, pale, hairless legs was nearer than her next breath.

Lenora instructed her own legs to run, farther than they'd ever run before. But she only ran in place. She stopped doing it when she saw how absurd she must appear.

"This ain't gonna be any more fun for me than it is for yew," Dell said, "'cause *you* is truly one ugly woman. But I needs all the magic I kin git afore I'm on thet 'long, lonely road' yew said I have t'be on." His partly gloved hands bent her head back so he could peer down into her face. The pain in her neck was excruciating. His face wore an expression of disgust, but he still kissed her.

"I can help you if you let me go," she cried, trying to avert her head and gaze.

"Yew'll help me now when I don't," he argued. Effortlessly, it seemed, he stripped her clothes off and threw her on the sofa. He pinned her there, squinted closely to survey her whole body. "So tell me—are you a dwarf or not?"

"No, goddamn you—I'm not!" She thrashed about but with no greater success than she had enjoyed when she attempted to run. "I'm a perfectly normal woman—just *little!* Stop hurting me before—"

"Well, thet's okay," he said reassuringly, patting her bare shoulder and freeing himself from his shorts with his other hand. "I think yew still got *some* magic."

The psychiatrist had a moment in which she rediscovered her usual flair for analysis. It happened in much the same way that an experienced soldier facing unavoidable combat may think of home, orders given him by his company commander, and the quantity of ammunition he has left. What she perceived shocked her more than anything else that had happened or was now happening to her:

As Dell forced his way into her, he was functioning with full masculine sexual prowess, yet it was entirely independent of the workings of his brain or his emotions—if he had any, any at all. He neither disliked nor hated her, he did not even *want* her—but he wanted something he fancied she possessed, and his body cooperated fully with him in doing what he had almost mechanically instructed it to do. While the pain began for her, she tried to make her own mind concentrate on the great thumbs he had concealed—preserved, chosen to keep warm or comfortable—because she knew he would almost certainly kill her—strangle her—with them.

Dell finished, then shoved himself up on his arms, his plain, customarily inquisitive face beaming down at her—and at where they were still joined—with measurable enthusiasm and pride.

"I don't know if I got any of yore magic yet," he exclaimed jubilantly, "but I think the genital stage worked jest fine! Yew agree?"

She could only weep and turn her face to one side, forgetting his great thumbs.

"Tell me, how I can hang around reg'lar folks without gettin' shot or locked up?" he asked while still lying on her. "Yew can see I'm po-lite." No answer, so he pinned her cheeks with his fingertips, stared deeply into her eyes. "Yew tell me thet now!"

"B-but I don't *know*." Lenora's obligation to answer him evoked all her pain, discomfort, and shame, and she started to sob.

Dell sighed. Lifting himself off her but not far enough for Lenora to rise, he reached over to her bookshelf, picked up the phoenix statue, hefted it. Opening her eyes, Lenora believed with terror that he intended to insert it in her.

But Dell merely sighed again, shook his horsey head from side to side. "Thet is purely too bad. What good is a shrink who don't have answers for the really big questions, 'specially when she's given up all her magic?"

Only then did she realize that he meant to swing the weighty piece at her. The awareness was short-lived, as was Lenora. His first swing had been experimental, to gauge the weight; his second caved in the side of her face and her temple. Using thumbs was for killing plain people, not people with magic.

Dressing quickly, Dell paused just once to

glance into a mirror in Dr. Middel's bathroom. He didn't want to find out if he looked different after having sex, but if he had changed as a result of acquiring magic.

Then he was patience itself as he set fire to a newspaper he found, placing it at Lenora's feet. A fine idea occurred to him and he set the blood-stained phoenix in the midst of the flames, as on a funeral pyre, and watched it burn as long as he could do so safely. The effect was interesting, because it took awhile for the statue to become fully ignited, and Dell had the notion once that it might just spread its wings and fly away.

Dell was departing the burning house when he wondered if the idea of destroying the evidence of what he'd had to do might have passed straight into his mind at the second he bashed Dr. Middel's brains out. It was hard t'know just how the magic worked.

He was only eighteen, after all.

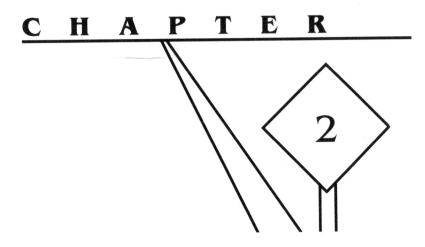

C H A P T E R 2

(A period of time beginning shortly after Dell first experienced magic up close and encompassing roughly a dozen relatively groping years.)

For a while after killing Dr. Middel, Dell settled for running over the things he had learned from her and attempting to decide if the long and lonely journey she had predicted for him should start just by going out to hitch a ride or perhaps getting his own car or truck and doing the driving himself. What he didn't question was anything he'd learned from the dwarf lady.

The trouble with hitching, though, was that you always put yourself in a vulnerable position. A lot of real perverts prowled the roads, just looking for teenage boys to hit on, and while Dell figured he would wind up killing half or better of the people who gave him lifts, he didn't want to screw any boys or men. Fact was, you purely could not trust strangers these days.

Getting his own vehicle was probably the right idea, but he only had two methods: stealing or buying. It hadn't been exactly profitable in the juvenile center.

Getting some money to buy a vehicle was not impossible, but it would definitely have to come from Mom. If he took her stuff, she was more unlikely to call the cops on him than anybody else. But Dell doubted she was earning much as a whore these days, not only because she was homely as sin and her body looked as if she'd dropped twelve or thirteen brats instead of only him, but because of the sickness she'd picked up. Mom just wasn't aging gracefully, Dell felt.

He had seen his mother ten months ago, at the juvie center, and her skin was so leathery then Dell thought it might make a better lady's purse than a face or arms.

But it wasn't just her looks, it was her shitty attitude. During that visit she'd bitched about how business was so bad because of the economy that she'd started doing corners and strip malls she'd thought beneath her only ten, twelve years back.

Returning home was a fairly nostalgic experience for Dell. For several days, or even as much as a couple of broken weeks, total, he'd been able to view the hundred-year-old structure on the hill at the outskirts of town as home and had felt more or less at peace within its walls. He and Mom had lived there for almost three years, prior to the time he attacked Mom's john, but the house had seemed such a ramshackle lean-to then—likely to collapse upon itself if a tornado ever decided to blow into town—that Dell was generally inclined to detest it. His mother's pride in how she'd managed to put a down payment on the place, with her salary from what she'd termed "starring" in two movies (regularly shown in adult bookstore video machines that cost a quarter for a peek), had alternately amused and disgusted him during his early teens.

Nonetheless, Dell had found the daytime quietude of the house a haven once when he'd boosted some grass from a fellow student, again when he'd hospitalized a dean of boys, who then sent the police after him, though later the dumb shit refused to press charges because Dell was only fourteen, and once more when his mom went to some overnight orgy and Dell was left by himself. He'd done nothing particularly special or notably illegal, but it had been kind of nice with nobuddy around to look at him as if they were criticizing and had t' be pleased so'd he have food t'eat.

Part of the way up the twenty-five steps to the

front door, Dell hesitated to recall those few enjoyable moments, and one autumn night especially. Today was a steamer, but then it had been cool, just nice enough. He'd managed to get his hands on some beers (even though he usually hated being drunk, 'cause he was afraid of what he might do, like get arrested when his guard was down). He downed a few and then took off all his clothing. Being naked always made Dell peculiarly excited, as if anything were possible. He had more beers and then went out on the top of Mom's hill—still bare-assed—to tell the whole guwdamn world off. He'd yelled crap like, "I'm Dell from hell and yore gone notice *me* or yew'll purely wish t'Gawd yew had!"

Afterward, he finished the beer and got miserably sick to his stomach. The following day he reflected deeply on his hangover and the way that most people he met tended to make him sick came to mind. If not ill, so disgusted it came to the same thing. It was the ordinary folks he'd known who drank a lot—people without an ounce of magic to 'em—suggesting to Dell that they boozed it up in the hope of finding magic for themselves. But he wasn't ordinary—he was Dell from hell—he didn't *need* any damn booze to be special!

But it'd been a wonderful night anyhow.

Mebbe it was special 'cause Mom wasn't there, Dell mused as he went up the rest of the steps.

You could have knocked him over with a feather when his mom opened the door. She was wearing the uniform of a Hardee's girl!

"Yew're out of jail," Mom said, right off. "And yew're back."

He ignored her. "What are yew doin'?" Dell took a step back to see if Mom was wearin a *real* uniform. "Yew got some customer who wants t'make it with a countergirl?"

"No, I do not," she said with indignation. Then her somewhat lopsided smile tried to be endearing. "At juvie I tole yew times was tough. Son, I had t'get me a real job." Shrugging, frilly things on her shoulders moved. "Don't be mad at me, Dellie. It's just till the e-conomy is better. Then I'll be the mama yew re-specks again."

And the part of yore body that belonged up top goes back in place, he thought, but kept it to himself. He grinned. "Yew gonna let me come inside or not?"

She eyeballed him for another second, finally stepped away from the door. "Well, if yew got to," she replied. "But I can't stay. I got t'git t'work soon or I'll be late for my shift and git docked."

"Docked, huh?" he said with a smirk, pushing past her into the house. "Never heard that word for it afore." He glanced around with a proprietary air, saw the place didn't look any different, which was not the best news he'd heard. "Weeeell, I s'pose I'll hang around till I git my bearings—lessen you mind." She wouldn't, Dell thought; *she wouldn't dare.*

She trailed him closely as he went and sat down across from the TV, the same one they'd had before he went to juvie. He gave off waves of disapproval and tension, like body odor; she wished he wouldn't look at the romance novels and soap opera magazines she'd crammed into a rack next to the chair—as if there were something wrong with being a romantic at heart. She wished much more that she didn't have to stick so close to him because it telegraphed her certainty that he'd rip her off sooner or later and made her feel she was an even worse mother than she knew she was.

"It's wonnerful t'see yew again, honey," she said as he yanked off his shoes, let them drop to the floor. "But school won't let yew go back to graduate. I checked up on that, and Mr. Hockstadder, the principal, he said you've wore out yore welcome." A stench rose from the discarded shoes and she couldn't be sure if it was her worry at having Dell back or the stink that brought tears to her eyes.

But Dell was leaning back in the chair, relaxing. His expression startled her, because he didn't look pissed by what she had said. Was Dellie finally growing up? "I don't need that guwdamn high school," he said, scratching his armpit. "See, there was a real ugly shrink at juvie—purty smart, though—who tole me what I should do with my life. I got to wander, find myself. So I'm gonna be a travelin' man and I'll hit the road sooner'n yew can wink." He smirked at her with his good eye. "Reckon yew know a whole *lot* about travelin' men, Mom. Right?"

She didn't answer right away, so Dell just went on looking, and smirking, at her. He thought she seemed sort of frozen in place, like a dinosaur. She was probably no older than thirty-five, but she was older than any woman Dell had ever seen in her dumb Hardee's dress with practical old-lady shoes instead of heels. Well, if she was turning respectable, she wouldn't have to kick those shoes off fast. "They got jobs, too, Dell," she said finally. "Travelin' men don't jest travel, y'know? They's workin' at *somethin'*."

Dell gave her a sigh. "Bring me back a big order of fries, Mom," he said. He leaned forward to turn on the TV. "Yore growin' boy needs him some grub."

He watched her from the corner of his eye. Nodding at last, sweating, she was starting toward the front door, looking as if the world were pushing down on her shoulders. Hell, she might go straight down into the hill and be buried alive any second— which wasn't a terrible idea, now that Dell thought of it.

"She died, honey," Mom said, stopping. Her big eyes, which were once her best feature, got bigger. "The psychiatrist I think yew were talkin about got burned up in a fire at her place."

"I heard," Dell said.

"I wondered . . ."

He glanced across the room to where she'd put on a coat over her silly uniform, she was sort of staring, but trying not to look like she was. "Yew wondered what, Mom?"

She didn't answer. Another second or two passed; she turned the door knob and pushed, and more hot air rushed in. Not even working yet and she was sweating like a pig. "Hey, Mom," he called before she was gone, "yew got yoreself wheels now?" There was no rush about things, but he'd been learning that a fella helped himself by planning ahead.

Mom's face looked as though she were getting gas pains or something, but she nodded. "It ain't much of a car, a'course, but it keeps goin' forward."

He studied her with his unmatched eyes, knowing he could hold her there indefinitely just doing that. Then he smiled, turned his whole attention to the old TV. "Well," he said amiably, "thet *is* the main thing, now ain't it?"

Two weeks later Dell was off on his "long and lonely road" in his old lady's car. Since he'd beat her up pretty good, he figured he had a decent head start. She wouldn't be able to crawl to the phone before the next day.

When he was far enough away from the house on the hill that he figured the police wouldn't connect Mom's license plate to her ex-juvie son too quickly, he stole his first van.

But before that, Dell put a big rock on the accelerator of the car and sent it flying off a cliff. Dell purely did not want his mom to get the car back in good enough shape to drive, so he enjoyed watching the vehicle wreck and burst into flames. He even imagined his mother was inside it, and that made him feel real good . . . for a minute.

Whores whore, jest like lawyers practice law, the teenager thought as he hot-wired the van, then peeled off in a more or less southeastern direction. Besides, they didn't have no business givin' their diseases to decent folks at Hardee's.

For the next six years Dell did what he called "livin' off the land." Sometimes he went bowling late at night when the leagues were done and rolled line after line alone, able to focus so completely on his own game that there were times when he even amazed himself, then remembered there was no one around to share his successes with. In many ways, that was fine with Dell, who considered himself independent; the term "rugged individualist" would have sounded just right to him if he'd heard it. He had always been alone, except for Mom and a few men he dimly remembered spending a week or so with. Other kids had found out who his mom was, told *their* moms, and then they weren't allowed to be pals with him—but it was okay for them to call Mom and Dell names, so he'd hurt as many of them as he was able, as bad as he could. Back then, when his mother was young and healthy enough to care if he whipped another boy and would tell him not to do it anymore, he'd told himself he missed having friends, but he grew out of it.

Fact was, Dell thought, he was so damned much better than anyone else he had ever met or ever seen on the television that just about everything he needed in life could be summed up as getting more magic, getting tail when he wanted it, and having enough to eat. And all three things had been in pretty short supply before he went to juvie and offed the ugly little shrink.

So Dell began his career as a traveling man with these basics constantly in mind, even if their order kept changing, and he was much more able to get grub and tail than magic. Still, Dell figured, he wasn't doin' bad for somebody who was little more than a kid. It made sense that the authorities of four states were looking for a man with his description. After only a few years of traveling, just the list of the cars, trucks and vans he swiped must have been as long as a big dude's arm.

What he couldn't figure out was how to cash in on the reputation he was working so hard to build—to make TV and the newspapers—without being caught, or without stopping by a police station somewhere and leaving his full name.

Yet the first two or three years were not without satisfaction and occasionally fulfilled Dell's urge for the same feeling he'd had back when he was bare-ass on his mom's hill, daring anyone to come get him if they objected. And always there was the pleasure of having nobody around to supervise him.

Yet the shortcomings of his present, totally solitary existence were evolving laboriously, slowly, in Dell's mind and could not easily be ignored.

The principal shortcoming was that he didn't feel free to murder any more folks than he absolutely had to.

It was a question of being practical, that was all. Dell reminded himself of it every time he was on the road, getting ready to make a score: Aw-thorities were more likely to get bent out of shape over the job of investigating a bunch of bodies stacked up at the morgue than looking into crimes of larceny. It was common sense.

Which was why Dell always wore a stocking over his head, sneaked up on the person he was going to attack, then made sure they were faced *away* from him—so he could partly strangle them, get *that* much fun out of life. And it worked like a charm! Mainly, he used the magic he had learned from Lenora Middel, the stuff about his strong thumbs. What she'd told him gave Dell the confidence he would be able to rise to the top in his line of work if only he held on to his self-control and didn't off too many people. Also, little girls, old ladies, and nuns *couldn't* be raped. Best bet for just robbing folks or stealing their vehicles was teenage boys, 'cause no one much liked them; the next best bet was men Dell's own size. *If yew keep to yore plan and remember whose neck yew got between yore thumbs*, he reminded himself, as if it were a litany, before every score, *the aw-thorities purely won't mind too much.*

But the last three years of Dell's first flush of adult freedom sometimes found him forgetting to let *go* of necks in time, or just squeezing too hard.

Something was missing and he thought he knew what it was: he simply wasn't having a lot of fun in his work anymore. He might be burning out.

The reason for that was he kept running across so many people he yearned to go ahead and choke right to death—Gawd, it happened when he was having his grub, getting gassed up, or taking a leak, almost anytime—so much that Dell began to wonder if indeed he *was* living out the fine destiny Dr. Middel had predicted for him. After all, the ugly little shrink must have been smart enough to know he couldn't get to be one of the baddest men who'd ever tooled around on the earth without becoming well known—without kicks, without killing *many* human beings!

Of course, she had also said he was some kind of fucking *freak*—an animal who wanted to control folks but couldn't control himself. That was why he'd set out to prove her wrong, to use her magic the *right* way, and not go off half-cocked about murder or rape. And he didn't cotton much to how the newspapers called other dudes who did what he did bad names, shit like "self-serving savages," "violence prone," "mad dogs," "antisocial loners," and "vicious sociopaths."

Where was anybody standin' up for folks with different needs? Where was there a living *soul* who tried to look at it from his position? Christ on a crutch, it wasn't as if he didn't serve *no* use to the world—not when there were so many people out there that a man in his line of work could easily see *needed* killing!

Sometimes he thought about that fellow Starkweather, who Dr. Middel had told him about. When that memory came up on the lonely highway, Dell felt a kinship and some envy for Charlie, who'd had a woman to travel with him. Well, Dell realized with a sigh, old Lenora had been purely right in warning him that his life was going to be one of loneliness.

At the times when he thought this, Dell had two

ways for chasing the blues. Number One was to park his stolen vehicle of the time where it would be fairly safe from cops and addicts for the night, then daydream that he might someday find his picture in newspapers, even on important wanted posters. It was sad to him that J. Edgar Hoover, the F.B.I. boss, had died. These days it was hard to get good help, so Dell couldn't be positive the new director would have the smarts to realize anybody as young and clever as he was was out there, committing all *sorts* of crime. And sometimes, too, he daydreamed that he might need to learn more. Not that he couldn't read, if he ever found anything worth reading, but he might make himself happier if he was able to *talk* with women—real smoothlike, soo-ave they called it—before he put it to 'em.

The second method Dell used to combat loneliness was rape.

Right from the beginning, both with Dr. Middel and the first girl he picked up after juvie, Dell wanted the women he took to think of all they did together as dating. Mom had taught him to be polite by always asking her johns what they "preferred" and keeping a democratic price list, so the females Dell forced into his current vehicle were treated with every courtesy. He told them exactly what he was going to do next, no surprises, and what they were supposed to do, and he always warned them that he wouldn't hurt them any more than he needed to, if they would just leave his stocking mask alone. He wasn't some macho man who didn't know a fella was s'posed to treat females with respect before, during, and after he'd screwed them. Why, there were many, many times after rape when he said he'd drive the woman home—or wherever they wanted to go. How much more did a man owe a piece of ass? For the life of him, Dell couldn't grasp the fine points of why females took it so hard no matter what he did. Shitfire, he'd even tried to converse with the pretty ones when it was over.

Then he figured it out!

The small bit of magic he had taken off the dead ugly shrink had made his life a whole lot better, true. No one could argue with that 'cause no one had caught him yet in a single adult crime! Dell from hell had been correct about believing in magic, but he just didn't have enough yet.

And it was possible there was a great deal of *other* magic, all around him every minute of the day and night, that a committed man like him could also seize. . . .

But maybe he needed to become smarter—not "smarter" exactly, because he knew most of the main things about life, but better *educated*—in order to *see more* of the hidden magic!

And maybe, if he did get to where he could recognize it and take it whenever he pleased, he could become just as famous and important as Dr. Lenora Middel had thought he could! To be fair about it, she might be ugly and she might be dead, but that little shrink was the only one who'd seen his potential—the only one, including Mom, to *believe* in him. He owed her that much, by Gawd—fulfillin' himself and bein' the most famous, the most feared, sumbitch on earth!

So going after a regular diploma didn't make any sense, maybe, but he definitely needed to know more of those "fact" things, open up the world of magic to ole Dell and become a man of the world—a man for *history* students to learn about—which would pay back the little punks who'd called him and Mom dirty names ever since he was small!

And mebbe—jest mebbe, Dell thought on the night he was choking a fella from behind so he could trade in his wheels for a different model—*mebbe I can git myself a nice virgin girl to go with me on my travels once I'm smarter and I got even more magic. It'd be awmost like goin' to church ever week jest to improve myself thet much!* It seemed perfectly obvious to Dell that anyone in the world who made himself that neat was bound to stop being lonely and be happy.

The guy he was strangling ducked down suddenly, his face all blue, then ran off, leaving behind his Subaru with the keys in the ignition. Dell had been so wrapped up in the new-and-improved Dell from hell in his mind's eye that he'd almost choked the fella to death!

Chuckling, feeling young and foolish, Dell got in behind the steering wheel and started the motor. He stared through a side window at the night, imagined it was loving him back. But he didn't put the car into gear.

A virgin girl of his own, for heaven's sake—he

was getting as romantical as Mom with such notions!

Still, when he thought about it, filled with the zeal of self-improvement, there were *all kinds* of females. A few were law-abiding and made a fuss about it. Lots more had to have a regular income—some way to live—and they weren't always as particular, whatever they wanted you to believe. Take Mom, for example, who hadn't been a whore before she was nine or ten.

Then there were women who craved putting roots down somewhere. Even Mom, with her ramshackledy house on the hill, was like that. Now that Dell thought about it, there were nearly as many different sorts of women as there were men—maybe.

So there just *had* to be a young gal somewhere who had a yen to ride around in a whole gawdamn fleet of vehicles—and who had a hankering for a fella who would look out for her, if she kept her nose clean—and who liked the excitement of staying on the road, meeting different kinds of people, for a little while, at least.

If I had me a girl like thet, Dell thought just before he was busted, *I do b'lieve the en-tire worl' of magic would spread out right before me—jest like the girl would do it!*

"Keep your hands on the steering wheel," said the cop, standing next to the man Dell had almost choked. A police automatic was aimed right at young Dell's left temple from maybe half an inch away. "Next time you rip off somebody's car, buddy, you might want to consider driving it away."

Damn it to hell! Dell thought as he climbed cautiously out of the Subaru. It wasn't fair. There he was, planning his next career move—discovering exactly how he could really make something of himself, and Mom's romantic streak had gotten him thrown into the slammer! Now there was one more thing to kill the old lady for.

Dell admired the efficiency of the officers at the jail, if not the way they'd never heard of him. It took no more than a few hours after being booked and tossed into a cell to realize the slammer was definitely not the same as juvie, and no more than a few days for him to see that the ugly dead shrink, too, had turned into a hoodoo who was doing her best to get him, from beyond the grave. It was as if all the women he had tried so hard to be nice to were ganging up on him, alive or dead.

It underscored for Dell the need to make himself impervious to their harm by learning all he could—even if he didn't plan to listen to anybody's advice for a while. The way Dell saw things, he got along fine so long as other people butted out and didn't try to tell him anything. There had to be a better way to learn magic and knowledge than listening to other folks bullshitting and boring his ass!

The man who prosecuted Dell told the judge and everyone else in the courtroom just what Dr. Middel wrote about him during his final interview with her.

So by the time the fat public defender assigned

to him had said his piece and the judge was sentencing Dell, he wasn't listening, he'd tuned out. He was speedily sent to the facility where he was scheduled to spend his next several years, and that was that.

Upon arrival at the prison, Dell made his first mistake immediately after he was shoved into his permanent cell and a guard locked the door behind him. He imagined he was the only occupant of the barred and unlit room. He'd just taken a whiz in the lidless toilet he located in the dark corner and was zipping up when he felt someone staring at him. Glancing around, and seeing no eyes in the murky blackness of the cell, he groped his way across the space in pursuit of two beds, whose faint outlines he could just make out.

"Hello . . . whitemeat," said a voice from the vicinity of the second bed.

Dell's eyes gaped through the bleakness of the tiny room. Filled with unfamiliar fear, he was able to discern another pair of eyes unblinkingly looking back. Beneath the level of the man's head was a sizable mass of a human body, which appeared to lack legs until Dell realized the fellow had drawn them up and was languidly clasping them below the knees.

"I got me a name," Dell protested, trying to regain his composure. "I'm Dell, and—"

"Names don't mean diddly in here till y'earns them, boy." The face Dell couldn't clearly see produced a sigh. "Sweet Jesus, you aren't even thirty years old. Streets ain't safe no more with babies outside, killin' folks."

Dell was rooted where he stood. Where he came from, a white man was supposed to have no use for black folks and, since Dell had almost no use for people even with the same color skin he had, he'd been able to go along with that particular rule with no trouble.

This black, though, had him a rumblin' bass voice made for lullabies or spirituals and sounded at least as sure of himself as Dell. Judging from the attitude in the man's voice, it didn't seem likely to find him singing songs to babies. Dell caught his breath.

"I ain't no kid," Dell said, "and I don't give a fuck if you tell me yore name or not." That much boldly said, and deciding to edge closer—you couldn't tell what you could take from a man till you'd seen him—Dell supposed he ought to say something more polite. "Besides, I'll turn thirty years old in here, and—"

He stopped a few feet away from the seated man when he realized he was carefully gripping a crudely made knife in his large hands. What light there was in the cell rushed to the blade.

"This is a two-man cell, meat. You need not draw near enough to me for a kiss." Teeth flashed in a grin, but it was impossible for Dell to judge whether it was friendly or humorous. "After we been together awhile, I thinks you'll be able to remember ol' Lloyd B. without the need of greater intimacy."

Not really knowing what he meant, Dell cleared his throat. "Whut do the 'B' stand for, Lloyd? That your last name?"

"Perhaps I took it for the same reason Malcolm chose his 'X,' eh? To escape the tyranny of a slave ancestry? What d'you think, boy? Or perhaps my last name *is* 'Bee,' and it's merely your ear that messed up."

"Mah ears is as good as anybuddy's," Dell snapped. He squinted into Lloyd's gathering shadows. "Whut's it like here?"

"Long, whitemeat," said Lloyd B., his chuckle pointed this time. "*Very* long."

Dell nodded, abandoned small talk. He turned to the empty bunk, untied the mattress where a cord held it together, even found a pillow of sorts wrapped in it. Grunting, relaxed, he placed the pillow at the head of the bed and stretched out. The mattress was like Scott tissue. Without taking off his shoes, he slipped his arms beneath the pillow as well as the back of his head and shut his eyes.

A hulking brown mountain hovered above him with such stillness and suddenness that Dell didn't have the faintest idea what was happening. When he strove to liberate the thumbs he thought of as powerful outward symbols of his primary magic, the pressure on his arms was acutely agonizing. He would have cried out with pain except that the older man on top of him had somehow managed to cover his mouth, too.

Dell's entire, nauseatingly selfish and evil life began to flash before his eyes. It was a shock that he was seeing it with detachment and a feeling of near revulsion.

"This is a start on what will happen to you in this joint if you fail to *hear* me, whitemeat," Lloyd B. growled, mouth inches from Dell's right ear. "*You* must be *my boy* from the start, this instant! Y'all are *new,* son—fresh. There'll be twenty, thirty bad cats after yore pasty ass!"

Dell was horrified. But he found the corner of his mouth open; he was able to speak. "Lloyd, I jest don't wanna be no prevert!" For the first time he caught a glimpse of his cellmate's face. "It ain't thet yore a nigger, or nothing *personal* like thet—I swear! If I *wanted* t'be a prevert, yew'd be my choice. But—"

"*Listen to me,*" Lloyd B. commanded. "I'd sooner stick my fine dick into a hole in my *mattress* than let it come within five *feet* of your worthless anatomy!" He relaxed slightly, glanced into the shadows. "If a man is intelligent, there are many ways of becoming someone's boy in this place."

Dell was finally able to make out the man's eyes, moist-looking and black, as if Lloyd B. might have cried himself to sleep a few times; they swam in little oceans of white and pinkness. They were wide, those eyes—not just big—and the forehead above them was short before becoming a nice even line of tightly curled ebony hair. Lloyd could have been forty years old or sixty.

"Here's what I wants from y'all," Lloyd drawled sarcastically, "Dell-the-meat. To find out how very

smart I am, provin' it by doin' the shit I ask y'all to do.''

"But yew said—"

"*No sex*!" Lloyd B. said, snapping off the words. "Whether you goes straight or gets worse than y'all are awready, I want all the boys who share my cell to be *smart*." Dell saw he was smiling. "Cuz I damn sure don't mean to spend eight or nine years of my valuable life with no dirtbag dumb honky. This is my *my home*!''

Dell paused as if to think and there was re-newed pressure everywhere on his body. "Awright, awright," he said, hurting till Lloyd had rolled away and was on his feet, standing but ready to fall upon Dell again. Dell massaged one aching wrist with the other hand, worked his way to a throbbing seated position. "So whut *are* you, Lloyd B.," he inquired, "some sorta gawdamn teacher?"

The black looked down at him another mo-ment, studying him. Then he turned his face so he could merge with the shadows and seemed to be nodding as he did so. "May be, Dell," he rumbled, returning to his bed. "May be. A *damned good* one, very possibly."

When he lowered his bulk to the mattress, Lloyd laughed. "Or it could be I gets off on showin' little whitemeat sandwiches how fucking little they know and how wrong all the Mister Charlies were to believe *I* was the ignorant one!"

Dell fell asleep wondering what it was that this nigger wanted to teach him, and what his game *really* was.

Eventually his right thumb slipped naturally between his lips and he sucked noisily on it for the rest of the night, while he dreamed of power and death.

CHAPTER

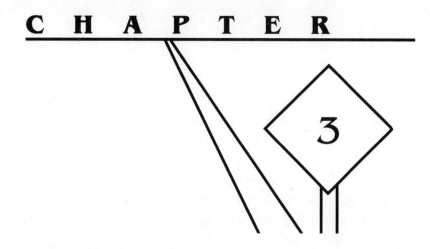

3

(A passing look at the life of a girl who might very well like the idea of riding around in a lot of cars and vans with a man very much like Dell.)

The physician had examined his woman patient from head to toe—"from A to izzard," as he liked to put it—and he'd been unable to pinpoint any malady visible either to X-ray or the naked eye. He had recommended a vitamin but without any confidence that it would make the woman feel appreciably better. Not, in any case, about life.

Now he knew where her problems lay and where he should have begun his examination, except for the fact that he was no psychologist, he was just an aging small town doctor. "You and Ewing once wanted several children, Natalie Grace," he said, folding his hands over his vested abdomen. "But there's only the one child. Honey, what happened to that dream?"

She was still youthful, still pretty beneath the strain on her face. For a moment it appeared to Dr. Lidbetter that he wouldn't be able to draw her out. Natalie Grace McCaulter worked for his friend Ardo Simpkins, over at the Second Cherokee Rose Baptist Church; she was an educated woman and a good Christian who wouldn't like airing her problems, especially not when they were connected to her only child.

"Kee," she admitted at length. For an instant the new lines in her face vanished, drawing her skin taut over her wide cheekbones and making her high, pale forehead look as if it might burst open. "Kee happened."

He attempted to elicit more from Natalie Grace—some specifics—but about all Marley Lidbetter got from her that afternoon was a reluctant admission that there were times when six-year-old Kee simply didn't appear "normal" to the mother. Lidbetter would have pressed Natalie Grace on that, even though he knew mothers of only children were the world's greatest worriers, except for several

60

very good reasons: Natalie Grace had told him during previous office visits of little Kee's antics. Marley had even made a complete record of them in his patient file.

A mother who had longed for a child—even if it was by a woman-chasing husband who wasn't worth spit—didn't feel anything except guilt by revealing family secrets concerning an adorable-looking daughter who was just starting school, particularly when the mother was deeply religious and believed much more in the answer to her prayers than she did a gray-haired country GP.

He and Rev. Simpkins had felt Kee McCaulter was different somehow from the day of her birth, and had already discusssed the girl a dozen times. So it was hard for Lidbetter now to imagine Kee had done anything significantly stranger or more inappropriate since he'd given Natalie Grace her annual examination only six months before.

Of course, I could be wrong, he admitted to himself, peering through the window of his first-floor office as the exhausted young mother got into her car, clutching his prescription as tightly as if it had been a tether, a lifeline.

Cherokee Rose, Georgia, was a town small enough that people brought rumors and gossip to him much the way they'd paid his daddy—also a family physician—with produce and hams during the Great Depression. Marley tried not to pay any attention—*tried not to let myself pay attention*, he corrected his thoughts—but he heard things from other folks about young Kee. Some said she was the moodiest little creature they'd ever seen, one minute running around like a wild Indian and the next minute staring into space, paying nobody any attention. Mrs. Bohannon, who lived near the peanut farm Ewing McCaulter inherited from Big Ewe, said Kee hated to be stared at, batted her tiny hands in the air when she believed people were watching her, and one day even struck the Bohannon woman for doing it. More than one resident of Cherokee Rose had told Marley they didn't let their children play with Kee, said she was an "exhibitionist" or a "show-off," and Kevin Durham had come right out with it on his last office checkup and asked when somebody was going to "get smart" and "put that sassy brat where she won't get other kids in trouble."

And Kee was a mere six years of age.

Dr. Lidbetter opened Kee's file, a separate one from her mother's, to remind himself of what Natalie Grace reported or he himself had recorded. She'd fought being weaned harder than any toddler in Marley's experience. So Kee had begun pointing to her mother's breasts in public and making odd little noises in her throat and with her lips. Natalie Grace put her foot down, but Kee took to chewing her fingernails—not in the customary sense of nibbling at them, but munching on them till they actually bled. The mother had put iodine on the nails at Lidbetter's advice, but Kee went right on chewing till she was getting sick from the stuff. *N. G. so desperate she nursed Kee one more time*, read Marley's handwritten report. *Gave N. G. bruises but Kee ceased clamoring for the breast that day, went straight to baby food.*

And that, Marley thought, was real will power. Not to mention getting her way at all costs.

As a toddler, Kee had taken off her diaper to follow a Mr. Softee ice cream truck over a mile away from the farm. The driver took the infant home, gave her a free cone, and Kee didn't seem to notice how hysterical her mama was.

Lidbetter's own comments about the child merely indicated her glowing health, except for two items: The first was that she didn't seem to mind anything he did to her during examinations except when he looked into her eyes. She'd barely sit still for the little light and, since she appeared to have perfect eyesight, he had never pressed it.

But now that Marley remembered it, Natalie Grace had told his friend Ardo about Kee insisting upon attending a funeral service with her mother. Kee said she wanted to see what dead people's eyes looked like and, to Natalie Grace's horror, the child had peeled back the body's eyelids to find out. Kids did inexplicable things at times, but that had seemed pretty morbid.

The other observation the doctor had scribbled down was his amazement over the way Kee had passed from being an almost obesely plump new-born to a little charmer within months. Kee was two then. He'd made light of it with Natalie Grace, but she'd sworn Kee considered herself ugly and some-how willed herself to lose the babyfat nearly over-

night. Marley had found that absurd; now, he wasn't
so sure.

Of course, part of all the McCaulters' problems,
including the mother's exhaustion, stemmed from
Ewing, the father. His brain was surely about the
size of one of the peanuts his daddy had grown
successfully, since the farm he had left young Ewe
was quickly being run into the ground. McCaulter
kept saying Jimmy Carter would buy the farm any
moment and make them a terrific profit, but that
was doubtful. Ewe was mainly an unfaithful bag of
wind who definitely wasn't the right pa for a child
like Kee. *Or maybe he's the ideal pa and the girl just
takes after him*, Marley ruminated.

He spent the rest of the day trying to get the
worn-out Natalie Grace, her strange offspring, and
backward husband out of his thoughts. No one had
ever told him how he was supposed to forget about
patients for whom all the medication he had to offer
was upward of sixty years of existence. By bedtime
he wondered if the time would come when all he
could do for poor Natalie Grace was write a piece for
the *AMA Journal*, to caution other people. Caution
them about what? Dr. Lidbetter asked himself, just
as he rested his head on the pillow.

About being religious and educated, too,
maybe—or that and marrying a selfish, rutting
clown of a man so you increased your chances of
having kids who were neither fish nor fowl. Or
closing your eyes to it when, after the child came
along, you and your mate had nothing in common

all at once—so the child wasn't able to get clear signals from anybody, and just grew.

Or grew bizarrely, living in a private world in which, increasingly, she couldn't tell the difference between fantasy and reality, her weird dreams and notions on the one hand and the expectations society had on the other.

All of which might prove to be patent nonsense, Marley realized as he was beginning to doze off, except for two things he believed he'd learned were God's own truths: not many six-year-olds used to come along who seemed as if they were nearly born to be bad news to everybody around them . . .

And when the news got as bad as it was going to get, the one who would pay the most heavily would be Natalie Grace. Because, the doctor thought, that was the way of this world. The mother would pay. Where the kids were concerned, she always did.

When she was nine, Kee drank most of a six-pack of beer belonging to her daddy, threw up on a new front room rug, and Daddy beat Mama because she'd been working at the church and away from home, unable to stop Kee from doing it. It didn't matter to Ewing that Natalie Grace went to her job everyday and Kee had said she would be staying after school to help her teacher.

At ten, Kee was caught stealing from the collection plate at the Cherokee Rose Baptist Church. Then she was caught stealing a jacket from the cloakroom at school. Rev. Simpkins didn't say anything much because Natalie Grace worked for him, and Miss Zenniger, hearing from Kee that her mama and daddy didn't have any money left for warm jackets and she was *so* cold, forgave her—except for a note that she sent to Natalie Grace and Ewing. Natalie Grace tore it up before Ewe could see it since the previous bruises he'd put on her hadn't yet faded.

Kee began her eleventh year of life by dreaming of a Prince Charming of her very own and buying a diary, with allowance money, in which she could record her every thought. She printed "MY BOOK" on the cover with a black crayon.

When her mother stumbled upon it one autumn morning and read some of her daughter's early entries, it became the first time Natalie Grace discovered how wise she had been in deciding to have no additional children.

Ewe was at work—more or less—in the fields, Kee was at school—or supposed to be—and Natalie Grace herself was too ill with the flu to go to work at the church. Alone in Kee's bedroom, flooded by fall sunshine, she almost didn't look inside the diary. Natalie Grace knew it sharply violated Kee's privacy, but she also understood that the girl hadn't once shown her any reason for trusting her, even for five minutes. Perhaps, Natalie Grace hoped, it would forewarn her against the child's next mischief.

"Everyone stares at me all the time like Im a dumb freak for what I think or somethin," one page of the eleven-year-old's diary began, "so I got to noticin eyes. Dogs eyes and peoples eyes an all kinds." Natalie Grace frowned, glanced up at the many pictures of Kee McCaulter in the bedroom. There must have been a dozen. There were no photographs of any other McCaulter present. "In human beans growed up eyes has seen so many people and things jest the way they wants to see them that they got vales over there eyes and cant see anythin the way it is no more. I been wonderin if dead folks who turn into ghosts cant go to heaven since they dont have *reel eyes* no more and cant see where there goin."

Taken by itself, that entry might just have been a little girl's fantasy; Natalie Grace understood that. But Kee had written more:

"I sawed my friend Sue Elenor's mama in the funeral home the other day and wondered what she'd see if she opened her eyes then. Mebbe dead is the way to be, or for some folks. Sue Elenor's mama didn't watch me. Not yet anyway but shed be a ghost now anyways." Then Kee had scribbled in the margin, her handwriting tighter to fit the space, "If my mama and daddy was dead too they couldn't watch me all the time. Or if they did, I wouldden have to know it."

Another entry: "Daddy's still waitin for that President Carter to by the farm and everybody in town nose that wont happen, even Mama. I hate rich folks who got everything and I hate Daddy and Mama for *havin nothin*. Well, they could get somethin if theyd *get it*! I saw a nice coat at school I wanted and I took it and teacher didn't do *nothin*.

What do I care about lil letters on a old cardboard anyhow?'' Then, in an ink of a different color, ''Mama goes to church and they says not to steel or you won't go to haven. If I'm jest gonna be a ghost with diffrunt kinds of eyes someday, what do I care about that eether?''

Still standing, Natalie Grace kept thumbing through Kee's book, remembering as she turned the pages that Kee was a child, the diary entries meant that Kee was becoming older by days and months, and that time was very different to children. The next place at which she paused read as follows: ''Sue Elenor said we shud go have sex cause wes old enough now, and she said Willie somethin (I think Fawkner or somethin) would give me fifty cents to take off my pantees, a dollar to do that and play with his thang.'' The entry shocked Natalie Grace to the core and she nearly threw the diary across her daughter's bedroom without reading another word. Her heart was beating wildly when she stared back down at the childishly scrawled pages, read what Kee had written next: ''It warn't no big deal but i got my dollar. He didn't have no more money though.''

Natalie Grace felt as if she'd been hit in the stomach by a baseball bat. But search as frantically as she'd ever searched for anything, Natalie Grace found nothing more in the diary about her daughter's direct participation in sexual activities. For an instant she was content to focus on how abominably Kee spelled and wonder how a nearly illiterate child could conceivably be her own.

Then, reading more, she discovered that Kee

was developing an incredible fantasy life, which exceeded anything she herself had conjured before or after her marriage to Ewing McCaulter.

The horrid truth was that Kee, who wasn't even a teenager yet (Natalie Grace's yearned–for *key* to deciphering God's pattern for them on earth!), was imagining sexual acts that Natalie Grace and Ewing had never considered trying. Natalie Grace confessed to herself that Ewing and she had tried two of those acrobatic feats early in their marriage, but even Ewe hadn't wanted to experiment with the others from fear that the two of them might get stuck.

Kee went on about more of her budding desires and opinions:

"I don't think boys is any good for hard stuff like that cause Sue Elenor says they aint got no controls and its like someone trying to eat a whole cake or pie, there eyes is bigger than their stomaks. We both think you got to find a older man, one with lots of x-peryance. One whos done a hole lot of thangs in life and got hisself reel cool. But evin Sue Elenor dont beleeve what I tole her last night that I dreamd about."

Natalie Grace found her concentration deepening at the same time that her heart was racing faster than it had raced before.

"I seed a man jest like I was thinkin about comin to town and takin me away with him, a man mebbe as old as Daddy but a *reel man*, not like Willie Fawkner, not like Daddy. A man whos done everything, even hurt people who got in his way who has a big car or somethin and dont care if I drive arown with him and if we *cloz up all them watchin eyes and make them ghost eyes* that dont see nothing reel no more."

"My God," Natalie Grace prayed aloud in her little girl's bedroom, then felt regret that she had mentioned the Almighty in a room where her flesh and blood had such dreams, created such terrible desires.

Yet she did not want Kee to know that she had slipped into her private world, telling herself that, by admitting nothing to Kee, she would be able to return for updates from the diary and at least keep abreast of developments in the child's life.

She did, however, try to share her frightening discovery with her husband Ewing.

"Kids're diff'rent these days," he said over morning coffee. Kee had already departed for school. "They hear a lot of shit we didn't hear when we was kids. More common-ist in-doctrination."

"But she's been *stealing* again, she took off her panties for some *boy;* she has her own evil *beliefs,*" Natalie Grace argued. "And she wondered what it would be like if we were *dead*! Ewing, she dreams of wanting to r-run off with an older man and . . . *kill* people! Damn it, you idiot, I'm afraid K-Kee is *crazy*!"

He scratched avidly under one flannel-clad armpit, sighed, and stood up. "Mebbe I'm an idiot, but I ain't no Russkie commie red callin' my daughter crazy. *You're* the one who's so smart, *you* figger it out. I got thangs t'do besides mope about a goofy kid's daydreams.''

The main thing Ewe had in mind doing that day, he did—once Kee was in school and his wife-bitch was off to save her soul or somebody else's at the church. Ewing entertained a currently blond woman named Bonnie Lee Hardacre in his and Natalie Grace's bathtub and then their bed.

He didn't even hear Kee, whom Miss Zenniger had sent home from school for failing to do her homework and then sassing her, quietly enter the house.

Kee swiftly realized what her daddy was doing and observed him and the lady she didn't know through a crack in the bedroom door for as long as he lasted—it wasn't long—and advanced the education that interested her with intense and delighted fascination.

And after Bonnie Lee Hardacre put her things back on and went home, Kee just let her daddy discover her there.

"Y'know this is blackmail, honey," Ewing told her.

"Oh, Daddy," Kee howled, kicking her skinny legs in apparent amusement, "yew always say the funniest things!"

He stared back at her awhile, trying to decide whether to smile along or not. For the life of him, Ewing had never quite understood his only child. It would have amazed him if anyone had suggested that was like failing to recognize his own face in the mirror.

J . N . WILLIAMSON

It wasn't more than several weeks later—a period of time Kee enjoyed immensely because of the pretty jacket and other things her daddy bought for her to Natalie Grace's numbed amazement—before Ewing's only similarity to his daughter was the fact that their fundamental attitudes on life remained largely the same. To Natalie Grace's dismay, Ewing fell severely ill, and Kee stayed the very image of bursting vitality.

Neither Kee nor Natalie Grace knew what ailed Ewing because he did his level best to keep the nature of his illness to himself. He would have succeeded, too, except that Kee happened to over-hear a conversation Ewe had with one of his few male friends. The gist of it astonished Kee.

The whispered news was that her daddy's after-noon dalliance with the yellow-haired Ms. Hardacre had left Ewe (he confided in his friend) with a sick-ness that could ruin his sexual life—and other aspects of life, as well. It might even kill him.

The eavesdropping Kee had never been so dis-gusted in her whole short life.

Any man whom she had dreamed about in her heart of hearts would *never* have fallen sick because *he'd done it with a girl.* The way Kee had been raised, men were supposed to be stronger than women—and that included their germs!

Soon after Kee had two further dreams about the brave, bold, older man who was gonna save her from a boring life like Mama's and take her off on the trail to good times, which she believed she'd been born to enjoy.

But awake, Kee knew she had to begin laying plans just right in order for her dream man to know where she was and come after her.

She was damn sure he wasn't hanging around Cherokee Rose, Georgia.

First, she got Willie Fawkner's telephone number from Sue Elenor and called Willie, asking him if he had more than a dollar this time. "Not much," he told her, "mebbe a quarter more'n that."

Kee said okay, that was enough if he wanted to go all the way. "When?" Willie asked for want of anything more quick-thinking to say, but he didn't sound bored.

"Right now, 'cause I got to see if I got the hang of it," Kee said, remembering what Bonnie Lee Hardacre had done with Daddy.

But her private reason for making it now, so fast, was that Kee had suddenly realized that getting her older man to tune in to her, to *sense* that she was waiting for him in Cherokee Rose, might depend on her not being cherry anymore. Why would a real man, a man of the world, want to drive around with her and have fun if she was only an ignorant virgin who needed to pester him all the time?

She got her dollar and a quarter, but twelve-year-old Willie let her down in every other way. Imitating Ms. Hardacre, Kee got Willie so excited he never did do what he was supposed to do. He never even really got started! Whether that counted as a consequence in making her dream man sense her existence, Kee was unable to judge. Feckless Willie had let her down so badly Kee was really pee-ohed, and if he hadn't been lots bigger than she was, why, she might almost have killed him.

So Kee tried to figure what went wrong and learned Willie had smoked some grass to get ready for her. It was then that Kee joined the millions of grownups who were anti-drug, even if her reasons weren't remotely the same.

She swore she'd never do drugs when all they did was make it hard to get a little nookie. Besides, the older man in her dreams was bound to have *some* standards—Mama couldn't be wrong (she thought doubtfully) about *everthing*, and Natalie Grace had been after all her dozen years of life to believe in *something.*

Then she wrote about her experience with Willie in her book and put it back in the place where she always kept it.

"I finely did it today, went all the way with Willie," Kee's entry read, making Natalie Grace— who was reading it just a few hours later—think she might swoon. She slumped down on the edge of Kee's bed and continued to read.

"It was only a buck and a quarters worth but it was fantastic and I practicly heard that ol cherry pop in 2 when he penitrated me. It was right after I went down on him, but I didden do that long cause he tasted sort of funny, like peanut butter somebuddy left out in the sun too long."

Natalie dropped the diary, Kee's book, and fanned herself with both hands until she was able to pick up the book again.

"That ain't true, *Mama*," the diary continued,

"I jest put that there for you but I tried to do it with Willie and he warn't no good. No more than Daddy is."

Natalie Grace's eyes protruded and her accelerating heart achieved new and terrifying rhythmic heights. It took her another second before she could fully comprehend that the *brassy little bitch* had *dared* to address her in such a manner!

"See, I stuck somea my hair on my book reel good, with lotsa spit, and ever time I did that, the hair wasn't there no more. I knos Daddy don't want to read nothin so it had to be you peekin in my book.

"If I'm wrong," Kee's scribble continued, "it won't hurt none to put in here that Daddy's sick 'cause he did it with Bonnie Lee Hardacre *right in yore own bed*! I think you should know about it but I couldden figer out any way to tell you, Mama, x-cept this. I bet Dr. Lidbitter can tell you morea the truth if you wants to talk to him."

Natalie Grace let Kee's book fall to the blanket of her bed. She made no effort to close or lock it, as she had in the past. She simply stood, took a few seconds to make sure that her legs would support her, then wobbled out into the hallway and her future.

Natalie Grace had had—at last—enough.

It was one thing for Kee to take advantage of Ewing's willingness to side with Kee in order to laugh at her, and it might even be all right for Ewe to believe in his daughter so much that when he heard the little brat was writing dreadful things in her diary, her "book," he wanted to buy her presents to make her feel better.

But it was something else entirely when the crazy little tramp decided to interfere in her parents' married life, claiming that her very own father was sick with a venereal disease! Natalie Grace was furious, ready to demand that Kee apologize to both her parents and then begin to live *properly*, *decently*, like a normal little girl!

Humiliated by Kee's taunting personal message to her about sealing the damnable "book" with her hair and spit, Natalie Grace went looking for her daughter, hands working—clawing—as she began to poke into every possible hiding place in the house.

Then she remembered that Kee was in school.

And it occurred to her, with such a sudden, dismal sense of fairness that she stopped walking and the anger seeped out like air from a punctured tire, what else Kee had said in the diary:

"I bet Dr. Lidbitter can tell you morea the truth if you wants to talk to him."

Natalie Grace did not want to do that at all. While she moved as though sleepwalking toward the nearest telephone, she told herself something would absolutely *have* to be done about the girl's abysmal spelling. And, when she dialed Dr. Lidbetter's number and was tensely listening for him to pick up, Natalie Grace wondered for the umpteenth time how an educated woman could possibly have given birth to such a stupid, illiterate, conniving little—

The elderly physician answered and, when he heard what his caller wanted to know, tried to tell her something about doctor-patient confidentiality. Then he wilted in the face of Natalie Grace's tears and his own disapproval, both of Ewing McCaulter and his pretty, free-as-air-and-looking-for-more daughter. "Your husband has syphilis," he informed Natalie Grace. "Of the most degenerative kind, Natalie Grace. It will affect his vision—and other parts of the body. I was debating whether or not I should let you know, since you're his wife."

She heard the rest of what Marley had to tell her—no, there wasn't a way in the world he'd picked it up from a toilet seat, there was just one way he could've gotten it—and found herself sitting on the floor by the telephone stand when the conversation was over.

Because, Natalie Grace knew, the conversation wasn't the only thing that had ended.

Kee, listening in on an extension, had to drop the phone instead of hanging it up so she wouldn't be caught by the onslaught of triumphal giggling positively overcoming her.

C H A P T E R

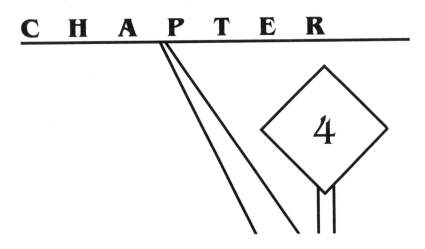

(How Dell first found education and a bit more magic but said, "No, thanks," for the time being.)

Dell had agreed to be Lloyd B.'s boy without remotely meaning it.

It was just the best way he could imagine to make his cellmate leave him alone for a while—long enough to size up the older man and determine how risky it would be to kill him if he had to.

True, Dell had reached the point of believing he

needed to know more than he knew—but that was when he was on the outside, free to pursue knowledge and magic the way he wanted. He wasn't about to let anybody else tell him what to do or even what to know, especially a black con who talked as if he was going to spend the rest of his life in prison. What had happened to Dell, he believed, was a bad break, a once-in-a-lifetime thing that he sure as hell wouldn't permit to happen again. He'd do the time and keep his nose clean, if the other fellas left him alone, and be back on the road when ol' Lloyd B. was six feet under.

Meanwhile, he'd just go through the motions of doing whatever his roomie told him to do—not that he was *scared* of the big man he was stuck with in the same cell; Lloyd had better not think *that* for a second! Dell just hadn't expected to be jumped, and now he meant to be on guard and not ever let himself be put in any more embarrassing positions. Like not being able to breathe.

Besides, noisy brawls in the cells got the guards real nervous. There was no gawdamn reason to wind up in solitary. When he, Dell from hell, was ready to improve his reading and search for the magic he needed, he'd do it. And meanwhile, ol' Dellie would be sizing up the joint and figuring the angles as he always had.

The next time Lloyd or any damn body even *tried* to get tough with him, they'd find out just who Dell was and the main difference between him and them:

If they was no other choice, Dell wouldn't mind just killin' them.

Fighting, Dell believed with all his heart, was really dumb. Two old boys tried to make smoke come out of their noses and called each other names they'd both already heard maybe a thousand times, and then they whaled away at each other till their arms were ready to fall off their bodies and they both had blood and bruises from head to toe.

When you had a chance to take out somebody who was causing you problems or somebody you hated, knocking him out was stupid. You *killed* him, then you didn't have to fret about what he might do when he came to next time.

Ol' Lloyd B. was slipping over onto his other side, letting out a big sigh as though he believed—while he was sleeping—some woman was next to him with her legs spread nice and wide. *Lord, Lord*, Dell thought, *jest imaginin' Lloyd imaginin' a bare-ass dream piece is gittin' t'be a turn-on!*

He'd make it all the way through his sentence, somehow—he truly would. And when he'd served it, when he was out on the streets again, he would by Gawd have himself as many women as he could haul into his vehicle of the moment! He'd have so many females he might not even *want* one for a week, *two* weeks—

But he'd go on having them anyhow, Dell decided—boosting just as many women as he did automobiles—because it was Mom's fault and that ugly dead little shrink's that he was in the joint right now instead of *improving* himself.

When you looked at it that way, Dell thought, resisting the temptation to pick up a jack-off magazine somebody had stuck between the bars as a favor to Lloyd B., prison life was hardening! After all, before they'd caught Dell daydreaming about finding some little virgin girl for his traveling companion, he had really held it down some, tried to focus on business.

Some of the guys in jail with him were disgusting about the magazines with the naked women, Dell believed. Last week a guy four or five cells away had cut his roomie bad because of a gatefold picture. All the first fella had done was want to borrow the girl—but the owner, Gawd Almighty, he'd left a cheek flap like a bird wing hanging from that fella's face, even tried to hack off one of his fingers!

No *way* he was gone get like that, Dell swore. No way even if he had to break *out* to get himself some the normal way! There had to be hundreds of women within a couple of miles of the prison to show a blade to or to half strangle. Hell, he wasn't even thirty years old yet; they weren't going to turn Dell into a gawdamn pervert just because the prison people thought they had all the fucking cards.

Lloyd woke up coughing. Dell's gaze shot to him, in case his cellmate had it in mind to jump him again. Fact was, the man wasn't hurting him, which wasn't what Dell had heard about colored folks when they couldn't get no tail. Instead, Lloyd B. had this interest in *learning* Dell. And so far, all he had really said was that the best thing Dell could do was learn to read. *Really* do it, not just know what was on street signs and all, but know lots of words.

"Words," Lloyd had said, "is what folks can use to make themselves superior to the rest of the animal kingdom."

"I'm already better than most animals," Dell said back.

"Are you?" Lloyd asked from his bunk, eyes like spotlights from the shadows that made a point of getting together in Lloyd's area. "Why is it, then, you can only whup them if you have a *weapon*? Animals have none."

Dell snorted, sort of snickered. "Yew sayin I can't beat up no cats or dogs? *I* got t'be scareda cows, 'n sheep, 'n animals like them?"

"Whitemeat, you is one dumb-ass honky piece of *shit!*" Lloyd B. said. And Dell wanted to go for him, but he got the idea Lloyd was talking black again just to piss him off. "You are incapable of replying even with the most rudimental gawdamned logic." Lloyd leaned forward on his bunk. "If humankind lost its weaponry and the animals of the wild *massed*—if they elected to come at us with the single objective of wiping every one of us *out*—they could do it in hours. Hours!"

"Well," Dell answered, thinking this was the silliest talk he'd ever had, "I s'pose if I had enough of yore books lyin around—and if I could throw 'em fast enough, hard enough—I could be king of the jungle, right?" He fell back against the wall, laughing. "Shee-it, Lloyd B.! What good're books and learnin crap when somebuddy's tryin' t'kill yore ass?''

Lloyd B. just shook his head. ''You're *mah boy*, Dell-the-whitemeat-of-all-turkeydom—and we's gonna go to the prison library together, you hear? I'm gonna *teach* you what's important about reading if it's the last thing I do in this joint!''

''Jest because you don't wanta be with no dumb-ass for years,'' Dell had remarked, ''that right?''

Lloyd's startlingly deep, intense eyes found him and almost pinned Dell to the wall. ''That's the only reason *you're* gonna get, Dell *boy*. If I has *other* reasons, they's none of your mutherfucking *business*. You got me?''

Dell had let it go at that. Ole Lloyd, he was only a joke, nothing more. There wasn't a doubt Dell could take him, beat his black ass into the floor if he wanted. For now, having Lloyd B. as a roomie was almost fun, kind of. At least he beat boredom. There was no reason to lose control and kill him yet.

One morning, awaking in an independent mood, Dell didn't wake Lloyd B. to tell him they were opening the cell doors for cons in their quadrant to shower. For the time being Dell reckoned it was high time to get better acquainted with the joint. Maybe he would take time to wash up and maybe he wouldn't. At the juvie center he'd found a lot of opportunities to make things nicer for himself by circulating, letting the boys know who was boss by whipping a few wimps into shape. He figured hiding himself away would do no good but that knowing any slammer really well was smart, in case he ever tried to take a permanent walk away.

There was also the fact that a man could never know where he might find himself some magic to take.

Though Dell noticed a lot of men behind bars who looked purty large, and strong, he didn't see anybody he was 'specially impressed by as he swaggered behind a guard toward the showers.

But it did occur to Dell that morning to wonder why there weren't more inmates accompanying him and the uniformed man. Once they passed through a door to the showers, he noticed that there weren't a lot of places for showering or shitting, so it made sense that the joint would let the men in on a staggered basis. When the guard called "ten minutes" and stopped outside, there were only three other fellas present and a chill swept down Dell's backbone as if cold water had been sprayed on it.

Crap, who needs to keep purty jest for another dude? Dell decided as the other men stepped into the bath area without him. Dr. Middel had thought BMs were gawdamn important, and he figured he'd have plenty of time now to get well-acquainted with his bowels, maybe even learn to *control* them—make 'em move when *he* told them to do it. A toilet stall was to his left and had considerably more appeal to him just then than showering with three strangers and no guard around.

After Dell was inside, dropping his shorts, the latch on the door made him feel even more content that he'd made the right decision. Sooner or later he'd have to wash up, he knew, but there wasn't any *big* rush to it. *Ackshally*, Dell thought, *the more I stink, the more nobody's gonna do—*

"I know you're hiding in there," a male voice interrupted from the other side of the door. "Come on out when you're ready. I won't hurt you."

A pair of bare white feet showed beneath the door. They still glistened with water from a quick shower.

Glancing around from his seated position, Dell noticed the grafitti on the walls at his sides. Half the messages and crude drawings had been carved, not inscribed with a pen or crayon. There was nothing unusual about that outside the prison, but Dell thought the guards took blades away from his fellow prisoners. The discovery spooked him.

"I may be a leetle while," Dell said as if the speaker with the dripping feet had only asked to use the toilet. "I'm new in here and I got all backed up."

"Don't let that worry you, hon," the other man said reassuringly. The suggestion in the voice made Dell sweat, caused him to shoot out a hand to make sure the latch on the door was secure.

But it wasn't. Just as Dell's fingertips made shaky contact with the gadget, the door swung back against his naked knees, kicked in, the blow numbing his legs.

A short man of about forty with a face like a chipmunk stood above Dell. He wore nothing but a towel tied loosely at the waist and it was already tented. Instinctively, Dell squeezed his aching knees together and fumbled for his shorts, simultaneously trying to look above the protrusion in the stranger's towel toward his face.

"You can come out and get it nice and slow," the man said in a rasping voice which was also fuzzily confidential, "or you can have it rough— very, very rough."

Moving more carefully and deliberately than he ever had before, Dell arose, pulling his shorts up with him, his towel and bar of soap in the other hand. He was relieved instantly to learn that he was quite a bit taller than the intruder. "Nothin' personal, but this ain't my thang. So I reckon I'll jest pass on yore offer."

The fellow with the chipmunk face only smiled more widely, confidently, and padded one step to his left.

That revealed *another* man. No towel, stark naked. *Mebbe*, Dell thought, *because there ain't towels big enough t'hide a king-size cock like thet.* This guy was taller than the first man, too, decently muscled, with black tight curly hair all over his body.

"I'll be first," announced the small one with the towel. He sounded as if he were choosing up sides for a game. "Then Calbert. And—"

"Yew didn't say whut *yore* name is," Dell reminded him. He was trying to see if a running start might get him through the two men, and it didn't look promising. He told himself he wasn't really afraid, he could probably take out both perverts.

The towel-clad leader beamed at Dell. "*I* see! You want to know the name of your *first*—to put in your very own love-book!" A hand darted out with astonishing speed, the fingers patting Dell's cheek. "Bless your heart, honey, Randy understands." He drew the hand back, cocked his head. "My best friends call me *Real* Randy."

Dell nodded, couldn't think what to say or what to do. But he knotted his fingers in his towel, wondering if he couldn't at least belt one of them with the hard soap at the end of the towel before they got him. If he did, he'd kill the other son-of-a-bitch by strangling him, even if the aw-thorities gave him life for it!

"You didn't let me finish," Randy said. He stepped back a pace, inviting Dell to leave the stall, his tented towel as unswerving as steel. "I'm first, *then* Calbert"—he put his fingers to the knot in his towel, began to undo it—"and Big Emmitt will be third!"

An arm like a python descended from behind Dell—behind the toilet stall—clutching at his shoulder. Truly scared shitless, Dell looked over his shoulder and saw the head of number three—a man who was probably seven feet tall—peering down at him. His blond hair hung down past his wide shoulders.

At the moment Emmitt's fingers began to clamp down, Dell swung the soap-loaded towel like a baseball bat, hitting Calbert directly in the face. Blood flew from his broken nose and Dell shoved his way past the nude man out into the shower area.

But Real Randy's reaching fingers, the nails scratching him badly, caught Dell's arm and threw him back against the stalls.

Randy had removed his towel and it hadn't been his erect penis that tented the cloth—it was a knife, from the prison kitchen.

A butcher knife.

"I asked yore name," Dell said, up on his toes and still gripping the towel, "'cause I cottons t'know the name of the men I *like* t'kill." Calbert was still blinking and bleeding, trying to clear his vision, so Dell would have to work fast—take out Randy, the short man, before Big Emmitt came around from behind the toilets. He thought again of yelling for help but figured it would do no good. "Mebbe Emmitt'll git me, but I'm gonna make yew eat that hog-sticker!"

"Come on, Calbert, it's just your *nose*," Randy said. Suddenly his eyes looked wide, wild. He had the butcher knife pointed at Dell as if it were a revolver. "Get your butt *out* here, Emmitt!"

Dell had a split second to act when Real Randy shot a glance behind him at the yellow-haired giant, who was just lumbering into Dell's own view—and Dell used his opportunity well.

He feinted with the towel—showed it, as if he intended to swing it at Randy's face—and the smaller man ducked his head while simultaneously jabbing at Dell with the knife.

Dell caught Real Randy's wrist—the one that supported the butcher knife—in his left hand and forced Randy's arm down, throwing him off balance. The objective wasn't to make the knife shake loose, but it did.

The objective was to smash his right fist into his

attacker's face, and he did, still holding on to the wrist as Emmitt slowly ran forward to help his companions. When bone began to snap in Real Randy's wrist, provoking a squeal of pain, Dell let go, picked up the knife from the floor, and whacked at Randy wildly as the man fell backward.

"Ohh*gaaaaaawwwd*!" the small one howled in agony.

But then Calbert was on Dell's back as though from nowhere, trying to force him to the floor.

Blindly, Dell hacked with the butcher knife, *behind* him, not caring what part of his second assailant he penetrated.

Then nothing was on Dell's back but air and the breath of a second man, who was screaming in pain.

Dell didn't dare look around. Big Emmitt— gawd, he probably *was* seven feet tall, and most of him was muscle—was only a few yards away. The blond giant wore nothing but a jockstrap that somehow looked obese, and tears stood in his eyes. *Real* tears . . . for Randy, his leader in the prison scheme of things, who lay next to a shower stall with a bloodied face of infinite agony, trying to hold himself together. Water overflowing from the shower was pink and becoming redder by the moment.

Dell held the butcher knife just the way he'd practiced using one in front of his mirror as a boy, jabbing it in short, aggressive motions at the enormous Emmitt. As Dell began to back up, trying to make it to the door, he saw that the fair-haired giant

Then he was falling again, dropped like a stone, his head thudding against a crapper door.

"This one is *my boy*, cocksucker."

Dell peered up groggily, trying to find out who was talking. All he saw then was Big Emmitt's jock atop hairless legs like peeled birch trees.

But then the tree was uprooted—taking off. Leaving!

It was very quiet in the whole area for a second.

Dell could see again, and what he saw, in the open doorway, was Lloyd B. Fully clad in his prison uniform. Unarmed. Respected enough, clearly, that the murderously grieving Emmitt had even understood the threat Lloyd hadn't needed to utter.

"Dell. You owe me."

"Yessir, I purely suppose I do," Dell croaked. Hurting everywhere, he started getting to his feet. Lloyd B. hadn't moved from the door to help.

"And Dell," Lloyd said again, folding his arms, "you *are* my boy." He paused. "Isn't that true?"

Standing, Dell took a step, tottered. "Why, shore, Lloyd B.," he said, mustering a grin. "A'course I am."

"Reason I asked," the older man said, "is because Calbert there is probably goin' to survive. Your new friend Emmitt, by the bye, is not the most trustworthy gent in this establishment."

"I hears thet, Lloyd," Dell said as he joined Lloyd B. at the door.

"Very well." Lloyd B. stepped aside to let Dell precede him. "So long as you remember the rules, meat. After you rest awhile, we still have time to go to the library before the lunch hour. You does *want* t'go theah, *doesn't* you?"

"Lloyd B.," Dell said, "thet's ex*ack*ly whut I want, too."

It was the first time in his life that Dell did what he was told, even though he didn't intend to let it become a habit.

Yet he did believe it was possible for him to learn something useful before the chance came to pay back Lloyd B. for embarrassing him the way he had.

As the weeks in jail became months, and the months gradually but inexorably turned into the years of Dell's sentence, he kept his part of the bargain with Lloyd B. a lot of the time and began to develop his limited reading skills. He already knew the alphabet, and something of phonics; he could spell almost all of the three-letter words and could have written a letter if he'd even known anybody who liked him and whom he liked enough to want to do that.

Then some john had sliced up Mom a little— nothing permanent, but she couldn't work awhile— and that was when young Dell had found out what his mom was. He learned it from some other boys at school who figured out what his mother did for a living—but part of the time they made it sound like there was somethin' *wrong* with whoring and part of the time like it was Dell's fault, somehow. It got worse when a couple of kids told him he didn't even know who his daddy was; that pissed him off *real* good, because they was purely right. He'd pestered his mom for a while to find out but all she'd done was tell him a different story everytime. When other boys started saying he didn't know, Dell knew for a damn cruel fact that he didn't.

So then he hadn't had much interest in learning until he got his idea about the importance of magic, and figured out what kinds of magic there were:

First was the kind you just got your own self, and the kinds Dell believed he'd got, by being born, were havin' lots of strength in his thumbs and not minding killing people. Fact was he liked it. Sometimes (when he was doing it) he had a clear picture of Mom in his head, and sometimes he was trying to see what his daddy looked like, and sometimes he just felt good to look at the person he was killing, partly as a reminder of what dying itself looked like.

Recently, like right before he'd gone to jail Dell hadn't thought about anything much at all. More and more, he was starting to notice, the real pleasure of it came to him later. When he was alone and had the time to remember all the details.

Then there was the magic other folks had, which you could take for yourself if you knew how. Trouble was, Dell saw fewer and fewer folks who seemed to have any magic to take—especially in the slammer. A man had to have some standards about things and not kid himself or the magic wouldn't come at all. Now, Lloyd B., Dell figured, had some magic. Outside the joint he would probably have killed ol' Lloyd by now just to get it.

But the funny thing was, Dell had the impression that Lloyd B. was willing to *give it away*, and that was something he couldn't remember ever seeing much of, except for maybe one or two teachers he'd had back in grade school. In fact, deep down inside, he knew that was the real reason he was permitting Lloyd B. to tell him things, point out what he might want to read or even study next. Darkie or no, Dell had to admit, the ol' fella *knew* stuff.

There were even times, late at night when the jail was dark, when Lloyd B. said things—facts, they were—that interested Dell. Made him feel sort of smart all over.

And there were times when Dell was truly alone, with Lloyd out on a work detail, when Dell knew that books were the tools for getting every bit of magic he'd ever need—when he would stare around the otherwise empty cell and get excited because, with a head full of knowing, he could almost see through the prison walls—imagine himself becoming things he'd never thought of being.

One day, about five years into his relationship with his cellmate and not long before Dell would be released, Lloyd B. said out of the blue, "I was a teacher, meat—a real teacher."

"Yew was?" Dell asked, startled. "I mean, 'you *were*'?" he corrected himself before ol' Lloyd could do it. "When? What happened?"

"It was a long while ago, at a high school." Just that second Lloyd also looked like he was seeing beyond the prison. "As for what . . . went wrong, that's my affair." So Dell tried to get him to go on, to say what he'd done to get himself arrested, but Lloyd B. simply frowned and pointed to another book they'd brought to their cell from the library. "Read, whitemeat," he said as usual. "Learn. Learn."

Which was hard because Lloyd hadn't wanted Dell just to be a better reader, right along he'd urged Dell to learn about a whole *lot* of crap—not just words from grade school, but high school, too, maybe even some facts from college books. And whenever Dell hadn't understood, he'd point with his finger to where he was stuck and Lloyd would look, then cut off his jive talk to lecture Dell.

More and more—because this *was* another kind of magic, maybe the hardest kind of all, whether it ever paid off the way the other kinds did—Dell found himself falling into the habit of looking things up. Purely *reading* a book, to have fun with it, though, was something he hadn't gotten the hang of. He supposed he had a long way to go before that was possible and he supposed he'd never live long enough to *get* there, either. But he sort of *liked* facts, Dell discovered, because they were more honest than folks. If you wanted to know when something happened or who did what to who, well, you went and looked it up—and when you checked it out in lots of the library books, why, the answers stayed the same *every time!* That, definitely, wasn't the way with people, he believed.

One morning he got curious about Jack the Ripper, a famous murderer, and found ole Jack's story told the same way every single time—the number of whores he knocked off, the dirty Whitechapel neighborhood where he nailed them, the fact that Jack hadn't ever been identified or caught. Why, it was like . . . like church, these *facts*. And the facts were like church bells ringing in Dell's head! They were *reliable*, unlike Mom or the other kids back in school—and it made him feel good, as if he were finally all grown up—a real *man!*

But the finest things in the whole guwdamn world, Dell decided, were words—plain words—and around the time when he was due to be paroled at last, he made up his mind to share the way he felt with somebody else. With Lloyd B. Just the thought of telling an ex-teacher made him all trembly. It was like an athlete confiding in his coach.

The reaction he got from the ageless black was one Dell hadn't dared to hope for.

"I am mighty happy to hear that, Dell," Lloyd said.

Dell was stunned. He wondered how many months had passed this time while Lloyd B. called him "whitemeat," or maybe just "meat," and not by his name. Sometimes it was just "boy."

The ex-teacher arranged himself on his bunk so that his back was comfortably leaning against the wall, folded his hands in his lap—he had been reading, too, an important looking book about some black educator named Washington—and his entire face appeared to emerge from shadows. Dell was startled to see how much more lined it was since they'd first met and how much gray was sprinkled in

Lloyd's hair now. It made him think of a coal mine with streaks of silver you might find if you got lucky.

"Words," Lloyd B. intoned, "are the true keys to the kingdom. The curious thing about them is that each one has the most *precise* meaning imaginable—and yet, as a man learns to speak properly, with a respect for words, he can make them do almost anything whatsoever to his own advantage. He can *play* them, Dell, as if they were the instruments of a mighty orchestra. Or he can *im*provise with them, as if in a jazz band."

This puzzled the shit out of Lloyd. "I don't think I understands, Lloyd B.," he confessed.

"That," the teacher's voice rumbled, "is because you have not yet advanced to that level of your education. And it is why I have succeeded in procuring a good-bye gift for you, boy."

Dell rocked back on his cot in total surprise. "Yew got *me* a *present*?"

Lloyd B.'s eyelids narrowed. He looked like a black Buddha. "I see from your face you are not usually the recipient of gifts." His hands separated, fluttered. "Don't come unglued over it, please." Breaking their shared gaze only when he was sure that remark was sinking in, he stuck a meaty brown hand into his shirt and slowly drew a paperback book into view. "This work, Dell, provides *all* the keys to the kingdom. Potentially, anything, just as I said. And by employing the proper combination of its elements, a man may make anything of himself."

"A better crook, too?" Dell inquired. He was anxious to read the title of the book but his roomie's

fingers were concealing it and Lloyd B. hadn't relin-
quished the present as yet.

"I said, 'anything,'" Lloyd B. sighed. "I see no
reason to qualify my description." He'd seen nothing in Dell in all those years to suggest a sense of
humor, but maybe that had been his idea of a joke.

Then one at a time, Lloyd's fingers pulled away
until the paperback book was fully in view.

"Is thet a *dictionary*—a dictionary of my *own*?"
Dell asked. He tasted the concept of it on his lips,
then stared up at his mentor. He whispered the title
of the dictionary the way some men might have
spoken their wives' or girlfriends' names. "*The Book
of Webster's . . . !*"

Smiling briefly, Lloyd B. tossed it across the cell
to the younger man. "To judge by your expression,
you haven't *ever* received a gift before. Well, this is
one—a parting gift to keep you better company on
the road of life than you're likely to pick up on your
own."

"It's—it's jest *swell*, Lloyd B.," Dell said, gripping the paperback in his hands. He was unable to
do more than merely stare at the teacher.
"I'm . . . real glad t'git it."

"All the words of mankind are in this book,"
Lloyd said quietly. "Every one that will make you
sing or make you cry, fill your dumb little brain with
certainty when you need that and bring you the
wisdom of doubt when you require that. *Select* those
words well when you're around another man, or a
woman, and you will give an impression of undeni-
able power."

"And I'll really *have* thet power, Lloyd B.—thet magic—right in my pocket whenever I need it."

"If you don't use this gift, and *other* books," said Lloyd, rising and standing above Dell, "you'll just come right back here." He flashed his teeth in what appeared to be a true smile. "I can respect myself because I started you out, whitemeat—because I'm no preacher and a man can't teach what he doesn't know—but I'm warning you to use your book, and your mind, or you'll be back in this cell before I'm used to you being gone. There, now. I've done my bit, my thing. I can do no more."

Dell jumped up, mad, and scared, too. "No," he said under his breath tightly. "I *won't* be back, no matter whut!"

"And *when* you *are*, boy," Lloyd B. finished, his smile widening, "when you've returned and I make you my boy *alllll* over again"—the graying black man spread his arms as if in anticipation of embracing Dell—"I'll make goddamned fucking *sure* you learn what I'm telling you."

Dell stared back, wondering if this was the time to take him. But he'd want to take him all the way *out*, to get his magic, and that would mean Dell would stay right where he was—maybe forever. "Whutever you say, Lloyd."

And when the shadows were spreading over the cell and the prison lights were beginning to dim, Dell was half-asleep when he heard old Lloyd B. saying—maybe to him, maybe just to himself—"That'll be the time when you learn about the phoenix, whitemeat. The *phoenix*, boy—your destiny."

And Lloyd B. laughed, thunder pealing in the darkened cell, his lips parting, permitting the lightning flash of his pure, white teeth. *"My 'boy'*—and the *magic* bird, the *phoenix!"*

Dell wasn't sure when he woke up the next day if he'd dreamed it or not, but he'd sucked one thumb so hard there were teeth-marks in it and small drops of blood; and he remembered, for sure, a nightmare about a big bird engulfed in flames, flapping its wings faster than he'd ever seen any bird do anywhere.

For some reason, he was reaching for it with both arms when he awakened.

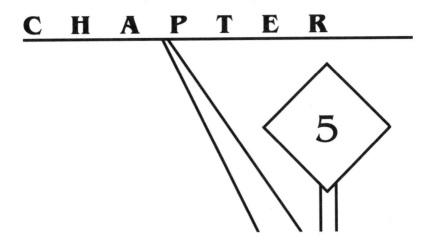

C H A P T E R 5

For a while—perhaps as long as a week—it was fun for Kee simply to know that she'd bested the mama who'd always let her know (one way or another) how superior, how much *smarter* she was, than her daughter. Or her husband, or anyone else in the family, or maybe just about everybody in Cherokee Rose, Georgia. One of Mama's favorite games had been just sighin' a lot, and another one had been sorta *starin'* at people when they made mistakes— mistakes which (Natalie Grace's expression always said) Mama wouldn't have made if she'd been doped up and unconscious and havin' one of them out-of-body experiences Kee sometimes read about in *Fate* and elsewhere.

Well, now Mama had made a big-time mistake by thinkin' she could trust Daddy not to have messed around on her, and another one by believin' she could jus' read Kee's very own book whenever she felt like it! Her own property was very important to Kee, even if other folks' wasn't, and it had pissed her *off* to find the hair with spit on it missin'! Mama had been the one to tell her that sneakin' around behind folks' backs was a awful thing to do. Well, now Mama had found out how right her very own words were: "When you try to poke into other people's business, that's saying how much cleverer you are than they—but even if you get away with it a dozen times, eventually people will find you out for the petty sneak you are."

So now Mama had to admit to herself (whether she ever said anything about it or not) (and she didn't) that she was a dirty ol' petty sneak, and Kee loved it—

Except that she herself had stopped being the center of attention 'cause Mama was spendin' all her time thinking about Daddy and how he'd gone and screwed Ms. Hardacre. But she didn't even come right out and face Daddy with it, maybe because Daddy kept gettin' sicker all the time and Mama was too nicey-nice to hit on him then. Or maybe it was jus' because Daddy was still bigger and Mama was afraid he'd get close enough to hit her again. Of course, Daddy was already startin' to go blind. Mama probably didn't have the guts to bawl him out, 'cause of that. Sometimes he didn't even know it was Kee who came into his room. Other times, if she was real quiet, he didn't even know she was there! She thought that was lots of fun, seeing Daddy stumble around like it was dark or something.

One day after school, Kee had the notion of finding out jus' how blind her daddy really was, so she snuck into the room he called his den, where he was drinking some beers and makin' believe he was watchin the TV, and went all the way across the room to him on tiptoe. Kee couldn't believe how neat it was to walk right *up* to her old man while he sat in his chair like a dumb ol' rock, sayin' somethin' out loud—sort of mumblin'—about there being shadows in front of him. Matter of fact, Kee thought he acted sort of *scared*, like maybe he thought Jesus or the Angel of Death was comin' to get him.

She took one of his beers—one he'd already broke the tab on, 'cause the noise would probably tell him there really *was* a person in his old den, and drank it straight down. Mama and Daddy both said she was too young to drink, but Kee figured that with Daddy it was mostly because he didn't want anybody to have *his* brews. When she was just about to the bottom of the Bud can, she looked at Daddy and wriggled her butt at him. And when he didn't catch her doin' *that*, she turned around and wiggled it right in his face!

Then she put the empty can right where he'd try

to pick it up when he was ready for his next one, and tiptoed out of the room, pressing her fingers to her mouth to keep from giggling.

Daddy'd probably figure the Angel of Death or one of those Apostles Mama talked about a lot had plumb *stole* his beer and drank it afore *he* could!

In her bedroom that afternoon, Kee had the daring idea that would liberate her from havin' to do anything Mama and Daddy ever asked her to do again, but she didn't act on it right off. It was a real wild, sort of crazy idea, even for her, and Kee just put it in the back of her mind (where most of her devilment came from) and kept it in reserve. But she knew then, anyway, that if her idea worked, she could get even with both her parents for all the shitty things they'd done to her, once and for all, and what's more, set it up so's she could be freer than any other girl she knew.

Maybe then her life wouldn't always be such a big bore-ass. Maybe then, in fact, she'd have done such a really *worldly* thing that the older man she dreamed about would sense it and come take her away!

For approximately two years, Kee didn't feel she had enough motivation to haul out her idea for evening things up with her folks.

It wasn't that there weren't times when she *thought* about going ahead and doing it, but it was something you could only do once, and life was sometimes interesting enough during the two years that she didn't need to waste her idea yet.

Part of the fun part of life had come from

watchin' Mama and Daddy lose it, and kind of change the way they treated each other, and things. For a time, Mama took to goin' to her bedroom practically all the time when she wasn't hangin' around Reverend Simpkins at the church. (Kee wondered a whole lot if Mama and the Rev weren't gettin' it on. He was older and all that, but Mama seemed old to Kee, too, so maybe it didn't make any difference when your hair got gray like old snow and the only thing you had to make you look like all your skin wasn't falling down around your feet was wrinkles. Wrinkles, Kee thought, looked like makeup in Hollywood—fake monster stuff jus' to make you look ugly.) Since Daddy had the syph and all, Mama wasn't givin' him any, Kee was sure of that. He didn't look much different—the clothed part of him Kee could see—but some of her girlfriends had told her he had scales like a dragon or somethin' all over the body, and that his thang probably had so many sores on it that it didn't even *look* like a penie no more. For a time she really craved getting a look at it, even tried hidin' in the bathroom for when the old man took a pee, but Daddy always sort of fell all over the bathroom gettin' ready for his whiz and sooner or later he found her there, when he ran into her.

Often, Daddy moaned and whined quite a bit. She guessed it hurt him to have a leak now and that really told Kee what a sissy her old man was gettin' to be. First he couldn't keep from gettin sick after doin' it to some blond woman, now he was gettin' pain from havin' a piss!

Anyway, Kee felt sure ol' Reverend Simpkins would have tried by now to put the make on somebody younger like Mama since she was hangin' around him all the time, and sure Mama wouldn't have touched Daddy even if she was wearin' one of them suits of armor!

And what Mama did in her bedroom—Daddy generally kept himself in his den, close to the beer and the TV he couldn't see very well, and he almost *never* worked so they had even less money than usual—was read the Bible and pray a lot—out loud, now, and even *more* of the Bible than she had read before! Kee heard parts of it she'd never imagined existed, and, when she snuck in and checked it out in Mama's copy of the Good Book, she discovered Mama was even reading the *Old* Testament! Which (to Kee) had to mean one of three things: Mama was seeing some Jew man, 'cause they were the ones in Cherokee Rose who read the old part, except for the Rev; or Mama was getting so desperate for help that she would try just about anything; or Reverend Simpkins wanted her to learn enough about *all* the Bible so that he could marry Natalie Grace someday when Daddy had passed.

Well, Kee had come to think just about *anythin'* was all right with her—whatever Sue Elenor or Willie Fawkner came up with, for fun, Kee was sure ready to try it—but the very idea of having a Rev for a new daddy was completely beyond thinking! It had been bad enough, letting him preach little sermons to her when Mama asked him to talk with her. Having him around the house all the time, free to tell

Kee how bad she was whenever he took a shine to the notion . . . well, the very chance of Mama doing it with Reverend Simpkins, then *marrying* him, contributed heavily to Kee's final decision—to try her really *bad* idea on Daddy!

The other part of the last two years that kept Kee occupied was her private life, and the way she had stopped being a little girl, and finally got to be a teenager.

A lot of it just happened and Kee didn't have anything to do with it. That was the period when her titties and pussy hair came in, and Kee couldn't remember when she'd been more excited about anything in her whole life! Well, the hair between her legs had already been there for a while—but it was finer, neater, and prettier after she had titties, Kee was ready to swear to it!

And getting tits was the finest thing that had ever happened in the history of the world! It was true she had begun getting them before she was fourteen, but they were itty-bitty, little girl things so they didn't count—or maybe she just hadn't noticed them much. It was as though her nipples had swelled up with mumps or something and spread out, like sore-spots on her chest. Mama had made a big deal about them and bought Kee a "training bra," but Kee though that sounded like trying to make the track team or something. Then Mama told her all about the "purpose of breasts," nursing babies and all. Well, Kee had just about passed out at such a notion. She remembered Sue Elenor's little twin brothers, and the idea of them hangin' on her breasts, smellin' like puke, was revoltin' for sure! ("Breasts" was definitely what they were, too—not titties, though Kee thought *titties* was a friendly, playful word, unless you wanted to be glamorous at the time, and sexy). Well, Kee knew all about the real purpose of her breasts; she didn't need Mama diggin' out the old fashioned bullshit when she'd see what men thought about them a hundred or more times since she was nine! You just had to watch fellas while they were lookin' at magazines or watchin' the TV.

So Kee had walked all around her bedroom naked, struttin' before a full-length mirror, practicin' ever which way she could . . . dipping over to watch how they sort of fell forward, but not very far, not all sloppy the way she imagined Mama's were . . . and then she wound up before the mirror, lifting them and squeezing them together—like she was offering big ol' fruit to her dream man, the older fella of her visions. (Kee knew, by now, that they were visions she was havin'. They were like knowin' about dead people's eyes, and stuff, and they told Kee how special she was, because Sue Elenor didn't know enough to put under a pea shell about any of these really neat things, including visions!)

As to when her titties would be complete—real enough that a fella might like to have a taste—Kee couldn't figure out. It seemed sort of weird to her. More than a dozen of her years she didn't have shit on her chest; then, overnight, they were there. Maybe they were . . . *magic*, in a way. Like dead eyes starin' and tryin' to see you-all, and how she knew her older prince was practically on the way to pick her up in his big car. Maybe there was a whole *lot* of magic Kee hadn't heard of, right on the outskirts of dumb ol' Cherokee Rose!

In the meantime, she had hardly been able to control herself until she called up Willie Fawkner and asked him if he had a couple dollars and wanted to see her new titties.

Willie took a long while to answer. She supposed that was because they hadn't seen each other in more than a year, even though Kee and Sue Elenor talked about him sometimes.

"I thought you-all sort of *had* titties, last time," Willie said at length.

"They wasn't *nothin'*!" Kee exclaimed, breathin' hard into the telephone. "I got *real* ones now, Willie Fawkner!"

Ol' Willie got silent again, like he was thinkin'.

When Kee figured out what it was he was thinkin', she spoke right up. "Oh, I remembers! Yew couldn't git it in that one day and jus' comed all over everything. But that was okay." She would show Willie how sympathetic she was. "You was only a kid then, Willie, only a *boy*." Next up was the part that would surprise him and make things fine. "See, I don't want yew t'even hafta take it out of yore pants this time, 'lest y'wants to. Here's the deal—I want t'know if my new titties give you a hard-on. Okay?"

Willie coughed and sort of laughed at the same time. His voice was kind of high still, and he sounded like a girl on the phone. "I don't colleck from my paper route till Thursday night, Kee. I just got about seventy-two cents." Willie brightened: "But I'll give yew that just to *look* at 'em if y'all want."

Kee paused, mildly disappointed. There was a bra she'd seen that pushed your titties up nice and showed half of the nips, and seventy-two cents wouldn't buy it. Then, suddenly, she had an idea. "Yew got any friends at all?" she asked. "What if you got mebbe nine or ten boys t'put up around seventy-five cents? You *mus'* know a few other fellas."

"Well . . . it *could* work," Willie said. "An' we could meet at the paper station right after Mr. Ligget goes home, 'cause he lets me lock up."

"Shoot, Willie," she told him, "I don't mind if Mr. Ligget sees 'em, too, if he's got seventy-five cents. I on'y want t'know if you boys'll get horny when y'sees my titties. Awright?"

It turned out all right—except Willie Fawkner and the other boys didn't want Mr. Ligget to be around, as if they figured he wouldn't want to see her new breasts or the like. That was a little disappointin' to Kee because the man who ran the paper station was at least forty years old—maybe *fifty*—and she could have been checked out by someone as old as the fella she dreamed about.

Still, each and every one of the boys who came to see Kee—Willie got more than nine or ten (when the word got around), he got seventeen of them, three or four only in grade school, who must have spent their *whole allowance* (which Kee felt was very flattering)—and each one swore that her breasts made them *really* hot. When she finished her survey and was starting to slip her sweater back on, she even got another quarter from Willie and his best friend, Scott, for letting them *feel* her. Only once each, too!

Kee made a mental note that she had tapped a brand-new potential income source.

Well, life was more interesting than it had been for a while, what with different ways to mess with her titties and even her pussy and listening to Mama and Daddy get *real* silent a lot of the time (and also hear Daddy beg Mama once or twice like a sick cat to do it with him), and worrying about Mama maybe getting hitched up to the Rev if Daddy kicked off.

But then Willie Fawkner snitched.

He told his mama not long before Kee's fifteenth birthday what she had done for him and his friends, and Mrs. Fawkner came over to the Second Cherokee Rose Baptist Church where Mama was working, and she was *mad*.

Her Willie, Mrs. Fawkner said, was getting grades worth snot, and he was buying dirty books from some older boy and ripping off *Mister* Fawkner's magazines; and now he had pimples all *over* his face; and Mrs. Fawkner had warned Willie (she told Reverend Simpkins) he'd probably go blind like that disgusting and sinful Ewing McCaulter if he didn't stop his "unnatural practices"; and Willie began to blubber like some bitty kid and *told* his mama why he got horny all of the while.

Well, now, that was positive *proof* to Kee that her titties were as sexy as she thought—maybe *all* of her was sexy even!—which was definitely good news. But Mama, she hadn't felt like that at all.

"You are exactly like your scabrous and scurrilous father," Mama had said when she got home and told it all to Kee. Daddy was around, too, when she said that, and he kind of squinched up his eyes as if he might like to slug his wife if he could *find* her! But he was all puny, now, like Kee and Mama knew. So Mama, well, *that* was the time Mama found out she didn't have to kiss his ass anymore. In fact, when she'd said what she'd said about the two "s" words, she'd looked him straight in the face—as if he could see her!—and kind of fired bubbly, teary words at Daddy. "Do you *see* what your sinful example has done to our daughter, Ewing? Do you *see* how the wages of God must be paid even unto the generations?"

"Gawdamn cunt," Daddy replied. He craned his head in just about every direction; finally he was lookin' at nothing but the door leadin' to the kitchen (which didn't really make him seem a whole lot mean or tough). "Gawdamn cunt."

"You bastard!" Mama said. Kee liked that, because she'd never heard Mama swear before. "It's your warped and evil desire for—for what you said that's put all of us in this hellish situation, don't you realize that?"

Daddy said, "Gawdamn cunt," to the doorway again.

"Can't you see your little girl is *trying* to lose her immortal soul just as fast as she can?"

Daddy started to repeat himself yet again but leaned back in the chair in his den as though he'd got tired. "S'not my fault. S'yours—you psalm-singin' ole douche-bag." His sigh seemed to begin at the start of time, kept runnin' over all the years, and wound up with a peek into the cemetery plot Mama bought for him recently. "Yew jus' don't know the fust thang 'bout raisin' a daughter with some spirit to her—some i-dee of what bein' a woman is about!" His eyebrows lowered quite a bit, and he spoiled it by droolin'. "Yew and your fancy edication, 'n yew don't know how t'be a woman." He laughed then, or Kee thought that was what the sound was. It was sure messy, she knew that. He swiped at his face with the one hand that didn't have sores on it yet and stuff from his mouth and his nose and eyes got all smeared together. "My Kee's gone be *awright*, bitch—she's gone be *fine*! Why, yew're jus' *jealous* of her—ain't yew?"

"You must be out of your mind," Mama said, "even more so than you've *already* become!"

"Jus' stay off my daughter's back—let her have some breathin' room—and she'll show yew jus how t'*be* a woman someday—iffen yew *watch* her close!" Daddy sniffled real hard, turned his head slightly so he was lookin' at a lamp, and grinned—probably at her, Kee decided. "Come over here and give yore daddy a big kiss, sweetie-pie!"

"Kee, stay right where you are!" Mama said,

standing in front of Kee. "You mustn't *touch* your father. Not until—until he's better. All right?"

That's all right with me, Kee thought. She hadn't moved an inch.

"You will not see Sue Elenor or *any* of your friends for one month, Kee," Mama went on. "You will come home straight from school, go to your room, and work on your studies. I'll talk to your principal and explain that what happened was *Willie's* fault, that you are still—in the most important sense of all—a *good girl.*" She stared dubiously at Kee. She wasn't in the mood for questions, Kee supposed. "And you will see Reverend Simpkins again just as soon as I can make an appointment for you—and you will *attend church* with your mother *every* Sunday from now on." Mama drew in a trembly breath. "Am I making myself clear?"

Kee glanced toward her father, but he was trying to open another brew and still hadn't even doped out where they was. "Yes, ma'am," Kee said, the wheels of her seething, busy, feral young brain turning, chugging, churning. "I guess so."

"I will make you," Mama said, "a decent Christian young lady if it is the last thing I do."

Kee said, plainly, "Yes, ma'am." It sounded polite the way Mama liked.

Had Dr. Lenora Middel survived her untimely encounter with teenage Dell several years before Kee was even born, she might have been able to apply some of her original but untested psychological theories to the Georgia fifteen-year-old.

She would almost certainly have needed to be at her professional best to create any profile of Kee other than a rudimentary sketch.

To begin with, Kee had no animosity toward Natalie Grace, her mother, and hadn't started to hate her until she was old enough to crave considerably more freedom than Natalie Grace was about to give her—especially since Kee's personal concept of freedom was to do anything at all that occurred to her. Natalie Grace's basic crime, in her daughter's eyes, was precisely that; Natalie Grace was not only an educated woman, but she cared enough about Kee to have learned to see the girl for what she was.

And there was also the fact that Natalie Grace McCaulter tended to be brutally honest. Part of the reason she had sought employment in Rev. Simpkins's church and fully participated in its activities after returning to Cherokee Rose with a diploma was to learn humility of spirit and thereby acquire the tact to go on living with her husband, Ewing. Otherwise, she was inclined toward exposing him for what he was.

But because Natalie Grace saw no reason to be humble around a small child, and didn't realize until Kee was almost fully grown that she was either a female echo of Ewe or hopelessly mad, Kee came to see her mother as a tradition-bound blowhard and a bullying ninny.

Or, to put it in the simplest way, saw her as the only human being who prevented Kee—day in and day out—from running wild.

From pert and pretty Kee's standpoint, she

meant no particular harm to anyone, she just found everything excruciatingly boring unless she was "havin' fun," and her only definitions of fun were the things she could do with her own body or her own mind. The time when she crippled the neighbor lady's dog by hitting its hindlegs with a two-by-four belonging to her daddy, Kee hadn't hated dogs. She had just wanted to see what its eyes looked like when it was in pain. Of course, she'd told Mama and Daddy the dog was tryin' to hurt her so she had defended herself. And it wasn't her fault if Daddy had believed her, just as it wasn't her fault if Mama hadn't. But it sure hurt *her* a whole bunch when Mama said she was a liar and a monster because mothers were *supposed* to believe their little girls.

And it made Kee scared for a while when Mama said she needed "professional help," because she thought maybe Mama would have her locked up somewhere with really crazy people, but nothing came of that, thanks to Daddy, who said he "had a reputation in the community" and "no daughter of mine needs no damn head doctor."

Kee knew which one of those ideas of Daddy's was his *real* objection.

Had Dr. Middel peered down from some heavenly abode and silently written her notes about the McCaulters, she might or might not have faulted the parents to a marked degree for failing to find help for their daughter.

But she certainly would have recorded that Kee and Dell, the youth who'd killed her, had a lot in common, despite the fact that Kee had so far murdered no one and that she, unlike Dell, was psychopathic. Each was as eager as a cocker spaniel to be petted and permitted to do any damned thing and each of them could be remarkably winning, cute. Each of them knew that, too, of course.

Kee—again, unlike Dell—did not know that killing was wrong because she was simply incapable of understanding it. In the frenzy of her desire or the grip of her fantasies and hallucinations, the portion of her brain that was meant to contain that old-fashioned thing called a "conscience" was rarely but not permanently smothered by fantasy. Dell, unlike the teenager, not only knew that most of the things he did was wrong, he reveled in it—because as a sociopath, *he* alone was *everything* of any importance in the whole history of the world. He saw life with perfect clarity.

And if Dr. Middel had made those notes, glanced around her , and realized Dell's outlook on life had deprived her of half of her own life—and recognized the fact that Kee McCaulter had the capacity to create even more carnage—she might have concluded her study in this fashion: Society could not afford to have people like them around any longer. The kindest thing to do for all concerned was to put the bastards to sleep.

So there was nothing personal about the perfectly abominable thing Kee had finally decided to do. She rarely even noticed anyone else—and preferred not to—so it was more a case of wearing permanent blinders to the realities of the world than of hatred.

So while she tried to wait for her own version of Mr. Right to show up, the grand idea Kee'd had when she swallowed Daddy's beer without his seeing her came back into her thoughts as if it had been yesterday when she first dreamed it up. That was the case, in an odd way. Even she had observed the strange manner in which time worked for her. Except when life was intolerably boring, there weren't a lot of minutes to time, nor even days. Primarily, her brain kept track of time in terms of the moments in her existence when she had been pleased or displeased, when her experiences were exciting or a total bore-ass. School and her home life were almost completely boring, so quite often she didn't notice them at all—almost as if time had not taken its customary toll during such periods. Had she been as analytical as Dell wished he could be, she might have formed the theory that she'd spent absolutely none of her appointed lifespan during the long stretches of boredom. She might even have been right.

It seemed to Kee that she had every good reason to put her plan into action now, what with Mama havin' grounded her ass, makin' lots of threats about haulin' in Reverend Simpkins and stuff. When excitement was what you went after with your whole heart, the certainty of tedium—mixed up with a whole bunch of criticism—was the very worst kind of threat.

And once she'd planned everything all the way through, Kee knew she could make it happen without even havin' to put in a whole lot of work.

It was after Christmas and New Year's, just before the first important tests were going to be taken at school. Mama hadn't taken down the Christmas tree and it looked awful—not because it was so old its branches drooped, but because Daddy—even with his very poor vision—insisted on goin' out and choppin' the tree down—"a real one, not onea them phony commie trees"—just as he always had. Mama and Kee had gone out with him to make sure he didn't cut down another farmer's pet elm, or maybe a cow, and it was so cold they were quick to agree when Ewing—squintin' like a madman and kind of gropin' the trees—finally made his selection.

The house was hot as hell the way Daddy liked it these days and Mama was off bangin' the Rev—so Kee imagined—when the instant of gettin' her idea goin' began. She'd already made the phone call that was at the heart of the plan, so she knew everything was truly set up jus' so!

She still had on the new for-real bra she'd bought with the money she earned from Willie Fawkner and his friends, and the skirt Mama knew was the one she liked most to wear to school, when she went into the den. When she got up close to Daddy, who asked, "That you, darlin'?" both a generic term that covered his womenfolk and the high probability that he meant Kee, since he kept callin' Mama a "gawdamn cunt," she dropped her blouse next to his chair.

"Whatcha watchin', Daddy?" she asked.

"I think it's a rerun of 'I Love Lucy,' but it might

be 'Mayberry,'" he answered, lookin' toward the doorway again. "This fuckin' picture tube's goin', Kee. If your mama'd git a *real* job 'steada runnin' errands for ol' man Simpkins, we could live decent again." He sighed deeply. "I gotta get back on mah feet *soon*, or everthang arown here's gonna go t'hell. A honest workin' man cain't afford t'get sick no more."

"Yew reckon," Kee inquired carefully, sounding as if she was almost idly askin', "All Mama's doin' for that old man is runnin errands?" She spread her skirt in the most ladylike of fashions and sat on the arm of her daddy's easy chair.

Ewing's glance swiveled around, startled, to squint at his fifteen-year-old daughter. "I don't wanna hear no trash-talk like that, darlin'," he snorted. "That ol' Reverend, he couldn't git one up for *Eve*!" He appeared to make out a shadowy form. "Yew really think somethin' funny's goin' on?"

"Gosh, Daddy, I wouldn't know 'bout stuff like that," Kee replied demurely. Daddy was a fright to look at these days, especially up close. She'd been careful to choose the arm of his chair that was near the least-mottled side of his face and his cleaner hand. Why hadn't anyone done what they were supposed to do after she phoned 'em?

"Well, baby, I'm still more'n enough man for yore mama," Ewing boasted, patting her leg. Or patting *at* it. If his aim became much worse, his actions would be indecent. "Ah know she bitches a lot, but that's 'cause she ain't got our spunk. She ain't a true McCaulter like yew is."

Someone just entered the driveway! Kee reached behind her, unsnapped her bra, let it fall noiselessly away from her young breasts. Then she draped it across Daddy's lap, unnoticed by Ewe. "I'm sorry yew been sick, Daddy," she told him. She was talking louder because she'd heard footsteps outside. Now there was a key in the lock of the door, so Mama was first, just like she'd planned. "Kin I have a lil' kiss?"

"Honeybun, yew shore can!" Ewing cried with gladness. For a moment, Daddy was speaking with real *affection*. The effect on Kee was stunning, pervasive.

For then she wasn't even in the room anymore, she was somewhere else—a yacht maybe, or a huge car! And it was no longer her daddy sitting in the chair, it was a different man—a tall, handsome man of the world with a mustache and muscles everywhere and even cute buns! Kee blinked, tried to remember her plan. But this wasn't a daydream, she thought—this was *actually happening*—and the inside of the huge automobile or big boat was absolutely *bee-yoot-iful*, full of expensive things Kee had always dreamed of. "Come, my darling," the tall, handsome man beckoned to her, "come to your lover's waiting arms."

Because a part of her mind retained the plan, Kee hauled up her skirt as high as she could just as the man in the chair reached out for her, and Kee leaned forward to present a startled Ewing with a kiss that had nothing to do with daddy-daughter osculation. Except now he was some handsome stranger who . . .

Yes, he *was* Daddy—because this dream man couldn't *see* Kee, just the way Daddy couldn't. He was *blind*, any damn fool could tell that from his eyes . . .

Mama's due now, Kee's memory reminded her. She shook her head in an effort to make the other reality, the hallucination, go away—and exactly at the moment Natalie Grace McCaulter saw them from the doorway, Kee yanked Daddy's zipper down, crying loudly, "Noooo, Daddy, *noooo!*"

Mama was across the den floor like a jungle cat! But instead of throwing Kee aside, as Kee had anticipated, Mama gently extricated her from Ewing's unseeing bewildered embrace.

Then she slapped him across the face with all the fury and frustration she'd stored up for more than a decade.

Stifling a giggle, Kee remembered to enact the next part of her plan—and it was the hardest part, other than having had to kiss Daddy on the mouth, because she knew she couldn't really cut loose laughin' as she wanted to do more than anything else she could remember. There was *more* to do—and Kee'd already heard the second person she'd called on the phone coming into the room.

She gave her Mama a little bitty shove—so *she* was sort of lyin' in Daddy's lap—then slipped out of her own skirt.

Kee didn't have on a stitch when she climbed back on the arm of Daddy's chair, put an arm around Mama and one around Daddy—and smiled prettily for the pictures her good friend Sue Elenor took of their family. Mama and Daddy didn't even see her.

And after that, it was okay for Mama to go on whalin' the tar outta her old man. They just thought Kee was tryin' to get them to stop fighting.

Right up until they saw the nice clear snapshots Sue Elenor had taken in exchange for Kee's promise not to involve her in the Willie-Fawkner-and-her-new-titties mess, that is.

Kee didn't even have to point out any of the better features of the photographs to Mama or, after she'd mentioned Miss Zenniger and the principal at school, Mama's boss, Reverend Simpkins. Daddy didn't know what in Hades was comin' down, but Mama had had enough education to get the message.

There would not be any of that "grounding" stuff or listenin' to the Rev's private sermons any more. No, there would be a *whole lot* of freedom now for Kee—startin' with the way she didn't want to go to high school anymore.

There was plenty of time to wash her mouth from where Daddy had kissed her, and Kee did, over and over. She also began to wonder a great deal if what she'd just done was worldly enough to reach the older man of her dreams, magnetize him, and get him to come find her.

It had to be fairly soon. Even with her newfound liberty to do what she pleased, Kee knew she'd probably start getting bored again before long.

She decided she would even settle, for now, for the handsome man with the mustache to come back. Where he had come from and where he'd gone didn't matter, really.

Not a lot did matter but havin' fun.

C H A P T E R

(Dell exchanges liberty for another opportunity to learn and discovers the phoenix.)

The money they gave Dell when he was released from prison—along with a suit of clothes—wasn't enough to buy a motor scooter, so he realized immediately that it would be hard to set himself back up in business. Wheels had to be the first consideration and, even if he knew a whole lot now that he hadn't known before he was busted, even if he was a grown man who'd learned not to daydream but to go out and take the things he wanted, then leave no witnesses—this wasn't the time to see how original and magical he could be.

But the ticket money the prison also gave him took him only far enough south that everybody in the fleabag town knew he was an ex-con just by lookin' at his suit. So Dell took the rest of his cash to buy a couple of pairs of pants, some cheap jeans, and a jacket with a lot of pockets.

The goal was to look pretty much like anyone else the first time he tried to rip off his new vehicle.

Changing clothes in the nearest men's room, Dell remembered to stick the paperback Lloyd B. had given him in one hip pocket. It hadn't been any bullshit about how much he'd come to like words and he knew a *vol-u-mi-nous* number of them now, Dell had found that out just by using a few on some other cons, even a guard or two.

But it was only Lloyd and the parole board who believed he had any notion of changing his lifestyle, not Dell himself. Not Dell from hell. True enough, his roomie had imparted good advice. And most of the magic Lloyd B. had to offer came without Dell even having to kill his ass. The vocabulary Dell possessed now would've blown Mom's mind—*not to mention all them other facks I learnt at the liberry*, he reminded himself as he zipped up his new pair of pants. But there was another word he'd memorized from *The Book of Webster's: moderation.* "'Avoidance of extremes,'" Dell muttered the definition to himself, "*stayin' calm, 'within reasonable limits'*—

like not throwin' aside a perfectly good career as a travelin' man when he might have enough smarts to do it right this time."

He already had himself an initial plan. Any fool would've known his first job was to get a vehicle because an American man in this day and age wasn't piss on a shoe without one. In that sense, Dell figured he was like apple pie, the flag, and Mom. All grown-up men knew you had to be able to get out of town fast and not stay in one place long. Magazines Dell had read with Lloyd B. in the library had called this a "mobile generation," and after Dell had looked those words up, he'd been dazzled by the wonder of facts all over again. Gudammit, that was *true*! So it wasn't his fault if the prison folks had been too cheap to give him enough money for wheels.

Somebody like the ugly dead shrink should wise them sonsabitches up so men who got released didn't have to go back to a life of crime till they were *ready*.

Then he had to get himself a woman because it appeared the road to goin' perverted began when you lacked female com-panionship and had to re-sort to pornographic crapola. No men *he* knew ever suggested *abstinence*, a word Lloyd B. used once, which Dell went and looked up. That was bullshit. God gave a man a dick and balls to be used, or why else did you have 'em? You used your legs and feet to walk, your eyes to see, and your nose to smell and make snot. Since women was the sex that liked decoration, *they'd* have been the sex with gonads if man wasn't meant to fuck every chance he got and when he felt like it.

So after Dell had balled a woman and was ready to go to work in his new vehicle, he would go kill Mom. (She didn't have any magic, he assumed, but *wanting* to do her was on Dell's mind greatly these days, so it made sense to clear his thoughts and not take the chance of havin' his brain fucked up when he got back to work for real.)

His work—as Dell mentally laid out his plan—should begin deep in the South this time. He'd had some dream a couple of times about that part of the country. He also had some weird sort of hunch that what he was lookin' for in life would be found down there.

After all, a whole lot of what he was (Dell figured) was a wayfarin' stranger like he'd come across in a book from the library. Or mebbe a knight on a croosade except what he was questing for—*quest* was another word he'd found, and on his *own*, without no help from ol' Lloyd—wasn't a grail. He had never found time to look up *grail* anyhow, but he supposed it was like gruel, which Mom had fixed him sometimes. Anyhow, *his* quest was magical, like a whole *lot* of the ones he'd read about. Maybe all he needed was a shield, maybe a sword, too, to wind up as romantic as anybody traveling the highways today!

But it was shitty and nearly embarrassing to have to get started again by hitching a ride, then just *taking* the vehicle away from the driver.

They wasn't no class to it, no fuckin' way yew looked at it, Dell thought again when he'd hooked himself a series of lifts that took him as far as Ashland, Kentucky—nearly on the West Virginia border. He hadn't hitched a ride in a single automobile, truck, van, or mobile trailer because he hadn't seen one worth stealing.

Tuesday just before noon, though, Dell might have taken an old red Granada he was hitching in simply because the TV ads he'd seen in jail stressed Ford's reliability. The problem was, just when he was thinking about overpowering the driver who'd given him the lift—a middle-aged fella in glasses who had nice gray hair—the man told Dell he wrote books. "For a *livin'*?" Dell asked, nearly as astonished as if the man had turned out to be Noah Webster.

"More or less," said the older man, chuckling. "My wife might argue the point. Let's say we *try* to live on the money I make from writing books."

"Well, sir," Dell responded at once, extending an arm toward the driver, "let me shake your hand! Literary per-son-ages have nothin' but my respeck."

The driver allowed Dell to wring his hand, grinning. "I always thought there might be real readers out there somewhere. Have you read—"

"See," Dell interrupted, "whilst I was in the joint with Lloyd B., I figgered a upstandin' man had to have a code of standards. A'course," he chuckled, "until Lloyd made me look it up in *The Book of Webster's*, I thought a code was jest for spies. But it means 'a body of syst-e-mat-ic laws' or 'a set of principles.' So I got me a whole set of my own. They's real syst-e-mat-ic, too."

"That right?" the writer said. He looked nervous all at once, though Dell didn't know why. "How much farther you going, Mr. Dell?"

"Yessir, I don't get drunked up and I'm allus on guard against preverts and I don't hit on old ladies, little girls, and writer fellas." Dell peered out at the road and the Kentucky hills. "Might as well get out at the next town."

"Glad to hear it," the writer murmured. He added, quickly, "About not hitting on writers, that is. And," he added, just as swiftly, "that you have a code of conduct." His toe tapped the accelerator, increased the Granada's speed.

"Knights go on croo-sades, I learned. Godfrey led the first one and killed thousands of Muslims and Jews in 1099 A.D., so since he was from Bouillon and they named soup after him, I figgered what was good enough for Godfrey was good enough for me."

While it was pleasant to make a real writer's acquaintance, even know they could probably have gotten to be friends, Dell's encounter brought him no closer to his major goal of obtaining a vehicle. But he got luckier around twilight on his second day out of prison. Standing on the edge of a tiny fleabag town he had never heard of, feeling as if life was passing him by and moonlight was piddling all over him, he sensed an engine humming in the distance. Then there was a car getting closer, the headlights becoming bigger, brighter—and Dell had a purely psychic feeling that this would be the one!

When it stopped on the berm, fast with no sound of brakes, Dell gasped.

He couldn't be sure about the color at night, but he thought he was staring at a red Jaguar automobile.

He saw the flash of a woman's face as she kind of slid across the cockpit seats to open the door— and he couldn't even remember raising his thumb to hitch a ride! "Anything I can do for you, big guy?" she inquired.

"Yew could give me a lift if yew'd be so kind," Dell shot back fast, polite all over. "Ah'd purely appreciate yore courtesy."

"I guess you find all kinds on the Kentucky– West Virginia border," the driver remarked, then gestured. "Hop in."

"Yes, ma'am," Dell allowed, hopping.

He was startled at how low his ass sunk down. For a minute he felt like he was sitting on the road! Then she was going through the gears, his door slamming shut with velocity, and Dell figured he might as well be riding some rocketship.

He was the luckiest man on the face of the earth to be getting himself a vehicle as *fine* as this one!

The next job was to check out the woman driver to know if she wasn't *too* far from his type (he had a list of preferences that showed how absent of snobbism he was). He'd have her as well as her car. He was unrushed as he turned his long, horsey head around to eyeball her, starting at the legs and working up.

When he made it to her face, Dell blinked twice, then closed his eyes. It wasn't only because she felt his gaze on her and stared back just as openly, as brazenly.

The driver of the Jaguar earned fine marks up and down Dell's list of preferences, but looking at her *face* . . . well, that was something else. Right then he could not make himself figure out *what.*

"D'you see anything that interests you?" the woman asked. She was still looking at Dell when he opened his eyes and, for a second, he wondered if this rocketship was set on automatic pilot.

"Well, ma'am," Dell said, "t'tell yew the truth, I hasn't seed—*seen*," he corrected hisself, thinking about Lloyd's learning), "any young lady as fine as yew in quite a spell." Dell swallowed, decided not to add he hadn't been around any ladies at all for a long while.

"Then what's wrong?" She smiled. The shiny look of her teeth made her seem platinum all over. "I'd almost think you've seen a ghost."

Mebbe I have, Dell thought, squirming on the most comfortable seat he had ever found in a automobile—if this really *was* a car. Even the dashboard made him think of a rocketship. Swerving his glance back to her and, since she didn't appear to mind a lot, he ran a second check on the platinum-haired driver: Something starry over her chests that almost didn't make it up far enough, the color: silver. A teensy skirt he'd like to push up, except it wasn't long enough to go anywhere but off, the color: silver. Legs headed in the direction they were headed and bound to get there first, wearing silvery stockings. Dell wondered for a second if she *could* be the pilot of a rocketship or from the future, because he'd never seen anyone but old people who were pretty much silver everywhere, yet she *wasn't* old—he'd bet his ass on that!

He gave her a precious fact. "Ma'am . . . yew look jest like my mom when she was a girl. Or, sorta a girl."

"Say what? *I* look like your mom?" Amused, she fell forward over the steering wheel, and Dell thought how nice it was going to be when her pretty hair did that over something other than a steering column. Merriment dispersed, she gave him a hard-eyed look. "Why am I listening to such dumb lines? Don't you understand why I picked you up back there?"

"Yew *do* look like Mom did!" Dell argued. His bad eye oozed, but it was dark enough in the Jag's interior for her not to see it. "Guwdammit, I ain't no liar!" She'd pissed him off so he chose to hurt her a leetle right then. "Mom's a *whore*, ma'am—born t'screw, if you don't mind my sayin' that word. But she looked okay, too, when I was little." He knuckled the weeping eye. "For a while, anyways."

It had got dark and she was still shoving the accelerator down, going faster because she was mad, too. "What the fuck d'you think *I* am, you fool?" she demanded. "I'm in a car like this; I brake, call you 'big guy'—not very original, I'll grant you, but I have other crap on my mind tonight—I'm wearing *these* clothes, and then I ask you if you see anything about me that interests you!" Her hair danced when she shook her head. "Maybe Phil had it right when he told me to invest in business cards!"

Dell, turned aghast by denial, sat straight. "You ain't no whore."

"Yes, I am," she nodded, driving faster now, if

anything. But she was looking out her windshield most of the time.

"Yew *can't* be," Dell argued. "Yew ain't!"

"I am top of the line, though." She turned her head and spent too long a time making eye contact. "Okay. If I really remind you of your mom, that has to mean one of two things—you wouldn't touch me if you could get it free. Or you're so hot right now your nuts are scorching that bucket seat. Which? And tell me now, okay, so I can drop you off if it's number one. Working girls can't waste the prime hours on mother-lovers."

Working girls. The expression torched a hotspot in Dell's memory. "I *will* take it for free, ma'am," he said quietly. His tone of voice made her look at him again. He thought he'd still be polite as long as possible. "Mebbe you are a whore. Yew talk like Mom. But I'll keep an eye on my *own* nuts, if yew don't mind."

She got the message at once. "You get *nothing* free from *me*, asshole," she said. Her foot crammed the accelerator down and the powerful engine reacted instantly. When Dell glanced out the window, he couldn't tell what he was seeing as they blew past. "You smart enough to notice my speed?" Her silvery capped teeth were like lightning. "Make a move, and I'll *really* open this baby up!"

Dell promptly turned sideways in his seat and put both hands on her breasts.

She tromped on the accelerator again. "Sooner or later, creep"—he couldn't believe she wasn't scared as shit of him!—"the fuzz'll pick us up on radar. Then you can explain to them what you were doing.'' She smiled, amazing Dell, and took one of his hands to move it between her legs. ''Or we can discuss price instead.''

Dell thought about it for a moment, he truly did. He was going to kill her for insultin' him, but fair was fair. Trouble was, he'd been told what to do for a lot of years. Besides, there were two other big facts to be considered: First, he was broke. Flat busted. Second, he didn't only want to *have* this whore—he meant to have her *car* too!

''Ma'am, I ain't got me a speck of mother love,'' he explained. ''So thet would not be no problem, awright? But I ain't got no cash-money neither. So I'm afeered that thet's that.''

He started to squeeze her crotch—to push in with his thumb so hard he sort of hoped he wasn't making a permanent dent where one didn't belong—and at the same time he gave her a big kick in the right ankle with the toe of one of his shiny new shoes.

Well, her foot came straight up off the accelerator as he had known it had to do, the Jaguar began to slow immediately, and he shoved her back against her seat, then grabbed the wheel. ''I thought you made a real nice try,'' Dell complimented her. He was polite as he eased the sports car toward the shadowy berm of the road. ''Yew know, it's gonna be better like this anyhow, ma'am, 'cause they's only about one thang you coulda done for me in this bitty ve-hicle 'n I wants *more*.''

The Jag rolled to a stop, the glossy tail end partly out on the road. ''I think you broke my ankle, you big son-of-a-bitch," she complained. She opened her door, gripped her lower leg with her hands.

"I reckon I'm a *real* son-of-a-bitch," Dell said mildly, distracted by the task of checking where they were. He saw his magic hadn't left him at all! All he saw were farmhouses, 'way back from the highway; no businesses, nothing. He also observed a nice little bunch of trees before you could even get to the farmhouses. "Even so," he added, "it ain't the place for women t'call men thet—'specially no whores. Lessen they's sigh-chi'trists, too. 'Member thet."

That was when the woman tried to get away. Ignoring her pain, she limped out on the road with surprising speed and craned her neck looking for cars coming. But this was a country road leading out of a tiny town that no one left except for visits to Mom for Sunday dinner, taking the crops to market, or possibly to seek privacy for an illicit tryst. *I wonder if I've bought it, this time,* she thought, wild with panic but trying not to let this weird john see it. They sensed fear like wolves. *I should've gone to Detroit the way Phil wanted.*

She didn't fight him when Dell was there, grasping both her arms and half lifting her—*Jesus, his hands were hams!*—then slinging her on his hip like an animal he'd shot (or roadkill) and trotting toward some trees at the edge of the road. *One more bastard who doesn't pay. God, make that all this is. I can handle that.*

For a while, it seemed to be.

"I ain't real fancy so yew do whut I tells yew,"

Dell said, "then I'll ride yew back t'where we met." He took his new pants off, careful to fold them neatly, hummed to himself. He'd stopped under some trees, but some nice moonlight was coming through for him to see by. "Some girls say I'm sort of old-fashioned, but let's jest start with reg'lar fuckin'. Okay?"

Where we met? the woman thought. The crazy talked like they were on a *date*.

Then he was undressing her methodically, even draping her skirt over a convenient branch. Somewhat relaxed, she touched his shorts and tried to slip her fingers inside.

And he *lost* it. She was dry as a bone, dry as remembered love—all Sally thought of sometimes on her day off at the hotel—but he was hurting her badly though she had managed to get her fist between him and her breasts so he wouldn't crush them. The pain surprised her for a second since the hick bastard's cock was barely bigger than a boy's. Then she remembered the way he'd crammed his thumb against her, hard. *You're a pro, Sally,* she told herself, *act like one and don't let him see you're hurting.* "Wow, you're good," she said, tacking on a gasp, "you're something *else*, baby, you're almost too *big* for me!" Christ, he hadn't put a rubber on his little weenie, all she needed now was some cornball looney tunes' *brat*!

"Jest bounce," Dell mumbled, pushing her fist away to hang on to both breasts, "and don't talk dirty."

All right, damn you, she thought. Sally thrust up against him hard. She had seen other johns rock back on their asses while their tools merely went off like low-grade fireworks when she did this. Dell went off, but not on her stomach or in the air.

He sat in the grass, panting some. "Thet was okay," he said, getting his breath. "But yew could do a better job by stayin' with me ever inch when I'm comin'."

Jesus, he's doing a goddamn review of my perfor-mance! "Maybe my work would improve if I got paid." She couldn't resist it.

But she soon wished she had. Sally had sat up; now he was knocking her over on her back, there were sharp twigs or something under her, and he was *sitting* on her chest, for God's sake—poking his thumbs into her throat! "Yew ain't Lloyd B.!" he said. "Yew don't know nothin'! Don't yew tell me nothin'! I bet my mother's better'n *yew!*" The strength of his thumbs was shocking, unexpected, like everything was this crazy night. But then he released her, rolled off. "Now. Make me git up again."

Sally sighed, struggled to her knees. "I'll try, but I'm not a rocket scientist."

"With that car of yorn?" Dell scoffed, chuckling. It was the first time she'd seen the way one of the john's eyes was a little off, and dripped. Before she lowered her gaze and went back to work she prayed he hadn't gotten any of his eye shit on her. "I got me some real special fuel all saved up!"

Time passed drearily for the most part. Eventually, he didn't want any more—that was what he said, as if he had been filled up with dessert—and went back to being the drawling, outwardly polite creep from the Jaguar. *Christ, he'll be something to tell Phil about*, Sally decided.

Dell did everything but mend the clothing he'd torn and then helped her get dressed. For the first time she felt it was safe to breathe freely, but she was also cold, colder now than she had been. That surprised her enough that her professional instincts were momentarily alerted. It was probably only that she'd been a hooker forever; she was getting a bit long in the tooth now and was aware of that. You didn't begin as a new girl on the streets at fourteen and hang in there till you were almost twenty-five without survival instincts *and* a little all-purpose fear.

She walked back to the car with him, knowing it wasn't her car anymore unless her pimp Phil knew some sheriff in this nothing county who would make a sincere effort to find it. The main thing was, she had survived. He hadn't strangled or shot her. That was the main thing—that is, if he didn't *have* something or she wasn't pregnant again!

"Y'sure you can drive this boat?" she asked from the passenger seat after Dell had gotten behind the wheel. "It's four speeds forward, on the floor." Her hair had come loose, the wave was gone, she felt like crap, but she smiled fondly at him as, fumblingly, he got the motor running. Both his eyes blinked, as though he'd forgotten the Jaguar's power, its distinctive, beautiful purr. God, she would miss it! "Let me show—"

He slapped at her extended hand and arm. "How do yew put the top down?"

Obediently, though she was freezing in what was left of her skimpy outfit, she showed him.

"I want t'thank yew," he said gravely, slipping the transmission into second instead of first. Sally was glad it wasn't third gear. "I thank yew for yore favors, too."

She laughed charmingly, careful not to let it sound as if she was making fun of him.

Unaccustomed to the sports car's cornering ability, Dell, trying to negotiate a U-turn on the highway, barely avoided ending up back where he'd started. He grunted, straightened out the Jag's nose, and touched the accelerator with his big, heavy foot.

The G-force shoved them both back against the cockpit seats and Dell stabbed at the brake. Because the pedals were slender and not separated as far as an American vehicle's, he hit the accelerator simultaneously and the great engine wailed in confusion.

Yet after that, Sally was startled by how her rapist adapted to the smaller, swifter car's demands. Maybe he'd been a chauffeur; he'd had a lot of experience in driving *something.*

And she realized the yokel probably *was* taking her back—dutifully keeping his goddamn *word* as if he hadn't just *raped* a woman! "You're getting the hang of it fast," she said tactfully.

"Gittin colder'n a witch's tit," Dell noted, his tone of voice grumbling but not, she thought, hostile. He was poking at a button. "Top won't go up now."

"Maybe you didn't—"

"I did whut you showed me!" he exclaimed. "Sumbitch is stuck."

She nearly asked if he wanted her to demonstrate again what to do, but in reverse, then saw that would be a mistake. Fucking had made his temper worse, if anything; his moods changed faster than she could keep track. She caught a breath, held it. "What do you want me to do about it? Not that I don't agree, I *do*—it *is* getting cold." She assayed a youthful laugh. "You should try it sometime when all you have on is—"

"*Pull* on it," Dell interrupted, gesturing behind them with his thumb. "Pull on the gawdamn top so's it'll come loose."

For a moment she sat perfectly still, regarding him. He might have been nice-looking except for the eye. And except for . . . she didn't know how to finish the thought, though, and abandoned it. But she knew her top *never* stuck, this was all some kind of ridiculous macho mistake. Doing what he demanded meant climbing up on the seat, facing backward, stretching her arms . . . it would only make her colder to be exposed that way. "Would you mind slowing down? Just a bit?"

"Whut?" He looked over, the wounded eye working, as if he'd been aroused from deep thought. "Whut do yew want?"

"*Could you slow it down?*" she said. They were going so fast she'd had to shout.

"Shore!" His lopsided grin was back. He eased up on the accelerator immediately. "Thet any better?"

Sally got on her knees in the passenger seat, nodding. She reached back, then found that her arms—wind was biting into them like fishhooks—

couldn't quite make it. She pushed forward and practically sprawled on the rear of the Jaguar above the trunk. Her knees on down were now dangerously the only portion of her body left in the seat. Swallowing panic, she stretched her arms and her body farther—touched the folded-back top with her fingertips—

A long, strong arm immediately fell across her back, pinning her in place.

"Yew think I'm a idiot," he said accusingly, just loud enough. Oddest tone of voice she'd ever heard.

"I don't!" Sally had to scream. She was close to being entirely outside the car.

"Yew said I use 'dumb lines', and called me a 'fool.' Well, mebbe yew're one of them *luckies* who finished up high school. But I'm tryin' t'learn."

"That's w-w-wonderful," Sally cried, struggling to get back into the seat. The bastard's arm felt as if it weighed a ton. Sally weighed one hundred two.

"Yew called me a 'asshole,' too." While he spoke, he appeared not to be paying attention to his driving and the Jag was fishtailing a little, but he was also continuing to slow his speed. The eternal optimist, effectually mounted like a trophy on the back of her automobile, wondered if he might not mean to stop soon, just to rip off another and more violent piece of her. "Also called me, I think, a creep. And I didn't purely cater to thet, either."

"Figures of speech!" Sally shrieked. It was getting easier to scream because, despite her surge of hope, she was also experiencing another surge of terror. Facing away from the front, she realized they were passing a strip mall she knew. They weren't far from town. "Those words didn't mean a *thing*. Please—let me get back in?"

Dell made a humorless noise that sounded like "hawh-hawh." She caught a glimpse of his eyes when he stared back at her. "Words mean almost everything," he said. "I'da drove yew home, but yew're jest like the other ones. Dumb, too. A idiot."

"Honey," she said, "I'm *sor*-reee." Hard to sound humble, gentle and womanly, and beery sexy when you were screaming. But he *was* going slower still, that was something. "Let me back in and I'll do you *real* good, sweetie. I'll show you tricks no one ever showed you before!"

"I'm gonna drive this here car t'Mom's home, kill her ass," Dell called back. "'Cause she's a whore. Woulda done her years back, but I didden have the magic yet."

Sally fought a yearning to scream. "I'll bet we could make magic together if we *both* tried," she said, abruptly realizing she hadn't had to shout or scream, that he had the speed down to forty, maybe. But of course, he did; they were nearing the city limits, he didn't want to get arrested—as if any fuzz driving around might not *notice* a living ornament on the top of a sports car! Was he totally insane? "Look, my ankle still hurts, let's stop at a drugstore for an Ace bandage, then head for my place. You'll be glad y'did."

Dell stared straight ahead. He hadn't interrupted her again because she'd told him they might make some magic. Well, he was no fool, all they'd done in the trees was fuck and he hadn't learned one gawdamn thing. The whore still figured she was smarter than he was!

"Mebbe you oughta use *yore* magic for *flyin'*," Dell suggested idly, slowly lifting his arm from her back.

As he shifted into second, flooring the accelerator, then into third, he let her go completely.

He'd heard some sports cars went from zero to sixty so fast you couldn't believe it was happening! And they were *right*, he marveled, and slammed on the brakes, because he'd just remembered: Folks could survive terrible accidents if they had magic, or their souls were clean.

Dell backed up, gunning the engine so hard he ran over the whore when he got to where she'd fallen.

The way she was lying, white bone sticking out of her neck so she had that silvery look all over again, any fool would know she had a dirty soul and no magic at all.

Dell opened the door on the driver's side, put one foot in the street to get a mite closer to her. That way, she was looking up at him exactly as they were all supposed to do. "Yew did, too, look like Mom," he informed her. "She's gonna look like yew when I have done kilt her ass!"

There hadn't been a great deal of noise—Dell had learned that people thrown out of cars landed nice and soft—but he heard a car motor returning to its sporadic imitation of life a block or two over, so he shifted into first and peeled away.

They would find strips of rubber on the street beside the dead whore, but it was her car and not in

Dell's name, and he'd swap the thing right after he . . . visited . . . Mom.

Jags were nice and all, but they were too small for a whole lot of thangs, Dell decided.

But times like this—*hours* like this, when it was dark like it was when you were going to sleep at night and knew you'd be sucking on your thumb soon, dreaming the *good* dreams you never ever had during the daytime—and also times when you killed or hurt somebody so bad they never *could* forget it—kind of made Dell glad he was at the wheel, being a traveling man. Because it was *your* light that broke the night, cut it in two so both pieces were yours like two sides of a coin; and you were all by yourself the *only one* who knew what you'd just done; and if you got real horny you could unzip your fly and sorta pull it out—still flopping but with some good old steakbone to it—and you didn't need no gawdamn perverted fucking *pictures* of naked women . . . to . . . to—

Dell had to get help at a gas station because he didn't know the Jaguar's ways, and he paid for it with the credit card he found in the dead whore's purse. He come upon it on the floorboard just when he needed money for gas. There wasn't much cash but that was fine, he hadn't even wanted to use her credit card. Nobody in the whole gawdamn family had ever took charity. But it was use the card or off the fella who'd gassed him up, and he'd been fairly nice.

Sitting in the Jag's driver's seat, Dell remembered how Mom had written him in prison. She would be *real* surprised when she saw him again. Her letter said she was washin' her hands of him. Well, he wrote back (before he learned to look up words he didn't know how to spell), "One more pieca shit sayin Bye don't mean nothin," adding, "but washin *yur* hands clean wood take alot of damn soap!!!!!"

Then Mom had writ to him again—*writ-ten*, he told himself—and that made him think of *The Book of Webster's*, and he was concerned briefly he might have dropped his copy when he took his drawers down back in the woods. He found it where the dead whore had sat. He took a Kleenex from the glove compartment and wiped the paperback off before he left the gas station.

Dell ate breakfast in a Waffle House that was open late, or maybe early, twenty miles from home. He took the dictionary in with him, began leafing through. *Mr. Webster, he must be one smart man*, Dell thought. Lloyd was right. He needed to study more.

Dell's good eye stopped at the word *merit*, his bad eye hurried into companionable focus, and Dell smiled, feeling almost peaceful. "Reward due," read the definition, plus "excellence" and "virtue" and "intrinsic rightness or wrongness." He didn't know the meaning of "intrinsic" and he'd have looked it up but his flapjacks were coming. But it seemed like *magic* had made him find a word *real* fast that fit him.

It hadn't taken long to drive from the little woods where he'd got the fancy car, but he was getting tired by the time he was drivin' up the block toward the familiar house on the hill. Dell noticed the neighborhood was looking older and junky, too, with cars or tires parked on lawns and one house with a homemade sign for earthworms. The idea of just taking a jalopy from a yard came to mind, but there was no style to that and they wouldn't be sitting out there if they weren't broken-down. Probably a bunch of minority folks had moved in on Mom and there went the old neighborhood. Of course, they were different from Lloyd B. Lloyd had talked about bigots and Dell knew they were never smart like Lloyd and him.

The old house on the hill was so high up he'd been eyeballing it from blocks off. Driving closer, he saw there were no lights on inside. He guessed Mom had stopped whoring so she could go to work at the restaurant, but Dell didn't like the look of it. There was just something about the place this morning that he didn't cotton to.

So instead of parking outside, he drove a couple blocks in the direction of Hardee's and left the car in the street. Cops weren't generally good enough to find their own ass that fast, but this was the new, ever-vigilant Dell, and you could not underestimate your opponent and expect to win the war. He'd read that in some military book in the library. He would just walk to the place, do what he'd come to do, then walk back—nice and easy—to get the Jag.

Or mebbe she's got new wheels, he ruminated as he returned to the house, the only man on the streets at that hour, *an' I can jest pick 'em up 'n go from there.* The small-town authorities would play hell not knowing where a fancy car like the Jag came from, and he'd be hundreds of miles away before they found out he'd been drivin' it.

As for fingerprints, well, Dell had learned from Lloyd B. that there was hardly any talk between police forces of different cities or states,and some of the bitty little towns didn't even keep a fingerprint file— because some of them didn't even have no computers!

Dell stared up at what had been home, sort of. He remembered Mom putting out a red porch-light once, but he'd punched it out, fast. As he saw it back then, a home was not a house. Whistling, he started climbin' the steps, remembered he hadn't slept and decided there was no rush, he could have a nap before he killed Mom. She couldn't run fast enough to get away when he got up, that was sure! Dell hammered on the door with his fists, waited the tenth part of a second, then yelled, "Git *up*, Mom— it's yore boy Dell!"

Nothing stirred inside. *"Mom?"*

For the fraction of a second Dell wondered if he'd run straight into that Jim Rockford TV fella or somebody like him in Ashland without knowing it, and this was a set-up, a trap. Hell, mebbe the dead whore had been the fucking governor's wife or something. You found whores everyplace. He listened intently, did it with his ears and his long body pressed against the front door and used the ear that wasn't there to try to hear somebody slipping around at him from the back of the house.

Nothin'.

Dell tried to look through the windows on either

side of the door, but the first one was so shitty dirty he didn't even see his own face.

Through the other window Dell saw nothing—not because he couldn't see into the house, but because there was nothing to *see!*

Not a stick of furniture remained in the living room, including *his TV!*

"Mom!" Dell shouted again, louder. Once more, till his voice broke: *"MOM!"*

When there was still nothing and nobody stirred, he ran around to the rear of the house to look through those windows—except only one was on ground level. Fighting anxiety, he pressed his face to the nearest pane with his eyes big as a boy's, found the window was clear enough to see through—

And the only things remaining in the familiar kitchen were the cabinets and the sink, both built-in. Also, a calendar on the wall—with last year's dates.

Facts came rushing in at him like a gawdamn SWAT team—or bees, yellowjackets—and there was no way Dell could avoid confronting them. Mom had moved while he was in prison.

His mother had left without telling her only son where she'd gone. She had no right to do that to him!

Dell's reaction was essentially what Dr. Lenora Middel might have expected—it was normal, for him. He hoisted a rusted lawn mower he had mowed grass with maybe twice when he was twelve or thirteen and half-shoved, half-threw it through the kitchen window.

Then, for the shortest instant, he considered goin' inside to trash the gawdamn puking stinking whorehouse where nobody had ever given him a chance—not one, fucking *chance!*—and where nobody had ever even *liked* his ass.

In Dell's ear, he heard Lloyd B. quoting from *The Book of Webster's: "Adjust*: 'to change so as to make fit, suitable. To settle rightly.'" And again, "'To adapt . . . oneself.'"

Trying to sort things out and feeling badly treated, Dell went as far on the hilltop as he could get, standing near nothing but a kid-sized wall and a big drop. He peered down at the town, ready to cut loose some of his innermost feelings. *"Yew git yore sorry ass back where it belongs, Mom, yew hear me?"* (A pause, in hope of getting a reply. But there was none.) "You lissen up, yew *mothafuckers* down there, this is *Dell* from *hell!* Yew ain't gone mess with *me* no more, 'cause *I'll* rip *yore gawdamn* gonads *off iffen yew even think about it*!" His volume had kept increasing.

There was a reply to that particular expression of his heartfelt feelings.

"Hold it down, you crazy fuckhead, this is Delray from De-troit, and I'll blow you off that mother-humpin' hill *with my Browning automatic if you don't shut your mouth*!"

Dell nearly fell off the hill. This neighborhood was shot to *hell!* And nobody even stepped out like a man to let him know where he *was.*

Christ, he didn't even know what way Mom had gone—but there *was* a way! Magic pumped back into Dell's veins. There *was* a way "to make suitable, to settle rightly" with this source of his newest frustration—the same gawdamn one that gave him *all* the worst times of his life:

Mom. Who worked *at nearby Hardee's.*

Dell fell twice on the long flight of steps leading down from the closed house, once rolling several steps and hurting one ankle. *Fuck it*! he thought, when he was on the pavement.

But he didn't have to hop. After several yards, the throb in his ankle went away, and he felt better as he drew nearer the tiny new mall a few blocks off.

Yet not one ounce of the murderous fury, the frustration, the desire to adjust his situation was siphoned from Dell's brain.

He was out of breath, the ankle still hurt some, he had a headache to match his mood, and his pride was screeching like hooty owls by the time he'd burst through the restaurant door. Dell sort of fell the rest of the way to the counter.

She was eighteen, everyone but teenage boys thought she looked fifteen, and she believed she could pass for twenty, easy. "What'll it be, sir? Breakfast?"

"No," Dell gasped, anger making it harder to git his breath back. *"Mother."* He shook his head, felt how sweaty and sticky his hair was, knew he needed a bath this week. *"Want—*my *mom,"* he said, madder because it didn't sound like any kind of man's command.

The teenager was bewildered. "What's her name?"

Dell told her, got his breath back. "Yew git her *out* here, girl! *Now*!"

She seemed ready to cry, or to run. "I'm sorry, I don't know who she *is*, sir."

The countergirl didn't have to run because she had raised her voice slightly and a manager was appearing beside her, drying his hands. Dell saw from his name-tag that his name was Bumstead and his senses reeled because the world was changing around him. "What seems to be the trouble?" the man inquired in a pleasant, tenor voice.

"My mother works here"—the teenager mentioned the name, then rushed away—"'n I wants t'talk to her." Things were better; he could breathe again. But why was Dagwood wearing a *mustache*? He looked more like Mr. Beasley, the gawdamn mailman. "Jest . . . talk!"

The manager reflected, snapped his fingers. "Your mother *did* work here, sir." Then he frowned. "Apparently you weren't in regular touch. Y'see, one day, she simply—"

Dells' arms went out. He tried to squeeze the manager's scrawny neck but his bowtie came off in Dell's hands. "Iffen yew tell me she *died*, I'll bust yore ass so bad yew'll shit outta yore bellybutton!"

"Violence won't be necessary, sir." Bumstead retrieved the snap-on bowtie from where Dell had thrown it on the counter and began trying to put it back on. "It was some two years ago, I think—possibly three—when—"

Dell felt his face turning red. It didn't do that often, he knew, but he wished it would. It scared crap out of folks. Casually, he turned sideways to a cart loaded with tomatoes, onions, lettuce, and pickles. *"Where* in *fuck* did *my Mom* go?"* he demanded—then used one big hand to sweep everything flying. It made him feel a bit better to watch it fly awhile, then bust all over the floor.

"Please, sir, I understand your concern," Dagwood stammered fast, getting no closer, "but your mother was alive when she left us to get married."

"Whut?" The way redness was suffusing Dell's face now might scare them but it also scared *him*— and that made matters worse. "Yew're sayin my gawdamn whore mother found somebuddy t'marry *her?"*

Customers at tables rose and quietly began to empty their trays into garbage receptacles. They either stood and waited several careful yards from the cash register or slipped out the nearest door, apologetically shaking their heads in the manager's direction.

Dagwood was braced. "I've answered your questions but now I must ask you to w-watch your language or leave." Part of the bowtie was back in place; the other half hung like a broken wing. He swallowed hard. "Your mother . . . *eloped.* Didn't say a word to us, just put down the fry basket—at the same time that a man named Archie Busey stopped frying hamburgers—and the two of them left. Together."

Dell pounded his fist on the counter and a number of things fell over. "How do yew *know—"*

"An assistant manager named M-Mary found a note in the ladies when I sent her to inspect." Dagwood's head went left to right like a ragdoll's and Dell, seeing it, decided the head and neck ought to work like that all the time. "I must say, your mom got pretty careless with her duties before she—"

Dell threw him back toward the kitchen, and Mr. Bumstead's feet or legs didn't touch the ground till he got there.

He followed up by deciding to trash the place. He was makin a pretty good job of it, when two objections to finishing came up. First, he suddenly knew he had to get an address for Busey—for *Mr. and Mrs.* Archie Busey—since he now had got himself *two* people to kill!

The other interruption was the arrival of the gawdamn authorities. Two uniformed cops came through the door fast and both of them had drawn their service revolvers, and they were aimed at Dell.

Dell looked around for a weapon, but he couldn't find anything that would do as one.

He just saw the young countergirl stepping away from the phone. "Thank God you got here!" she gushed at the cops, standing behind them.

Handcuffed, Dell had to pass the girl. He said softly, "I jest wish you was at least eighteen years old. Maybe I'll git to see yew later."

But he knew that would be quite a while.

"What took you so *long,* meat?"

"Jest leave me alone, Lloyd B.," Dell growled, brushing at his short-sleeved shirt where the guard had touched (and guided) him. The man had seen that a lot and didn't look impressed. Dell sagged down on his old bed, a bit surprised it was available. But Lloyd's mocking eyes across the cell reminded him of what a short amount of time he'd spent outside, free. He plumped his pillow as though he were trying to destroy it.

Hugging himself, Dell rocked back against the wall at the end of his cot. Fuck! *One time* he got pissed and now he'd have to do that time they knocked off when they gave him his early parole.

Of course, it could have been a whole lot worse. As far as he knew, the authorities hadn't tied him to the ripped-off Jag, so they hadn't connected him to the dead whore either. Had they learned about either of *them*, he'd have been outside next around the time of the Second Coming!

"You know and *I* know you did something a hell of a lot worse than bustin' up some restaurant," Lloyd B. intoned like a mind reader. He hadn't glanced up.

"How yew know thet?" Dell asked. "I just got here!"

The older man tapped his temple with his index finger. "Ah knows, boy. Ah gots my *ways.*" He winked and went back to his reading. For the fifth or sixth time Dell wondered if Lloyd B. went back to talking jive for fun or because he had to. "Ah knowed y'all was comin' before *you* knowed it, meat." Looking up, his wink was real smart-ass. "I got spies *evahwheah*, mothafucker!"

"Yew got shit." Dell dismissed him with a wave.

"True, 'cause I got my whitemeat boy back like I said I probably would—and do you care to know *why* I expected you back? Because you're just like the cats who read two chapters of one of the Gos-

pels and decide they have *religion!* Five minutes outside, with temptation, and they got *dick!* But you, why,
you are one lucky honky." The patois disappeared.
"Dumb as bedrock, Dell, but distinctly fortunate."

"Fuck it!" Dell tossed his dictionary at the cell
wall. "I thought I'd ask yew t'teach me more, but if
thet's how yew think of me, jest *fuck* it."

Lloyd turned a page in his book. "All right."

Dell froze in place on the bed. "All right?" For
an instant it seemed as though everybody was turning against him. "Now, hold on."

"I'm holding." Lloyd B. didn't look up for a long
while. When he did, Dell saw he was wearing
glasses. Rimless glasses! His face was still mostly in
shadows, and even his eyes were hard to see; the
glasses were *real* thick. "What is it?"

"Well, I thought yew might tell me about thet
bird." Dell ransacked his memory for details. "It
was—well, sort of magic or somethin'."

Lloyd B. had that teacher look and his brows
were raised. "You'd like to learn about the *phoenix,*
and how you may use your *Webster's* to convey the
impression—when you encounter others—that you
might truly be a human being?"

Dell almost got pissed at the question but bit his
lip. "Yes." He nodded his head. This uppity sumbitch
still had magic to give away, and he wanted it. "I do."

"Go pick up *The Book of Webster's,*" Lloyd said
with an incline of his head in the paperback's direction. "And never let me see you mistreat a book
again in my presence."

Dell brushed the book carefully, then blew on

the edge of the pages. He went back to his bunk and sat down, slowly. *Someday I'm gone kill this nig iffen I fry for it,* he thought.

"Look up the word *phoenix*," Lloyd B. rumbled. His index finger rose. "*Don't* make my earlier work with you a sham by looking under the letter F!"

"Warn't goin' to," Dell grumbled, lying. He made his thumbing thumb go out of F and look for the letter P. But there was nothing starting "pfee" at all. "Can't find it, Lloyd B."

With a sigh, the former teacher spelled the word and then repeated it with a near certainty that Dell's brain hadn't yet truly recorded the correct spelling.

"I shall tell you about that ugly bird, boy, and spare you the—ummm—*spare* definition such an abbreviated dictionary surely provides. *Then* you may read it. But I shall tell you in the colloquial form you may be most able to grasp."

Dell had already read, "n. (Gr. *phoinix*) *Egyptian Myth*." None of that made a lick of sense. He stared up attentively at the older man.

"Every man," Lloyd B. began, "has the options—the choices—of the great phoenix. Except he doesn't know he does."

Dell liked that. It sounded like magic.

"When someone hurts yore ass, whitemeat, you can stay hurt—or you can change into somethin' else." Lloyd, enjoying his own patois, winked a second time. "See, if they hurt you so bad it *kills* you, y'all are *definitely* gonna change into somethin else anyway!"

"Whut?" Dell inquired. It was once more getting

dark in the nation and therefore the prison and therefore in the two-man cell. As Lloyd spoke it was as if he
became swallowed up more by knowledge and what
he had loved to do when he was free than by shadows, and he alone appeared lighter, brighter.

"For one thing, boy, *dead* whitemeat. Rottin' into
nothin' but worm food!" He rolled his eyes back. "For
anotha, young massa, mebbe an angel. Mebbe a demon." He laughed in spite of himself. "You certainly
don't remind me of any angels *I've* read about."

"Well, mebbe I'll be a demon then," Dell said
slowly.

"Y'all're shittin' me!" Lloyd B. howled and went
on laughing for so many long seconds that Dell joined
him. "You're in *prison* again, son—Calbert's still here,
and he's gonna *git* y'all sooner or later! Dell, ain't no
demons who *swish*, don' you know that? Maaaan, a
demon, he's a *bad*-ass dude. Don't take no shit from
nobody, boy! Demon, he ain't even *got* an asshole—
ain't even got him a dick! If he did, *he'd* know when to
use it and when not, he wouldn't let no hunk of his
own *hide* tell him what to do!"

Smarting, scared, Dell called the teacher a name
but just with his working lips. Even Lloyd B. couldn't
see in the dark. "So whut the fuck is a phoenix?"

Lloyd's face appeared to soar so near his own
that Dell imagined the old darkie *flowed* at him!
"Why, meat, *he's* a bird who always rises again—
that's what! He's the *boss* bird—them scientist folks
even named a whole constellation in the sky after
him!"

"Where does yew go t'see him?"

"Well, boy, it's highest in November. In the southern hemisphere."

"So it ain't a *real* bird then?" Dell asked, innocently enough.

Lloyd B. struck him across the face and the force of his blow drove Dell off the cot to his knees. "Don't give me no mouth, lily-white motherfucker! Don't call me no *name*, either, 'lest y'all got the guts t'say it to my face! The *real* phoenix, it lived in the desert. In Arabia. For nearly five hundred years, they say. But it didn't like how it was turnin' out, Dell." He was helping Dell back up to the bunk, patting his arm. "It felt old, hurt—used up *all* over. Other birds'd been beatin' its ass. Know what it did?"

Dell just said, "Whut?" 'cause his whole head hurt and he'd been caught off-guard again. Lloyd had slapped him so fast there wasn't time yet even to *hate* him!

The teacher stood erect. What remained of distant illumination from the guard station caught him in the back and made him seem tall, mighty. Great. "It made itself a big ole mess of wood, and twigs, and set fire to it. Then that ole Phoenix began *fannin'* the flames, son, beatin' at them with its wings . . . until the fire, it jest came *up* arown that bird!" He threw his graying head back, spread his arms wide, and laughed. "Burned itself clean *up*!"

Dell stared at him. "Fuck," he said, pissed without knowing why. "Well, *fuck*."

"But *out* of the ashes, Dellie . . . whitemeat . . . *outta them ashes came a new*, different *bird*—a young *bird*. Bigger 'n stronger 'n sassier than ever!"

"Huh?" Dell asked.

Lloyd B. patted Dell's cheeks, reached down and hugged his head. " 'Cause the *bird* had decided it was time to change, son! *It* had decided—all on its own—*when* to change, *when* to begin over—and then, why"—Lloyd gave Dell a big juicy kiss in the middle of his forehead—"it plumb flat-out *flew away*! Free. Freer'n it had ever been *before*!"

"I'm a son of a beech," Dell exclaimed, marveling too much to scrub off Lloyd's kiss.

"Yes, you are." The teacher had turned, but he turned back now. "The moral is—you can even change *that*."

It wasn't that night or the next morning when Dell fully became aware of what he had seen pictured in his Webster's dictionary nor when he experienced his revelation.

He was too busy feeling sorry for himself. By the time the courts got through with him, he figured he'd be more than forty years old when he got out of prison.

But Lloyd B. continued to be at his back, protectin' Dell from the perverts who were after him, and as the years fizzled out and passed, there were other choice targets who replaced the maturing Dell in the desire of the ever-changing, ever-present minority that liked to bully the younger men.

Dell was also successful in making himself less sexually compelling, when the prison finally put in a weight room. No one hit on fellas with muscles that showed. Dell, no less bored than any man except those like Lloyd B. (with fairly high intelligence quotients and a wider range of interests), worked out once or twice a week. He had the sort of frame that rarely developed conspicuous musculature; Dell had always been stronger than he looked. When the actual improvement of strength in his biceps and his grip and his thriving desire to murder were combined, it became an increasingly lethal mix—one Dell was entirely aware of.

It was during one of those moods when he was marginally more eager to get his ass out, to find wheels and kill than he was to have a woman, that he was flipping through the pages of *The Book of Webster's* and had his greatest revelation.

Dell hadn't been studying, he'd been bored.

But his thumb stopped on the page with the word *phoenix*, and the definition, read for the first time since ole Lloyd's lesson, quickly triggered his new moment of enlightenment. After some crap about the source of the myth in Egypt, Dell read: "A bird which lived for 500 years, consumed itself in fire, then rose, renewed, from the ashes."

He sat transfixed, churning inside. It was what Lloyd told him, yes—but now he could only peer blankly at the picture as the wonder of revelation began and instantly filled him with rising awe.

This phoenix was the *same bird* Dr. Lenora Middel had owned—and *he'd* bashed her brains in with the statue. He hadn't even seen, or recognized, all the magic that had been there for him, *right from the beginning!* He had taken only *part* of what the ugly dead shrink had possessed.

Which meant that magic, like the good feeling you got from having sex, was *deep inside.* A fella had to reach in, real deep, and *pull* it out!

It was just like the way you had to open *The Book of Webster's*, and draw *its* magic out—even *search* for it, if you wanted to find it all.

Words—and facts—and magic . . . they were almost like some sort of religion, he decided, simultaneously shivering and sizzling up and down his body.

As that year began for Dell, for the very first time he started to pay attention to what Lloyd B. said and to make the first effort of his life to improve himself. He'd thought he did it before, he'd *believed* he had— but now he knew he hadn't even begun. The possibilities for growth, he saw, were beyond calculation.

By the time he got out of prison the next time, Dell realized, he ought to be smart enough to steal from everybody and to kill *anyone* he wanted, and *get away with it.*

Lloyd, though, kept getting older as time passed. Maybe it was the glasses that did it. But sometimes the old teacher didn't even say a lot that made sense to Dell; sometimes he just squinted at his own books, scowling, not saying a thing.

But one day Lloyd B. had the idea for Dell to open up *The Book of Webster's* wherever Dell's own thumb decided—"doing it at random," Lloyd called it—and gave Dell the magic he needed to *not ever get himself caught or shot, no matter what!* But, if he *did*, to know how to escape. Forever!

Dell opened the Book up—flipped once—then stopped.

He'd been keeping his eyes shut, but now he popped the lids up, and looked.

"'Vi-car-i-ous,'" he read. An adjective. "'Made by substitution; suffered or done in place of another; a *vicarious sacrifice*.'"

Dell's bad eye began oozing.

He continued reading the fascinating definition. He already had an idea of what a "sacrifice" was.

"'Enjoyed by one as a result of his imagined participation in an experience,'" *The Book of Webster's* declared, ringing with the sort of authority Dell had always dreamed of having, "'not his own.'" Dell read it all together and put mental italics under the final three words: *not his own*.

Not his own sacrifice. But, *Enjoyed by one*.

Dell's heartbeat nearly ceased. Was he gettin' it *right* or should he ask Lloyd B.?

But the answer to that lay in the last words of the definition: "Filling the office of and acting for another."

Had Dell ever believed in anything beyond himself before, had he ever felt reverent toward anything, he would have fallen down on his knees to thank his Lord. Because now his whole future was laid out before him!

The word *vicarious* and its definition had supplied the answer to what had stumped Dell ever since Lloyd described the bird that burnt itself up, because one thing Dell *never* meant to do was harm so much as a square inch of his *own* hide! But he'd learned about the way people said things met-ophorically, too, and so he knew right then what the phoenix bird had really done:

He'd got *other birds* to step into the flames for him—and that was what Dell would do, too.

His wonderful *Book of Webster's* had said he could become a better, different dude—always win-ning, never hurt, and never stopped—by getting other folks to take all the punishment and the pain *for* him—through *vi-car-i-ous sacrifice*! It was also *fine* to enjoy rapin' and stranglin', because that was just "a result of his imagined participation" since he'd been imagining doing those things for most of his life!

You just *substituted* a person when you were in trouble or felt bad—you just let them "suffer or do in place of another"—Dell *himself.*

And you got to be a new, bigger, stronger, sassier bird than you were before—whenever *you* wanted!

Other prisoners opened the Bible at random and read whatever they saw. Then they accepted what they read as inspiration, solace, advice. From that moment on, Dell knew he would always do the same with *The Book of Webster's.*

Part II

HELL ON WHEELS

C H A P T E R 7

After he'd learned about the magical phoenix, *vi-car-ious* sacrifice and all (Dell still had to say that one word slowly to get it right), he spent so many years hunched over library books—*The Book* always close by—that he was almost s'prised to realize his release date was coming up soon—and with it, turning forty years old.

Other men in the prison dreaded reaching the age so much that Dell decided one day there must be something *magical* about forty.

In a really old volume in a corner of the library where almost nobody ever went, Dell discovered the fact that some people believed numbers were magic.

And the first *big* number, the occult book said, was Four. Four was the elements of nature—fire, earth, air, and water—and the points of the compass.

And it was also the first number of *completion; wholeness.*

In astrology, Dell found, number One got thangs going, Two sorta firmed 'em up, Three kind of spread the news to everybody else.

And *Four*, well, that number made absolutely everything *permanent.*

So if he was *ten times four* he was whole now, he was a really *complete* man, ready to leave the prison and show everybody just how much he'd learnt!

And with his knowledge about sacrifice and the phoenix, he was real eager to get out there and learn whether he had the key to somethin' purty close to immortality—or if he was *already* immortal.

Of course, he'd added a whole shit-load of knowledge to the magic he possessed, and Dell's awareness of that—how he could go on pickin' Lloyd B.'s brain right up to the minute he was released—was why (he supposed) he had never gone ahead and busted Lloyd up. That and the fact that Lloyd was starting to look even older by the time Dell was leaving.

But the ex-teacher didn't hesitate to stay on "meat" to the end, telling Dell he often used words from his new vocabulary wrongly, that they sounded "mangled." Even worse than that, there were times when Dell's aging instructor told him *not* to use big words at all when he talked! He'd ask why, and Lloyd would say, "Because you haven't heard or read them in use by people for whom it's second nature. You don't always gits 'em *right*, whitemeat, and they can become sources of deri-sion." Dell asked him to hold on a minute, whilst he looked up "derision," memorized that word (and its approximate definition), then told old Lloyd, "But iffen they laugh at me I'll jest *kill* 'em. So whut diff'rence do it make anyhow?"

Lloyd had no answer for that, so Dell slapped his hands together and then hit the wall and tried to give a high-five to Lloyd because it was the first time he'd stopped his favorite darkie cold!

Which in turn told Dell just how well he'd learned logic from the books Lloyd had made him read over the long years. It was even kind of appeal-ing to think about re-frainin' from strangling some-body once and trying "sweet reason" on the fella— that term was one he'd picked up just from hearing Lloyd talk.

But after Dell was free again and had money in the pocket of his new cheap suit—a size larger than the one he got years back because he'd filled out and because pumping iron put on some muscle—he knew there was no way he could experiment with sweet reason right off. First things came first, and Dell had a much more important experiment to try.

That was to make folks *substitute* for him, espe-cially when he got a bellyache or his head hurt, because that'd be *fair*—not to off anyone till he was really feeling bad (except in the line of business, of course). Then, if his hurting went away, he'd *know* they'd made a successful sacrifice for him, and he'd have that wonderful magic under his belt for good! They would've "Suffered properly for another," just like *The Book* said!

How he got his first set of wheels on this release was a bit different than what Dell had previously done.

He waited at a bus stop for a halfway decent car to stop for the traffic light. It was dusk in the same bitty town he'd had to start from before and he knew that, after rush hour, there wouldn't be a whole lotta traffic. Just in case cop cars might be hanging around, he refused to take either of two passing jalopies; you'd never outrun police vehicles in one, and Dell was working on the idea that he might *never* let the aw-thorities arrest him again. Magic was no gawdamn use in jail except to keep perverts at bay.

Then a boy about the age Dell had been when they first sent him up was sittin and waiting for the light in a Chevy that looked as though it might have a coupla years left in it.

Well, the age of the kid was almost an omen. Dell figured he'd begin with this 'un even if he did prefer Fords and vans.

"Move over," he told the boy at the steering wheel after sidling around the rear of the automobile so he could be on the driver's side.

"No," the driver said promptly, astonished but brave. "Eat shit!"

"I *did ask*," Dell said, sighing. The window was rolled down, so he punched the boy in the face—partly on the nose, partly on the mouth. Then he yanked the kid out of the Chevy while he was tryin to focus on getting his hankie out—his nose was bleeding somethin' fe-rocious—and tossed him into the street.

Dell hesitated, deciding whether he himself was hurting anywhere and also if the boy could identify him later. But the radio was on and the youngster on the pavement probably hadn't looked straight at anybody except a dealer or a teenage girl since Santy Claus. Dell felt just fine.

"The worl' is a pur-ilus place, in case yew did-den notice," Dell informed the boy after he had gotten into the car and turned off the radio. "Next time yew gits a ve-hicle from yore daddy, be mindful of ever *one* of yore senses and all the strangers around yew." He lifted one hand over the lower part of his face, tapped the accelerator while it was still in park. "Yew might run into a *bad* fella, next time."

He was purty pleased with himself when he was on the highway again. It made a grown-up man old enough to be the brat's daddy feel good to get off some sound advice now and then. "Some sweet reason," Dell said, aloud, smiling. Time then to make sure the "participation" he was imagining another man experiencing instead of his was—for a fact—just how the word *vicarious* was defined. Dell drove to what passed as a suburb of the burg, utilizing his new-found reasoning abilities once more, since he didn't want a lot of people watching what he was going to do next.

Finding himself on a boulevard of newer and larger homes than he'd seen anywhere else in town, Dell wondered if there were any people living there at all. It wasn't later than seven o'clock in the evening and, till he'd driven around for three-four minutes, he couldn't dope out where everyone was. It was way past supper, no one was hanging around on corners selling shit or even rapping—*hell's bells, they isn't even no real corners!*—and there were absolutely *no* whores on the streets. Shit-fire, there weren't even cars and tires in the yards!

Then Dell got the drift of it, the fact that these were newer houses cluein' him in.

This was where rich bitches and their husbands lived in this burg. Why, lots of them didn't even have children—a genuwine outrage! There was nothing for them to sell because other folks did that during the daytime, *for* them, and most of the vehicles they owned were put away in garages and *locked*!

The neighborhood was downright *spooky* it was so different.

It made Dell feel like puking to finally spot an old man riding his ass around on a power mower—no hurry, a leetle here, *zip-zap*, more over there. *Je-sus, the rich ole fart had alla time in the world.* Yet he hadn't even hired a poor man to do the work. He was so fucking tight he mowed his own grass!

Fired by social conscience for the first time in

his existence, Dell thrummed the Chevy motor, then headed the automobile straight for the elderly man on the riding mower.

This was a tricky shot. If he caught too much of the lawnmower with the front of the Chevy, he could wreck it and he'd have to hightail it out of there on foot. Dell had a glimpse of a woman much younger than the rich sumbitch watching from the front of the house, then had two swift thoughts there wasn't really time for: Was there a way to smear the old man—drive over just him—and not cream the car, snatch the young woman, and fuck her before swapping the vehicle? Secondly, if he had to run away on foot, was the bitch one of them athletic cunts who ran marathons and would chase him straight through the center of town till the authorities caught him again?

Now the wealthy old fart on the mower was coming into view like a dumb animal rushin' at a good hunting rifle. Calculating cautiously, Dell cut the wheel of the Chevy to the right and had only a second to brace himself for the impact before they were colliding!

WHOP! It worked, he'd done it!

Dell saw a white hairpiece lift off as if it intended to fly away, a pair of spectacles that fell under the car's rear wheels—and then the bulk of the demolished old body was propelled several feet to where it hit the yard, rolled over twice, and didn't move again. Dell's car motor shivered as if it was scared, coughed as if it was ashamed and wanted to die, *caught.*

And he was hesitating just long enough to yell, "Dell from hell!" at the woman who came running down from the house.

By the time he was laying rubber to get out of the rich-bitch neighborhood, Dell was pissed at himself for mentioning his name. He wouldn't have done it, but the woman wasn't nearly as young as he'd believed—just made up nice—and that had pissed him. He sped around a corner, almost out of the suburb.

And two more good things happened: Number one, he knew he felt just fine—*great*—and that meant this kind of sacrifice worked, *vi-car-ious* killin' did substitute for all his prison memories and miseries.

A teenage couple was strolling along a sidewalk right before he got to the main road as if they were fuckin' *volunteers*—as if they *wanted* to fill the office and act for another!

Well, a man had to have a bit of pleasure in life or he got himself stale and boring. Even Lloyd B. said so.

This time he wanted to use the Chevy like it was a bowling ball and he was taking out the last two pins—meaning, he hoped to strike the two kids, who were holding hands, sort of *between*, about where their hands were together. Of course, the vehicle wasn't a fucking torpedo! He'd hit their bodies, too.

But you also had to learn everythang that might be useful later, Lloyd said—and he could always go back after he hit the kids and stomp them if the force of the old Chevy didn't finish 'em to start with.

What Dell really wanted to see was if two standing, straight-up, narrow things, a whole lot like bowling pins, would shoot off in different directions the same way, or just plain fall down. Squinting hard with one eye weeping, he let his mouth drop open and flattened the accelerator.

A clean strike! Braking on the other side of the young couple, Dell smiled but quickly lost part of his enthusiasm. They hadn't known he was coming so they hadn't screamed. About all the sound there was when the Chevy hit them was a sort of "splat" mixed with a cracking noise. He peered at the couple in the rearview mirror, appraising his job: The girl, she might have been kicked out a foot to a foot and a half, just like a bowling pin. And the boy had rode the wind a solid six-seven feet before hitting somebody's fancy lawn ornament with the back of his neck. Just about where the spine gets a good start, which was neat.

One of the two kids moaned. Dell heard it just when his good spirits were returning and, his old habits shouting to get out of there, automatically revving the motor.

Then he remembered how much magic he had now, and paused.

Could the girl still be breathin'? Dell wondered, leaving the car in gear. Slowly, he opened his door.

Jogging back, common sense told him to check the boy first. Little shit might have a piece—besides the one he'd been humping!

Once again, sweet reason—and magic—were good as gold, since the boy had been the one moaning and pissing and making a ruckus. There were internal injuries, clear as glass, and one arm was almost *off*. The kid looked as though his whole side had never had any ribs at all because it was all caved in. The young son-of-a-bitch had got himself up on his other arm, though; appeared to be trying to crawl after the girl. Interesting, with his neckbone like it was.

Dell just pushed the boy's head back on the well-mown grass with the sole of his shoe, then glanced around to see if anybody was coming. Nope. Fucking hotshot neighborhood didn't even have any security!

Dell booted the kid in the temple with his other foot, balancing on the brat's face to do it. He did that a few more times—six or seven, actually—then had to wipe off his new shoe on a bush close by.

The girl, well, she had on an indecent blouse that stopped above her bellybutton. Her fancy designer jeans (her upper half was mostly on its back, but it was easy to make out the cartoon animal on the hip pocket) were probably more red now than the white they had been, and more red was coming. Dell noticed she was holding something in her fist, stooped to see what.

It was one of the boy's *fingers*. Now *that* was one for the book!

Dell used the toe of one shoe to push up the girl's blouse. She had nice tits, he reckoned. You couldn't be perfectly sure about that when they had bras on. Hers was simple. White, not see-through. He had a tussle with himself for a moment over that, but finally made himself go back to the now-wrecked-looking Chevy without taking the dead girl's clothes off. She was definitely dead; he'd finally noticed that.

But he'd have to get him a woman soon, there was just a limit to what any man could stand.

But there might not be *any* limit to how much magic he had, Dell thought after he was back in the Chevy and had seen maybe three county-mounties pass him without even looking his way. Sure, he'd have to swap vehicles yet tonight, just to be practical—but that didn't have anything to do with how easy it seemed to be now to run folks down whenever he felt like it.

Just maybe there was another way to sort of test his magic—by seeing how many *more* people he could kill before anybody even seemed to notice that there was a stranger in town and, at the same time, keep the Chevy going so he could drive somewhere else before he traded it in!

The answer to how many more victims turned out to be three, and then there was just under a quarter of a tank of gas left—and the old kiddie-car was starting to look as if it had turned over four times on a dirt track. Leaving the rich-bitch neighborhood behind, Dell had to chuckle, thinking how the kid he'd took the Chevy off of might get blamed for the half-dozen people he himself had killed. Maybe that would reinforce the lesson Dell had taught the little punk!

Now it was darker and Dell from hell was all alone, bothered by no one; and even though he hadn't screwed a woman during his little spree, he felt pretty gawdamn good about this fast new start in life—in particular, how he'd made his new magic work. Sure, he couldn't be absolutely sure that no one could kill him until the authorities gave 'er a try, but there was no hurry. They sure couldn't *catch* him! He was in a hurry about finding a bitch—the right bitch—somewhere, because just rubbin' his cock had made it swell up like a gawdamn balloon!

Someday, 'cause I'm like the phoenix, I'll git me a new one, Dell thought, looking for a service station. He zipped up, as psychologically unfinished and dissatisfied as he could remember. He couldn't go to a men's room with his pecker beating him there by an inch and a half. To get a new one, he'd either have to set himself (or maybe just *it*) on fire. Or do that to some other fella; the vi-car-i-ous thing.

But when he *had* got himself the new one, Dell reflected as he was gassin' up, stooped to hide his hard-on, there would be several changes made in it: First , he'd be the one in charge—not it! He'd say, "Harden up, leettle guy," and it'd do it. Shit-fire, havin' a penis was like havin' some evil boy brat out of a horror movie attached to yourself; it was hard to slip up on anybody with one, when they knew where to look, and it woke up at night making demands on you more than any gawdamn woman ever had!

What else he wanted his new pecker to be was smoother. Purty. Every one he'd ever seen had been all wrinkled. It wouldn't get purply on the end either, it'd stay the nice pale pink it generally was. And the new one might be a wee bit smaller, too. The last whore he fucked who said he was almost too big for her wasn't the *first* to say that. Dicks weren't made for hurting, Dell figured, not most of the time anyhow, though there were notable exceptions. If he needed to waste some bitch, or wanted to, he'd use a weapon or his thumbs like any man was supposed to.

A guy paying for his gas ahead of Dell—Lloyd B, had told him how to gas up his own car and explained that it was cheaper if you did—got into some talk about what kind of vehicle he drove. While he and the service station dude were talking, Dell took a peek out the window. A *van*, he thought, then thought some more—real quick. *Vans got a pisspot'a room. Yew take yore girl in back an' not git grass stains all over yore clothes.*

What's more, Dell realized, practically glowing with the realization, *yew could jest about* live *in a van*. Rippin' off vans'd be distinctive, too. Stylish. A way to get a reputation for oneself . . .

He waited in the Chevy till the man got back in his van—the fellow was fifty but big, might have been a professional athlete when he was young so he would offer Dell a little exercise. The man fired her up. Dell got excited again.

He was probably already immortal since no cops were stopping him, but if the man in the van turned right, he'd be on the road where Dell didn't know a good way to pull him over and he'd have to give up his new plan.

But if the dude turned *left*—back toward the burg Dell had just gone through to find the gas station—he had dreamed up a plan while he was in prison, and he couldn't wait to try it!

The guy went left!

Dell followed the van like a shadow. Nobody paid attention to Chevys or Fords. They weren't fancy as a rule, but that was a good thing about them. What was good about the big guy's turning left was a stop signal—and that it was night once again with nobody apt—he'd fallen in love with that little word, *apt*!—to be out. Now he'd find out if this experiment would work, too, if the big fella got the red!

He did! Ready, Dell stopped feelin' his new boner, stayed in the lane behind the van, and tapped the accelerator two, three times, slowing the Chevrolet. What he was going to try would mess up the Chevy some, but who gave a fuck? He was heading to his favorite car lot to trade up right then, and he was the *only* one with the bluebook!

Dell whispered to himself, "Easy, *eeeeasy*," letting the kid's car inch closer and closer to the rear end of the van. The Chevy brakes still worked if you pumped them, but that wasn't the plan. *Easy, eeeeasy*, Dell told himself—

TAP. And hit the van. Not *crash*, or *grind*, or any kind of blowup noises. Just TAP.

The big fella was out of the van in a flash, just like Dell had figured he would. Quite slowly—with perfect deliberation—Dell opened the Chevy door and climbed out. The van driver was squinting down at where the junker had bumped—*nudged, actually*—the ass-end bumper, and he was turning redder than the stoplight!

"Don't you have any goddamned brakes in that piece of junk?" he demanded.

"I do," Dell said. Then the lie. "But they don't work good."

The other driver had pushed back his suit coat and had his large hands tucked at the back of his belt. "I guess there's not a lot of damage," he grunted.

Dell said, "Not yet."

The softly uttered tone got the older and larger man's attention more than the words, but he ran them back in his head, finally went back to looking at Dell.

That was far too late.

Dell kneed him in the nuts. His head came down as it was supposed to and Dell had an elbow ready. It hit the fella's nose, hard enough to put him on his knees. But he wrapped his arms around Dell's legs as though he was trying to get his head cleared and fight back.

That was somethin to be respected—but later. While Dell was driving the van. "I gots t'kill yew," Dell said. It was explanation, not any real apology. "See, I wanta keep yore van awhile. An' I gotta take yore money 'n credit cards, too." He brought his clasped hands down on the big man's head (the top, mostly, but part of the back, too) from over his head.

This way, he believed, the fellow knew there was a reason for it and wouldn't hate him too much after he died and went wherever he was going then. He got the man's billfold before turning to the van.

Dell wanted to try his new vehicle so much that he went ahead and got in, even though its previous owner might still be breathing. Just like the boy in the Chevy (which was abandoned and forgotten about now) he'd left the keys in the ignition, the motor runnin'. Sheer magic!

Dell adjusted both the rear- and side-view mirrors, saw the big man scrabbling along the street. Not after but away from Dell. *Looks like a crab crawlin'*, thought Dell, locating reverse. He hit the pedal hard.

Crunchy sounds under the wheels, Dell mused, cocking his head in approval after the van rolled lumpily over its owner. *Kinda like biting into a unopened candy bar, so yew got the noise of cellophane tearin' and yore teeth bitin' down into almonds at the same time.* Pleased, Dell drove forward again . . .

Far enough away, Dell came upon a map. He also found a drink cooler and let out a real happy sound like a kid findin' presents on Christmas morning. He threw out the beers, but he could put milk in the cooler. Dell liked milk a lot, and it was healthy for you, too. He'd buy some soft drinks, too.

The next thing Dell had to do after getting the van (he hadn't driven a mile) was to check out what was in the dead man's billfold, and that was *more* magic. Good ol' plastic up the wazoo—and almost six hundred dollars cash-money!

Then Dell found the gun. Hidden under the seat, a .44 Magnum, it had been placed there in case some baaad robber come right up to the window! Dell's hilarity damn near made him bust the passenger seat off since he had to hold on while he laughed.

Biz-ness comes first, he reminded himself, and started studying the map under an overhead beam. He scanned the southern states in their many shapes and depicted hues to decide which one he'd head for. Then his lingering hunch or dream about an interesting girl down there triggered an older memory, one from his late boyhood.

He had purely cottoned once to the idea of finding himself a young, purty virgin who'd like to have a strong man who'd make her keep her nose clean and look out for her, too; get kicks riding around while he made sure they met different kinds of people; have a few laughs to share. Not no permanent thing, Dell decided, not no marrying, of course. It'd just be till he found her boring and had to off her. Meantime, she'd satisfy his sexual needs and let him focus on business, properlike.

And where was he most . . . *apt* . . . to find a virgin girl? The Deep South! Even today, in a sinful time when nobody much knew his place, it could still have some purity to it. The awareness of how smart he'd got awed him. My Gawd, the magic he'd got was startin' to tell him things he needed to know even before he tried to dope it all out!

Soon after midnight the radio brought Dell news about the dead folks he'd left behind in the small, snooty town—its name escaped him just then—and it plain capped off the day! The stupid announcer reported only five deaths, though, not the neat half-dozen. Dell frowned, his fine humor momentarily darkened. *Lessee*, he thought, recapping. *They was the ol' man in the wig on his mower. The teenagers holdin' hands—and fingers. A Hardee's curb girl whose neck I wrung by reachin' through my window and hers jest to' see if I could (and 'cause Mom had worked at Hardee's).* That was four, and the announcer hadn't even said how Dell left the money for his food on the ledge—plus a nice tip, which fast-food folks weren't even allowed to take!

Then he'd seen some daddy walking his kid on a tricycle and the kid had looked cute. Dell was sure he hadn't smooshed the kid, too, because killing children might reverse your magic—Lloyd had said so once and it made good sense. On the other hand, if he *had* killed the tiny tot, too—by accident—why, that'd make a half-dozen right there! Besides, he'd sure as hell kilt the colored on the bench in the town square where he had parked the Chevy, got out, sidled over, and asked if the man knew how to spell "lexicography" or knew the country where the phoenix lived. When he hadn't, Dell had broken his neck with a tire iron before the fella even got up. So that *was* six!

Only thing Dell could imagine as he passed through the ass-ends of Tennessee and then North Carolina—the spree had given him confidence he could reach Georgia before he had to get more shut-eye—was that the authorities must have just decided the black was no good and not *reported* him to the news folks. They hadn't even tried to find out. Well, he was starting to understand what Lloyd B. meant about bigotry, and it was a disgrace to Amurica!

Or some pervert mighta took off with the man's corpse, Dell mused.

Inside the Georgia state line, Dell read the state's motto when he stopped at a roadside rest stop for a whiz: WISDOM, JUSTICE, AND MODERATION. He could live with that; it *was* him!

He was beat now, he'd worked hard, he wouldn't even feel like killing anybody unless he got bothered or there was a good business opportunity to it. Finished and zipped up, Dell went back to the van knowing he was satisfied every which way but the sensual. He wished he'd have the energy to study *The Book* awhile when he got where he was goin', but he knew that was unlikely.

The real question was: Where *was* he going? And where did he want to park the van for the night?

He didn't have an answer till he had driven God knew how much farther, deeper into the state. Then he saw a nice little church on the outskirts of another burg. He'd be sleeping in his van for the first time and he knew there was no safer spot to pick just then than the parkin' lot of the Second Cherokee Rose Baptist Church.

Bedding down on a foam mattress, concealed by velvety red curtains on runners, Dell stretched, yawned, and patted *The Book* (placed within reach on a second pillow beneath which was his new

Magnum). Pervs, sickies, and weirdos did *not* hang out around churches, so he knew he was perfectly safe. . . .

Dell reared up, pulled the curtains back enough to peek out of. Just in case.

One of his thumbs was in his mouth within minutes.

Then he was waking, not because of the morning sunlight warming his face—though it was—but because an *eye*, fringed by long lashes, was peekin' back at him!

And because the purty girl who had the eye was tapping on the windowglass maybe four inches from Dell's nose.

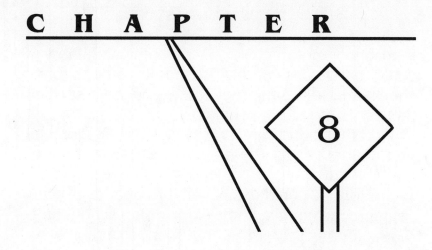

C H A P T E R

Strangely scared, Dell tore open the door nearest to the snooping girl all the way. Sometimes he'd almost bit his thumb off by dreaming about the authorities catching him asleep in some car he'd stolen or Mom filling his head with the contents of a shotgun, and once or twice he'd woke up shaking because he'd seen all the folks he'd ever offed like ghosts in his nightmare—zombies, maybe.

But he had truly never figured he'd wake up with no girl seeing him sucking his thumb or with a hard-on or nothing. It was different somehow if you'd banged them first. (And if you'd already shucked or kilt 'em.) They knew you were special, then!

Yet that didn't explain why he felt scared or why he just looked out the door of the van instead of jumping out and getting her, Dell knew that.

Before he could decide what to do, the girl was wiggling by him like some skinny high school half-back, entering the van without so much as a howdy-doo, and sitting in the patched-up captain's seat as if she'd been born with the right to do it!

Mebbe she was, Dell thought, backing up from the door and turning around to size her up. *Mebbe she belongs t'the big fella I took this vehicle off of.*

She said nothing about that, though, just got busy fingerin' everthing she could reach. Dell noticed she wasn't eyeballing him at all but was touching and prying at the upholstery and the ashtrays and makin' the seats turn around, and locating the drink cooler. Looking into it, she seemed kind of disappointed to see it was empty. *Well, one thang*, Dell decided, at last, *she ain't seed this here van before.*

While she was messing, Dell took a good look at *her*.

It was probably the longest time he'd ever taken looking, especially when he liked what he saw at a glance but hadn't even jumped her yet.

The girl had come out of the church—Dell dimly remembered hearing a door shut, and the van was the only vehicle in the lot—and was dressed like nobody Dell had ever seen attending a house of worship. No one got any upbringing anymore. She had on a blouse with colors brighter than new blood and it looked as if a big animal had ate out most of what went at the top. What blouse there was fitted closer to her skin than a flex bandage and moved the same way, with the skin. No way Dell could picture did she have a bra on.

The girl's jeans were orange, except for a white part that covered the crotch, and fitted tighter than the blouse. Her feet were bare even if it wasn't quite spring—girls he was seeing since gettin' out must want to get pneumonia—and her feet were long with more lines on the soles than a chimpanzee's. Her toes looked like she could hang by them, but that was sexy to Dell, kind of. Girls who had real long toes sometimes had nipples three, four inches in length when they were hard.

It wasn't what she wore, though—it was her, and how she *was*. Watching her poke into things it was as if she were naked . . . and she didn't care that he could see her. No, that wasn't quite right because those topless pussies, they didn't care either. Dell felt himself frown while he tried to figure the rest of it out.

Then he had it! Topless dancers either wanted you to watch them but wouldn't fuck you unless you had something nice they could *get*—or they hated doing it, private-like, but they had to pay for their men's dope. But this here girl—she *liked* to be watched and *she purely wanted t'fuck*!

It didn't occur to Dell that Kee was underage—

too young for his scruples—even when she was looking back at him with at least as much intensity of interest, because she had well-developed breasts.

But when it did occur to Dell that he wanted to rape her, and he hesitated only because there probably were more people inside the church, Kee bounced down from the captain's seat and skittered up to peer into his eyes. He was amazed when she put her hands on his cheeks and pulled his head down so that she could have a closer look.

"I was *right*," she said exultantly. "You ain't got no veils over yore eyes! Leastwise, not *one* of them."

Dell had thought she was goin to kiss him. Her comment was one more surprise. "I reckon I don't," he admitted.

Kee laughed. "Silly!", slapped his face very lightly, and went back to her exploration of the van. "Yew didn't even know what I *meant*."

He almost said again that he purely hadn't known, but that sounded dumb. "Well, I ain't no lady, so a'course I don't got me any veils on my face." He noticed she was peering down at where he had spent the night. The amount of curiosity she displayed continued to keep his customary rap-a-cious reactions at bay. "Was thet a insult or a compliment?"

"Yew got a *bed*," she drawled, marvelingly, "A bed in a *car*!" Then her expression was that of a flustered child aware that she had chosen the wrong word.

"It's a van," Dell announced, and began working his way back to her. "'A closed truck or wagon for carrying people, furniture, and so forth.'"

She fell to her knees on the thin mattress but looked up sharply as he approached. Her fingers touched the pillow where his head had lain. "Gol-*leee*, yew're smart." She continued to stare up at him.

By standing above her he was able to squint down at even more of her young breasts than he'd been able to see while she was squirming around on the chair. Dell recalled, without breaking his stare, that the velvet curtains were open only a few inches and would close. "I want t'thank yew," he said politely, planning his next move. It was possible she just might like doing it with him. It was a real long time since anybody had.

"Why, yew're a true man of the world, ain't yew?" Kee asked. Her gaze finally dropped, but without leaving his body. She giggled. "I gave yew a hard-on, didn't I?"

Dell looked up from her breasts to gape in astonishment and search, frozen in place, for her eyes. But now she was poking into other things— including the space under his pillow.

Kee found the Magnum, pulled it out, and leveled it in Dell's general direction. "Is this a honest-to-God gun?" she asked. It wobbled in her hand. "Gosh, I'd be afeered I'd blow my fuckin' head off if I kep' it under *my* pillow.

"Gawdamnit to perdition!" Dell howled, dropping to a crouch and sticking out his arm. But he yanked it back each time Kee poked it at his hands, because she was still holding the weapon uncertainly by the grip with her index finger on the trigger. "Give me thet!"

"I'm *trying*," Kee said honestly, thrusting it toward him once more with the barrel first.

"Will yew quit pointin' it at me?" Dell shouted, batting at the Magnum again with his hand. "I ain't hurt yew none!" Abruptly, he lost his balance and sat down hard in the space between the last row of seats and the sleeping area. "Damn yew, that's a deadly weapon!" Desperate, Dell wrested the firearm away from her and leaned back against the seats. Just as soon as he could do it safely, he was going to kill her!

Kee bounced forward on her knees, a rabbit with ideas on its mind—or maybe a *Playboy* bunny-girl for whom the centerfold was only a means to an end. She kissed him full on the lips, inexpertly yet with passion of a kind Dell had never before encountered. "Yew got the most *un*veiled eyes I ever did see. They don't hide. They's *livin'* eyes, not dead ones—even if yew *is* a little cockeyed." She reached down and cupped the astonished Dell's already responding terrific trio. "Yew know, yew could be the man of my dreams!"

He tried instantly to get ahold of her. She was wriggly as a eel, though, and retreated to the mattress at the back of the van without any suggestion of either coyness or fear.

He got up on his knees to follow, tossing the Magnum aside—but stopped when he noticed Kee massaging her breasts. Kee didn't take anything off, but when she purposefully leaned forward to giggle in a mixture of wonderment that this was truly happening, and delight that she'd had the guts to enter his van, Dell saw almost everything she had on top—and Kee knew it.

Dell hadn't *known* there was a girl like this anywhere. If she didn't yell rape like the rest of them always did, he kind of hoped he wouldn't have to hurt her much for a while. He might even decide to hang around town a few days.

Thinking he was being playful, Dell groped for her blouse, meaning to tear it down the front.

Kee sat up first, pure and earnest as an angel, and pointed to the Magnum Dell had cast aside. "If I let you do what you wants . . . will yew do my mama 'n daddy for me?"

Dell's hand stayed raised to her blouse without touching it. "Do . . . *whut* to 'em?"

Then he realized that she was pointing directly at the .44 Magnum.

Dell was dumbfounded. "Yew ain't askin me t'*shoot* your mother 'n father, are yew, girl?" he demanded. Kee's head bobbed up and down. He arose, moved to the closest seat and sat down as if someone had pushed him. "Great Gawd a glory, are yew *crazy?*"

She shook her head in answer to his second question. And all the while she was studiously peering down at herself, at the tight-fitting, brilliantly hued blouse, tweaking her nipples through the cloth. She was so serious in her work she seemed as if she expected to be graded for it. "Well, it's *jus'* the two of them," she drawled, "and Daddy's got the syph real bad—so it ain't like it'll be hard. He might not even *see* yew." But Dell didn't quite seem to get it. Kee dropped her hands and arms, dejected, and threw herself tummy-down on the mattress. She'd spent her puberty dreaming of an older man who'd ride in and save her from the bad knights of her boring life. Dell was supposed to say, "Sure, I'll murder your folks for yew"—and off they'd go! Kee's tall, brave cavalier wouldn't be like Daddy, so *she* wouldn't be like Mama. They'd drive all over the world, he'd show her things she'd never heard of and she'd do things for him that stupid Willie Fawkner never dreamed about even when he was getting his dumb pimples! Dell's expression of amazement was really disappointing.

"My mama wasn't ever arown," she said experimentally, rolling over and stretching her arms above her head, arching her back, "'n I might as well've had no daddy."

Dell glanced back sharply from where he sat. "Yore mom's a no-good bitch?" he said, trying to figure her out. "Yew sayin' she's a *whore*, girl?"

"Kind of," Kee allowed, and yawned. "She does it with Reverend Simpkins 'cause Daddy can't get it up no more or somethin', with his sickness 'n all." Suddenly she stared at Dell, young and bright eyes opened as wide as she could get them. She could read him better than she could ever have read any old book. "I feel a teeny bit sorry for Daddy so I want him murdered nice 'n fast, okay? He'd have eyes like yourn now, without veils—more like dead folks'—'cept he's nearly blind." Her sigh was as calculated as the original blueprints for hell. "Yew're s'posed to be magic, see? Like in my dreams 'n shit."

"*I was*?" Dell said, thinking hard. He was holding to the armrests of his seat.

"Or know a *little* magic, anyhow," Kee replied. She rubbed herself between the legs as if she had developed a slow but not particularly annoying itch. Just one to be dealt with. "So when I come to church this mornin' t'see Mama—she's here *ever*day, to be with that ole rev I tole yew about—and I saw your neat *van* . . . well, I b'lieved yew'd come to Cherokee Rose, Georgia, like a knight in shiny armor. Not *every* man got the balls or the magic to kill anybody!"

"I knows some magic," Dell allowed. He was starting to sweat and his heart was beating quicker. "Go on."

Kee tugged the tail of her blouse out of her jeans and patted her naked belly. "Yew left that teeny little space in the curtains over yore window open, and when I peeked in, I saw how *handsome* yew are 'n all"—she sat back on the mattress, hugged her knees to her chest and kept her eyes as wide open as any small child's—"and I jus' had t'welcome yew to our town. Especially when I saw the handle of yore gun stickin' out from under yore pillow."

Dell pursed his fleshy lips. He was pretty sure now she wasn't part of a trap any authorities set up. So the only reason to hesitate was because it didn't seem *natural* being asked by a girl to kill anybody. Besides, it was as though she was acting like his boss or somethin'! Before he did dick for her, he had to get a few things straight—and not just what he slipped *to* her!

"Yew are cor-reck, I *am* magic," Dell said with dignity, "an' I am jest like a knight. That's the pure truth, and I reckon it would be po-lite t'say *yew* may have more magic than anybuddy I seed in one long fuckin' time." *Which I will make her give me, one way or the other.*

"Thank yew, sir," Kee said sweetly. She'd gone on playing with her tummy and had pushed her jeans down a bit as if wanting to find out if the itch she had begun in a lower region.

Dell touched the corner of his upper lip with the tip of his tongue, washed it across. "I *will* kill yore whore mama an' yore poor blind daddy for yew so yew will know for a *fack* how magical I am."

"I *knowed* yew was my knight!" Kee cried, looking up with her marveling expression in place again. "I jus' bet yew're shiny all over!"

"But"—Dell raised his index finger—"I wants t're-ceive my proper payment *now*."

"To screw me?" Kee asked.

"I think that's best," Dell said judiciously.

She stood up, appeared to prowl around some. "I on'y wish we could fuck right now," she said, sighing. But—to Dell's horror—Kee already had one hand on the handle of the nearest door.

Then, when she had the door pulled open a fraction, Kee's face was suddenly bright as a silver dollar. "I got it!" she said. "You know about down payments, Mister . . . ?"

"I know," Dell snapped. "Call me Dell." He almost added, "from hell."

"Well," Kee drawled, dancing toward him in girlish exuberance, "this is what I jus' come up with . . . Dell." She wasn't even out of arm's reach where she halted. He didn't think he'd ever eye-balled a female who looked more alive, or plain willing. "I could show you my titties right now—like a down payment. Then yew git the rest after my folks are dead. What do yew think?"

Dell expelled a huge sigh, glanced away from her. "Yew would purely not like t'know what I'm thinking," he told her truthfully. He looked back, staring up from under his eyebrows. That had freaked a few folks in the past. "Whut's yore name?"

"Kee. It's really a religious name, kind of," Kee answered promptly. "I'm Kee Dora McCaulter. It's sort of like 'a *key* in a golden *door*.' To heaven." Kee ruffled Dell's lank hair with her hand, grinned. "Tell yew the truth, I added the middle name and that part."

He snatched her wrist and held it to his head. "Girl, I can fuck you ever way I wants right *now*— and they's nothin yew can do t'keep me from it."

"But yew ain't doin it," Kee said brightly. 'Cause *yew* wants t'shoot my parents, too—and yew don't know what our *address* is!"

Dell felt his fingers tightening on the girl's wrist, his thumb digging into that vein right under the heel; and she was grinning as though she was having the best ol' time. Her fingertips were even *patting his head*! Dell grinned despite himself. "Yew're smart," he acknowledged. "I allus ad-mire thet a whole lot."

"My mama thinks I'm dumb as gravel. Yew want to let my hand go now and see my tits?"

He nearly laughed. "Let me help yew," he offered, again putting his fingers to the hem of her blouse.

"That ain't how I want to do it," Kee replied, scampering into the space between the fixed seats and spreading her feet and legs. Dell realized she could be seen by anybody looking in from the front of the van—there was sunshine behind her—but if she didn't care, Dell thought, he sure as shit didn't mind.

She hooked her fingertips under her blouse, began to pull it up, and got the giggles.

"Yew chickenin' out?" Dell called from the rear.

Kee got control of her hilarity except for a few snickers and then explained. "I was jus' thinkin, there oughta be some music goin' 'da-DA!' for yew to see my ta-TAs!"

Dell chuckled, closed his eyes for an instant, and when he opened them again, the girl was naked to the waist—past that, actually, because she hadn't hitched up her jeans and everthing Kee had was on view to within maybe half a foot of her pussy.

Dell found he had a wad of spit in his throat and that hawking wouldn't make it go away. Kee was the prettiest leetle ol' thing Dell had seen since he slipped in to watch Mom doing it when he was eight, maybe nine. Kee raised her arms way over her head, knowing that made her breasts rise higher, and then turned left, and right, and left, and all the way around in a circle.

This Kee was purely weird, Dell thought, but she was making *him* rise higher than he'd been since he caught his first girl coming out of junior high school and put it to her where the track team had practice.

"Thass all I got," Kee said, stooping to retrieve her blouse and putting it back on. "On top, that is."

"How much to see what yew got down there right now?" he asked. He wanted to stand but felt awkward about that just then.

"I *tole* yew!" Kee laughed music like Lloyd'd listened to sometimes. She was looking through the van windshield, toward the church. "Yew gits t'see and do everthang yew wants once yew done your part of the deal. But I think yew're gonna be a happy partner 'n all."

Dell headed in her direction. "Ain't happy even one leetle bit, girl."

She sprinted, giggling, along the edge of the van as if going back to the sleeping area. She looked as though she wouldn't mind a game of tag, Dell realized with incredulous disgust.

But he merely took his seat in front of the steering wheel, scrubbing at his bad eye. It was weeping openly now. "I said I'd do yore mama and daddy, 'n I will. But I ain't goin' t'shoot no fella who can't see." He sighed heavily, started the engine. "Well, where d'yew live?"

J. N. WILLIAMSON

She rushed back to the front to plunk herself into the captain's seat again. "The streets're all funny in Cherokee Rose," she said. "I'll jus' show yew how to find it."

Dell made his queer humming sound as he drove, for several blocks. He'd probably have put a tape on—the van's previous owner had left some—but Dell (he didn't know why) had never liked music. He'd never liked a lot of things other people did; he knew that. He'd never once heard a comedian who could make him laugh, and he'd bragged about that in prison.

When Kee drawled "Turn here" next time, he also knew she had taken him around a big circle—as if she imagined he wouldn't be able to find the church or her home again!

He looked back at her, meaning to belt the little bitch one.

She was sticking gummy pieces of paper in the form of flowers on the sides of the drink cooler and humming to herself.

"I reckon this'll be the first time I ever kilt anybuddy t'put 'em outta their misery," Dell muttered, and sighed.

The dig didn't register on Kee for half a second.

When it did, she kicked up both her legs and her bare feet did a crazy dance in the air. "Oh, *yeeew*!" she exclaimed with affectionate abruptness, reaching forward to give his neck a big bear-hug.

"Careful, girl," he said, trying to keep a straight face. "If yew strangle me, you won't have nobuddy left t'kill yore folks."

She dropped back in the chair in an attitude of instant decorousness. "Yew are gonna blow Mama away, aren't yew?"

"If thet's whut yew prefer," he said solemnly.

"Try to shoot her in the mouth if you can," Kee suggested. "She been givin' me so much of it it's sheer wonder she's got any mouth left." Again she leaned forward. "How are yew gonna do my daddy if yew don't shoot him?"

He shrugged, found her forearms and hands on the neckrest behind him. "I don't rightly know." He glanced at her in the rearview mirror. "He *is* sightless, correct?"

"'Sightless!'" Kee exclaimed. "I'm sure gonna learn a lot from *yew!*" She put her round little chin on the neckrest beside his head. "He kin make out shadows'n the like."

"Yore daddy feel yew up or anythang like thet?" Dell inquired. The van had turned, on Kee's instructions, upon a road clearly leading into the countryside. Scarcely anyone was around, but Dell knew the walk to the Second Cherokee Rose church couldn't take more than ten or eleven minutes if you had to go on foot. He saw Kee, in the mirror, shake her head no.

"Well, then, tell me the ve-racious truth, Kee. What's the real facks about why I'm offin' yore parents?"

She fell out of his line of sight and became so silent—so absent of motion after her frenetic non-stop performance ever since she had entered the van—that Dell felt as if she'd jumped out. He was starting to wonder if the back of his neck was safe when she gave him his answer. "I'm bored," she told him. "Dellie, I am so fuckin' bored I jus' cain't think of nothin' else to do, unless it'd be killin' myself."

"Yew got yore whole life ahead'a yew," Dell said pontifically. It didn't even occur to him to wonder if it was true.

"Ah knows *that*."

When he twisted the rearview, relocated her image, she had her arms crossed and didn't look quite as pretty as she had. She was so sober. "I knows whut yew mean, girl," he confessed. Then he felt her breath on his cheek and saw her little index pointing for him to turn in at a farmhouse. He hoped her pussy would be somewhere nearly as hot as her breath was. "Why'd yew have me come here 'steada pluggin' yore mama at the church?"

Kee brightened, made a noise midway between a giggle and a real laugh. She sounded too embarrassed to answer. "I want Mama to come home 'n find Daddy dead. So she'll have a sort-of surprise before *she* gets it." She slid over and was openin' a door by the time Dell had braked. "Mama never even knowed I been sentamental jus' like that since I was real teensy."

Dell killed the engine, got the Magnum, and stuck it in his belt. He took it out again immediately to be sure he'd put the safety back on. "A parent's purely lucky t'have a chile as consid'rate as yew are these days." He caught Kee's arm as she was alighting. "When's the bitch comin' home? I ain't got all day."

"She allus comes home for lunch—sort of," Kee answered, heading along the gravel toward the porch of the frame house. The laugh she gave Dell was a teasing string of mostly melodic bells. "Don't worry, Dellie, after my ole man's gone, I'll bet I kin thinka ways to keep you ennertained!"

He trailed in her wake, shaking his head faintly once more. *Dellie!* Mom was the only one who'd ever called him thet much and he'd thought for a long while he hated the name. The girl was a whole lot like Mom, too, except Kee was a thinker. A little strange, but definitely a thinker. Mounting the porch, he had a new idea: Though it had never occurred to him for a minute, maybe he should think about going into business while he was still young. Kee would stay a right nice piece for years if he kept her off drugs and treated her good. Some pimps he'd met in prison had done all right for themselves, and—

Dell nearly ran into Kee's back as he realized they were both inside the house now and she was being quiet like a good girl so they could get to her daddy without any trouble. He had to hand it to her, she had her act together! Besides, this was business, too—the one he knew best.

On tiptoe Kee took him to a kind of den with a TV goin' to beat hell. *Woulda thought he was hearin' impaired iffen I didden know he was*—what was the nice word?—*sightless*, Dell thought.

There hadn't been no more surprises from her

like he'd got in the van, and there were no more till he was close enough to Kee's daddy to see him. Then there were two things wrong from Dell's standpoint.

First, the man was a gawdamn drunk! There were beer cans everwhere you could look, lined up on the floor like the tin soldiers Dell had wanted when he was little and almost as many cans—unopened—waiting for the sumbitch on an end table. All that made it more fun to contemplate doing him. Immoderation was an awful thing around young people.

The second item Dell observed didn't make his plan for *choking* Ewing McCaulter to death—he hadn't mentioned the method to Kee—easy to think about. It made it real *un*tasty. Because this man had fat, busted-scab, running sores up and down his neck and most of his face—and the notion of getting his hands around a throat like *that* was enough to make a fella lose his lunch and last night's supper!

"Daddy," drawled Kee (loudly enough to be heard over the TV squawk). Dell turned panicky and froze in place. "It's yore li'l sweetie-pie."

The ugly man in the chair spilled the beer he was drinking and his foot kicked over a can that wasn't empty in his haste to hold up arms that weren't the skinniest Dell had ever seen but might have made the Top Ten. "Hey, honeybun!" Daddy cried. He looked really happy, even though he was looking somewhere else and not at Kee. But then his expression changed. "Yew come home by y'self or did the cunt bring yew?"

If Kee hadn't been waving for him to cross over

and get behind her father, Dell might have laughed out loud and had to shoot McCaulter after all. Grinning at Kee, his head turning both in amazement and a feeling he had that this could be the start of something really *bad*, Dell took a second to quietly pick up a lamp. Then he tiptoed toward the girl's daddy as quiet as a mouse. *But it'd be a shame t'waste a nice dancing-lady lamp*, Dell reflected, looking down at where he held the lamp under the lady's boobies.

Once he was right behind the revolting fella— just as Kee sat down on the arm of his chair, talking away while she winked at Dell—Dell tensed his muscles and yanked the cord out of the lamp. It made a ripping noise.

So Ewing glanced up and around—more used to identifying the origin of sounds than he once had been—and *smiled* straight up at Dell. "Did yew bring home a friend for Daddy t'meet, princess?" he asked Kee, patting her knee and leaving his hand there. "Is this one of your gal friends?"

Positioning his hands just so, eager to practice his skills with a *garrotte*, Dell wound the lamp cord tightly around the seated man's throat and tried, politely, to answer Mr. McCaulter's questions. "I'm somebuddy new to meet, and I'm—"

Dell had to stop talking right then because the sumbitch in the chair was about the same age as he and fighting strangulation with quite a lot more strength than Dell had anticipated. He'd meant to tell Ewing he was Dell from Hell, but the only thing that came out clearly was the single word "Hell."

Except for lacing her fingers with fascination and squeezing them together as if she were doing Dell's job, Kee merely watched for a moment in rapt attention. Then, suddenly it appeared as though Daddy was going to get up out of the chair and as if her knight in shiny armor was losin' hold of the cord.

So Kee sat on Daddy's lap, ground herself down onto him, giggling while she used all her weight to keep Ewe McCaulter in place.

And it really *did* help Dellie, what she did was *enough*! She'd pitched in like a adult to help her dream man out, and it was she who'd finished Daddy off, in a way. Kee's pride was tremendous. And Dell, he even said she was a big help soon after that—which would make her job of explaining to him just what they were going to do next, after they left this crummy old house for good, that much easier.

Dell stepped back, dropped his hands (which were hurting from keeping ahold and not touching the dead thing). He didn't know whether to look at how the girl was panting or the way her daddy had the cord sunk *real* deep in his neck.

"Yew was *wonnerful*," Kee said to him, her eyes big as two blue saucers. "I am so *proud* of yew!"

"Yew wasn't so bad yourself," Dell grunted. He glanced around, both his eyes looking sort of flat, like the little bottom part of saucers. "Where's the bathroom? I need t'wash my hands real good."

"'Course yew do," Kee replied with huge understanding, patting the back of his hand. "And maybe take a leak or somethin' after such hard work." Hurrying forward like a young hostess, she skipped from the den with Dell following and halted at the foot of the stairs to point up. Then, as if it were an afterthought, Kee said, "Wait, I'll show yew where the bathroom is. I gotta couple of teensy thangs I need to do in my room anyhow."

Roundly perfect bottom switching like the tail of a pretty new mare, she led the way, chattering about gawd knew what—Dell didn't, because he was just watching.

"Yew go right through that door," Kee instructed him with a nod to the right. "I'll be down the hall a ways if yew want a *thing*—but I don't think yew will, since Mama had me put out clean guest towels on'y this mornin'." She put her hands on her waist. "Mebbe Mama's a tiny bit psychic, too—what do yew think?"

But Dell had gone into the bathroom and closed the door.

Kee turned with no disappointment whatever, took a single step.

She stopped when she heard Dell's flat voice. He hadn't opened the door. "Yew reckon yew could com-plete yore part'a our bargain before yore mother pre-sents herself?"

"Afraid not," Kee replied. There was no hesitation. She was already two steps down the hallway. "I jus' remembered, Mama said she had to take Daddy t'see Doc Lidbetter on her lunch hour, too."

When Kee got to her bedroom, she threw herself on her bed and buried her face in her pillow. She knew she truly ought to shed a tear or two for Daddy, but the ones coming from her eyes and wetting the pillow were tears of true joy. Joy, and victory, too—because her bestest dream was beginning to come true! Her Dellie was every goldang thing she'd hoped he would be, even better (except for his eye), and he was gonna be *perfect* after they'd ridden around on roads awhile, and he got to know her well!

She got out her book to make an entry. This time she dated it. She even circled the date with lipstick. "Dellies his name & hes cum into my life at last!!!!! His real good eye don't got no vale atall and i'm sure he sees things the way they is, like I do. Hes got a neet car, a closed truck for carrien people & things, but I dont thank hes rich yet, but he *wants to be & he'll do it!!!!!*" Kee added several lines beneath her excited phrase. "He wants to fuck me like I duz him but hes a busnezz man & I got to wate till hes shot Mama. Or he will go away." She lifted the pen. Then, "I wunner if i'll miss them."

Kee paused to think, tip of the ballpoint pen in the middle of her tongue. Running out of room on the page, she had to squeeze her final remark into the space she had left: "Dellie wants to cloz up all the watchin eyes & make them ghost eyes like I do i'm sure!! I feel he awreddys got *lots* of x-periance doin it to but he nedes *me* to help no who to pick."

Her book became the first thing to go into the suitcase she packed next. She accomplished the task in a couple minutes, went quietly to the door of her room, and opened it.

"This's yore bedroom," Dell said. It wasn't a question and his tall body, planted firmly in the doorway, left comparably less space for Kee to squeeze around him than she'd had to write in in her diary entry. He had used water from the tap to smooth his lanky hair back and had apparently scrubbed his face hard because it was red. He looked like a man who'd swam a hard race. If he saw the suitcase Kee had in her hand, he didn't comment on it.

"Yew got yore gun handy?" she asked. " Mama'll be home any time. Yew didn't leave it in the bathroom, did you?"

"I got it right here," he answered, patting beneath his belt buckle. The pat appeared to Kee to go all the way down to the tip of the barrel. "Yew gave me *one* look; yew got *one* killin'." Dell took his other hand and touched the white section of her jeans that swept under her legs. "I think I got a right t'make it two looks now."

She gasped at his unexpected touch, but didn't let it show much. "Yew saw *both* my ta-tas so yew got two awreddy, Dellie." This was Kee's most reasonable tone. "An' my bellybutton made three!"

He had to contemplate that one. When he did, Kee took a single step away from him.

Afraid she was *apt* to run for the door, Dell attempted to pen in the lithe girl without using force. Sure, he could go ahead, overpower her—but that wasn't what they'd talked about, neither of 'em. Groping for her hand that wasn't holding the suitcase—what the hell did she have *that* for?—he coaxed Kee's fingers in the direction of his fly. "Why don't we jest get everthang out in the open an' let Mother Nature take her course? Sort of see whut happens?"

Kee felt the metal lock at the top of his zipper under her fingers. She also felt her Dellie surge like a teeny ocean wave or somethin' and truly hoped he had an Atlantic and not a puny Pacific like the boys she'd knowed so far. "I *could* do yew now, Dell," she said at last. "But I'm afraid yew'll turn out the way Willie Fawkner did when I took off my panties for him, lessen we takes our own sweet time."

"I didn't think you was any gawddamn gyp," Dell swore, pulling his zipper down, "an' it's my prerogative t'make sure yew don't turn into one!" His dictionary defined *prerogative* as "an exclusive privilege," Dell remembered, "one peculiar to a rank or class." The way he saw it, their deal gave him that privilege (however peculiar it seemed, even to him), and both killin' folks and screwing girls was *definitely* part of his rank.

Kee saw Dell's thang more or less spring into sight like a salmon trying to flop its way upstream. Then he had his hands on the zipper running down the front of her jeans, and he was tuggin' hard enough on it to rip it out, and a second female voice called Kee's name from downstairs. Dell's .44 Magnum promptly dropped out of his pants to the floor.

"Hold on, Mama, I'm comin'," Kee shouted, and bolted for the bedroom door. She banged her getaway suitcase against the door frame as she glanced back at her shiny knight. "For heaven's sakes, Dellie, put that away now and come shoot Mama. We got us a *deal!*" Then, "Stay put, Mama, I got a surprise for yew!"

"Dammit, I'm tryin'," Dell growled, honestly. Everytime he popped his penis back into his pants, however, it jumped back out again. The Magnum wouldn't remain in his belt until he managed to zip up, and that was another problem. "I'm gonna have to re-sort to *The Book* t'look into the pro-prieties of this, though."

"Yew ain't got time!" Kee hissed from just outside the bedroom door. "Dell, if she sees Daddy before I can get there t'watch, I won't even care if yew shoot her. And then our partnership is *off*!"

She ran for the stairway, clunking the suitcase against the walls, hummin' one of her mama's favorite hymns real loud.

But Mama wasn't waitin' at the foot of the steps. She'd already begun heading for the den!

"Kee, what in the world has been happening up there?" Natalie Grace was on the verge of goin' in where Daddy was. But she had turned when Kee breathlessly sprinted up beside her.

"I was jus' writin' somethin' in my book," Kee said, trying to get her breath. She sidled around her mother into the den without making any effort to conceal the packed suitcase.

If Carter had jus' whipped ole man Reagan, Kee recited the ancient family litany in her mind as she carefully blocked her mother's view of Daddy inside the den, *we might truly've become one of them new-koo-loor famblies like Jimmy talked about so much.* Maybe it was a red commie scheme like Daddy'd believed all along. *Where in goodness's name is Dell?*

As though growing suspicious, Mama tried to look around Kee. Kee shifted her upper body as if they were doing a new dance together. "Kee, I've accepted that you—have your precious new freedom," Natalie Grace said softly. "And I understand you don't like being . . . questioned. Honey, I can't stop being concerned about you." Tentatively, she touched her daughter's cheek. "If there's someone in your bedroom, c-couldn't you at least tell me whom?"

Kee was amazed. Tears were in her mama's eyes. *Real* tears, puddlin' in the corners! For the first time it passed through Kee's mind that everything could've been Daddy's fault, that Mama was just bossy, and stuck-up—and religious.

"*I'm* the 'whom,' ma'am," Dell said, as po-lite as possible.

He'd startled Kee nearly as much as he had Natalie Grace. The former forgot to keep her position in front of the late Ewing McCaulter. Smiling just a little, Kee edged uncertainly toward the man who owned the van. Her dream man.

Natalie Grace saw Dell then, spinning around in shock when she heard his voice. What she saw was a rough-hewn scarecrow of a man with slicked-back wet hair, his shirttail partly out, his zipper only half up, and a firearm in his hand. She thought fleetingly of how the weapon didn't look comfortable on him, or natural, and of a Psalm she'd always loved. A corner of her mind began reciting it and kept it going.

Natalie Grace saw her sick wreck of a husband next, head thrown back, his neck apparently adorned by an odd red necklace. He was in his chair with his legs sprawled out before him, calling her no names at all. He was merely *staring*, she realized when she had gone another step closer. His eyes were as hateful and sightless as ever. *More* hateful, and sightless, than when she'd left the house that morning. Natalie Grace said, "Ewe," with sadness she thought had left her for good. "Poor Ewe."

Kee said Dell's name, then nothing more, because she didn't know what else to say or if she wanted to say more, and she didn't know if she should utter another sound. The house was so quiet it felt filled up with ghosts. Strangely, Kee felt that one of them might be her own.

"I looked in *The Book* under 'agreement,'" said Dell. "It's bein' of the same opinion or bein' in harmony. I b'lieve we re-tain the same opinion."

He fired the .44 and a slug—missing Natalie Grace by a yard or better—shot the dancing-lady lamp, which he'd put back on the end table, to smithereens.

Dell fired again. Because he was pissed at destroying the lamp—and missing—his shot was even farther off the target. Kee, head lowered, darted toward him in a wide, arching path, afraid a bullet might strike her. The automatic's explosive sounds were deafening in the small room.

Natalie Grace only glanced up briefly from her

husband's corpse. The madman had said something about *"The Book."* What could he possibly have found in the Bible that supported what he had done—was *doing*—here?

With Kee beside him, trembling and excited, it finally dawned on Dell that he could walk closer to his motionless target and have a better chance of hitting her. He did so, humming and muttering a heartfelt complaint about the girl's choice of weapon. "She don't even look *skeered*," he got out intelligibly at last. "Why don't yew jest go up to yore room awhile an' let ole Dell handle this?"

Unanswering, Kee began to cry. Dell saw that right off when he glanced down at her. He *had* thought of raping the woman first.

So he forgot about aiming at all and blew an enormous hole in the middle of Kee's mother's face, noticing only that the bitch's lips were moving up till the time she didn't have any to move.

"Killin' ain't the same this way, gawdamnit!" Dell opined as he put those things of the McCaulters' with resale value in the trash bag he'd had the wide-eyed Kee bring from the kitchen. "It's my unsolicited o-pinion thet contract killers is purely crazy."

Kee had stopped crying. But she felt less in-clined to jump around than she had earlier in the day as she helped Dell make the wisest selections about what to take. There wasn't a whole lot there of value, truly. But she supposed she had finally experienced life—and been completely unbored—

for the first time. "There isn't nobody else I want yew to kill," she told Dell with as much poise and dignity as she could muster. "It was jus' them."

"Well, sure, yew say thet *now*!" Dell said with scorn. "I knows women, girl. Next thang, it'll be a grampa or a aunt yew want offed." He shot out a finger. "I ain't killin' no children, git *thet* through yore head right now!"

Kee looked up, touched. She'd almost forgotten for a while Dellie was her shiny knight. "I didn't know yew was a man of principle, too," she said. She began to cry soundlessly. "I on'y wish yew unnerstood this stuff is part of *my* shit, too, and be more sympathetical." Kee searched his long, scowling face tearfully. "I'm a orphan now, Dellie. A *double* orphan."

Dell filled the trash bag with a clock he'd had his eye on ever since arriving, but then stared down at Kee in fresh astonishment. The drip in his eye subsided, clearing his vision.

He saw a real pretty girl he wanted awful bad, and he had held up his end of the bargain. "C'mon!" he told her. He wasn't in a mood to be polite now. Pinning her hips to his own lower body and grinding against her, he dug strong fingers into her buttocks. "It's time now, Kee, so yew git *hot*!" She hadn't flinched, so he added, "We ken do it here or we can go somewheres else in the house if the corpses bother yew."

Kee saw two sets of properly dead eyes—three total, to be honest, since Mama didn't have both of hers anymore—were watchin' Kee one hundred percent now—not like they had when they were livin' and refused to see Kee like they were supposed to do. "I cert'iny wants to screw you now," she said, the first lie she had told Dell that she knew was one, "but don't yew remember?"

"I remember we is *partners*," Dell said, hard as stone from head to toe.

"Dell, Doc Lidbetter was gonna see Daddy this afternoon."

"Well, he prob'ly still will." He yanked her blouse up high, made blubbering noises against her chest. "Might be awhile afore he checks thangs out, though."

"The doctor's comin' *to pick up Mama and Daddy!*" Kee exclaimed. She kissed him on the end of his nose, rubbed briefly against his already sagging bulge with her hand. "I'm shore I told yew *that*. Doc Lidbetter's truly prompt, too. He's due any minute."

Dell shoved her hand hard enough that she nearly fell. "When in hell yew ever goin t'pay up, Kee? Jest tell me *thet!*"

"Why, tonight," Kee said sweetly as she regained her balance. She took one end of the plume of hair that tended to fall over her shoulder and put it back in front. She fancied the idea of one hunk in back, one in front. "In the van—when we's faaar, faaaaaaar away from ole Cherokee Rose, Georgia— safe as teeny bugs in a rug!"

Dell's weeping eye wept. At that moment no idea of any nature occurred to him. He was a complete cipher.

"Now, I packed my suitcase to go with yew an' it's got a see-through negajay I've never even had on. But it don't hafta be on *long*." She raised the suitcase, started toward the front door without a backward glance at either the dead bodies or the living one.

"I never said yew was goin *anywheres* with *me!*" Dell shouted.

"Dellie, you *must* have," Kee called, "'cause you warned me 'bout not shootin' no children for me 'n said I'd pick a grampa or auntie next time. So if there's a next time—well, then there's got to be a *next* time."

He followed her to the door, started drawing the Magnum out of his belt, wondering if he might just use it one last time that day.

Kee did something magical with the zipper of her jeans. She'd stopped at the door with her back to him, and next thing Dell knew, she was showing him the cutest little butt he'd ever seen! "We'll go absolutely *ever*where and I'll do *ever*thing yew asks me. Yew can use a girl like me, Dellie." Recollections of what Dell had once hoped he'd have sifted through his brain and made a new pattern. In some ways, he realized, this Kee McCaulter was the girl of his dreams.

But she'd take a lot of trainin', too.

CHAPTER

9

"Looks to me like we've got a gee-damned savage son of an illegitimate seacook right here in Cherokee Rose," said Police Sergeant Yarbro. He'd been through the room with a fine-tooth comb—which is to say, everywhere the detective had let him look—and he was as excited as a teenage girl on her first big date.

The detective said nothing by way of reply. The way he stood, barely inside the den where his gray-blue eyes were able to see everything "in context" (as he'd put it), he might have been taken for a statue or a man who liked what he was seeing.

"Natalie Grace was a decent woman," offered Dr. Marley Lidbetter, motioning to Kyle Yarbro's men to bag the bodies for him. He was getting on in years and wanted to retire, but the county talked him into doubling as its coroner instead.

"Some say somethin' was goin' on between her and Reverend Simpkins," Yarbro said helpfully with a sidelong glance at the detective. He stopped just short of winking. But it was close.

"I'm aware of who started that rumor, too, Sergeant," Doc Lidbetter said. He helped seal Ewing McCaulter's bag, then straightened his back with some arthritic difficulty and gave Yarbro his sternest look. "Ardo's been my friend for over twenty years. If I hear that rumor spreading under circumstances like these, I'll have a little talk with the chief. Make myself clear, Sergeant?"

Kyle had a pre-thirty face that had never waged a war with acne but still managed to look mottled even when he wasn't turning red. "This here's police work, Doc." He got a little red then. "Yew cain't ask—"

"*I* can *tell*, Yarbro, not ask," said the carved figure in the doorway. "And I am. Telling you to zip your mouth before Dr. Lidbetter has to close it for you—inside *another* body bag." The detective came off the door like something hard being chipped away from it. But he veered before he reached Sergeant Yarbro, strode to the shattered pieces of a lamp, and instructed another office to bag them. "He wasn't a very good shot, was he, Doctor?"

Lidbetter glanced around in some surprise. Neither the police chief nor Kyle Yarbro had ever discussed a case with him except when they bugged him for the results of an autopsy. Now this out-of-town feller was doing it, and the old man was caught with his crustiness down.

"Make it 'Marley,'" he suggested. "I see that the cord the murderer used on Ewe came from this lamp. But I thought it just came off while he was chokin' the poor bastard."

The detective minimally shook his head. "No. It took strength to tear that cord out. When he had, the alleged murderer replaced the lamp on the end table—and shot it." The beginning of an expression Marley Lidbetter couldn't read trembled once on the younger man's lips and went into hiding. "Right *there*," he said, indicating the baseboard. "Kyle, make yourself useful," he ordered the sergeant. "Get a knife and pry out that slug . . . unhurriedly. Pretend one of your parents was just shot or choked and you'd really like Atlanta to run a decent ballistics test."

"They'll jus' show it come from the same weapon as the bullet in the woman," Yarbro grumbled, but under his breath. He did what he'd been told because his superior, frozen once more into statuary, was behind him. He added, "Mama's already dead."

"But if it doesn't show that, it may indicate more

than one person was involved," the statue said, explaining himself more to the doctor than to Yarbro. "Marley," he said, "let's chat a minute. If your work is done here."

"I'm afraid it is." Lidbetter turned, wondering if this sleuth from outside Cherokee Rose could prove to be a caring as well as a thorough man. "Can we do it in the fresh air?" Anticipating agreement, Lidbetter began wending a path through the house. "I knew these people. Including the missing girl— brought her into the world fifteen years ago. This is the worst crime to happen in this town during my whole lifetime."

"The fact that you've spent your life in Cherokee Rose is why I want to talk with you." The detective held the front door for Marley, abruptly realizing the doctor had been a taller man in his youth. Now the shoulders that preceded him through the door and angled left to a porch swing looked as if he'd spent his years accumulating them in a bundle on his back. Maybe old men at some level believed they could keep them there and find a way to draw them out, someday—like tuxes worn to proms or other apparel of the young.

The detective noticed the doctor had fallen silent, content to sit next to him and let the swing move nearly with their breath, and that seemed like a good idea to Kirk. It was an old-fashioned way to become friends, of sorts—shared silence—and Kirk could use one in this town. He could especially use a friend now that he was obliged to take on a murder investigation, since each one he'd investigated before had resulted in his being asked to accept a reduction of duty, or to move on.

He had imposed statuelike poise on himself because he had once been so eager to prove himself that he'd sometimes reacted too quickly—and he had not liked how he had behaved. But he'd hated the sight of lifeless bodies so much that he had pursued the most likely perpetrators relentlessly, usually found them, then had to kill them. That had never been his conscious intention, so he'd concluded it was either because of the name his parents had given him at birth, or because something queerly methodical in his mind preferred balance: dead body left back there, the new dead body responsible for it over here. Not a perfect match but better than without.

Under pressure, Detective Douglas had left big city police enforcement behind in the hope of solving every purse-snatching, pettily larcenous, wife battering, domestic squabbling, and high school football skirmishing crime America's small towns had to offer.

"You said the dead woman, Natalie Grace, was a decent woman," he reminded Lidbetter. "You said nothing about the dead man."

"Because he wasn't a decent man," Lidbetter said, then frowned. "I don't want to go on any report, or record, speakin' ill of the dead. This is between us?"

Kirk studied the homely, honest face. "In all probability, let's say. Why did he look like that? What was wrong with McCaulter, Marley?"

"The cause was *treponema pallidum*, syphillis. Worst kind, the third stage; the nervous system, creatin' *tabes dorsalis*, primary eye disease, muscular weakness, personality change, and piss-poor judgment—or maybe that's what starts the cycle. He didn't get it from the last tramp he bored, he jus' thought so." Lidbetter swatted his knee irritably, squinted at the sky. "Spring's coming, but it sure takes its sweet time about it. Prick was blind, you know."

Woman he "bored," Douglas thought, liking the quaint term. "I didn't know, but I wondered. The perp had to've sneaked behind him to use the cord." At times Kirk got a tic or something in his face, near his mouth, and it was back. He hated it. When people noticed, they also saw the damn cleft in his chin. If they hadn't thought of the movie actor when they heard his name, they did then. He wiped his face with his handkerchief, but it wasn't perspiring. "Mrs. McCaulter worked for Reverend Simpkins?" He saw Lidbetter nod. Kirk sighed. "I tried to halt that rumor in its tracks because crap like that—pardon my language—muddies up police work as much as for reasons of ordinary decency."

The doctor sighed, too. "But you want to know about it anyway."

"I don't want to. I *need* to, Marley."

Lidbetter turned his head to squint at Kirk Douglas. "What do they call you, Detective?"

He smiled, crammed his handkerchief into his

breast pocket any old way. "They call me 'Kirk,' Marley. What else would they call me?"

The physician snorted. Then he took the cigarettes he'd forbidden himself to smoke from his breast pocket and shook out one of the three in it. He offered one to Kirk, reluctantly as the devil, and felt relieved when it was refused. He'd been down to two or three regular Camels five times in the last two weeks but he was in no hurry to finish them off.

"I wouldn't know where to start," he said, "about the rumor." The smoke he sucked into his lungs was like an old friend he had trusted who had somehow gone wrong without knowing he had; it felt loyal, in a way, to keep the companionship.

Kirk crossed legs that were as sturdy as a piano's. He was too short ever to be any sort of actor he'd seen in the few movies or TV shows he watched, and his eyes were so widely spaced he looked like the front of an old Buick—in his opinion. "Neither you nor Kyle Yarbro expressed one word of concern about the missing girl, the victims' daughter. How good a place to begin would that be?"

Marley strove to make a painful cough sound smoother, like a rough spot in his voice that he might simply speak over. "About like countin' your meld in a pinochle game after the cards have all been dealt and before you bid."

"You delivered her. Isn't that what you said?"

Half-forgotten memories smoldered like cigarettes improperly stubbed out. "Y'can't send a man to the gas chamber for that when you're merely the attendin' physician. Kee was round as a butterball turkey, Detective." He looked up suddenly and both his expression and what he said were as much a surprise to him as they were to Douglas. "She looked like she found life boring from the start. *Ad*-ult bored." He coughed. "Jaded."

The detective turned his well-spaced eyes to the sky, read off old newspaper headlines he'd clipped and studied frequently enough that he knew the facts behind most of the stories. MAN HELD FOR BURNING PARENTS—but the "man" was eighteen and he'd been too high to find his cock at a urinal. CHILD, 9, STABS DAD—but Dad was an abusive bastard, even if Kirk had never proved it.

There were other stories, other headlines. About children no older than Kirk's own Annie-pie, now living with his ex-wife in Oak Forest, Illinois, children who peddled drugs there were no names for yet—or children who sold their bodies. Or who joined gangs and shot other children because they lived a block or two away.

He'd never heard of any newborn monsters, though. He wouldn't believe there was such a thing until psychiatrists proved beyond a shadow of a doubt that sociopaths were born and not made. Anything else meant either that God made mistakes, a view Kirk could never consider for a moment, or that ecological nightmares began in the womb these days.

"Did I get it right that"—Douglas glanced at some notes—"Kee is fifteen?"

Doctor Lidbetter stripped his Camel the way he

had learned to do it in the Army a long time ago, watched the remnant skip in the McCaulter grass like little pixies. Lord Jesus, he was getting whimsical with the years—and soundin' like a total idiot to this out-of-state Sherlock. "My impression was that she had no morals, no . . . no *something* that most of us have at birth. She'd be fifteen now, yes. But I think she's psycho, not sociopathic."

Kirk liked this old man but his obvious animosity toward the girl, Kee—well, it seemed more than that. "Marley, did Kee have a juvenile record?"

"I don't think she's ever gone to juvie, no," Lidbetter sighed. "Kirk, I didn't say she murdered Natalie Grace and Ewing. And it wasn't just me who felt the way I did about her when she was born. Reverend Simpkins felt the same."

"But what has she done?" Douglas pressed.

Marley rose creakily. The Douglas kid was short, but he had a stocky build to him, good eyes and manners. But he wouldn't want to hear about the way Natalie Grace claimed Kee had willed her baby fat to go away, how Natalie Grace had been so scared of her own daughter she'd stayed with Ardo, working, as many hours as possible. That just made the pathetic woman sound more neurotic than she was—had been. As for the rest of the mother's problems with Kee, he himself had told Natalie Grace they were usually pretty normal, even, in some cases, advanced. Hell.

"Spring's just about here, Detective," Marley rasped. "It's a good time to get out on the open road, feel your oats a little."

Kirk put his handful of scribbled notes into his suit coat pocket, nodded. Apparently there was nothing Dr. Lidbetter had for him except grudging notions or preoccupations of the past—and probably some excellent advice about health matters, if Kirk should ever feel under the weather. "I guess it's beautiful here in the spring."

"You're figurin' there's a god-awful murderer runnin' around loose and he took Kee with him just long enough to rape and kill her. You're a decent man—any fool can see that—so you hope t'catch him before he does either of those things."

Kirk nodded.

"Welllll," Marley told him, "I share your ambition—assumin' you're right. But if you're not . . ."

Kirk stood up, too. "Don't stop there. *Please.*"

The old man put just the first joints of his fingers in his jacket pockets, arched his back to loosen old vertebrae. "If you're wrong, Kee went with him 'cause she wanted to do it, Detective. And if the murderin' son-of-a-bitch *only* killed Ewing, I'd feel sorry as all get-out for him."

"God Almighty, Marley, she's still a child!" Kirk exclaimed. The physician's attitude was as ugly as the things Douglas had seen in the big cities. "Any bastard who'd slaughter the parents, then force a fifteen-year-old girl to go with him—who will maybe have to *watch* while he kills still more innocent people—isn't worth considering a human being!"

"That's a helluva attitude for a lawman to have,

if you ask me," Marley said levelly. Then he was on the driveway, headed for his car.

"Detective Douglas, got a minute?"

Kirk saw Sergeant Yarbro hulking behind him and he had that hotshot, shit-eating smirk he wore on his mouth when there was a chance he'd done something right for a change. Kirk lifted his eyebrows and waited as patiently as he could.

"One of the boys—Junior Kisner, the guy with the mustache?—knowed the McCaulters pretty good. Went t'church with the missus awhile, he says."

"Come to the point, please," Kirk said, rankled by Lidbetter's inclination to spread rumors, old tales. "What did Officer Kisner tell you?"

"Ain't so much what he tole me as what he *knowed*." Now, maybe this big city prick would realize there was already gee-damned good detectives in Cherokee Rose before he put his fancy nose into their affairs. Douglas—'n the way he tried so hard to look like that actor-fella! Kyle figured he could take either one of the Kirks on a rasslin' mat and have enough left to eat a big lunch. "Junior, he may have fancied ol' Kee a little—not that he'd lay a finger on no *child*, unnerstand—"

"Of course not," Kirk said. He was watching Dr. Lidbetter's four-year-old black Caddy leave bursts of dust clouds behind as he headed for the main road. Annoyed by too many things for his own health, Kirk changed his concentration to the rose garden at the side of the house. It had gone to seed. While he knew next to nothing about gardening, it gave Kirk the impression that no one at all had worked in it for a long while. Was that because of Ewing McCaulter's syphilis—probably an unmentionable disease in this place, a horror nobody could directly address—or were there actually other problems in the family?

"So he noticed most'a the clothes the girl wore. Said Kee'd been gettin' a whole lot of new thangs this last year."

Reluctantly, Kirk returned his gray-blue gaze to the taller and younger man. "*Yes?*"

"All those clothes are *gone*, Detective," the sergeant said in a rush of words, "or most of 'em, leastwise. Along with a few toys Kisner remembered from the girl's childhood, an' some makeup."

Kirk Douglas nodded almost absently, pretended to blow his nose in his handkerchief. Then he pressed the clean edge of it to his jawline, looking as thoughtful—and as bored—as he could. He knew it appeared to Yarbro that he either hadn't heard what he said or didn't care, but Douglas didn't give a damn. The redneck bastard had made his implications clear enough for a moron to follow— that young Kee had voluntarily packed a bag and then left with a vicious killer who'd just wiped her parents out of life like subtraction tables scrawled on a blackboard. It was the same intolerable concept the doctor had attempted to plant in his head until he'd been obliged to come up with something concrete to condemn the child. Well, what could you expect from townfolk who apparently considered a woman a bad mother and an arrogant bitch because she graduated from *high school*!

Well, he wouldn't forget what they'd told him. And he wouldn't forget the two men from Cherokee Rose, Georgia—policeman and doctor—who proposed such things. But who in hell was supposed to speak for the children? (Who'd take care of his own faraway Annie-pie if *he* got killed and these men were correct, and if the country was made up mostly of men who always tried first to blame the children?)

"Get this 'Junior' with the eagle-eye to talking to merchants, service stations, whoever runs a business close to the exits from town," Kirk ordered Yarbro. "The perp either lives here in town or he entered it *in* something."

"Coulda been a hobo. Walkin' ain't crowded." Kyle frowned. "Why Junior an' not me?"

"Because he 'knowed' Kee McCaulter," Kirk said. "And see if you can find a recent picture of her for him to take with him. I want to locate her and the perp before he harms her."

Yarbro said okay, turned. "I think you mean 'alleged perp,' don't you, Detective?"

Douglas only half heard the sarcasm. He was already making a mental list of good law enforcement people he knew about elsewhere in Georgia and in the neighboring states. There was zero reason to believe they hadn't made it out of town, so he'd need to enlist cooperation if he was going to leave the county to pursue Kee and the son-of-a-bitch who'd abducted her—and by God, he *wasn't* going to "bore" her!

And when Douglas found them, he'd shout once at the goddamned pervert, then blow whatever he had that passed for brains all over the road!

Unless he was very, very cooperative.

C H A P T E R

It wasn't quite one o'clock in the afternoon by the time Dell had driven the van a couple of miles from the McCaulters' house and realized two things.

The first was that they were running out of gas and he didn't have any choice than getting more or swapping the gas-guzzling cocksucker for other transportation. Since he wasn't anxious to be seen in Cherokee Rose, he'd have preferred the latter, but the pert and bright-eyed girl perched on the captain's seat behind him posed a problem. Dell felt purty sure she was telling the truth and wanted to be with him—if he hadn't felt that, he'd have gone ahead, fucked and killed her back in the house—but he wasn't sure how she'd behave during a business transaction. Then there was the fact that between her suitcase and the jam-packed bag of goodies they'd took he couldn't rip off just any old car. He needed room.

The second momentary concern he had was getting into the girl before he exploded. Or got so tense he lost his control and did something dumb enough to wind up with Lloyd B. for a roommate again—assuming Lloyd was still there.

So even after he got the van gassed up with no one saying shit to them, he found an old weeded lot in a block so run-down and shitty-looking it almost made him homesick. There were empty houses with the windows boarded up on each side of the lot and nothing across the street, so it looked real safe for a quickie.

He tried to make the girl stand up on the mattress at the rear of the van and drop her drawers, but Kee didn't have enough room to *really* stand up, and she fell down twice! Finally, while she was hunched over—facing him with one arm thrown out so's she could balance herself with a hand on the ledge of the back window—she got her jeans mostly down to the ankles, then started trying to kick one leg off.

A new boner was making good progress and Dell reached out to pull off Kee's gawdamn jeans—

And damned if company didn't show up! Kee'd pushed part of the velvety curtains back while she was gripping the framework of the rear door and when she glanced out of the very same window, *there* was some fucking friend of hers!

"*Sue Elenor!*" Kee shouted, turning around just when he yanked the jeans off and left her bare-ass. Then Kee started *hammerin'* on the window like a crazy person.

"It's my oldest and truest friend, Sue Elenor, walking home from school." Kee offered the explanation as she turned her head, her eyes like chunks of blue torn out of the sky. "Dellie, it's like the answer to a *prayer*!"

To Dell's amazement, she went back to staring out the crack in the red curtains, screaming and knocking on the window some more. "*Sue Elenor, you come here—*I wants yew t'meet the man I saw in all my dreams 'n visions!"

Dell craned his neck in the hope of seeing the girl, too—

But the rear door flew open and unceremoniously dumped Kee out into the vacant lot.

Jesus on a as-cendin' cloud, Dell thought, scrambling outside, too, *if anybuddy sees this gawdamn girl without her pants on, they'll sure as shootin' take me for a fuckin' pervert*!

To Dell's further chagrin, Kee got up real fast and *started running* after *her friend!* "Hold up, Sue Elenor!" she screamed at the top of her voice—"it's jus' ole Kee!" She was sprintin' like a two-tone filly toward a deserted building, waving her hands and arms over her head, her fanny wiggling so cute it made it hard for Dell to concentrate on what he had to do.

He stopped where he stood, dug the Magnum out of his pants—and fired it straight into the air. Twice.

Kee froze where she'd got to, then put her arms up again, as if she was surrendering.

"Git yore ass back in thet van!" Dell said, half-walking, half-running after the girl, tearing off his shirt as he went. He never did see Kee's friend. He was only lookin' from one side to another, then tying the sleeves of the shirt around Kee's bare waist. "Yew tryin' to get us arrested?" he demanded.

"No," Kee answered shakily, guiltily. She hauled herself back inside, the front of Dell's shirt drooping on the floor of the van. "It's on'y that Sue Elenor 'n me, we done shared jus' about everything, and I wanted her to'see that *my* d-dreams and visions came true—and how perfeck *yew* are."

She was climbing back in her jeans, zipping up fast as if her mom or daddy told her to go to her room, and Dell spotted the tears running down her cheeks. It was the second time he wondered how old she was, but this was the time to establish who was going to be the boss out on the lonely road.

"Don' yew think we oughter high-tail it outta here lessen somebody s-seed me?" Kee said.

"Thet's whut I was goin t'do," Dell said as irritably as possible, turning and walking toward the front of the van. Motor running, he checked to see if anyone had seen them or if Sue Elenor had gone to get the authorities. The coast looked clear. *Thet was smart'a her*, he decided, and finally headed out of town, glad to put Cherokee Rose behind him.

Mebbe the girl can be some help since she keeps her cool unless she gits a hair up her ass. "Yew ain't cryin back there, are yew?" he called from behind the steering wheel.

"No!" she exclaimed, lying.

"Git up here in your captain's chair where you belong," Dell commanded, reading a state sign with arrows telling him how to leave town. "I wants you t' ob-serve for me, be my navigator, in a manner of speakin'." He glanced her way when he heard her plunking herself down and had to grin. She didn't bawl like some bitches. She cried cute in a way. "I figger we'll go northeast toward South Carolina, mebbe go through Charlotte 'n Winston-Salem 'n head across Lenoir into Tennessee. I got that much planned jest *glancin'* at the map." He'd left it out on the deep panel behind the steering wheel.

"Golly, yew're smart," Kee whispered. "We gonna get somethin' to eat before we hit Ten-o-see? I'm gettin' powerful hungry."

"'Before,' the word is 'before'—not 'afore,'" Dell corrected her. "Naturally we're goin t'git a meal—*dine* somewheres. But first we need t'make tracks. Put some miles between them 'n us." He groped behind him, patted her knee. "Yew got a lot t'learn, girl."

Kee sighed. "Everbody says that. I reckon it's the truth."

Dell turned his head around, fast, to ask, "Yew

willin' t'learn? Cause thet's the first step—along with whut yew said about acceptin' thet yore iggorunt as dung."

Kee nodded. Dell looked through the windshield in time to keep from getting smooshed by a semi. The driver and Dell exchanged pleasantries as the semi passed and then he told the girl about the smartest gawdamn black man he'd ever met, Lloyd B. "It wasn't thet I didden know mosta the *basics* 'bout readin' an' writing, jest like yew knows 'em. But I purely had not figgered out thet facks was the same from time t'time, not like people; they's *allus* honest, 'n they don't change on yew the way folks do. Yew follow me so far?"

"Uh-huh," Kee said quietly.

"But the *big thang*," Dell said, heading down the road, the sun setting at his back, getting in a real fine mood, "is words. I figgered thet out! An' when I tole ole Lloyd, yew know whut he said?"

"Uh-uh," Kee said quietly from the captain's seat.

"Well, first he called me by m'name—not 'boy' or 'whitemeat' or nothin'—and then he got so he awmost sounded like he liked me some. 'N he tole me, 'Words is the keys t'bein' a king.' He said, 'Words is like music instruments'—yew know, like a snare drum or a gee-tar?—'and a fella who speaks properlike can play with whoever he de-sires to.' And he give me a present, old Lloyd B. did." Dell tried to see Kee's expression in the rearview or by glancing behind him but her seat wasn't at the right angle. "He give me *The Book of Webster's*, girl."

Then Dell looked back again when he heard an odd noise and saw Kee had fallen asleep where she sat, sliding over with an arm on the floor.

He backhanded her in the face with his right hand, unhesitantly knocking her applecart for ass plumb off her seat.

"Why'd yew do that, Dellie?" She got to her knees woozily, holding the angry red splotch on her cheek, and began to blubber.

"Lest yew wants another one like it, missy," he said, feeling ooze on his own cheek from his bad eye, "pay attention when I'm talkin' about *The Book*. Unless yew *wants* t'be dead whitemeat 'n hauled away on a fuckin' stretcher!" He snuck a peek at her, reached behind to give her his handkerchief. "Here. They's a leetle clean spot on one corner."

She took the handkerchief but settled for holding it by the edge with the clean spot and letting the rest of it hang. "I'm s-s-sorry," she said almost inaudibly. "I think it's swell of yew to teach me things. I'm jus' hungry."

"Thet's awright, Kee," Dell said, full attention returned to the abruptly darkening road. "And I'm sorry I had t'swat yew one, but hittin' is a important teachin' tool." He sighed, heard his own stomach rumbling. "We'll let that be the lesson for t'day and get some grub. First, though, I got t'find us a pawnshop an' sell somea yore mom 'n daddy's loot."

After Dell had driven another six, eight miles, he risked another glimpse of her and saw Kee had gone to sleep again, this time with her cheek on the seat while she still knelt on the floor of the van. Dell had to marvel at the girl. He supposed she was nothin' but a kid.

Dell picked a little town with a name that sounded like it'd have a pawnshop in it—Fredericksburg, Georgia—then took the next exit. He was thinking about taking Kee somewhere real nice for supper, to put her in a suitable mood for fucking, when he saw some bumper stickers on cars that Dell considered disgusting. PREMATURE EJACULATION IS JUST A MATTER OF OPINION, read one. Other vehicles passed, headlights on. Dell, frowning, strove to get his bearings in the unfamiliar town, trying to scan the signs on storefronts as he wheeled the bulky van through the narrow streets. GEORGIA'S JUST ON MY MIND (BUT I'M STILL TRYING!) was another sticker that distracted Dell. When he finally saw both a sign on a shop reading RUBIN'S PAWNSHOP and a diagonal parking place right in front of it, Dell was road-weary, irritable, and too slow to prevent another Chevy from scooting in ahead of him.

Worse, there were no other parking slots within visual range and since Dell wasn't entirely convinced Kee wasn't pissed at him for hitting her, he didn't want her to wake up in the van and not know where she was. If she would run away buck naked, she sure might do it with her clothes on—if only for spite.

He'd just have to make it snappy.

Dell intentionally parked the van so that it blocked the Chevy that had taken his slot, left the motor running and the Magnum on one of the other seats, then hauled the garbage bag filled with the McCaulters' possessions to the entrance. The fella who'd stolen Dell's chosen slot actually held the door open for him, and the polite Dell said, "Thanks."

I look like gawdamn Sandy Claus steppin' outta a chimbly, Dell paused. He stepped in front of the Chevy dude and set the huge bag on the owner's counter. "Wants t'sell alla this crap for yore best price."

A half-bald man behind the counter—Dell figured him to be the pawnshop owner—barely looked up. When he did, it was to look at the sack as Dell began lifting Kee's folks' things out. "So much," the owner said, eyes blinking real fast like he read a lot, "so many things."

"I've just got a watch I'd like to pawn," the Chevy man said at Dell's side. He added, a trifle slow for Dell's critical ear, "But it's a good one."

Dell ignored him except to get one arm in front of him. "It is a heap, that's fer shore," he answered the owner. He watched the man sort through loose silverware and plates, the TV Kee's Daddy had been pretending to look at, a clock-radio, more. The man did it with hands too nimble for expectations, glances that scarcely touched the objects they held or lingered an instant while the fingers picked other things up, or pushed them to the side.

Suddenly the man said, simply and very plainly, "Forty-six dollars—ninety-seven cents—take-it-or-leave-it."

"Yew ain't seen alla it," Dell pointed out, one brow drooping.

"So you didn't take this from the Taj Mahal, don't blame me." The owner shrugged and leaned forward slightly to take the Bulova watch the Chevy man—who looked like a new sailor or soldier to Dell, he had a head shaved as if he was waiting to be electrocuted.

But the shop owner's hand didn't get to the watch. Dell's hand got to his wrist first.

"I tole yew I wanted yore best price."

"You've got it, you've got it," said the balding man. "Remove your hand please." Dell's thumbs were digging in.

Dell caught a glimpse of the only timepiece in the shop that appeared to be running, a clock behind the counter. The girl was waiting along with supper and fucking. "Yew can jest about reach that cash register whilst I'm holdin' on. I wants yew t'do thet n' take out all the cash money."

"Look, buddy," the soldier/sailor said.

Dell hit him on top of the head with the clock-radio and he fell to the floor and stayed.

The pawnshop owner belatedly did what he had been told, and his eyes were blinking fast again. "Take it all, here, I don't want it." He was making a face because Dell knew his wrist hurt a lot, because he'd stuck a powerful thumb where it would do the most good.

"Don't *want* it all," Dell said stiffly, using his free hand to scoop up half the bills from the counter. "Yew can sell this junk iffen you don't notify the

aw-thorities; yew'll make out awright." He sum-
moned his most aggrieved expression. "This here
was a honest biz'ness transaction 'n you screwed
'er up by insultin' me."

He went ahead and broke the man's wrist in
two places.

When he saw the bald owner fall to the floor in
pain he figured there was no need to run to get out
of the shop. The van was visible through the big
store window so the girl was probably still there.
"Yew can never be too po-lite in this world," he
called back to the injured owner.

When he got to the van, Kee was still asleep and
he didn't mind if she stayed that way as long as
possible. He climbed in behind the wheel, then
realized he'd have to wake her up after all.

The young guy with the Bulova watch and
shaved head was running out in front of the shop.
Well, he was on his *way*, he wasn't there yet.

Expressionless, Dell reached back to get the
Magnum.

Kee drifted off into sleep and a weird miasmic mix of
dreams, nightmares, and what she thought of—
sleeping or awake—as her visions.

Kee had run into a set of circumstances and
obligations she'd never encountered before, not
even previously envisioned with any degree of ac-
curacy. They'd left her seriously confused about
what she wanted to do now.

Never once before had Kee Dora McCaulter
been remotely confused about either the steps she

preferred to take next or the things (and the circumstances) she wanted to have.

The larger reason why she had felt an overwhelming need to go to sleep while her Dell was talking about his dumb dictionary was because she had almost *always* gone to sleep when she was bored (which was mostly why she had stopped going to high school) and because she knew he wasn't going to let her wait to screw him until she was truly in the mood. And Kee had nothing left to show Dellie in order to stall him.

And there was a last teeny reason she had dozed off even after he slapped her: Kee had hoped she'd have a truly neat vision of herself doin' it with Dell—one that would tell her how she could go on postponin' their first romantical night together till she was fuckin' *ready.* It wasn't because he wanted to hump her in the van, that wasn't it; there was a mattress and nice red drapes and all.

It was—and this was also why Kee got herself so confused in the first place—because *he* was the one who was doin' the decidin' and tellin' her what *he* wanted.

She hadn't allowed anyone else to choose the when or the how—or for that matter, the *what*—ever since Sue Elenor had taken those pictures that looked like Daddy n' Mama 'n her were gettin' it on. And Kee, really, *truly* did not intend to let even Dellie make choices like that, not as long as she could figure out ways to be boss!

Now it had been almost okay for Dellie to bash her in the face and nearly chip a tooth. She hadn't done what *he* wanted her to do or listened at a time when she hadn't had anything better to do anyhow. She might still be just fifteen years old but she knew marriage, even romance, was a two-way street.

Kee had a dream about playing with her teddy bear when she was tiny and one about the nice trip she took with her folks to Atlanta when her daddy thought that ol' Jimmy Carter was going to buy his farm; she dreamed of the once-nameless man of her dreams (only now he had a bad eye and hands like grapplin' hooks), discovering her new titties—but the nipples were snakes coming out and their heads were just like Mama and Daddy's; and also about whole fields of peanuts that were really shells with eyes inside, staring at her.

She dreamed a short while about the way Dell had offed her folks. Kee was asking her dream man not to choke Daddy *all* the way, just until he turned blue, but Dellie did it anyhow . . . and then Kee saw Mama coming in (in her nightgown) and Reverend Simpkins was begging for Mama's life, saying, "I have not fornicated this woman, I have not fornicated her." But Dell unloaded the one bullet that blew Mama clean in two, then started hitting the Rev around his head and shoulders. . . .

And she had a nicer dream, then, seein' herself making the cheering squad at school. Which she hadn't. Because she hadn't gone out for it, and because she knew for a fact they wouldn't let anybody like her—Ewing McCaulter's girl—on a team where a lot of boys in uniforms that showed their cute butts off might start puking while they were playing, because they were afraid they might get themselves the syph some way.

So she started having some other dreams about killing folks even while she knew she wasn't truly sleeping anymore. When she woke, she saw that Dell had his gun, and he was *shootin'* like a crazy man! Dellie was emptying the Magnum on some old car they were blocking. He hit all four tires, even if it *did* take him more than four shots, and he blew them all to smithereens!

Then Kee saw both a loose stack of money lying on the seat next to Dell, and a cute boy—*he might even go to college somewheres*, Kee thought— running out to his car. Kee sagged back against the captain's seat with her hands pressed together and had to laugh her head off at the boy's terrified expression.

Dell popped back into the van, slipped into first gear, and drove away. "He was po-lite enough to hold the door fer me so I jest decided not t'kill him," he explained. "He ain't goin' nowheres anyhow on four flat tires."

"Lookit all this *money*!" Kee cooed, reaching forward to count it.

Dell slapped her hands hard. "Don't yew be touchin' thet. girl. It's up t'the man in a relationship t'handle the finances. We'd best git thet straight up front."

Mumbling something midway between an apology and a curse, Kee climbed back onto her customary perch and fell silent. Actually, then Dellie was probably right about what he said. Daddy had always handled the money in their family, right up till Mama didn't want him handlin' nothing.

Dellie looked smug, sort of happy, Kee noticed. His bad eye wasn't drippin' a drop. He wasn't drivin' fast to get out of town, either—where *were* they?—so she decided everything was all right. Kee wanted to ask Dell what had happened in the pawnshop but he seemed locked up in his own mind, so she guessed he hadn't had to shoot up the pawn shop. She felt kind of proud, choosing such fine things from Mama and Daddy's shit that Dell had earned money for them. But something else was bothering her.

"Dell, that ole boy who yew didn't shoot—won't he 'member what we look like an' tell the policemen so's they might ketch us? Mebbe we should go back 'n kill him."

They were just returning to the highway, so Dell took the girl's question in a friendly manner. Girls didn't know diddly anyways. "In regard to the second part of yore query, Kee, who gives a fuck? After we eat ourselves some grub, we're goin t'trade this vehicle in. Although I'm going to keep my eye on another van." His profile showed his bad eye winking in her direction. "The bed in back is good and convenient—which is why I ain't swappin' right *now*, if'n yore curious about thet, too."

"But what about that cute boy *identifyin'* us?" Kee repeated. "From what I heard, them po-lice isn't 'zactly romantical, like we is."

Suddenly Dell was sitting straighter in the driver's seat, his shoulders marginally more squared
than usual; but even that transformation was so
subtle the girl on the captain's seat didn't recognize
it for a minute. All she could see of him was his right
hand on the wheel, and the knuckles were whiter
than Kee had ever seen knuckles go. Though the
speed of the van remained the same, Kee's ears
caught the sound Dell made sometimes of half-
humming, part mumbling, and a chill went down
her spine so fast and so cold she nearly asked Dellie
to close his window. Quietly, surprising herself by
how silently she made herself move, she swung her
young body to the left in order to catch sight of Dell
in the rearview mirror.

It was the worst pus she'd ever seen his eye
produce. It was just *rollin'* down his cheek and
looked as if it was getting in his mouth before
continuing to drip a teensy river all the way to his
chin and then into his collar, where it disappeared.
She hadn't noticed till then that one end of his collar
looked as though it was a different color than the
other.

"Give me *The Book*, please," Dell said.

She realized he was looking right back at her, in
the rearview, and made herself smile purty. "What
book's that, Dellie?"

"*The* book!" he shouted, pounding the steering
wheel so hard with his fist she thought it might
come plumb off and they'd crash out in the middle
of nowhere. "*The Book of Webster's!* Move yore
stumps, girl!"

Kee moved them. "Here," she whispered a second later.

Dell wiped the upper part of his face on the shoulder of his shirt, studied the dark highway briefly, then—guiding the van with the heels of his hands—opened the dictionary.

"'I-den-ti-fy,'" he read aloud. "'The state of being the same.' Yew 'n me look the same, girl?"

"We sure don't," Kee said honestly. "That's a fact."

Dell's upward glance again swept the road. He waited to continue his lesson until three cars passed. Dell looked back down at the open book. "'I-den-ti-fi-ca-tion,' which is a noun, by the way. 'Anything by which a person or thing can be identified.'" Snorting, he closed the book and put it tenderly on the seat beside him, holding the money down. "Thet *young man* yew called 'cute' warn't eyeballin' no license plate, he was eyeballin' the Magnum. Also—yew jest a 'thang,' girl?"

Kee considered his question seriously. "No, Dellie, I'm more'n *that*."

"Well, he seed me in the pawnshop—yew got that part right—but I don't rightly mind it. He'll stay outta Dell from hell's way. Next time he won't park nothin' where *I* means t'park." Dell's chuckle was the nicest sound Kee had ever heard. "It's awright t'ask yore questions, 'cause how else yew going t'learn. But try not t'second-guess ole Dell so's he won't hafta hurt yew bad."

"Yessir," Kee said quickly, arranging herself primly on the captain's chair.

"Gonna 'treat yew to a fancy spread t'night, girl!" Dell declared, pointin' a finger. "We's goin t'dine right in there, at Steak N Shake, 'n yew can order anythang from the menu yew de-sires!"

Since Kee had privately arrived at the conclusion that she was suffering from terminal malnutrition, her reaction to Dellie's choice was completely honest. "Yew mean that, Dellie?" she asked, bouncing up and down on her seat. He'd pulled in already and parked close to the entrance. He was counting the money from the pawnshop, but smiling even if she *was* interrupting him. "I can get *anything* I want?"

"As long as it ain't some gawdamn 'cute boy,'" he told her, hopping out and opening her door.

She started out with the chili mac and a Coke, the double cheeseburger plate (plus a side order of onion rings) for an entree—plus a vanilla shake—and still had a teeny spot in her tummy, which she filled with a lettuce salad.

"Salads is helpful for yew, Mama says, an' Daddy says green food makes hair grow on your chest."

"Yore daddy, rest his soul," Dell said across the table from Kee, "was purely mistaken—I'm pleased t'say."

"What?" When she understood Dell's joke, she almost spat her last onion ring at him. "*Yeeeew!*" she joshed.

Dell's short smile was a masterpiece of mature indulgence.

He had gotten control of his quick furious resentment at being challenged by the girl on the strength of her idea. "Mebbe we should go back 'n kill him," she had said. How Kee had referred to "we," not just "you," might have brought Dell closer to gentle emotions than any other words he had ever heard spoken.

But the fact was he didn't believe Kee meant them any more than he'd meant most of the things he'd said to people throughout his lifetime. Pitching in and helping off your dad and mom was one thing—and he knew jest how she felt, because she'd hated their guts as he hated his mom's.

Helping him commit acts of *business* was something only one woman in five hundred could do.

At least her heart's in the right place, Dell thought, politely asking a waitress for more coffee. You had to be polite in a nice restaurant like this, where they gave you free coffee refills and put up with Kee and the way she ate so much. *Well,* he thought, sighing, *even good times comes to a close. We got more bizness t'discuss and then I gits to fuck her.*

"Kee, I got some thangs t'tell yew. Bizness thangs. If we's goin t'go on bein' partners, *I'm* the senior one. Yew got that? It shall be me, Dell, who makes alla big decisions." He took a look around to be sure nobody was near enough t'hear 'em. "*Yew* shall feel free t'*suggest* who we steal from. *If* we hits 'em, and *how* we does it, got t'be up t'the pro. Me. You unnerstan?"

"Jest as long as yew won't leave me outta the

THE BOOK OF WEBSTER'S

killin' part," she said, around a huge bite of salad. "An' some of the sex stuff."

Their waitress, a fiftyish woman stuck with closing that night, said, "I think it's sweet when a father takes his daughter out for a treat in the evening."

"She ain't my gawdamn *daughter*!" Dell exploded, his face red as the stripes in the American flag. "Order yore fuckin' dessert so's we can git outta here," he added to Kee.

"Well, what *am* I, then? To yew?" Kee inquired when the waitress, pale as the banner's white stripes, had her order for dessert and left.

"Girl, I don't purely know thet," Dell hissed, his head tucked into his shoulders to the best of his physical ability. He clasped her hand in his, squeezed. "I jest knows what yore goin t'be—soon, *real soon*!" He let her hand go, snorted, sat straight with his arms akimbo. "And I knows yew ain't got the—the intes-tynes t'kill nobuddy on yore own— and don't tell me about how yew sat on yer daddy's lap whilst *I* choked him with the cord neither. That warn't really diddly squat!"

Kee felt her eyes fill with tears. "Don't everbody hafta start somewheres?"

Dell hesitated, nodded.

She leaned across the littered table to him. "Yew got a book—*the* book—an' I keep one, *my* book, sorta like a diary. It's in my suitcase. Well, I said in my book when I was on'y a baby girl how much I wants to close up all the eyes that stare at me

251

alla time? 'Cause I think dead eyes is more honest 'n ghost eyes are mebbe even better.'' Her eyebrows, light brown of color and still lighter of texture, raised. ''Remember when we was first together an' I said yew have nice eyes? I never wrote down what I really dream about, Dellie.'' Kee leaned back slightly but still sat as straight, as earnestly, as Dell. Her last napkin had missed a streak of vanilla shake on her upper lip and Dell, his gaze falling, saw that her chest was moving faintly with the passion of what she was telling him. ''Leastwise, I don't 'member puttin' it down. It's the *next dream* I got, Dellie. After *yew*.''

''Spill it,'' Dell grunted. He had one hand in his lap.

''I wants to leave a mark. To show I was here?'' Her remarkable blue eyes cleared themselves of memory long enough to flash fire at him. ''Yew won't laugh, will yew?''

''Prob'ly not,'' Dell said. He didn't laugh at anything much, and he was noticing that the assistant manager was switching off the lights in the front of the restaurant. A darker place always made Dell hornier.

''It all began with me gettin' my feller,'' Kee said, pausing for a dramatic but genuine swallow. ''Well, I kinda *got* him now, so I can truly think about fulfillin' my *other* dream.'' Her eyes were so bright he could have read by 'em. ''Okay, don't yew laugh—but I want to kill at least *two folks* in ever state of the union! Don't say nothin' yet, okay,'' she went on, waving one hand, ''let me finish. See, by jus' drivin' through our great nation and seein' the sights, all of them monuments 'n instatootions—and jus' takin' time out for the killin'—I figger they'd awmost add up by *theirselves*!" She drew in a quick but ragged breath. "Would that give folks somethin' to 'member lil' Kee for, Dellie, or is I gettin' too big for my britches?"

"I think it would," Dell replied slowly, judiciously, concealing his surprise—"but yew *can't* drive t'Hawaii. I ain't sure about Alaska, but them *are* two of the states." He watched her carefully, dubious about her sincerity.

"There's more of my dream," Kee added, then lowered her voice to a whisper. "Yew see, I got me a real *'pecific goal.*"

He went on appraising her in his methodical, nobody-knows-what-I'm-thinking fashion. He imagined she was sort-of making this up as she went, and withdrew his hand from his lap to study her. He sensed Kee had a need for him not to regard what she was saying as foolish and he preferred to be polite. "Having objectives is always smart."

"Well then," she blurted out the rest of it, "my goal is a *even hundred* people. Kilt." Dropping her gaze, she flushed still more deeply. "That mightn't seem like a truly wonnerful total to yew, as a real travelin' man." She giggled abruptly, thereby eliciting a warm maternal smile from the waitress who arrived with the pie. It had whipped cream on top and Kee's eyes lit up, seeing it. "But if we did it *t'gether*, a profeshnal like yew and a mere slip of a girl, why—yew 'n me might jus' go down in his'try!"

For a moment all Dell could do was gape at Kee, knowing now she was sincere and filled with a fine thrill of anticipation. Rarely if ever spontaneous, or rash, he scanned their meal check, then threw a twenty-dollar bill on the table and tried to think Kee's dream through.

First, going down *anywhere*, history or not, had been on Dell's obsessive mind so long now that their waitress was starting to look better to him by the minute. Second and right after *that* was the fact that something in what the girl had said kind of made his *mind* horny, like he'd felt when everything was sparkly new and full with promise. Right after he had murdered Dr. Lenora Middel.

For most of Dell's godforsaken life he'd waited for the television and the newspapers and the F.B.I. to take notice of his work and all he'd got for his troubles was to be stuck in some gawdamn prison. It seemed like every time he'd sat down with the other inmates to watch TV, there was some fucking Bundy or Dahmer or a fucking looney tune holed up in some store who got all the attention because the asshole used an automatic weapon, then blew his own stupid head off! Shitfire, you could drop an atomic bomb on a country, but what did *that* really prove?

And while he was studying Kee—poking that pie into her mouth as if she were a porker or something—Dell felt the old recollection of what Dr. Middel had said, about a man and a girl who'd done the things Kee wanted to do. Charles Starkweather and Caril something . . . Dell dredged the names up—Caril Ann Fugate. It happened in 1958, even if people did treat that gawdamn Manson as though he'd *invented* murder! Well, Charlie and Caril Ann had offed her mother and some other people including a kid, as Dell remembered, then taken off in a car—on a regular spree. The authorities shot a carbine at Charlie, busted his windshield, and made him surrender. . . .

But then Charlie had become cool again. "You've killed ten people," the cop said to Starkweather, who corrected him then. "Eleven," he said real fast.

To stall answering Kee, Dell sipped his now-lukewarm water and eyeballed the gal across from him.

Caril Ann Fugate had been fourteen.

"Yew like it, Dellie?" Kee asked sweetly, and definitely he knew what she meant. Finally finishing dining, she was applying her lipstick but not doing it very well. She was squinting into the mirror something ferocious and putting too much on. Then her eyes sought Dell's above the compact. "Yew want to go down in history with me?"

Dell sighed, tried not to picture how another female he'd known had put too much lipstick on, or where she'd blotted it. The fact was, he had been out of prison *days* now and he hadn't raped anyone. Only killed some people. This was harder to handle than Calbert, Emmitt, or Randy had been in jail—but he had to admit that old Dellie wasn't getting any younger.

Maybe it was time to take on a worthy successor, teach how to spot the vulnerables, how to take care of the legwork and plan ahead—share the sex and even the killing.

Maybe it was time to start sort of . . . settling down. Enjoying life more.

For now, though, Dell decided to change the subject. He wanted to *cogitate* (one of the newer words he'd found in *The Book*). It was right between "cogent," getting to a point (which he preferred), and "cognac," some kind of fancy French drink. He figured he was a natural-born cogitator. "We're gonna have t'rub out half the people in the en-tire nation jest t'keep yew in double cheeseburgers. Yew'll git hawg-fat."

"Uh-uh," Kee disagreed, shaking her head. She belched loudly. "Practic'ly the first thing I learned when I was tiny was how to use my mind over matters to lose weight. Jus' cause I *wanted* to! Now I know how to keep from gettin' any old pounds I don't want. I just' 'member alla time how purty I looks *this* way!"

"Yew're sayin yew was fat as a toddler?" Dell asked, staring at her bright red mouth.

"I *was!*" She swung her legs out, prepared to stand. "Fat as an ol' piggy." She stood, sashayed toward the assistant manager waiting to unlock the door again—then go home. He stifled a yawn. "I was so fat when I was jus' a babygirl," Kee called over her shoulder. "I was possalutely ugly!"

"Well, girl, I disb'live that," Dell said as he went to pay their check. "I purely do not b'lieve yew was *ever* fat or *piggy* or *ugly*. Not never."

"I might jus' be more magical than yew've found out yet," she replied, giving the assistant manager a huge wink before edging out into the night.

"I am countin' on thet bein' the pre-cise an' perfeck truth," Dell said, partly to himself, yanking the van door wide open.

This time, when Kee got in, he patted her rear end and told her to sit right up front in the seat next to his own.

Kee turned on the radio and was began punching buttons like crazy. "It's nighttime," he said, starting the motor. "The way I sees thangs, we still got time to put a little more of thet romantical shit into yore life before we got t'trade this here vehicle in."

"Prob'ly," she said, still fiddlin' with the radio. She turned around and looked at Dell, hard, when he was driving back out on the road. "Yew didden answer me about my idea an' hist'ry an' all."

"I tole you it did not sound bad."

She sat as close to him as she could get. Her snuggling bottom and roving hands made it seem suddenly that she was much closer. "But yew didn't say if yew's *in* it with me, Dellie—if we's goin' to the hist'ry books together."

Dell tried to grab the back of her head and push it down. Kee merely giggled and slid back on her seat. "Yew do thet again 'n we'll go to a fuckin' *ditch* together!" he growled, urgently searching for a suitable place to turn off the road and park.

"Dell," Kee pleaded, hand on his forearm, "pleeeeeease?"

"Mebbe." Dell mopped at his forehead and eyes, mostly for sweat this time. "Mebbe!" Music blasting from the radio made it harder to think.

"Dellie?" Kee called sweetly, and her tone of voice was just familiar enough now to make him turn his head and look at her.

She'd removed her jeans. She formed the one word *"Pleeeease?"* with her lips and slipped her bare feet up on the wide dashboard. The fingers of her right hand dipped between her legs. Dell braked, stopped on the shoulder of the road. Reached for her, avidly.

A strange male voice that was as unexpected as if its owner had popped out of the dash said, "We interrupt this program for a special news bulletin"—and even Dell froze. Kee heard mention of a town she'd never heard of—Fredericksburg—and a holdup at a pawnshop, and injuries to its owner, and several gunshots being fired at a parked car. Then there was something about a "youth" who had described a van—including its license number. Kee's mouth dropped open and remained that way.

Further reference was made to an "out-of-town police detective named Douglas" who "urged all citizens not to attempt to apprehend" the people in the van because it was "thought to be a stolen vehicle used in more serious crimes in Cherokee Rose."

By then, though, Dell was shouting and carrying on so loudly Kee couldn't hear the tag end of the bulletin. But what she saw in his face was more frightening than anything she'd heard so far. "Don't say *one word* 'bout my not killin' thet boy at the pawnshop! I saw yew open yore mouth, but *don't yew say it!*"

"I was on'y gonna say I guess this means we can't have sex till we've swapped this here van," she said prudently, and slithered between the seats in search of her jeans.

Dell fell into silence like half a mountain falling into a creek. Kee had turned off the radio before she climbed in back. It was like being in a tomb with something still alive that wouldn't announce itself. "I won't fail t'do the necessary again, girl," Dell said. His voice made her glance toward the rearview mirror. In it Dellie's face was . . . different. He didn't really look pissed and he didn't look horny, and he wasn't handsome to her as he'd been.

Yet he was even more the man of her dreams that instant than before, like *both* her big dreams were becoming one. "To hell with 'sweet reason,' we's a *team* now, girl—just like yew wanted. I'm as good as immortal now anyway." He laughed and hummed, scrubbed his long face with his hands. "I almost forgot the *phoenix*—of course, nobuddy knows 'bout that 'cept Lloyd B. 'n me." He winked at Kee in the rearview, muttered under his breath. "What yew said yew want is jest *full-time 'vi-carious sacrifices' anyways*—'n they will jest guarantee becomin' a phoenix for ol' Dell from hell in spades! Besides, I got enough magic now—'cause I got *yew*. An' I'll get *more*, too!"

She started to reach forward to hug him but held back for reasons she couldn't identify. "I know yew will, Dellie."

"But we *ain't* goin' down in hist'ry, Kee," he said, catching her eye again, blinking and winking, humming some and making the other noises deep in his throat, "'cause we ain't goin' *down* at all!" He edged the van out onto the road. "They purely cannot kill no *phoenixes*! We can do *anything!*"

Part III

SPREE

C H A P T E R 11

Autumn was falling all over the place and, from the standpoint of Kirk Douglas, it was like being chased into a cave by a bear, being unable to see, and discovering there was no other outlet from the damned hole in the mountain. Even then, he might have been able to figure out what to do—build a fire somehow, even wrestle with the animal if it followed him in. But Detective Douglas, and the way he felt in his imagined predicament, was not alone.

He had a girl with him who'd probably turned sixteen recently, and she was defenseless.

Whether the ubiquitous and endlessly mysterious, frustratingly fascinating "Dell" was the bear in Kirk's symbolic plight or the bear was played by autumn itself, each leaf that fell and every degree of temperature that dropped and did not quite climb back to its previous level represented to the detective his own failure.

Maybe the goddamned serial killer (and that was what Dell was, now; every law enforcement officer who kept up at all was aware of it) didn't even know it yet himself, but he'd find something out all too soon for Kirk: Madmen who drove around in a procession of stolen vehicles, behaved as if they'd never heard of homes before, and took their prey off the roads or slaughtered them in towns they were passing through, *ran out of victims* when cold weather arrived. It drove the innocent people into their homes.

Which meant (in Kirk Douglas's experience) that human wild beasts were apt to go to ground—lay low, hide, seek shelter, seethe as much as the police seethed who were pursuing them—and wait for better weather.

The thought that turned every decent cop's soul on its side and made them try very hard to keep it from returning was that some killers just couldn't *wait* for warm weather, and therefore began to attack their landladies or pick-up lovers, so-called "friends," even their underworld contacts. When that happened—when that *tragedy occurred*, Kirk corrected himself—law enforcement got an unexpected shot at bringing the pricks to justice.

Picking up the trail had been so easy that Kirk's well-worn mental pocket of paranoia had, at first, distrusted the evidence. Dell left his damned fingerprints on everything as if it was a dirty glass; evidence based on another fact was that the creep had never petitioned the courts to have his juvenile record destroyed, so tracing his prints and getting a make on the sack of shit was easy as pie. Douglas now knew that Dell had actually gassed up before departing Cherokee Rose—where the girl Kee had been glimpsed alive—then headed toward Tennessee by a route that took them through both South and North Carolina. Getting help from police in other cities and states had been a formality for Douglas to observe; they'd all been cooperative when Kirk explained the nature of his pursuit. But to other homicide detectives, it seemed that Dell had a particular destination in mind. Or that he was painstakingly trying to shake them off.

Because Douglas had run into a couple of other serial types during his career, he gravely doubted that either viewpoint was right, even though he didn't voice his views. He believed *one of three* circumstances explained the bastard's route, seemingly random tour of America, as fall arrived:

1. Dell was blindingly stupid, possibly psychopathic, and simply preferred to drive aimlessly around, stealing automobiles and other vehicles, then snuffing out human life because he was com-

pelled to do it—and probably didn't remember much of it because he was too mad to do so;

2. Dell was a cunning sociopath who, in spite of his lack of education was amazingly shrewd and possibly intuitively brilliant in knowing where and when it was safe to strike. He killed not just because it eliminated witnesses, but because he had a perpetual hard-on against the human race; he was a hater, probably of everybody he could not perceive as possessing a few qualities similar to his own (meaning that the opposite sex, gays, blacks, Hispanics, and Asians were instinctively anathema to him). And once he got into a routine of *taking* life, it would be hard for him to find any other pleasures as fulfilling or as exciting as the stalking/killing process, or as satisfying in supplying a trophy;

3. There were facts he, Kirk Douglas, had not yet gathered or perceived which somehow *combined* elements of the first two theories—perhaps one *bridging factor* that might involve Dell's past or present associates, his view of himself, his own beliefs (or aberrations), or his own odd appetites—something *new* or *extra* that was currently motivating him.

Pattern Number 3 didn't surface until six weeks after Douglas had begun his investigation. He'd switched almost hourly between Number 1 and Number 2 and hadn't even devised Number 3 until it began to appear that Dell's pattern was changing. Or, more precisely, had been moderated, then slightly redirected, and finally kicked into horrifying high gear.

Though the son-of-a-bitch had gone on a devastating localized murder spree after his last parole—he'd been seen in the neighborhood, tentatively identified from mugshots—he'd reined it in for a while after that. Neither the pawnshop operator whom Dell robbed nor the sailor on shore leave whose automobile tires he'd shot out had been killed. The sailor had not only provided a positive I.D. but had supplied the license number of the stolen vehicle. To Douglas that implied Dell's temporary restraint; in turn, that ruled out most psychopathic qualities the detective had studied, because it eliminated obsessive compulsion in the familiar surroundings in which a psycho was most likely to go off. Maybe Dell heard about the sailor on TV or the radio and it had just pissed him off.

Douglas headed slightly northeast from Cincinnati toward Columbus, wondering why the vicious cocksucker was venturing in August, last month, from Kentucky into the Midwest.

It's almost like our Dell had other things on his mind, in Fredericksburg, Kirk thought, *a real, solid reason for wanting the money he boosted from the pawnshop. . . . as if he'd been diverted or even "gentled"—in some unknown way.*

After that, Christ, the monster had been diverted by nothing; he'd turned savage, brutal beyond belief. He'd veered from the pointless dumb acts of vehicular theft and rape—in which he was just as likely to let the woman go or drive her home as he was to murder her—to the deft crimes that were not only unfailingly fatal but so successful in their violent execution that Kirk had the impression Dell had become psychic. "Dell" suddenly seemed gifted with some weird sixth sense that enabled him to make his strike almost whenever and wherever he pleased, then permitted him to clear out before any local authorities could get a fix on him!

Worse, the public was beginning to get the same idea, fearing this useless piece of ostensibly human wreckage as infallible—and quite a bit worse than that, as some variety of *natural force.* He had seen that happen before once or twice, but usually the perpetrator had done his dirty work in a single state or, at most, within a certain region of the nation. "Dell from Hell" was what folks were starting to call him thanks to the media, and Kirk detested press tactics like that nearly as much as he detested the puke-bag himself. The chance of glorifying such scum when he himself had dealt with a few of the creeps one-on-one and seen how insignificant they were when they were captured and their weapons were taken from them infuriated Kirk. Celebrity fed confidence to the serial killer, and that could make law enforcement people reckless—especially at times when *they* were depicted as the ignorant country bumpkins.

He found that he kept thinking of his own daughter, worrying about the kind of a world young Annie would inherit after the bad guys had received all the good press for twenty or thirty years. He'd decided he would stay on the case even now, with the feds entering the picture because Dell had been crossing state lines. He had no choice. The only thing Douglas knew that was sicker than Dell's slaughter was the way the bastard's kind emitted an attractiveness of evil to people watching TV or reading news headlines. The evil itself tended to become glossed over when decent folks couldn't see the ruination and wreckage or hear the heart-rending stories of loss from the victims' loved ones. Somehow, he felt, the uninvolved but otherwise good people were inclined to *identify with* the soulless nonentities—infamous trash, not famous!—maybe as if they were acknowledging their own lack of importance.

Rumors abounded now that young Kee McCaulter was still alive and, according to completely unsubstantiated reports, was actually participating with Dell. Kirk also knew now that it had taken two people to kill the girl's parents—but that *didn't* have to mean that Kee was one of the two. After all, Dell could have enlisted the aid of a second man—a local, maybe, gone on his way since then or even taken out by Dell. He also knew about the Stockholm syndrome: Normal folks, trying to get along with their kidnappers to survive, began to side with the very slime that had stolen their freedom from them.

To Kirk Douglas, Dell was no natural goddamned force, he was no freaking psychic, and he was definitely not an infallible criminal. He was not literally "Dell from Hell"; he was not any fucking Antichrist! But if Detective K. Douglas had anything to say about it, Mister Dell would wind up being right in one way. For when Kirk caught up with the sociopathic woman-battering weasel, he'd be "Dell *in* Hell"!

Departing the Carolinas through Lenoir into Tennessee for a while, then driving to parts of Virginia, Kentucky, and the southeastern tip of Ohio, Dell kept them on the move. He wanted to see a bit of Indiana, too, before heading west to southern California—"to winter."

It was during that stretch of driving—in so many different cars and trucks and whatnot that Kee didn't even try to remember which vehicle they used at any particular time—that her Dellie kept his word to her, and she began to keep count—

And kept a nice, honest record of the accumulated dead meant to add up eventually to an even one hundred kills. One hundred sets of staring eyes that'd be closed forever.

At first Dell would *not* include any of the folks he had killed before their romance started. "They're mine, gawdamnit," was his first objection. "Yew didn't have nothin' t'do with them ones I got—sheee-it, yew wasn't even *born* when I offed the ugly dwarf sighchiatrist!"

But his objection set Kee to thinking, and she was ready for Dell the next time she brought it up and he told her, "I didn't even know yew yet whilst I was on my leetle spree in thet fancy-Dan neighborhood." Kee reminded him promptly that the reason he had gone on it at all was just *partly* because his dictionary had suggested he get sacrifices to "suffer properly for another," meaning Dell. It truly was not, she swore to him, only because he was experimenting with his new magic.

"It wasn't, huh?" he said, extremely dubious. "Well, whut *was* it, then?"

"It was *my* ex-perimentin'," Kee answered real fast. "My dreams, my visions, my—my *summonin'* yew to come be my white knight and save me!"

"Bull crap an' balls," he said instantly.

"*Why* then did yew drive straight to teensy ole Cherokee Rose, Georgia, 'steada goin' someplace else? Huh? Why *else* would yew go straight to where I was jus' *waitin'* in the Second Cherokee Rose Baptist Church parkin' lot for yew to show up? Huh? *Huh*, Dellie, *huh?*"

And though Dell stalled and fumed and got even meaner to the next sumbitch on the road who got in his way, he had no answer at *all* for her question until he'd looked into *The Book* and found, almost by chance, the word *dualism*. He told Kee about it, how it meant being "of two," and an idea "based on a twofold distinction." Well, somehow that meant something to Dellie, and he too seemed to know right *then* how the two of them was Meant to Be, because of how she'd known before she ever saw him what he looked like.

"'Destiny,'" Dell intoned from memory. "A 'seemingly in-evi-table suc-cession of events.'" And Kee told him right back, "Yew mean fate," and he nodded.

On such tiny gobs of shit as those was a lasting relationship born, Kee decided. Now Dellie knew she was every tad as magical as he was—even if her magic might be littler.

Kee felt convinced that she had to persuade Dell she was justified in counting the six folks he killed in the rich-bitch place in their joint total. The best way seemed to her to accept the task of killin' at least six people herself just as soon as possible—for starters. Dellie'd see then that she *could* have kilt 'em before they met.

When they got to some town just into South Carolina and were ready to make their vehicle trade-in, Kee decided it wasn't really offing anyone that was causing her breath to come extra fast and makin' her feel as if she might wet her panties, it was at least three other things: How *eye-deelistic* her Dellie was in what he expected of partners, so she was pretty afraid he might decide to kill her if she messed up; how full of *principles* Dell was, so she truly didn't *want* to let him down; and how plumb *excited* it made her feel on'y to know she was getting a chance to *do* somebody, *be* somebody! She knew it was the era of women's lib and all, but *her* career path was a mite harder than making it to the vice-presidency of a company.

She would have her chance to start proving herself in the town on the South Carolina–Georgia border that night.

Dell had been the one to see a car parked maybe twenty or thirty yards into the dirt road. The driver'd left the car door open a teeny bit and Dell saw a dim red light and backed up till the van could enter the road, then turned in.

Kee understood that what Dell mainly wanted was to make the swap, but she'd seen the same thing going on that he had: There were lovers in the car, making out. One of them was probably a girl. Kee's heart was making sounds like firecrackers and she told it to keep still while she was gettin' something she'd brought from home out of her suitcase.

Dell flashed the headlights as he pulled around in front of the car as if he was a cop and Kee giggled at that. She felt more relaxed because she didn't think cops drove vans a lot, so the lovers must really be going at it. Then Dell stopped, got out with the motor running, and went stomping over to the driver's side of the little car.

Kee got out her door and crept to the *other* side of the car. She caught Dellie's good eye, winked, and tore the passenger door open.

Kee watched a blond-haired woman rise up from the man's lap and ask, "What the hell?" Kee saw his thang, too, but she was so busy trying to justify herself to her fella that she didn't look at it long. "Shut yore mouth for a change," Kee ordered the blonde, "and sit up nice 'n straight. Keep lookin' at your man. His face."

Spellbound and silent for one of the few times since he met Dr. Middel, Dell just watched as Kee produced a paring knife, and holding it underhand but clearly meaning business, slipped her arm quietly into the car, on her side. Then with the blonde's back to her, Kee stuck the tip of the knife into her neck—far enough to draw a decent stream of blood!

The blonde yelped but went on dutifully facing her trembling date. "Whut the hell're yew *doin'?*" Dell demanded of Kee.

Kee answered him by flashing a grin and showing him the Magnum in her other hand. She'd brought both weapons from the van. "Acceptin' my share of the re-sponsabilities, Dellie," Kee said, keeping the point of the paring knife pricking against the blonde's throat. "Would yew make that feller git out, please, Dell?"

Both the driver of the car with his exposed but currently shriveled privates and Dell stared at the girl. "*I* does this part of the work, Kee," Dell called from his side. "Whut's got into yew?"

Kee raised the Magnum wobblingly, centered it more or less on the terrified man at the wheel. Everything in her warped little fifteen-year-old mind shouted that this was the pivotal moment of their entire relationship, that something terribly awfully important was comin' down right then. "Yew said we's a team, Dellie. Yew *agreed.*" She swallowed hard, felt cold sweat sting her eyes. "Yew gonna trust me and have him get out, or not?"

Dell looked at her hard with his eye blinking and his face in shadows except for the upper part of his long head. She heard him hummin', and mutterin', taking what felt like whole nights and days before he reached his decision. Between them, two human beings whose lives were being changed forever also waited; but neither man nor woman knew how they should hope it turned out.

Dell, his decision abruptly reached, put both his

big hands on the automobile's owner and dragged him out onto the ground.

And then he stepped back, smirking to himself, and folded his arms over his chest. A startled Kee caught a glimpse of his good eye and Dellie reminded her of an ol' owl, wise as Solomon, just waiting to see her next move. Already the driver was getting to his feet while Dell grinned and made no move to prevent the fellow from getting away.

Kee put a single bullet through the man's left ear at just the instant he churned his legs and started to run. From where Kee stood with one forearm resting on top of the car, he seemed to sort of disappear—exactly the say she'd always longed for her folks and so many others in Cherokee Rose to vanish from the earth.

"Be damned," Dell said, not without admiration.

"I'm a farm girl, Dellie," Kee explained, stooping to poke the point of the paring knife back into the hysterically crying woman. Kee had just enough control left not to kill her. "Daddy, he taught me all about guns in the good ole days."

Dell shook his head. Not much of the other man's head had showed above the car. The girl could have shot her mom a whole lot better than he had, if she'd cottoned to.

"Git in, Dellie," Kee said. "Go ahead." Holding the knife horizontally to the weeping blond woman's throat, she jerked her by the hair violently enough to provoke a new scream of pain. Dell was doing what Kee asked and she met his gaze in order to give him her biggest, proudest smile. But she also glanced down into the face of the bloodied woman whose hair she was pulling. "Dell," Kee announced, loudly enough for him to get the full impact of her news, "yew're takin' the place of the feller I shot!"

He gaped openly at Kee, sort of studied her to make sure he properly understood what she was suggesting. Then his shark's smile was back, he was sliding under the wheel and edging nearer to the blonde Kee was threatening. "If yew isn't the most corn-siderate gal I ever did see!" he praised her, reaching for the woman.

"The way I sees things," Kee said, jabbing at her captive again and poking in the direction of Dell's crotch with the barrel of the Magnum, "partners take care of each other. Sorry about the way her neck's bloodin." The blonde began making some new noises but Kee saw she had gotten the hang of it and knew her Dellie wouldn't mind such sounds too much. "My time of the month's come but I didn't want t'disappoint yew completely."

Dell grunted, "I'll return yore gen'rous favor soon's possible."

Kee fiddled with the passenger door. "It *is* what yew need, what yew wants, ain't it?" she asked.

But Dell didn't reply this time, so Kee closed the door as quietly as she could, then paused one more moment to stare through the window. She only watched the expression in her man's eyes, the way they were squeezed tightly together. "I'll jus' be out here, awright?" Kee retreated from the door, hesitated again at the rear of the car. "Take yore time,

Dellie. And—and honk the horn when yew wants me ag'in. Awright?''

"Awright!" Dell exclaimed. He reached behind him to slam the door on the driver's side. *"Awright!"*

It got quiet in the night then unless Kee wanted to listen to the sounds Dell and the blonde were making. She didn't, so she continued backing away for another several feet, still smiling but not meaning it as much.

And when Kee was far enough from the automobile they were taking that the red taillights looked like ground level demon eyes beaming at Kee without blinking, she sighed and wandered into the woods. She had personal business—*her* business—to handle in the next ten or fifteen minutes. The first thing involved a treasured souvenir her dead mama'd given her, a brightly-colored permanent tampon box. Kee extracted from, and used, the last of its contents.

Returning to the point at which she could again see the winking demon eyes, Kee had the Magnum and the knife in the waist of her jeans and had to move carefully to avoid being shot or stabbed. Her motion was deliberate and intensely quiet, too, as she approached the man she had shot. He hadn't fallen far from the car and Kee didn't want to bother her Dellie.

Kneeling in the grass and weeds—*quiet as any mousy, Kee,* she ordered herself—she pulled the paring knife from her waistband and finally inspected the dead guy.

The rim of the ear her bullet had passed through

was still there, mostly. Curious, Kee used two fingers under his hairline—the body lay face down—to raise the head slightly and peek. That side of the fella's face was sure a big mess, Kee noticed. Maybe the Magnum bullet had got itself snagged on the inside of his nose or something because he just had one eye, now. It was only the one Kee had seen first that could look at her the way she preferred to be seen, which wasn't much at all.

Kee stared half the length of the dead guy and nodded. Like she had thought, he'd never had the chance to zip up. *My first soo-vaneer,* Kee mused, beginning her work by moonlight. *My very own first.*

But it was a lot more, she reminded herself as she sawed. *Dellie and me can't count worth piss an' we posalutely* have *to know how many people we've kilt.* How else could they know how many more they needed for the even hundred?

Besides, Dell didn't cater to guesswork and he liked mistakes much less than that. *This* way, with souvenirs, she could just pull 'em out and count up any old time, and Dellie wouldn't get mad so often.

The new idea of making her feller give her a penny for every killin' occurred to Kee as a double-check before she finished cuttin' and walked over to their new ve-hicle—and it was a practical way to save money, also. Mama'd be proud of her! She could keep the pennies in the tampon box, too—just to *honor* her poor mama.

The jolting sound of the horn being suddenly tootled made Kee keep her arm and hand hanging at her side. "Yew done?" she asked, looking through Dell's window.

He said nothing and appeared tired to the girl but he was grinning. The woman had her hankie up to her face like she might be blowing her nose. Kee put her own head, shoulders, and arms through the window as if she was going to kiss Dell, but she wasn't.

She had the paring knife in her hand as she reached around him.

"That's *two!*" Kee cried as she wriggled back out of the window, clutching something roughly two inches in length and dripping red between her fingers. The blond woman collapsed against the dashboard, the base of her fingers on both hands pressed to her face and shrieking as her soaked handkerchief seemed to turn to flame, but Kee didn't think she would scream for long. "I need four to tie, now—or eight total. Right?"

Dell reached past the dying woman, wrestled with the door till it popped open, and shoved the body out. "Yew did good, girl, but yew got t'think ahead," he growled. "We would not wish to git too large a quantity of blood all over our new ve-hicle."

Those events, though, were back when it was still spring. Finding the sporty car had reminded Dell of the Jaguar he had once except it wasn't nearly as fast through the gears and definitely would not corner like the Jag, so Dell decided quickly to make another change.

They wound up making three more trade-ins that same night.

How they swapped one—a three-quarter pickup Kee'd been partial to (Dell, however, claimed that only blue collar workers drove such vehicles)—seemed to her to be one for their memory book.

Aware that he wanted shunt of the truck, Kee was the one to spot yet another van parked off to the side of the road while a man was inside a public phone booth, making a call. Instantly, remembering Dellie's fondness of the van he'd driven when they first met, Kee had a great idea—and they were still far enough away from both the van and the phone book when inspiration occurred to the girl.

"Yew hate this ol' pickup," Kee said from the captain's seat. She pointed straight to the phone booth as the truck ate up yards. "Why not jus' cream it?"

Dell gave her an immediate appreciative smile. "If I hit 'er dead on," he allowed, clearing his throat, "it could kill us."

"But it might not," Kee replied, bouncing on the seat with a sense of urgency. "It's mostly glass—I *think.*"

"Well, what the fuck?" The corners of Dellie's mouth turned up even more. "Mebbe I can sorter . . . *clip* it!" And then he tapped the accelerator after glancing around for other traffic but not seeing much because they were miles from a city and it was raining. "Hard enough, leastwise, t'git the phone caller—"

"Or pin him inside!" Kee finished gleefully, clapping her palms hard.

And that's what they did.

The sound of the crash alone was enough to break the mood of boredom Kee had felt for a few hours—and Dellie managed to hit the pay phone so hard that money just *flied* out of it, went shootin' up in the air like shiny fireworks!

Kee ran arown on the rainy road and in the grass beside it picking up coins while Dell made sure the man in what was left of the phone booth was dead. Then he checked out the van. "Looks like we got us a winner!" he called to Kee.

"Sure have," she answered, adding up the change before transferring her stuff to the van. "If I can count *him*, I done caught up with yew, Dellie—he's my six an' *we're* awmost up to a dozen together!"

"Go ahead," Dellie told her that night, "take him." He was having a fun time futzing with the different shit in their newest vehicle.

Which had made it the natural time for Kee to tell Dell (when they were on the road again) about the souvenirs she'd been collecting since the lover-boy in the sporty car. And where she'd been keeping them. And how convenient it was for keeping count up to her magic hundred.

"Yew're putting *parts* in the *cooler*? The ice chest?" Dell got so worked up he nearly piled up that van he liked so much. "We started out t'keep *milk* and *soft drinks*—and *beer*, in case we git any *real* company in here!"

"Don't yew stew about it," Kee said smoothly, "I'll accept the re-sponsability for changin' the ice whenever we stops to fill up." She had paused, pressed her lips with her fingertips. "Mama always taught me to be clean an' po-lite—jus' like your mama!"

Dell laughed out loud over that and it was like a page was turned in a book, another chapter begun, because he quit complaining about most things for the rest of the summer. Little by little Kee saw the man of her dreams get more contented, more like a husband, she believed. There were lots and lots of hitchhikers and many of them were female. To keep her "fella" happy, whenever Dellie spotted a woman he took a fancy to, Kee was right there to give him a helping hand.

There was a day when it was raining some and the sky was becoming as black as Dell's old, dark moods, and he and Kee saw a lady in a skimpy top and really tight, fire-engine-red shorts thumbing a ride from beneath a tree. Right off Kee saw Dell's eyes hone in on the lady's ta-tas, as if he hoped to see clear through her thin top, and Kee knew for a fact he was horny for her.

So when Dellie slowed down, it was Kee who leaned out a window to call to the redhead: "My daddy says yew shouldn't git near no trees when a storm is comin' up, ma'am. Yew want a lift with us? For safety?"

She peered with passing caution at the teen-ager, then took two slow steps forward. "Look at those leetle beauties," Dell said, under his breath. He was right, Kee realized; her nipples were out-lined clearly through the rain-dampened cloth.

Until then the van had been idling along. The

woman peered in as it came to a full stop. She had enough phony red hair to stuff a mattress but her big blues looked scared to Kee, as if she didn't hitch often. "I could use some help," she admitted hesitantly. "Is it just you and your daddy, honey?"

"Yes, ma'am," Kee said while Dell slid the van door open. "Mama couldn't make it on this trip 'cause she was feelin' sickly."

"Hop in," Dell said in a tone of friendly good humor. "Where y'bound?"

The redhead slipped passed the seat next to him into the back of the van with Kee. She told Dellie the name of a town but Kee reckoned he didn't catch it either; but he said, easily, "Thet's where we're bound, too."

Then, though he pulled the door closed, Dellie didn't put the van into gear. He was looking up the road to a cutoff that probably led to a farmer's house.

The rain came with a vengeance. It flooded the van windows, a deluge, yet Dell didn't turn on the wipers. In the rearview mirror, Dell slowly nodded his head to Kee. Then he edged the van forward, barely creeping, and Kee knew he was going to turn in at the farmer's driveway while she distracted the red-haired lady.

"Yew pore thing," Kee murmured, touching the woman's arm, "yew're flat-out *soaked*. Here, put my blouse on. We're 'bout the same size. I'm nice 'n dry."

And Kee undid the buttons of her shirt and was

out of it before the older woman could protest. She held the shirt out invitingly.

The redheaded lady glanced toward Dell, startled, but he was leaning forward over the wheel, wipers still off, squinting through the downpour as if the wipers simply didn't work.

"Don't yew look, Daddy," Kee called merrily. "This lady's gonna wear my blouse till we gets to our destination. Yew and Mama always told me to be—what's that 'H' word?"

"Hospitable," Dell said, staring straight ahead. "So-li-citous to one's guests."

The redheaded lady had her skimpy top off at just about the second Dellie made a right on the road leading to the farmhouse . . .

And his eyes, good and bad, were beaming into the rearview mirror at the woman's naked ta-tas at the same instant he both braked and switched on the windshield wipers. He looked so starved for her even Kee was dimly surprised.

Kee blocked the lady's escape through the door nearest to them, and Dell threw out an arm like the branch of an oak tree to stop her on his side.

Then, trying to retrieve her discarded top or Kee's shirt, she was squeezing between the seats, rushing for the rear door of the van.

As it came open and the redhead was ready to jump out and run, Dell was there waitin'. Before she could think what to do, he reached up, hooked his strong fingers in the red shorts that almost matched her hair color, and ripped them off.

From her position on the captain's seat, Kee

saw the tattoo on the lady's right buttock: MIKE'S PROPERTY, it read. And like any good souvenir hunter or collector, Kee knew what she craved for her cooler the second she saw it.

Dell was looking straight ahead and Kee noticed one corner of his mouth was kind of wet, as if it was leakin'. He followed the redhead back into the van unhurriedly as she retreated—until she saw that Kee was aiming the ol' Magnum at her head. Then the lady kind of tried to disappear, Kee thought, but it didn't work. Dell had one hand on her ankle, another on her other calf (as she sorta slid down onto the floor), and his first hand was up higher on her.

"'Intercourse,'" Dell said, kneeling and pulling his pants down. "'Noun. Communication or dealings between people, countries, et cetera.' I wish t'commence dealin' with *yew*, ma'am."

That was just about when the lady started screaming, and Kee got to watch. She was interested as hell in what her Dellie did. She knew he'd tell her to get lost if he wanted that.

"The male North American duck has a red head," Dellie said while he laid over her, then screwed his thumbs under her jaws till the lady's tongue popped out. "So do I, sometimes. But yore hair color's a fake."

Kee saw just how he did both things—screwed her and kilt her—remained there till the time when Dellie was really getting kind of red in his face, and he looked up over the lady's head—straight at

Kee—with both his eyes awmost comin' outta their sockets.

Then he gave Kee a big, big smile.

So she hopped out of the van awhile t'play in the rain.

Leavin' her shoes on, 'cause the farmer's house was boarded up and the porch was rickety and she didn't want t'git splinters in her feet, she took her bra an' the rest of her clothes off and did a purty little dance all arown the old farmhouse while the rain showered her face and she giggled like a teeny chile.

Well, they had lotsa laughs that summer. Sometimes they picked up male hitchers too because Kee enjoyed taunting and touching them till they thought they were going to get something they weren't. Because she hadn't wanted to have what she thought of as their "love juices" all over her and she still intended to save herself for Dell—if they ever found the right place and time—Kee simply wound up killing them. Anytime she needed help, Dell was there of course, but mostly Kee just signaled to Dell when the men hitchers were too worked up and excited by her to know what was happening to them and she couldn't get her knife out safely.

An exception was a brightly sun-lit morning when Kee just about had a fella where she wanted him and Dell—out of the blue—slammed on the brakes, then got out from behind the wheel and yanked open the door next to Kee's overtly aroused victim before Kee knew what was going on. "Get out!" he told the hitcher, a big man with long hair to his shoulders and a guitar he'd been carrying lying at his feet.

"What the fuck's the matter with you, man?" the fella asked, slowly doing what he was told. But he didn't seem that scared of Dell. "The little lady and I've been makin' out for miles. I don't see why—"

"Shut up!" Dell snapped, reaching in and removing the big guy's guitar. "He's *number fifty*," Dell told Kee. "I counted 'em up after the last one."

"Well, that's jus' fine, Dellie," she drawled, pushing her skirt down. She added in a stage whisper, "But I don't rightly think we oughter *ad*vertise it. Besides, I don't need yore help with my friend Brucie—don't yew think he looks like Bruce Springsteen with long yeller hair?"

The hitchhiker, hands fisted and pressed against his waist, asked, "What the fuck's coming down?"

"Yore gittar," Dell answered him, bringing the guitar over his own head and smashing it full on the pate of the other.

The man dropped to the dirt at the edge of the road, bleeding from his ears and dazedly shaking his head.

"It's *The Book*," Dell told Kee, casting aside the remnant of the instrument and pulling his dictionary from his hip pocket. "Now, everybody knows fifty is 'five times ten'—but right *under* 'fifty' in *The Book* is 'fifty-fifty,' which means 'even' or 'equal.' But *yew* been killin' most of the folks we pick up." His homely face was the picture of earnestness. "I got t'do my part in shootin' for a even hunderd—or mebbe it *won't count!* Mebbe it won't make me a true phoenix if *I* don't off close to half of 'em, personal like."

Kee almost protested, asked for an explanation she could understand.

Before she could speak, Dell was stooping to the man with long hair, slapping his face a few times to help him clear his head.

When it was cleared and the hitchhiker was getting mad, trying to rise, Dell wrapped his big hands around the man's throat, his powerful thumbs virtually punching holes on either side of the fellow's Adam's apple. Resigned, Kee jumped out to move to where she could see both "Brucie" and her Dellie clearly. The former was tryin' to fight back, to stand. The latter was humming his tuneless song as he planted his feet better, in order to dig in.

"Lookit his *eyes*," Kee whispered marvelingly. "They awmost pop out!" With an appreciative giggle, she stretched her head forward to kiss Dell's cheek. "We kin see the death come straight into 'em *together*, Dellie."

They did, too. And Kee still had her post-kill surgery to perform for her own fun.

There were also some big horse laughs that summer when Kee and Dell heard the name of the detective chasing her feller. (Douglas never did mention her, showing Kee just how unfair the ol' world was to pore womenfolk.) Right away, Dell had to buy some newspapers to see a photograph of a cop called "Kirk Douglas."

And then when he found the picture—Douglas was standing next to some other officers—Dell truly *did* fall down laughing. "He looks like he's their leetle boy!" he said, slapping Kee on the shoulder and back so hard she found bruises later. "*He's* the main one of all the aw-thorities sayin' they ex-pect to ap-pre-hend me '*imminently*'?"

Kee had to put off her own laughing till the next day because she hurt so much, but she sure did understand Dell's hilarity. Douglas-the-cop didn't even look as big and strong as Daddy had looked before he got the syph.

As the days became weeks, then months, Dell's moods continued to level of to a purty steady agree-ableness even if Kee noticed times when he just drove without hardly moving an inch and wouldn't let her hear the Top Forty on the radio and almost seemed as if he didn't need another soul in the whole world, even her. But she got accustomed to that and looked at the sights or napped or messed with stuff from her suitcase, like the blessed gift from her poor dead mama, which had a nice flower on it. Dellie liked hearing the news most of the time because it got to be what he called "even money" that they'd be yakkin' about him during the news-cast. He especially liked it when they called him "Dell from Hell."

Once, while it didn't make Dell pissed or any-thing, there was a mention of him along with Lloyd B., the negro he enjoyed talkin' about, getting paroled because he was old or sick or something. Kee had been drowsy and didn't catch all of that but Dellie, he got truly serious looking—right before he switched the radio off and got all quiet. Kee wasn't sure what that was about.

Otherwise, the rest of summer passed with certain occasions of excitement and delight for the now-sixteen-year-old Kee McCaulter that shoved boredom so far into the past she was gradually forgetting that she knew she wouldn't forget about her parents completely if she lived to be a hundred.

Right up to the moment when Dell decided to detour to Indiana and things got kind of ass-backwards, she'd almost thought she might.

CHAPTER

12

A low-hung van trundled over the flat American midsection east to west at a pace as calculatingly maundering as an oversexed tailor's measuring tape. That matched the driver's unrushed, unconscious level, where Dell was most confidently himself and where, mainly, he still lived.

Anyone observing the rusted-out vehicle for long—and close to Labor Day, there were still miles of hitchhikers like eyelets in an outflung cordovan belt—would have discerned two dissimilar facts:

The old gray van and its pair of occupants did not seem to be headed anywhere in particular, yet something about their doggedly maintained rate of speed suggested purpose.

Even when the rather cockeyed driver doubled back as they'd done for the female last weekend, yesterday for the male in Lima, no time had been wasted getting the hitchhikers inside. Efficiency, methodology, and purpose were still Dell's operational bywords and he seldom allowed anything to move ahead of them in his deeply-felt hierarchy of complex values.

Kee remained on the van's patched-up captain's seat unless they were stopping to pick somebody up. She kept a narrow container with a latch and a gardenia stenciled on it beside her. Sixteen now, she was pretty in an unexceptional way; it depended upon whether she moved hotly in sunstream or was washed weary by the fluorescence of the purposefully unpopular midnight diners where they stopped now, but sometimes she didn't look as though puberty was cold yesterday's big thrill.

Their methodology with hitchhikers worked this way: When males were invited into their world, Dell reached across to open the door and inclined his head toward the seats behind him, and Kee. None had objected so far. The few thumbing females were offered the seat beside Dell and, if they glimpsed the girl in the back at all, she seemed half asleep—sprawled across the captain's chairs, bare knees tucked foetally to her slight bosom. Kee always looked about fourteen or so on those occasions.

"Nighttime shore does come on early up here," Kee said one evening. Her sigh was drawn out, long-suffering.

"We's near the au*tum*nal equinox," said Dell. He did not look back or cock his head, but he spoke with his increasing, greater clarity. "Days *is* gettin' shorter."

"Dellie, yew want a brew?" Kee wiggled around till her unclad legs—rather too long for her overall height—could straddle the wide, capacious cooler between the seats.

"A'course, I don't want to brew.'" Dell's hands spasmed on the steering wheel, but he went on looking straight ahead. He switched on the low beams despite the fact that there was no need as yet, trying to make his bad eye focus along with his good one. "Why in the world would I de-sire t'boil, t'ferment?"

Kee kicked her heels against the cooler, laughed loudly. "Yew are so *smart*, Dell—honest to God!'

"Man who don't know his own language 'n how t'*employ* it proper is a gawdamn fool unfit for life." He patted the inside pocket of a new jacket he'd picked up, keepin' *The Book of Webster's* close to his heart again. "Man who knows it, though, rises above the herd like a eagle."

"Ain't that the pure truth?" Kee scratched her bare left knee, yawned. She'd learned how he absolutely loved that book eons ago now. "Well, can I have one, Dell? Dellie?"

"Not yet, Kee. Not till I pro-*claim* yew can."

She started to sag sullenly back on her set and had already folded her arms across her lightweight turquoise sweater, but she stopped. Some note in his voice was truly familiar. "Yew stoppin'." Snatching up the container with the gardenia, she jiggled it in her lap, laughed. "Yew *are*, right?"

His head nodded with enormous solemnity. The longer she knew him, the more she got used to how her Dellie looked, and she liked it. His hair was more mouse-brown than she'd noticed right off and his ears were set out from his big head, if yew saw him from behind. She'd also realized his neck got pink during situations such as this.

"It's time ag'in," he said.

Seconds passed, and . . . "See *him*," Dell commanded, his voice raised though he wasn't pointing.

Leaning forward, Kee saw a male figure with his back to them walking nice and slow by the right side of the road. Now it was dusk; shadows from distant trees moved ahead of them up the highway and the young man taking clearer form in Dell's low beam seemed momentarily nude. "Ooooh," Kee breathed. "He's cute."

"Yew got him," said Dell, tooting the unobtrusive horn of the latest van.

Shirtless, wearing cut-off jeans, the youth's long arms dangling at his sides, he had a gallon gas can in one hand and his drooping tanktop hanging from the other. He'd been sweating. He looked drawn into himself, mad; it took a second toot to get his attention.

Then Dellie was easing onto the berm two yards ahead of the boy, and he began loping lightly after 'em, Nike-clad feet kicking up white dust clouds, face relieved and jubilant. Dell had found he liked this part a whole lot.

"He's *real* cute," Kee breathed.

Dell, reaching over to open the door, greeted him. "Climb right in back, partner," he said with a grin. His drifting left eye was just partly visible at that angle and his thumb flick was a directional signal for the boy.

He got in next to Kee just as Dell slammed the right front door. Not gunning it, he pulled back on the highway, quick. This was the old road, he'd seen. To the east a multi-lane monster roared to the west—but *that* was over *there*.

"Gosh, am I glad you two stopped!" The kid grinned from the girl to the man hunched listening at the wheel.

"Yes, yew are," Dell agreed as if it had been a question. "So? Whut transpired?"

"Beg pardon?"

"I esked yew what happened." Dell sighed. "Did yore vehicle suffer af-flickin' disabilities?"

"Not disabilities. Not exactly." The hitcher tried not to notice Kee's stare. Heat she gave off fairly shimmered in the van. "My gas gauge is busted so I had to jog almost ten miles to a service station." Perched gingerly on the seat, he looked for his smile. "I forgot about the gauge when I left home Friday afternoon. Crap. I had maybe another three miles to' go before I would have gotten back to my old Buick—except for you two good Samaritans."

"We're just Americans," Kee said, surprised. "Like yew." Fading sunlight blushed one of her soft cheeks.

"Samaritans like in the Bible, I meant," the boy explained. "Remember?"

"Well, I 'member Mama mentioned a whole *heap* of foreigners in there." Kee sniffed.

"'*Sa-mar-i-tan*," Dell said expressionlessly, like reading it off a page. "'Noun. One of the people of Samaria. *II Kings xvii.'*" He said that "Double-I Kings, ex-vee-eye-eye."

It got quiet awhile in the van. But the nervous boy heard a clinking noise rise now and then from the girl's container. "What you got in there, miss?" he asked.

"It's jus' my tampon box Mama give me," she said. No longer shakin' it, she lifted it to the boy's coloring face for closer inspection.

Desperate, he turned to Dell. "My name is Negley, Lewis Negley? I can point out my Buick when we get closer," he said. When nobody spoke, he cleared his throat. "I'm returning to Indiana State, y'know? That's where Larry Bird played college ball."

The girl said, "Who's he, anyway?" Not the center of attention at the moment, she made a show of exhibiting her long legs by noisily planting both feet atop the cooler.

Lewis looked dazed. "Why, he's—"

"He was one of them overpaid N.B.C. atha-
letes," Dell interposed. "White boy tall as Gawd. I'm
Dell, the girl is Kee."

"It's 'N.B.A.,' sir," Lewis corrected the driver of
the van, too much a Hoosier to resist. "Gosh, he
took the Celtics to—"

"They's all ineffably overpaid." Without letting
his voice rise to display his anger over being corrected, Dell still sounded like thunder. "The others
had t'make Bird look good, let him score 'n be all
fancy, t'git white folks inta them seats."

Lewis really wanted this ride, but the pain of
resisting an argument with the idiot in the front seat
was acute for a basketball junkie like Lewis.
Evening wind whipping through Dell's open window might have brought messages, but he didn't
hear them.

"C'mere." Kee said, speaking from the group-
ing shadows. "Want to tell yew somethin'."

Lewis started to face her and her red nails,
much nibbled, clutched his forearm and dragged at
it till he had lowered his ear to her lips. "What?" he
whispered.

"Yew're awful fuckin' cute," came her stage
whisper back.

"Well" Lewis said, "gosh . . ."

"No, yew are truly a *hunk*." Kee licked the tip of
his nose and then bit the lobe of one ear. "Yew
wants t *'do* it now?" she asked. "Huh?" Her bite
genuinely hurt, but she had both her hands on
Lewis's right bicep then and he believed men

couldn't let women know they'd harmed them. "Yew might as well go ahead an' do it. *He* makes me do it *alla* time." Her tongue tasted the inside of his ear. "He's a pervert, Lewis—yew know that? He's a genuwine mo-lester."

"De-cade or two back," Dell said, clearing his throat, "there warn't no white men in thet league." He was still faced forward and probably hard of hearing, Lewis Negley thought. "Yew can check me out."

"Mr. Dell, I—"

"Nary a one."

"The ole cornholer flat stole my cherry," Kee whispered noisily. God, Lewis wanted to clap his hand over her mouth! At the same time, everything from her ragged widow's peak hairline and badly plucked brows and watery blue eyes to the pugnacious snub nose and the maddeningly pouting, kissable mouth challenged Negley. If she wasn't lying, he *had* to—do something. *What*, though, with a very mature-looking man driving a rickety van at fifty-five miles an hour? *Now* the girl seemed ready to bawl. "Ain't yew goin' to help me *atall*?"

"Mebbe yew're not a reader," Dell droned on. "Them N.B.C. gland cases, why, they're half-stealin' that money! Whut they gonna do for a livin' at retirement age, tell me thet!"

"It's gospel *truth*, Lewis!" Kee was filling up the interior of the steadily rolling van with youth and vitality, her sex, a hunger Lewis did not grasp the nature of, her disconcerting apparent vulnerability. "I *means* it, I don't lie!"

"Go on gawdamn welfare—thet's whut! Live on our tax dollars!"

Lewis was staring back into the girl's eyes, or trying to. She had a way of holding her mouth as if sizing him up, yet she was so emotionally charged her tampon thing that clicked slipped off her lap and she was suddenly pressing his cheeks between damp palms, the tips of her nails gouging his skin. The pain was negligible. "Lewis, I was a innocent virgin, and that ole mo-lester, he *kidnapped* me. Uh-huh! Now he's sexually abusing me straight across the whole fuckin' country!" Tears blossomed in her eyes. "Jesus, ain't yew got no hair on yore nuts, honey—what kinda man *are* yew?"

"Watch yore tongue!" Dell snapped back. "Mind your gawdamn language!"

Lewis's head spun forward as fast as it would go and his heart vaulted. This Dell was hearing everything she said! "S-sir, I'm no judge or policeman, God knows—but what she's been saying—"

The driver's horsey face appeared over the front seat. The bad eye was laboring; a car sped past with blazing lights and Lewis saw the lid flutter and viscous tears drop down his left cheek. "Keep outta whut don't con-cern yew, boy." He glanced back to the road, readjusting the van's position in the lane. "The girl can de*claim* as she pleases rel-o-tive t'sexual shit an' thet, but I *will not let* no chile curse in that manner. It is not proper. Kee, yew tell Lewis yew profaned, hear me? Yew was pro-fane and *perfidious*."

Kee nodded. She was quick about it but expressionless. "I been profane," she repeated, "and—what was that other two-dollar word, Dellie?"

Dell just emitted some low-pitched strange noise. Then he went on making it, Lewis realized.

But Larry Bird *had* gone to Indiana State, too. "I do want to help you," he told Kee with enormous caution, sweating. "But I'll have to have the exact truth if I'm gonna—well, help you . . . get away." His whisper was only for her and nothing human could have heard it farther away than the girl was. "How *old* are you? And where did it happen, the . . . rape?"

"I barely had my boobies, Lewis." Her eyes were huge, sheened. When they widened, Lewis imagined how lovely she was going to be one day. "An' I on'y had peach fuzz. Down there, yew know?" After glancing between her legs, she burst into inexplicable laughter—or laughter inexplicable to Lewis—and slapped her open palms stingingly on his bare chest. "Yew *are* cute, Lewis, I swear!" Then she let one of her hands drop, brush. "Cain't yew tell when a woman is truly joshin' yew?"

Lewis stopped breathing; at least, it felt that way. Crimson, he picked up the tampon container for her and then edged as far away as he could from Kee. "I never knew any girl who could possibly kid about something like that." It was anger and relief and, he sensed, a weird basic apology. For having been fooled. By a gag. Filled with the need to re-gather his senses, he craned his neck to squint through the windshield of the van, praying his car might be out there. "It'll be coming up any second now," he called.

"*Will* it?" Kee asked wide-eyed, and squeezed his privates and hooted with hilarity.

"Lewis Negley," called Dell, "yew just ig-nore the girl now 'cause she's a congenital liar." He'd just looked that word up. "She's the sort of bare-faced de-ceiver who allus makes up them jokes 'bout sex thangs." The wind was dying down; contrarily, Dell cranked the window up, bringing an instant wave of odors to Negley's nostrils which he could not iden-tify just then. "Chile, yew inform our rider of the truth. *Now.*"

"Awww, Dellie, do I got to?" Kee asked. She waited, but just for the flick of an eyelid. "Well, then . . . Dell here's my *daddy*," she told Lewis, modestly averting her gaze.

Young Negley gasped. Studying her intently, he said, "For real? Is that the truth, Kee?"

Kee's eyes rolled. She toyed with a strand of her hair and nodded with enormous sincerity. "I'm Del-lie's *on'y* daughter. An' we travel this whole, wide, wonnerful country, jus' the two of us." She began nodding and Lewis joined in, as if encouraging a four-year-old. "We go absotively *ever*where to-gether, my precious daddy 'n me. Seein' things."

"I think that's kind of nice," Lewis murmured. He relaxed slightly, leaned back.

"Uh-huh. An' Daddy shows me the sights—the great nash'nul monuments—and then, 'cause Dad-dy's truly *big* on what they call a 'well-rounded eddication,' we park somewhere . . . and Daddy pulls out *his* monument fer me to see ag'in!'' She folded practically in two with merriment.

Oh God, Lewis thought, eyes blinking as he tried to find *something* safe to stare at. Dell's head was once more a motionless icon above the neckrest. God, oh, God, how had he gotten himself into this mess?

Kee stayed so long in convulsions of laughter—at his expense—that Lewis began to wonder if she'd come out of them. Shrieking giggles that were like screams, gasping for air, she was white as snow and then red in the face. First her girl legs were in the air, kicking, then her feet were flat on the floor so she could pound on Dell's neckrest with her small, damaging fists—or anything else she could reach. ''Gollygollysum*bitch*!'' she said as if strangling. ''He b'lieved that 'un too!'' Finished abruptly with her fit, she wrapped both playful arms around the driver's neck, nibbled on his ear. ''He b'lieves everything I says to him, this old hunk of a boy, Dellie! Mebbe Lewis is that dumb—or mebbe *I'm* gittin' awmost as smart as *yew* are!''

A large right hand darted from the steering wheel, pinned Kee's wrist and the heel of her hand. Lewis saw how bony, how nearly fragile, his wrists were in contrast with those *paws*—thumbs that made him think of toes that chattering monkeys could hang from tree branches with. Dell shoved the girl back. Simply. Powerfully. She virtually sailed into her seat as if airborne, or rocketed sideways from a pad.

''It's just a little farther.'' Lewis rasped the syllables out. He'd pressed his body against the door merely to get as far from both of them as possible. The Kee–thing was crying softly, but Lewis didn't think she was hurt, couldn't force himself to *care* if she was. "It's an old Buick, two-tone. Should be about a quarter of a mile now."

Then a chilling question formed, unasked, in Lewis's mind and it shocked him so much the thought created words he could virtually see: *When we get to my car, will they let me out*?

"I tole yew t'tell him the truth, gauwdammit!" Dell's neck was fire-engine red. A small gland beneath an ear that looked like the wing of an albino bat throbbed noticeably. "Tell him, girl, or you won't git any of what yew de-sires!"

Kee's eyes were bulging when Lewis turned his head to her and her cheeks were filling, emptying, filling with air. "We're sort of . . . married, Lewis. Or almost, 'cause we's like man 'n wife." The whisper sounded genuine this time. "Or awmost."

The twitching gland in Dell's throat slowed, but he said nothing.

"I have not been a proper hostess," said Kee. Lewis suddenly felt something excruciatingly cold against his cheek and jaw. "Here's a"—Kee paused, blinking her long lashes—"beer from our very own cooler."

He accepted it, his gaze passing the cooler still open at Kee's feet. Something *sloshed*. He knew it wasn't beer. Kee closed the lid snugly, blocking his view with her soft shoulder, and raised her head to stare out the rear window with a rather dreamy smile. "What do yew know, we jus' passed us a old two-tone Buick."

Lewis looked too, urgently, and saw his car at the side of the road. Now dwindling into the distance like an exercise in artist's perspective.

"That was my *car*," Lewis yelled at the driver— "that was *it*!"

"I fundamentally b'lieved it might be," Dell said softly.

"Well—why didn't you *stop*?"

"Girl was bein' hos*pit*able." A quick, man-to-man wink of the good eye. "Little lady was fetchin' yew re-freshments, Lewis Negley. One must provide a opportunity fer one who attempts t'make amends fer her naughty gawdamn lies."

The Buick was lost in grayness, distance that grew as the van rolled on. Feeling numb, Lewis concentrated hard, came up with a suggestion. "C-can we pull off while I drink my beer? I'm a-afraid I'll spill it while we drive. Then, well . . . I c-can walk back."

Dell's face flashed into unspeaking profile and he was smiling. The smile was horrible, privately, secretively purposive.

Unanswered, Lewis tried once more. "*Please* pull over." Nothing. "Sir, just let me out." He'd nearly said *go* instead of *out*. "I'm expected at school, I can have my beer while I run back." Oh God, the cockeyed son-of-a-bitch wouldn't even *answer* him! Dell just kept driving, driving! "Sir? Mr. Dell?"

Kee howled then. It sounded just like that to

Lewis; he tore around so he could gape at her. The mounds of her high-placed small breasts were jiggling under the sweater that ended above a neat and staring navel; her pale belly was sucked in with such inexplicable amusement that it was concave, as fleshless as if she didn't eat. Both her hands were tucked into her crotch. "We ain't 'sort of married,' Lewis," Kee gasped. And the tip of a coated tongue oozed from her deep, wet mouth while the eyes above it and the pert teenage nose became night jewels. "Yew cute hunk—we're *partners*!"

The van shook, rocked and rolled, sent Lewis off his seat to clutch at a front seat for support. *A crash is coming*, he thought, whipping his head around to peer frantically through a window—

And the vehicle's tires rattled on the unpaved earth beneath them like a shaman's shaking sticks. They weren't on a road now, it wasn't even a path. Dell had decided to turn the van onto a field and they were bouncing across it, caromming off ruts.

Then—"This here is good"—and Dell braked so sharply Lewis's slender body rammed against the seat, partly tearing his breath away.

The driver's door clanged open. Dell dropped lightly to the ground, disappeared from Lewis's view.

"Let's go," Kee said, gesturing to Lewis to open their door.

He did, and started to get out, but Kee passed through the door on the other side of the van like a puff of smoke. One foot still inside the van, Lewis remembered arriving in a bus at the Butler Bowl in

Indianapolis for a football game. He pictured the camaraderie, the cheerleaders; he had heard and sung the fight songs, had considered it merely another autumn evening.

Dell pulled him out the rest of the way, chuckling. The man was only a little taller but rangy, long-armed, of a piece. A piece including the peculiar thumbs and powerful hands and skeletal wrists. "Yew de-sired me to pull off so I did," he told Lewis affably. The tone of voice was friendly, so polite that the young man dared hope, even glanced around at their surroundings.

A sifting glimmer of light worked mystical designs in the saturnine western sky. Here there was silence, there were no farmhouses, there was nothing that had been planted. When he looked toward the distant new highway—why had he wanted to avoid traffic?—there was only an occasional flash of illumination indicating the passage of unrushed motorists, each of them as unknowing of what was happening to him as his folks at home.

But just what *was* happening?

Kee. Coming out from behind the van, she was making sure she caught Lewis's eye before she skinned out of her sweater and stopped a few yards from him, naked to the waist.

Incredulous, uncomprehending, he glanced at Dell. The smile was back.

And when Lewis returned his gaze to Kee, she was completely nude.

Lewis was unable to find anything to say and just stared, slowly aware that the girl was striking a variety of poses for him. She gave him the impression that she'd spent time studying center gatefolds and was showing off, trying to be as sexually attractive to him as possible. What annoyed and also frightened him was that she was succeeding. Kee was no longer giggling—she took what she was doing quite seriously. Her young body formed an obscenely leering face in the unsure lighting—purplish nipples like the bottoms of beer bottles for eyes, the trim bellybutton as a nose, the darkly shadowed beard of pubic hair, spreading to her thighs in a whiskery smile.

"It would not be de-corous for us not t'*join* the young lady," Dell said. His own white shirt was already off and he wore an immaculate T-shirt, the sight surprising because the collar of his shirt was badly stained. Each upper garment was folded carefully and placed over an open van window. Lewis noticed Kee's clothes in a pile at her feet and she was scratching her armpit. When he saw Dell slip his belt out of the buckle Lewis realized he also had something else in his hand. His left was behind his back.

"Yew want another beer first?" Kee asked. First? Before *what*? It was getting cold out but neither the girl nor the man appeared to notice it at all. "We still got Schlitz 'n Bud Light in the cooler 'n there might be one Coors left. We can go back to the van."

"No, I-I'm fine," Lewis said. The beer in his hand from the cooler was unopened so he ripped the tab off, drank deeply, chuckled, and belched, chuckled tonelessly once more. (*I had my first beer with Dad. The next one with Karen.*) He drank again, hurting himself as he gulped it down. Finished, Lewis swiped his mouth with the edge of his shaking palm, shook his head in apparent appreciation. "Look, this has been *great*! I'd better start running back—it's not far from here, thanks to you people, but my lights aren't"—he paused—"great." Dell and Kee wore blank expressions. Like carvings. "I'll just take off now, okay?"

"No." Dell's flat voice came at him like an edged throwing weapon. "It ain't okay."

What he had in his right hand was an automatic. His fingers were folded around it and the thumb ran along the barrel like an additional sight. The left hand remained behind his back. Lewis's jumping eyes saw also that Dell's fly was open.

"We shall *as*-cend into the back of the van," Dell said like a tour guide, nose of the Magnum shifting minimally, directionally. He looked at Kee. "Yew first, girl." But she was already climbing up and in, eagerly.

Lewis stared at Kee's bifurcated rump, knew it was his turn next. Red velvety curtains—slobbering beast tongues—were drawn. Hesitating, Lewis felt the back of his ribs jolted by the impact of the automatic being jabbed into them. Dell muttered, "Christ on a crutch, Lewis Negley, yew got somethin' ag' in sexual con-gress?" From the highway a passing semi yowled as if rushing a belated warning. Lewis swallowed hard.

The van's interior lights were on and the un-

fathomable girl seemed gaunt and bleached, infelic-
itously freckled or blotchy. She had the mad-angel
face. He had seen naked women seldom, naked
women who cared nothing much about it anyway.

A simmering started in male bits of Lewis that
responded or activated connective glands which
most of his mind cursed as a betrayal. It seemed to
him that someone had tried to construct the body of
a perfect teenage girl, but allowed it to bake and dry
out in the sun too long until it had crinkled and
crisped, gone livid and somehow become too taut—
too hirsute as well—for what he had imagined an
eager but relaxed nude woman would be.

A makeshift bed with a foam mattress took up
almost all the space in the back of the van. It had
been tidily made, readied for use; a clean sheet was
pulled back evenly from two snowy pillows. And
lying next to them—a pair of gleaming garden
shears. Till then, Lewis had only been wondering if
he could make it with this girl, particularly at gun-
point. Seeing his narrow reflection in the shears, as
distorted as a face in a funhouse mirror, his head
began to throb.

"Git up on yore bed, Lewis," ordered Dell.

He obeyed, but instead of climbing under the
sheets, he knelt, glanced back at Dell—who was
also naked except for flamboyant bikini under-
shorts.

"I'm not taking off my clothes no matter what,"
Lewis said. Trying to watch Kee, too, he fumbled in
a pocket of his cutoffs, tugged out a crumpled five-
dollar bill. "This is all I got. I bought the g-gas." Gas

left on the floor of the van. (*Dad taught me to drive, I already knew how when I took the course*). "Just take it."

Kee did and pressed it beneath one of the pillows. "Yew cute thing," she giggled. "Yew got a *lot* more'n that, even if it ain't money. Don't yew worry 'bout gettin' naked, Dellie and me've seed awmost a *hunderd* bodies bare-ass now. We learnt a whole heap *about* the hewman body, too. Shit, them sciennists truly doesn't know, right, Dellie?"

"We thank yew for the do-nation, Lewis Negley," Dell said. He brought his left hand from behind him, displaying a tattered paperback. Strips of Scotch Magic Transparent tape held the cover on the book. The man still had the automatic in his right hand. He'd stopped talking for a moment and was partly murmuring something, partly humming. He had already shut the van door and now he was kneeling on the thin mattress. "'To *sol-em-nize,*'" Dell said quite distinctly. "'To perform a ceremony or solemn rite.'" His eyes showed above the top of the book briefly, the left fixed on the van ceiling—dizzyingly from Lewis's viewpoint—the right regarding the shaking boy with dignified amiability. "'To *dig*-ni-fy, as with a ceremony.'" He closed the paperback, tenderly. "'To *cel-e-brate.*'"

A noise from Kee made Lewis jump again. She had gone to get the cooler and was raising the lid, motioning to him. "Come on now, Leweeeee," she said in singsong fashion. Her smile was nearly the same as before; impish, not quite instantaneously detectable as mad. "Yew got t'have a new brew—I mean, a *beer*—as part of the solemnizin' stuff."

"Girl's right," Dell said, behind him. "Go on now. Pick whut yew want."

Lewis caught the gleam of lubricious animation in the older man's good eye. Setting his jaw, the youth crawled the few inches over the mattress to the cooler, peered down at half-melted ice swarming grayly on the surface, its motion mimicking life. Lewis looked like *crazy* into the cooler, completely ignorant of their purposes and wanting tremendously to understand them before he put his hand in the chilly water.

Kee got impatient and, grabbing his wrists while he was kneeling above the cooler, plunged them in. When she let his wrists go, one hand automatically closed around something ice cold and he pulled it out

In his palm lay something of limited length, something that felt grisly and looked wrinkled. It wasn't a can of beer. Lewis gaped at the dripping thing with eyes that wouldn't believe. His brain chose to remember Wally, his much older brother forever dead and gone in 'Nam; Wally's loss was what had transferred their dad's whole paternal concern and focus on him. Wally'd had a friend who wrote that Wally saw fingers lying by themselves in steaming jungle grass and Wally hadn't realized they *were* fingers—or recognized them as his own. People were used to seeing them *attached* and everything, they couldn't accept how small and slight they looked, freshly . . . removed.

"It's a gag," Lewis told Kee and Dell to let them

know he wasn't a fool who fell for dumb jokes, stupid pranks. But the nude girl was pressing her own fingers between her legs, leaning forward slightly and doing a piss-poor job of suppressing another insane giggle. And even then Lewis, frowning studiedly, couldn't accept it, hadn't even thrown the dripping thing back into the cooler.

He noticed, then, the choppy edges where it had been sliced, or sawed, off.

Lewis hurled the penis into the cooler as if it were a live grenade, and moaned. *Pick what you want*, Dell had said.

And Dell, the touch of him subtle this time, brushed against Lewis's back—*not with his hand*. Turning fast, Lewis saw the lanky man had removed the bikini shorts. "Yew needn't dis-robe, Lewis Negley," he said softly, "we'll do it for yew." Lewis saw spiky, short, graying hairs a foot away, marble-veined and twangy readiness. "Look, I ain't no perv. I jest don't like t'git any on my clothes."

"NO!" Lewis roared, hurtling toward the door like a football player trying for a saving tackle. Behind him there was the *snick*-SNACK, *snick*-SNACK of the naked girl's garden shears clacking like some forgotten prehistoric life form. He tore the rear door open, felt a small, grasping hand on his ankle. A glance behind showed the sprawled Kee—and the incomprehensible image of the naked Dell pinning her down, to the mattress. *"NO!"* Lewis screamed again, falling hard on the ground and jumping up instantly, running for the highway and then straightlining it for his car—*another* car—

anywhere and anyone else! He thought he heard the door of the van slam shut, but he didn't bother to look back and find out.

Dell shoved himself up off Kee's bare back and posterior, not without regret, making his infrequent sound of all-but-silent laughter mixed with the mutter and the tuneless hum. With no explanation he headed for the front of the van.

"Yew *ain't* jus' lettin' him *go*?" Kee scrambled up, thunderstruck. "Dellie—he's *Number Ninety-eight*!"

Dell sat in the driver's seat, fired up the engine. It didn't want to catch for a second and Dell's eye began to seep.

"Dellie—I *wanted him*!" Kee dropped into the worn captain's seat, folding her arms in pique. "That's why yew stopped me, ain't it? 'Cause I finely found another hunk, an' *we* hasn't found the right place 'n time for our romance yet! *Ain't* it?"

Dell shoved the accelerator to the floor, cut sharply, made for the highway without answering Kee. His unexpected fast start almost threw Kee out of her seat. She saw his face in the rearview. The bad eye was drizzling pus like rain from a thundercloud.

"Yew're goin' *after* him, ain't yew!" she shrieked in excitement. The terrible ride over the bumpy field ended and the van smoothed out, whined as Dellie put it through the gears. His hunched shoulders and the back of his reddening neck were like watching a man see a real good movie. The words he growled unintelligibly while

313

his hummed bloodlust formed the soundtrack. They were at a film-fest, a fun-frolic, and the van's headlight beams bleached stains on the road before them, turned the white center stripe into a washed-out bloody trail. "Go, Dellie," Kee shouted in his big red ear, "*go*!"

Dell went, poured all his practiced expertise into goading the old van to a performance it probably hadn't managed for years. His male member was engorged, erect—might be a grave risk if he needed to turn the steering wheel again—but he doubted Lewis Negley had done more than try to run in the straightest and most direct of paths. The question was whether he and Kee could catch up before Negley flagged a ride.

"Go, Dell, *git* him," Kee chanted like a cheerleader. "Go, Dell, *git* him!" She thudded small fists on Dell's neckrest, breathed hot in his ear, once bit the lobe and tasted the inside of his ear with the tip of her tongue. "*Git* that road-runner!"

Men didn't really run fast and it didn't take long. "There he is," Dell said softly.

The boy, running ahead of them, was tiring fast. He looked thin, frail, not very real in the bleeding headlight beams. He was still trying to lift his knees high, but they were moving in slow motion, as though in parody of a weary marathon runner. Both the girl and the man saw Lewis glance over his shoulder, at a shrinking distance, attempt to get more from his exhausted body.

"He is a blade of grass," Kee breathed, "a *weed*!

He's the last one left on Daddy's field and we're gonna cut him *down*!"

"He's a human animal, male," Dell corrected her, "who has been called Lewis Negley an' is yore ninety-eight now—our thang. And they is nothin' more t'this than thet."

They saw then where the young man had decided to go, if he could make it.

Half a football field away was his car, the out-of-gas Buick. For a second Dell thought Lewis was heading for it even if it wouldn't go anywhere, and exulted.

Then he figured it out: Lewis Negley was trying to reach an old drive-in theater where nine or ten vehicles were enterin' on a dirt road—close enough to see the kid, and help him.

What those cars *weren't* close enough to see was the pursuing van, because it was out on the highway and *they* were all bunched together, bumper to bumper, heading into the drive-in lot.

Dell had to decide whether to catch Lewis Negley when he was abreast of the theater or to go ahead and catch up just as the boy got to his car. What *wasn't* going to happen was Lewis Negley getting away.

So Dell slowed the van. Partly to consider, mostly to play with the kid. He tooted the van horn. Lewis glanced around and Dell made the motor to go *vroom, vroooom*. Lewis pumped his legs high; in the headlights, sweat came off him as though he was throwing buckets of water. *Toot, toot*, the van's horn said. Lewis looked back. *Vroom, vuh-rrooom*!

Dell made a sniffly laughing sound. The kid knew Dell was *pacing* him now! Kee started to clap her hands with joy, thinking Dellie would make the hunk get in—

Then she knew, that *wasn't* what Dell had in mind.

Realizing the crazy people could catch up whenever they pleased, Lewis was attempting valiantly to speed up, redouble his efforts, and leap into his car. The door on the driver's side was unlocked, and he had a big monkey wrench he'd kept under the seat for just such emergencies—except it wasn't for emergencies like *this*, Lewis thought hysterically. His lungs cried out for air as he strove to cover the final yards to his car. Well, at least he might brain one of the killers before they cut him up or blew his head off! Lewis gutted it out.

Dell gunned it. Lewis heard the increased sound, sensed the van closing in, imagined he heard tremendous winds gusting toward him, as if Dell and the mad girl had become elements of some natural cyclonic force.

Lewis thrust out his arm and his fingers groped for the car door as his spirit filled with a thrill of hope.

The door was open part way when the left front fender of the van collided with Lewis at some forty to forty-five miles per hour. Crushed, an outflung arm lay briefly on the top of the van; the vehicle was wedged against his broken body. Lewis's fingers were splayed. It was like the involunarily twitching hand of a drowning man who went on seeking support even while most of his life had trickled away.

Excited as hell, Dell fumbled for reverse, pulled the van back. Internal strands of Lewis extended from the body to the hood ornament. Dell and Kee had to stare, fascinated, enthralled, nearly smiling. When Lewis Negley didn't slip on down to the pavement, it became obvious why: one side of the corpse was either lodged firmly between that part of the Buick where the door was hinged to the chassis or the kid was basically *stapled* to the door somehow.

Dell tapped the accelerator, edging around the door and Lewis Negley. Redness on the van windshield made it a newly rose-colored night. Kee stared through the window as they passed, saw the way the youth's face was somehow raised, his eyes wide open. Blood pumping from his torn mouth went unnoticed by the cute ole hunk himself but she thought she saw his eyelashes move, as if Lewis Negley needed to close his eyes now.

Voices, shouting. Living folks leaving their cars to run out of the drive-in theater line, one or two already near enough to see what was going on. Shrugging, Dell cut the wheel fully to the right—snapping off the Buick door—and sped out on the road again.

"He *seed* us!" Kee pummeled Dell's shoulder. "Dellie, his *eyes*—they was still *open!*"

"He's dyin'." Dell said, "or dead. Flatted out like a bug on the windshield." They was in high gear now and he was remembering everything clearly. "That 'un was somethin,'" he chuckled, wiped his dripping eye with his bare arm. "We's gonna need t'stop 'n git us some clothes on soon, so's nobuddy takes us for perverts. Hand me *The Book*, will yew?"

Kee's eyes scanned the interior of the van wildly, blankly; finding the paperback, she passed it to him, but Lewie's face—at the end—was in front of her eyes almost as it was before they had driven away. Cold all at once, freezing, Kee found a sweater and pulled it over her head, fussed with it when it wouldn't go down and cover her navel. "He could identify us, Dell." She sulked back in her chair and crossed her arms. "He *could*." She got no response. "He might live *that* long, Dellie."

"Yew don't need t'have no souvenir this time, 'cause we'll both re-call Lewis Negley," he told her kindly. "Yew see his face when I said he didden have t'dis-robe after all?"

"I seen him," Kee said. Hugging herself harder, she squirmed down on the seat and began thinking of putting on her jeans.

"Well, he's *still* yore Ninety-eight, chile," Dell assured her.

"*Not*!" Kee argued. Suddenly she broke into tears. "I . . . I *liked* him. An' we didn't even git his thang!" Seeking comfort, she hooked his red neck with her arm and pressed her tear-streaked cheek to it. "My collection's all *spoiled*, Dellie. Would you drive back so we can be *sure* he's dead, and his eyes are shut? Otherwise, we's stuck on Ninety-seven, and Lewie don't count as *nothin'*! I won't take him unless I *know* he's a deader."

He didn't say a word, but Kee felt his muscles

tighten as if he were laughing at her. That pissed her but she held on to his neck anyhow, squeezed as hard as she could. She sure as shit wasn't going to share the five-dollar bill under the pillow with Dellie! But whatever she did or didn't do, Kee knew she could never put a penny for Lewis in her container with the gardenias and count him as ninety-eight. Some things were just truly morally impure.

"Kee, girl?"

She removed her hand from his neck, obsessing a lot about her cute Lewie's staring eyes. "What do yew want?" she asked sullenly.

"It purely don't matter." Dell's face was illuminated in the rearview mirror when a semi barreled past, and he was as handsome and as homely as ever, but he was still everything a girl could rightly expect. "It's in-con-se-quen-tial, like *The Book* says. Yew can even look it up yoreself if yew de-sires. Also, a *triv-i-al-i-ty*." Dellie shrugged, raised his right hand from his lap and put it behind him, over his shoulder, beside the neckrest. "An' ever one of them words means it jest . . . don't . . . matter."

"What if his dyin' eyes took pictures of us?" Kee said, but she put her hand over her fella's where he'd rested it.

"Well, why don't yew jest put it in yore diary?"

Yawning, he switched on the wipers. What remained there of Lewis Negley was washed away. Dell winked at her in the rearview mirror and, for Kee, for Dell, the rest of the world disappeared. "Nothin' matters—but the phoenix."

Before they put their clothes back on, Dell

parked in the woods and they lay near one another on the mattress in the back like tired-out children. He dozed awhile, slipped his thumb between his lips, and shivered. Kee covered his chest with one sweatered arm, warmed his lower regions with her own naked legs. This could have been the time, she thought. Maybe she should go ahead and do it with her Dellie, now or soon. Of course, she had to make him get some rubbers somewhere since that was the only responsible thing to do these days. Gazing at him, she didn't figure he'd need a maxi-size.

When Dell awoke, he comforted her too. "We'll just git us a couple at a time t'morrow or the next day—mebbe all three." He put clean shorts on, then his pants. "Three'd make yew yore even hunderd, wouldn't it?"

CHAPTER 13

It turned out to be easier to look at the boy crucified on the door of his old Buick, and to watch him carefully taken off it, then to talk with the dead kid's father.

Ernest Negley had been even older than Douglas expected, considering young Lewis's apparent age. When the elder Negley mumbled the information that he'd already lost his other son in Nam, Kirk got it—the college boy had been a midlife baby for Ernest and Esther. And the son who had been lavished with the care and concern, the love and support, the Negleys originally divided between two sons. Now they had no one but one another and the years would come rushing at them like black winged things—assuming either one of them had as much as a year left.

Just a few minutes into his meeting with Mr. Negley—the missus was "resting"—Douglas hoped they wouldn't have that much. Enough was enough.

Almost as bad (in some ways) was driving all the way to the small Hoosier town for the Negley interview and conducting it was that it proved to be nothing but another burden for Mr. Negley and a depressing waste of time for Kirk.

Ernest Negley described not only his son's girlfriend, Karen, but all his acquaintances so affectionately that they couldn't conceivably be connected with Dell from Hell. There had been the off chance Lewis might have met the monster or seen him with young Kee McCaulter prior to the highway encounter that led to Lewis's awful death. So Kirk had gone all the way from Ohio to small-town Indiana searching for a clue suggesting where Dell was headed next, and now he had entirely lost the trail.

Kirk drove away from the Negley home in a totally hopeless and disgruntled mood. His feeling of helplessness to prevent yet another nightmarish slaughter after which he would have to wait for the son-of-a-bitch simply to murder someone else, *then* rush to the death scene like a crazy bloodhound who couldn't get enough of the hot scent, was darkly repellent to Kirk.

Mainly, it maddened the hell out of him that another kid with his whole future ahead of him had been snuffed out, just like that. Truth was, he knew he had begun to identify too much with the families of the younger victims. And that was unacceptable, unprofessional; he would have been the first to let a new cop know it. It was just because he missed seeing his own daughter so much, that he worried constantly about her and often woke from dreams with some damned pervert's hands all *over* her, and him not there to—

Go over the facts you know so well you've actually memorized them, Kirk ordered himself. *Or stop for coffee somewhere and read them again, get your damn bearings. Look for tiny crap, weird details you've discounted because they're so mad.*

Dell's thumbs. Dell appeared to prefer murdering people with them. He didn't wear gloves; he left his thumbprints around like—like thumbing his nose at the authorities. The notion Douglas had was that Dell didn't get to kill with them as frequently as he would have liked, not that that kept him from running down—and over—his victims, stabbing or shooting them.

Well, research had turned up a few screwball facts. Back in the early 1800s there had been a pretty big market for human body parts, especially for the thumbs or the thumb bones of thieves, killers. The belief was that dead criminals had succeeded in accumulating a lot of loot, so ordinary citizens who wouldn't—maybe—harm a fly imagined that hauling a bad guy's severed thumb in their pocket could bring a few extra pounds or shillings their way.

Worse, perhaps, was the way women tended to grab at the thumbs and fingers of executed murderers, then rub what was called the "death sweat" on their faces and chests. All sorts of skin blemishes (those gentle ladies believed) would be cured, if they acted swiftly, got the digits while they were still hot—or warm, Kirk grunted to himself.

So if I was superstitious, he ruminated, deciding to phone the state troopers and see what they and the F.B.I. agents had turned up by interviewing witnesses in the drive-in across from where Lewis Negley'd bought it, *I might believe Dell has been evening up old scores from some earlier life.*

But I'm not, Kirk reminded himself, adamantly refusing to buy into the media bull that saw Dell as a virtual psychic Dillinger. The scumbag was a calculating, lucky creep and that was all.

Carjacking was all the criminal rage across America. But it was no freaking supernatural crime. In '91, 416 vehicles had been ripped off in Houston, Texas, by August alone—a 26 percent increase in a year. Dallas reported around eighty such thefts a month. The International Association of Auto Theft Investigators mentioned epidemics of carjackings in New York, New Orleans, both L.A. and Frisco, Chicago, St. Louis, San Diego, and Portland. Detroit was such a popular spot for the crime that creeps— *alleged* creeps, Kirk sardonically reminded himself— were said to be *going there* to pick up their wheels. No regular tab had been run on carjacks before late July of '91, but between that date and October 12th of the same year, upwards of seven hundred automotive "boosts" were reported—carjackers were ripping off some seven hundred vehicles *a week* in Motor City.

Douglas waited on the phone to be put through. *But there's a difference where Dell is concerned*, he reminded himself. The majority of carjack special- ists was raping and getting money to buy drugs; Dell *almost always kills the people he steals from, for kicks.*

He was looking at family photographs of Kee McCaulter and Lewis Negley, side by side in front of him, as he listened to a reliable recap of what eyewitnesses said about the way the college kid had been pursued—"tauntingly" "a damned cat-and- mouse game"—then crushed.

And the way Dell was in no hurry to get the stolen van off Lewis, did nothing whatever to help, just stared in open-mouthed interest at the horrify- ing spectacle.

Not just Dell was smiling, according to what Douglas was hearing on the phone. Pert, fresh- faced and sassy, sixteen-year-old Kee was said to have loved the sight, too.

Douglas remembered something he'd heard that might provide a tip on their next destination as he took the snapshot of the alleged perpetrator named Kee and tore it in two. He'd be all right, now. He'd be himself, fine, ready to go and prevent them from continuing their damnable spree indefinitely—in just a minute.

Another second and his vision would clear enough to drive. To follow—*them.*

* * *

Kee worked relatively hard—for her, she put quite a bit into it—to conquer the sense of foreboding that began to frighten and even possess her at the point of Lewie's departure from the world. She tried to turn her mind to other things as her Dellie drove, presumably looking for a new Number Ninety-eight (and another vehicle), but she'd had her own way so often and for so many years of her life that failure and old superstitious beliefs made it impossible to forget Lewis Negley's open eyes and fluttering eyelashes. Even when she scrawled an entry in her book, the words turned indecipherable whenever Dell stopped for a light or made a turn in the road. She found herself writing of "pain puddles"—eyes like shiny rain on the "conkreet" with "bitty peeces" of cement in the middles. One second she was convinced Lewie had took their pictures and the smart detective Kirk Douglas would figure out how to develop them. The next second she was starting to believe Lewis's ghost was floating right down the road behind them.

As early evening became deep night on the lonely highway, Kee fought the urge to spin around *real* fast—as Lewis Negley had when they passed his car—to see if there was a spirit looking in through the window at the back. She believed it could happen; Lewis might have sent his soul out of his body *right* at the second he expired—and if she *did* see him lookin' in, all there'd be was something shiny, and his cold, *rememb'rin'* eyes.

When it got to her thoroughly, Kee finally put

some pants on, feeling like a snake shedding its skin backward. Perched once more in her familiar seat, she breathed on Dellie's neck and ear without saying anything—good friends or lovers didn't have to talk, Mama had told her that—and then asked, "How d'yew know when it's time to pick another one, Dellie?"

"I know," he grunted, then resumed his silence.

"I jus' wish we'd go to some other state—any ole state 'cept this 'un."

"Yew don't even know whut one we's in now," Dell snorted.

"No," Kee 'fessed up, "I don't rightly keep track—but both of us like our books—*right?*—and the whole blessed na-shun is jus' like a book to me, Dellie. An' ever state is like a chapter—ain't that whut they calls 'em?" She waited and he didn't deny she was correct. "Well, then, ever time we go outta one state, then that chapter's *over*—right? So yew go into another one 'n that's alla *that*, an' yew can start all over again!"

Dell didn't even deign to grunt at her remark. Leaning back, feeling eyes on the back of her neck again, Kee wondered if there was anything that killed ghosts. She knew about using a silver bullet on werewolves and a wooden stake on vampires.

Something in her own thinking amused Kee and relaxed her somewhat. Her thoughts unaccountably shifted to her partnership with Dell and how fine it'd turned out, so far. She was still a virgin, but she sure felt grown up by running around with her dream man. She'd definitely learned a *ton* of shit she never would have learned by stayin' in Chero-kee Rose. Smiling sweetly, allowing her chin to droop to her breast, Kee drowsed. . . .

What do I do after we git Kee's even hunderd, Dell wondered as he checked highway signs, found he could probably get the girl her Ninety-eight and still reach his destination by afternoon tomorrow—*help her go for two hunderd?*

That would be okay; so would a thousand. But he was smart enough to know what Kee was too immature to know, Dell reflected. If you went to the well too often, someday you'd find somebody'd puked in it. It was even a strain, always addin' more on, mostly because it wasn't the fun he'd imagined it would be. With a woman along, it wasn't *purely* sneaking up on folks because Kee always knew where they were going to end up, and basically what they were going to do. Without her, he could've sought variety, spon-tan-eity.

Hell, he figured, *wimmen's allus the same, even when they's crazy!* Raising kids or offing people, they never got enough, and they had to nag. And they sure as shit wouldn't fuck you unless there was some special occasion coming along. Marriage was the only one he knew they even thought was special enough!

I should pull over, put new holes in her neck with my thumbs, screw her till she's even weirder, Dell told himself, *then leave her out in the field for wild animals t'put up with.* He had wanted a little virgin girl to ride around with while he took care of business, but not forever—not without *gettin'* something from it.

Yet . . . Kee *was* special, Dell had to admit (to himself if nobody else). That was the hard part. He was damned if he could remember if he'd ever had a real girl of his dreams, partly because he seldom dreamed, partly because that sounded romantical, like something his mama would have talked about, partly because he'd never consciously wanted anything from a girl but fucking her. Yet Kee had given him what they called a "new leash on life," also new lead in his pencil whenever Kee let him rip off a vehicle belonging to a female and she cleared out awhile. Trouble was, vans were good luck for him yet most of the ones he'd seen had men drivin' them!

Dell concentrated, squinting at the road before him: The thing to do was remember just why he'd agreed to let the little cunt come with him in the first place—then that the more folks he offed, the more vicarious sacrifices they made for him, the younger, newer, more powerful Dell from hell got. Along with the greater guarantee that he was becoming fucking *immortal!*

He swiveled the rearview mirror to check his own face in it. Any fool could see that the gray in his hair was getting darker now, over the ears. He had seen a crinkle in his face before doing the girl's folks—maybe two—not that anybody else had noticed, because you had to get *real close* to see 'em—and now they were gone. What purely astonished Dell was the way his bad eye was becoming good again, like *new!* Why, there wasn't a drop of pus anywhere on that handsome-rascal face of his nor even on the new shirt he had slipped on after his nap. It wasn't fitting to be vain, Dell knew, but it appeared to him in that rearview mirror in the uncertain lighting of his vehicle that he might never have looked better or younger in his whole life!

And he felt *strong*, too, he did—able to handle any man-jack who showed up.

Dell turned to see the way Kee looked, sleeping. One thing was for *sure*: She wasn't getting credit for the one he planned to off when he got where he was going. Nobody else in the *world* had the right to *that* kill but ol' Dell!

Getting Ninety-eight and swapping vehicles turned out to be so easy and largely empty of challenge that it should have been anticlimactic both to him and Kee, Dell knew. But it had the opposite effect, for reasons he did not desire to consider.

All he knew later was a feeling similar to what he'd known when he was sent to see Dr. Middel years before.

Kee awakened in time to see the next hunt begin, and to discover she was even getting her way about leaving the state of Indiana and entering another chapter of their partnership book. From Dell's standpoint the only thing wrong with the trade-in was that they had to settle for something other than a van.

It was a brand-new BMW driven by a man in his thirties who, drunk, had decided to pull off the highway to the side of the road and have a nap before he went on home.

Dell merely parked in front of the BMW, walked

around to where the driver was slumped snoring with his head against the driver's side door, and pulled the door open.

It hadn't even been locked.

Dell planted his foot on the man's chest to pin him to the ground and waited till Kee scooted over beside him. The drunk's head didn't seem to be clearing as fast as that of the formerly bored Kee. "Yew want him?" Dellie asked her.

"To kill," she asked, "or for a soo-vaneer?"

The word *kill* restored the prone man's alertness, more or less. "Who're you?" he asked. Repeating it, then, he managed to inject a slightly more aggressive emphasis to the question. Evoking no response, he grappled dumbly with Dell's foot and ankle.

Dell balanced on the man's chest, pressed on the man's groin area with his entire weight, and ground down with his heel. "Don't much give a damn," he answered Kee, restive. He looked up and down the dark road to check for traffic but it was late now. "Make up yore mind, girl. I got other fish t'fry."

"Hell, Dellie, yew prob'ly jus' ruint him for the cooler," Kee said in mild pique.

"Well, shitfire," Dell said, "take a look! Check him out for yoreself."

Brightening, Kee stooped, tried to unzip the man. "Hold him down, will yew? He's squirmin' like a fish." When Dell obliged, producing further squeals of pain, Kee checked him out. "They's some blood on it, and it's gonna git purple," she said regretfully. "I can use his *other* thangs, though." Kee glanced up. "Will takin' 'em off kill him, yew reckon?"

Dell had his hands full; the drunk was sobering up. "Sooner or later it will kill him—but the cooler's full of 'em. Why not take his eyes? That'd show a little imagination."

"Oh, *no!*" Kee exclaimed in horror. "Dead eyes really *see* things! I—"

"Awright, awright," Dell snapped, "hurry up or I'm goin' t'have to squeeze him. Jest do yore thang."

Nodding, dutiful to her Dellie, Kee went right to work. Unfortunately, the man passed out at once. Still, she got her Ninety-eight, and then the two of them found a bonus in the backseat of the BMW.

A nice-looking little black-haired woman who'd already passed out maybe an hour ago.

She would have been Ninety-nine except that when Dell stuck his head in the back to get a closer look, she reeked of vomit. "Whooo-*eeee*," he said, withdrawing and fastidiously holdin' his nose. "*Yew* haul her outta there. I wouldn't do her with a ten-foot pole!"

Kee, clamping the lid on her cooler, was irked by such an unpleasant chore. "Nothin' personal, Dellie—but it *ain't* no fuckin' ten feet!"

And that keyed their mood for the rest of the spree, because Dell got the joke, chose not to lose his temper, and his self-control initiated the start of a different series of experiences that neither of them would regret for the remainder of their lives.

"Kin I make this here woman Ninety-nine if yew

don't want her?'' Kee was busy hauling the woman out of the car and unceremoniously dumping her next to the man who, by then, appeared to be dead.

Dell observed the drunken woman's attempt to sit up while he thought about the girl's question. It was hard to concentrate, too, with the bitch fallin' out of her cocktail dress. He might have conquered his revulsion then if he'd been prone to changing his mind. ''It'd be more interesting to wipe off the paring knife,'' Dell suggested, ''then leave it in her hand—she won't remember jack–shit about how we look, so let *her* try to explain whut happened to the aw-thorities.''

Kee laughed, then cut it short. ''But she's wakin' up now, Dellie,'' she argued, pointing a finger.

Dell hit the woman on top of her head with one fisted hand. ''Now she ain't,'' he said.

And with Kee giggling like a mad fool, they frolicked up the highway in their new BMW, Kee giving him kisses every place on his face and neck. The expensive vehicle responded nearly as good as the Jaguar Dell had driven once—the way women never had responded to him—and the fun they'd had getting it made Dell feel damn near invulnerable.

As for Kee, she couldn't recall the last time she'd had a whole night of sleep—or one in a real bed—so she felt goofy, giddy. After Dell had slowed down, she started telling him her secrets. About the way she'd got money from Willie Fawkner and his buddies to check out her new titties. How she'd forgot to wear panties under her skirt when she tried out for the cheerleading team (this anecdote was a lie). The time she'd fooled Mama into believing Daddy was *incesting* her, and Sue Elenor took the pictures. About how wonderful it was for her Dellie to kill her folks on'y to save her ("Honestly, I think I might've gone plumb strange if I'd had to stay so bored all my born days!") and how much, real deep down inside, he loved her even if he wouldn't say so. And how *she* didn't care if she had penis envy because all the boys she'd known probably had tittie-envy.

And Kee told Dellie how she figured the two of them as just like regular mid-evil knights and she would put that right in her book for the whole world to see someday when folks wrote a history about them. She said she had dreams sometimes while she was napping in their vehicles about marrying Dell—being truly hitched, just like Mama and Daddy was. "Why, the amazin' *true stories* we'd have us to tell the teeny ones! They shore wouldn't think *we* was borin', would they?"

Dell had said nothing—nothing at all—during the entire period of time that Kee was revealing her most secret heart to him and he said nothing then, either.

So Kee, in her annoyance, brought up the subject of Lewis Negley again, simply to hear Dell's voice. "I'm still skeered half to death 'bout that Lewie," she said, sneaking a peek at Dell. "Lord A'mighty, Dellie, doesn't yew ever have dreams that makes yew so afeerd yew can't even make yore eyes open up?"

Dell had just caught sight of a sign indicating they were within a hunderd miles of the place and the person he had chosen to visit. First, though, they'd grab some shut-eye, get some rest so's he'd be fresh for what had to be done.

Stirring in his seat, Dell nodded his head slowly. "I got two bad dreams these days. First one's about Mom. I'm skeered she might die before I can find an' kill her."

"Is that where we're goin' now?" she asked. "To kill Mom?"

Dell sighed. "No, it ain't. Isn't. 'Cause I doesn't know where she's gone to." And that was one of the reasons he was headed where he was headed, since somebody was holding back the magic he ought to have to *know* where Mom and her new husband went. "Second nightmare I git is about some ol' man in a white beard comin' t'kill me."

"Well," Kee asked, "who *is* he?"

"I purely don't know, girl. If I did—if he's *real*— I'd go off him first."

Kee gave a musical laugh. "One thing for sure, Dellie, it *ain't* Uncle Sam—'cause we've awreddy seed more of his wonnerful country than practic'ly anyone I ever did know!"

Dealing with the likelihood that Kee McCaulter was not only assisting Dell in the slaughter of innocent citizens but had probably planned the murders of her own mother and father disturbed Kirk Douglas— more than he would have liked to admit—for the first hour or so of his renewed pursuit.

Then he began to put it into perspective in his professional memory bank and got on with his work.

Someday, perhaps when he was able to retire from this soul-poisoning ordeal he called a career, he might be able to begin sorting things out in his vastly troubled, most intimate thoughts. Now there was only the work.

Apart from the fact that he felt pretty sure where Dell and Kee were now headed, the brightest spot of his day was the realization that his own amateur-psychologist analysis of the male monster had worked out—or so it seemed to Kirk. Basically, he'd concluded that Dell was either a psychopath, a sociopath, or maybe some sort of damned hybrid—a mutant—of the two. He had preferred the analysis that argued for the sociopathic personality but problems with the bastard's pattern, and the way it had become more pointlessly violent after a history of occasionally letting his victims live, had opted more for the psychopath category.

But with the insertion of a participating teenage girl into the equation (*God, she was fifteen when their spree began!*), the jigsaw puzzle, it was possible at last to begin drawing some valid-sounding though tentative conclusions:

He *was* a sociopath. *Kee* was the psycho, and—well, their partnership was very nearly what you created when two people in love married—a new, *separate entity entirely*. Not exactly a child, more like the creation of a union, a relationship, which had its own priorities, its own needs and aspirations, its own moment of inception—its own *existence*, for the love of God—

And its moment of termination. Of death, cessation. Or so Kirk dearly hoped and prayed.

Together, it appeared, Kee and Dell had made a bridge between her psychopathic desires, compulsions, crazy dreams, and fears, and his rationalistic, cold-bloodedly pragmatic, completely egotistic and pleasure-seeking rover's personality. The wonder was that her sweeping range of emotions and his emotionless preoccupation with routine and method had ever jibed, clicked. Obviously, Dell had or could offer things the girl wanted and Kee had things he needed. And the obvious assumption to make about Dell's needs was tied to sexuality, yet he hadn't killed her—at least, not yet.

Kirk checked the highway signs, tapped the accelerator, wondered if he'd put his neck on the chopping block by not making sure the *federales* knew his destination. He might enlist the help of a local officer, but he absolutely wasn't going to allow the F.B.I. to take this collar away from him. He'd put too much into it. Possibly, he pointed out to himself, *literally* too much.

Odd, though, to think through the path of reasoning his own theories obliged him to consider: When a young couple got married, they almost never realized they were creating a "separate entity," a marriage. They were inclined toward loving each other, believed they did, they both usually meant well, but the awareness that a real "something," a force called "marriage," was the product of what the two of them made together *first*, escaped most people—whether they stayed together a year, ten years, thirty or forty or more years.

Douglas hadn't realized anything of the sort till after his wife divorced him.

But the thing was, whether marriage succeeded, failed, or any of the other qualities in-between—you never knew what kind of new and separate entity the two had created till the deed was done. Really good marriages were marvelous to behold, they warmed your heart or made you aware of your own drawbacks, but they were impossible to miss—they were still the hallmarks of any healthy society, what men and women could aspire to together.

Yet now and again you saw two people get together and create such a freaking Frankenstein monster of an entity that it drained the very life from society, and from those who had to be exposed to it.

That was what these two serial killers had invented together. An entity, a thing, that sapped the life out of everybody they ran into.

In the old *Frankenstein* movie, representatives of the town finally got together and went to the castle to burn up the damned monster. However pathetic he might have seemed, however much he didn't even understand the horror he'd brought people, they burned him up.

And that's what I'm going to do, too, Kirk told himself, looking for the next exit to Illinois. *Destroy the monster.*

* * *

It was getting cold and very late at night when Dell informed Kee they'd have to get a couple of hours sleep before they "finished the trip." Kee asked, "Trip to *where*?" but reached a deaf Dell ear with that question.

So she tried asking Dellie to stop at a motel somewhere because "they ain't no bed in this ole car," but got nowhere with that request either. "I've tried alla my life t'git t'be famous—an' I shared it with *yew*, too—an' now I'm like any sell-ebrity. I cain't jest go wherever I has a mind t'go. And neither can yew," he said. "Yew're my groupie."

That left the options of trading in again that night (which Dellie said it wasn't yet the time to do, meaning he was tired), breaking into some house just to find a bed for the night (which drew his sharp reply that "Serial killers ain't common burglars, we has a reputation t'uphold," at which point she'd asked just what that reputation *was*, and Dellie told her, "Yew cain't be everthang in this world; burglin' is for assholes who don't have as much eye-magination."

Or squinching up next to Dellie on the backseat of the BMW, not knowing whether they were glad for the company (to stay warm) or if they wanted to kill each other (so there'd be more room on the seat).

"Yew feel like givin' me a blow job?" Dell asked.

Kee, lying on top of him except for one leg caught under both of his, was feeling irritable. They were almost world-famous and still didn't have a place to sleep or eat a decent meal, and Kee wasn't in the mood for games. She knew it was important to Dell not to look like any ole sissy, so she said, "I'm only fifteen years old."

He didn't rear up and look amazed, or anything like she expected. "I mused on how long yew planned t'wait before informin' me of the truth. But dammit, girl, thet ain't it no more. Yew's *sixteen* years old now, not fifteen. I heered it on the radio an' read it in two newspapers. Yew would've, too, if yew read for shit!"

"Well, I truly *was* fifteen when we first met," Kee argued, stirring, trying to sit up and be indignant. "We didn't even celebrate my birthday back in July, and a young lady's Number Sixteen is a momentous occasion!"

His arm lay heavily across her waist, he didn't feel like moving it, and he sensed Kee giving up the effort to sit. "Best I can recolleck, yore 'Number Sixteen' was a fat-butt woman about forty-five in pants yew had t'peel offa her jest t'take somea her thigh for the cooler." Dellie sounded stern, but he was shaking a bit with amusement, not making his humming or muttering noises.

"The proper young ladies back home," Kee said haughtily, "still have comin'-out parties." She yawned hugely.

"I know thet," Dell said, "thet's why I asked yew about blowin' me—so's *I* could 'come out!'"

She tried to elbow him where it'd truly hurt, but missed. "I never needed any ole men or boys anyhow," she sniffed, leaning against him and stretching out the best she could. "Yew knows I'm psychic an' all, but yew don't know my *big* secret."

"Go ahead." He yawned, getting ready to tune her out. It was nice and dark and the BMW was tucked 'way back in the small private park of a fancy new apartment complex, and if any security suits showed up, he'd just blast them and drive off in the morning. "Yew got a big hairy *dildo* in thet suitcase?"

"No!" Kee exclaimed. She relaxed her face to tell her story as convincingly as possible and with as much dignity. "What it is—I can have me a orgasm whenever I wants to have one."

"*How*?" Dell demanded. "With *whut*—with *who*?"

"Jus' by—*wantin'* one!" she said airily, turning in order to see his face.

"Yew cannot," he said, inches away.

"Can so," she declared, lowering her eyelids, reopening them with an air of defiance.

Dell's eyes narrowed. "Go ahead," he said. "Do it."

Kee snuggled happily against his chest and into his arms. "I jus' did it," she said.

"*Whuutttt*?" He pushed her up, off him, wiggled out from under till he was on his knees and Kee was in a heap on the seat. "Yew did not!"

"Did so," she purred, eyes closed in contentment. "An' I was *great*, too!"

Dell groped at her jeans zipper. "Do it ag'in so's *I* can see it happen."

Kee shoved his hand, slapped it. "I know I said I could do it anytime but not after I jus' *did* it!"

Dell turned around with difficulty and got part of his butt on the seat. "I've had me mebbe sevenny or eighty women 'n I purely can't figger any of yew out." His instinct had been either to hit her in the chin for lying to him or to put his hand in her pants to find out if she was wet, but he knew for a fact where either one would lead him. And the girl was right: He didn't want anyone to think for a minute he was a pervert, even if that actor-cop Kirk Douglas *said* he was every now and then.

As for Kee's last surprise, well, he was onto her now. He'd stopped trying to fuck her ever since the start of spring when he learnt the truth. At least he got himself a free show whenever she ran around naked, and that kept him ready for the females they'd met. He just wished men'd pay women better so they'd buy more vans and other decent vehicles for his own tradin' purposes.

"I wish it could be yew, Dellie," Kee said, beside him. She barely spoke loud enough for Dell to hear. When he looked down, she was nearly asleep—and still the purtiest little gal Dell had ever seen. "I wanted yew t'be my first real fella but I mustn't talk a gallant knight outta his principuls. Yew'd make a fine husbin, though. An' daddy."

"I reckon that's a fact or two," Dell granted her, nodding. Moonlight was sneakin' in, messin' with her face, and he thought there was something funny about how she was conversing right then. He had no idea, though, how to find out what she was thinking, or feeling. "They warn't never nothin' I couldn't learn if I put my mind to it."

"Mebbe someday," Kee said groggily, small hands tucked under one cheek. "Mebbe in heaven. Yew never know."

Dell nodded once more, troubled, caught motion from the corner of his good eye.

He'd left his most precious possession, the dictionary, on a front seat—and what he saw was the cover of the paperback, Scotch tape finally undone and gone, drifting between the cockpit seats to the floor of the BMW.

The Book *was startin' t' fall apart*.

"Kee . . . girl . . ." Dell began, had to gulp and begin over. "I'm goin t'lose my magic if I don't go *kill* him—an' thet's where we're headin'."

"Who?" Kee's was the falling-asleep voice of a child.

"He knows all about the vi-carious sacrifice, too—hell, girl, he knows even more than *I* do. Why, he was the one who taught me about the phoenix." Dell extended his arm to retrieve the dictionary cover. Then he held it tenderly between his powerful thumb and index finger. By then, he knew every letter and every number on it, including the paperback's original price. "Thangs was fine, too, as long as he was in prison. Mebbe thet old man is usin' magic now hisself. Mebbe he's usin' it *ag'in* me, for all I know."

"Floyd?" Kee asked in a whisper, nearly asleep.

Dell snorted. "*Lloyd B.*," he whispered back, like a man chanting magical words to counter a curse. "It's all in the books in the library, thangs 'bout sorceror people 'n shameins havin' t'take over when the ole magicians git old and uppity."

I thought you liked him. By now Kee was actually sleeping but Dell had always enjoyed deciding what other folks would say if they were talkin' to him, so the conversation continued.

"Well, I did—much as I can like a darkie. Shit-fire, I ackshally add-mired him, girl. Jest like I add-mired Dr. Middel back when I was a mere kid." Dell sighed and leaned back against the backseat. In his absent manner he stroked the drowsing teenager's fanny, careful not to kick the cooler with his toe and create a clanking or sloshing sound that would interrupt his soliloquy. "Thet's got nothin' to do with those dreams I been havin'. Yew 'member the ones about the old man with the white beard?"

I 'member ever single thang yew ever tole me, Dellie.

Squinting through the gloom of the BMW at the ruined cover of *The Book*, Dell saw his deepest concern—his only real fear now—beginning to come to life. "Well, girl, he's either Jesus Christ—or the spirit of Noah Webster."

CHAPTER

14

Dell drove through Terre Haute into Illinois with the images of three signs lingering in his mind. One said that the Indiana city was the "Basketball Home" of Larry Bird; another, green sign advertised a hotel he owned, the Boston Connection, and was nearly as high as a three-story building. The third sign, depicting a sweet-natured man in a beard, advertised that JESUS SAVES.

The former might have seemed a good omen to Dell, because he and Kee were finally getting where

Lewis Negley was trying to go. The last sign, however, reminded Dell of his recent nightmare and gave him a twinge of unfamiliar doubt. It wasn't his fault *The Book* had begun falling apart on him. The combination of Bird, Christ, Dell's own fine recollections of what they'd done to the escaping Negley, and his awe of any man who knew *all* the words there were made him wonder if he could be making a mistake about offing Lloyd B. Maybe one or the other of these great people was telling him to go kill somebody else instead.

"I read up about Illanoise in prison," he told Kee just to change his mood. " 'Cause I knowed ol' Lloyd was from somewheres in this state. It got its name from red Indians 'n French folks an' it means 'tribe of soo-perior men.' " He glanced at where she was sitting beside him. "Maybe I should come here t'retire, too, if I ever does. 'Cause of the name."

Kee yawned. "Everplace I know *means* somethin'. Why doesn't they jus' call a town or state 'zactly what it does mean?"

"Well, *yore* state, Georgia, was named after King George, Capital I-I. It might take a while t'write thet on a envelope."

"I think Mama tole Daddy Georgia was named after some place in Russia. That's whut got him all pissed, and chasin' on Mama, 'n all." Her nose crinkled to show her distaste. "They would've named Georgia 'George' iffen he hadn't been a faggot, I s'pose."

Dell thought about that and nodded. "Imagine thet's what happened with Louisiana," he averred.

He was pleased to see Kee had changed clothes during their last gas-up. It showed she had some refinement and understood on her own what was suitable when they paid a visit to an ol' friend. She had on a lacy white top with holes and a bright red mini-skirt with zigzaggy orange arrows.

What Dell 'specially liked was how Kee had got her hair out of her eyes with a purty blue bow on top of her head. It made her look like the child of fifteen he'd wanted to screw right from the start even though she'd been cleaner then.

The small town they eventually found—Black Hawk, named for a war that ended Indian problems for the Illinois settlers—combined some of the state's major money-making features. Coal mining in the past had left much of the land barren, gray as a week-old corpse in the fall; hog farms the BMW passed added scent and sound to the meat-packing industry of—but never quite contained by—the distant north; and abandoned railroad tracks crisscrossed every thirty or forty yards like skeletal bones discarded by a manic chiropractor. All this was formless impression in Dell's mind, but did not go unnoticed. Black Hawk was so removed from any expectations of a Chicago-like ambience that even syndicate people had usually refused to drive that far south for the sake of burying a newly-dead adversary. Dell remembered all those things from a prison library book about organized crime.

"Jest smell thet air," he urged Kee, rolling the window down to inhale. "It's Mother Nature at her purest, girl."

"An' I thought Cherokee Rose was borin'," Kee said. "At least it didn't stink." She tucked her knees to her chest, wrapping her arms around them and sighed.

Dell left the window down as long as he could stand it. It was fairly balmy for autumn, but Illinois winds seemed to begin at the stockyards. Eventually, the smell was too much even for Dell. "We'll liven her up some."

"Yew got a address for the friend yew're gonna kill?" Kee inquired.

"Don't say it thet way, gawdamnit!" Dell said with a frown. "Yew mind yore manners whilst we's there, too. Jest follow my lead. We're only goin t'visit with ol' Lloyd—at first."

Kee glared out the window with conspicuous disdain. "I cain't see whut point they is to comin' here to off someone when Mr. Lloyd won't even make it a even hunderd." She turned back to glare at Dell. "Why couldn't we go ahead an' get the rest first and save yore friend for a bonus?"

"Lloyd B. saved me from a fate worse than death for a real man, he did. His book-learnin' was whut made me the man I is."

"B-but yew're gone kill him anyways," she said, baffled.

Dell nodded with great solemnity. "I am. I'll probably bust his neck jest as sweet 'n gentle as if he was my very own daddy."

"Sometimes," Kee said thoughtfully, "I purely believe yew like that—that ol' Lloyd B. better'n yew like me. An' he's black!"

Dell did not answer for a moment. They had driven the BMW into what he assumed to be the only predominantly black neighborhood in Black Hawk, Illinois. All the children he saw playing were black and the few adults on the street weren't white either. Searching for Lloyd, he craned his neck from side to side. "Girl, I don't know if I like anybuddy. I allus been too busy workin' to think about likin'. As for yore previous query, the radio did not cite Lloyd's street address. The only reason they mentioned him was *me*. But I knowed this would be a leetle town and I figgered it would not be hard to locate my colleague."

Kee didn't hear Dell's last couple of sentences. She was peering out the window and her eyes were getting glassy. "Why is they starin' at me?" She glanced back to Dell with an expression of bewilderment, fright, and fury. Dell noticed she shivered, as if the little ones' eyes were goin' straight through her. "Dellie, I absotively *hate* bein' stared at!"

"'Cept if yew have removed your clothin' and *wants* t'be stared at," he replied. "Might be they're eye-ballin' this fancy ve-hicle. Yew reckon that might be it, girl?"

"I jus' bet yew're right!" Kee said, feeling better immediately. She even wiggled her fingers at the next child, like some fairy tale princess riding in a fine carriage. Suddenly she spun on her seat, excited by the idea that had occurred to her. "Dell— whyn't yew go look up yore friend Lloyd's address in a phone book?"

Dell hooted at that. "Under *whut*, chile—the letter *B*?"

The two of them rode in silence for another block or two. Then when Dell was beginning to think about givin' some kid on the sidewalk a nickel to find out where Lloyd resided, something happened that seemed to him like the answer to a prayer—

Because, there he was! Lloyd himself! With a long rake and maybe the biggest pile of autumn leaves at his feet Dell had ever seen!

But Dell wasn't sure it *was* Lloyd till he'd driven by and remembered something of how the great teacher's eyes had looked the first time they ever saw each other. Big eyes, mean and wise as an owl, like he wasn't afraid of no man nowhere.

Now, in less than a year, everything *else* about Lloyd B. appeared to have changed. Dell noticed how bent over he was, and thin—he'd purely lost maybe forty-fifty pounds—and how . . . old . . . Lloyd B. looked.

Lloyd had grown himself a beard since Dell last saw him. A beard so snowy white he might have looked like Sandy Claus, if he'd been white.

Eager to talk, now, Dell fumbled their new car into reverse—he'd kept the BMW because he wanted Lloyd B. to see how well he was doin'—screeching the tires as they went backward. Then he stomped on the brake and turned to let himself out. He wasn't certain his old guru had even seen the car or him yet.

"Whitemeat." Lloyd tasted the word, made a

clear two syllables of it. He still had the long-handled rake in his hands and glanced inside the car, at the girl. "Been hearing quite a lot about you. And your little traveling companion."

"I mighta knowed I couldn't sneak up on yew, Lloyd B.," Dell said, chuckling. Nervously, he put out his hand. "Yew shore has changed, though." *That beard . . .*

Fall wind gusted without effect at the wiry growth. "The same could be said of you, meat, if the media hasn't got it all fucked up." Lloyd B. still held the rake, gripped it high to his chest with both hands; his now skinny legs, clad in work pants, were spread slightly and they still looked like most normal forces could not budge them. He had not accepted Dell's hand and he hadn't asked him into his house.

"Kee," Dell shouted as though unaware that her nose had been pressed against the BMW window since he left the car, "git yore stumps stirrin'—come meet Lloyd B!"

Instantly, the door flew back. She must have already been squeezing the handle. Lloyd, with no change of expression on his stony face, saw her jump out and come running. Within a few yards of him she slowed down, though, most of the curiosity in her animated face changing to wariness, tentative hostility. "Dell, I don't really think—"

"Lloyd B., I want yew t'encounter my . . . my travelin' companion. Kee." Dell was supremely hearty. He got his hand in the small of her back and shoved her stumbling forward. "Kee, this here is my add-visor and guru, Lloyd B."

She put out her index, middle finger, and part of the ring and Lloyd took them, briefly. No referee could have said who broke the contact first. "Dell, my most attentive pupil," Lloyd said, chuckling despite his better judgment. "Still mangling the King's English but still—endeavoring."

"I been endeavorin' all over the country," Dell said. Then his busy brain conjured twisted memories of himself as a lovable young con. "Are we going to stand out here 'n chat, gittin' cold, or are yew goin t'ask us in t'see yore house?"

Lloyd glanced with uncertainty from the familiar murderer to the white girl. She was something, the type who gave you more of herself to see than you wanted. Was there any real choice about admitting this pair and letting them sully the house his father left to him, the one thing Lloyd had in the whole world? On one side was the chance that Dell meant no harm, merely wished to brag of the dreadful things he and this . . . bad seed had done, then get the hell out of his life. Lloyd owed the authorities nothing.

Most of his life he'd striven to get a new trial, then a pardon. But they had finally let him go because his new attorney had applied sufficient pressure, and because he, Lloyd, was dying of cancer.

He had gone straight home when he was released. Dad, Mama, and Lloyd's own wife Flo had long since sanctified the place. And if he made a ruckus out front, the police might well take him along with these two. By the time the truth was known, his reputation would really be destroyed and the neighbors would never believe him again.

But, if Lloyd allowed his "visitors" to enter his home, they might well just kill him! Whitemeat was not the same. Something had made him worse, more overt. Maybe neighbors had already recognized him and his little "San Quentin quail"—the prison term for an underage female—and the damn cops would find these honky horrors having fucking *coffee* at Lloyd Benson's dining room table!

"Dellie," Kee said, shivering and hugging herself, "I'm freezin'." Her arms were goose-pimpled. "Kin we go *somewheres?*"

"Come on inside," Lloyd said on total impulse, laying down the rake next to his collection of autumn leaves. Most of them would remain where they were. "I was just tryin' to decide about my raking," he explained to Dell, walking ahead of them up the driveway to the flat stones which led over to his front door. The house was a small frame structure with a porch, old but always well tended. "I want to burn the leaves—my neighbors generally do—but somebody told me there's an ordinance against it."

"If thet's like a law," Dell said from behind the old man, "there can't be too much of a fine. I wouldn't worry about it none."

No, you probably wouldn't, Lloyd thought, tugging the storm door open for his "guests." He glanced back at them.

The bastard Dell was gaping open-mouthed at

the traveling mansion, an enormous vehicle, that Lloyd had parked by the side of the house.

"Gollleee, Lloyd B.," said Dell, familiarly ingratiating, chilling Lloyd with the nearly naked tone of avid greed, "is this here whut they call a 'RV'?"

"Yep." Lloyd stamped his feet on the welcome mat to keep from revealing his nervousness. "It's Jake's, my adopted nephew's. He asked me to let him park it here awhile." Lloyd had seen the glint in Dell's eyes as he stared at the RV; now he knew what crime Dell would try to commit before he left here. "C'mon, meat, your friend's teeth are beginning to shake."

"Thet ain't all she shakes," Dell said with a wink, brushing past Lloyd into the house.

"Oh, yeeew," Kee said, squeezing inside before the door slammed.

The living room was larger than had seemed possible on the outside. There was one easy chair that appeared to have been recently upholstered, another that had seen better days, an old sofa with a maroon throw draping it. . . .

And walls lined with bookshelves, the shelves crammed neatly—but certainly crammed—with books.

"Thet shyster lawyer musta got yew a purty penny when he sprung yore ass," Dell said admiringly, making a beeline for the closest shelf and tugging at a book. The volumes on both sides fell to the floor. Dell picked one up, slipped it back in a different place. "Looks like yew made up fer lost readin' time an' bought out a whole bookstore, Lloyd."

"Looks are often deceptive." Lloyd stepped forward quietly and bent to pick up the other fallen book. He was afraid Dell would step on it. "I got just what you got when they released you; still have my suit in the closet."

"Where did all these books come from, then?" Dell asked. He realized dimly that they were grouped by subject matter, then alphabetized by author. He sent his good eye sliding over to see the old man's face. "Yew come inta some big bucks somewheres, Lloyd B.?"

Lloyd tried to use a seemingly good-humored hand at Dell's shoulder to steer him farther from his treasures. There were no rare books there that he knew of, no first folios; he merely loved them. "Just the house, meat, and a lot of old books belonging to my dad, my mom, and"—Lloyd hesitated abruptly, certain he didn't want to mention his late wife in their presence—"and other members of my family. There's no one left of us now but me."

"Thet's a whole ton or two of magic yew got," Dell said. He sat down in an upholstered chair beside the end table that held an open book and Lloyd's reading glasses, propped his feet on a hassock. "Real magic. Mebbe yew should jest leave yore personal liberry t'me, seein' as how I'm a book lover, too."

He's serious about that, Lloyd thought with amazement, edging over to stand before his other old chair. His back was turned to them and he was trying to come up with an answer to Dell's incredible suggestion when, simultaneously, he perceived that the girl had left the room and was now returning from the kitchen. "Yew didn't have no brews in the fridge for yore guests, so I put on some coffee," she said. Pausing, she folded one palm over the other. "Anybody want a sandwich? I couldn't find any peanut butter but I saw some flat meat in the fridge."

"The word is beer, gawdamnit t'hell!" Dell exploded. "Yew want Lloyd B. t'think I'm runnin' around with some fuckin' moron?"

"I wouldn't worry about that," Lloyd murmured. "Kee, you might—"

Dell's palm, halting his remark, shot up. "It was nice t'make coffee, girl. But it's the *host's* place t'offer us a more generous repast—if he so desires." The bastard didn't even look at Lloyd when he said it. "Yew jest sit down on the couch till Lloyd *recalls* his hostly obligations."

Midnight welled up in Lloyd Benson's brain like a swift and deadly growth. He recognized clearly one of the games this untutored cretin he had made the mistake of befriending meant to play. He just wasn't sure of Dell's rules—of how deadly Dell intended to become to a man who had saved his life.

"If you'd spent thirty-more years in prison, folks, you wouldn't be expecting any company either." Lloyd forced an aw-shucks grin, detesting it, sat down in the chair. He was damned if he would let them have the run of his front room without him there to watch them, but he badly needed his glasses from the table next to whitemeat. "Go ahead"—he waved to the teenage girl—"make yourselves sandwiches if you're hungry. And I *could* use a cup of coffee."

Kee, apparently puzzled, stared blankly at the seated black man. Then, heavily, she sat on the edge of the sofa with her pale arms folded over her young chest and peered at nothing—unless it was something Lloyd did not wish to see.

Hostility, unvoiced questions, and enmity nobody in the living room remotely understood hung like smoke above their heads. Staring at the dusty toes of his shoes, Dell looked more thoughtful than Lloyd had imagined he had the capacity for. Dell, too, appeared older in spite of the brief period of time that had passed since they last shared a cell. His lantern-jawed face was gaunt and his long-ago damaged eye dripped matter incessantly, though Dell did nothing to stanch it. "Lloyd," he said, his gaze still on his shoes. "I notice yew don't talk darkie no more at all. Why, yew don't even sound like no black person."

Behind Dell light from a window beamed at the old man as if spotlighting him, putting him in the witness chair of some mad and hate-filled courtroom. "It just isn't necessary any longer . . . Dell." Lloyd maintained his manner of outward cheerfulness while his guts churned bile and pain gnawed freely wherever it could reach. "Remember, I explained about language to you?—how one may use it to fit in with any company—"

"But I purely don't think yew're fittin' in with the *present* comp'ny, Lloyd," Dell said bluntly. He hadn't raised his voice, but it was a command, of sorts, that was unmistakable. A part of it, unquestionably, was for Lloyd to stand and make those sandwiches, pour their motherfucking coffee. "Thet snow-white beard. Why d'yew s'pose yew ain't fittin' in now?"

"Well, it could have to do with the fact that this is my house and not my cell," Lloyd said. Still smiling. The smile felt frozen there, like a glacial blob of something pressed to his mouth by unseen hands. "Is that possible, d'you think?"

All three of them could smell the coffee—it was ready—and nobody moved. Lloyd was trying to keep from blinking, he yearned to move his head from the sunlight and Dell's one watching eye, and he was succeeding so far. Cold and hot, darkness and light, the will to kill and the will to live existed simultaneously in Lloyd's front room—*living* room—but they were like the meeting of matter and anti-matter, they could not co-exist long.

"If this was *my* house," Kee blurted out, "they'd at least be *peanut butter* for callers to eat!"

Lloyd, helpless to stop himself, laughed loudly. Once only, but loudly.

"*Shut yore face!*" The command was Dell's, and Lloyd, scared as much by surprise as because he was a rational man, stared at his ex-cellmate in the anticipation of immediate attack.

But Dell was looking at the weird, rude girl, jabbing his finger at her. "Yew go git coffee fer Lloyd B. 'an me *this minute*, or they'll hafta carry yore useless ass outta here on a stretcher!" He glanced at Lloyd. "Yew like it black?"

"No, meat," Lloyd lied. "I like it with lots of cream and sugar." He was able to break his careful surveillance of Dell by looking up at Kee, his own eyelids rapidly blinking. "If you please . . . miss." The sugar'd take her longer, the two of them would be separated.

She sniffed, turned in the direction of the kitchen. "I hope yew leaves big tips at least," she said airily.

Dell's unobstructed eye found both of his host's, and he nodded approvingly. "I was wrong, Lloyd B. Yore language hasn't really changed." Smiling he picked up Lloyd's reading glasses from where they lay on the table beside him and idly turned the shafts in his hand. "Yew still talk like a man. A eddicated man."

"Thank you." Lloyd found another grin somewhere. "You still mangle—"

"A eddicated man who made me his *boy*," Dell interrupted. He turned his horsey head forward and he wasn't smiling any longer. "They was a time I was fuckin' *starved* t'kill yew, Lloyd B. Jest about as bad and as soon as I could. Yew know thet?"

"Yes," Lloyd said. "When you needed me no longer, of course. To keep your pristine white posterior unsullied. Please be careful with those specs, Dell. If you still intend to kill me, I don't think it would deprive you of enjoyment for me to watch it coming. It might even enhance your pleasure—or does the word *amusement* come closer to it?"

"Yew're right ag'in, Lloyd B.," Dell said with a marveling sigh, and stood. He cupped the glasses in his palm, started across the space between them. "But it ain't—*isn't* thet I'm going t'kill yew." He reached Lloyd in his chair.

"Surely the girl isn't going to do it." Lloyd stared up, keeping his hands on the arms of the chair, refusing to humble himself by reaching—pawing— for the spectacles. "Surely you would rather see if your fabulous thumbs are actually stronger than all of my beat-up ol' black body, *prove* it beyond the shadow of a doubt, than give that *infant* the assignment."

Dell said, "Here," and dropped the glasses, unharmed, into the old man's lap. Careful not to brush against Lloyd's heavy white beard, he turned sideways and seemed about to return to his chair. But the damaged eye was weeping copiously in its exhibit of mixed guilt and willful self-blinding, and Dell was *pissed*. "Yew taught me not to be no gawdamn bigot and I *ain't*, yew mammy-jammer! I'd fuckin' love t'git my thumbs on yore black neck, but it's *hid* by thet fuckin Noah Webster beard 'n yew ain't got a muscle *anywheres* no more! Yew've purely screwed me outta my right t'hate yew proper, t'*do* yew proper!" He took two steps to the hassock, brought back his big foot and kicked it hard enough for it to bound off a book-covered wall. "Yew ain't even a *man* no more!"

"I'll show *you* who's a man!" Lloyd grunted, pushing himself up from the chair.

But Dell, whirling, knocked Lloyd back down

and hovered over him. Stabbing downward with his pair of index fingers, each enormous thumb was like a tightened scrotum. "It all comes down t'jest one thang, and yew know it—the phoenix! Thet's all that matters. Yew and yore learnin' taught ole Dell from Hell more about magic than anythang but thet ugly Dr. Middel an' leetle Miss Show-Her-Ass-But-Cover-It!"

"*Phoenix?*" Lloyd mumbled. He got his glasses back on any old way he could, tried to understand what the hell Dell was raving about.

"Don't pretend t'get iggurant on me!" Dell shouted. "Well, sir, once yew've done like the phoenix did, Lloyd B., yew'll be *young* ag'in—bigger 'n stronger'n yew've ever been before! An' it's *time*, now—time fer yew t'*renew yoreself* like you tole me about—so's I can tear yore fuckin' throat out, properlike, an' give it t' the girl for Number Ninety-nine!"

"Renew myself?" Lloyd both said and ruminated over the words, casual words he'd spoken in distant days he had done his level best to forget, words that were gradually acquiring terrible new significance to him. "Number Ninety-nine?"

Dell yanked Lloyd out of the chair with one jerk. "Stand up, gawdamnit!" he ordered. Dragging him forward for a couple of off-balance steps, Dell glanced through the picture window, past the porch with the old-fashioned swing, fixed his weeping gaze on the leaves Lloyd had raked into an immense pile. A few—a very few—had blown away. "Here's the deal, Lloyd. Yore goin' out there whilst the girl adds some shit that'll burn purty decent—and yew're going t'make yoreself *over!* Yew're going t'become the man yew have a right t'be, so I can *kill* yew when I'm ready—and if the magic don't work, then we're goin t'take yore nephew Jake's RV an' drive t'California in it!''

Lloyd dropped his big head on his chest, let his body sag in despondency. He seemed then to surrender himself completely to the strange experiment, but he asked wryly, "Meat, what happens if I decide to just *pass* on this glorious opportunity to enact Joan of Arc?''

"Lloyd B., we isn't playin' no girl games here and thet RV in yore drive ain't no damn ark. Doubt if it'd even float much.'' Fairly gently, Dell turned Lloyd, steered him past the kitchen entrance and toward the front door. A smile was back on his lips, the sort bestowed by people fortunate enough to maintain their mental health upon those who have started to seem simple. "I'm afeerd I'd jest hafta—''

Lloyd yanked away, free of Dell's powerful hands and thumbs, and took three swift steps to the rear. Dell was so startled he made no effort to charge after the old man. . . .

. . . whose feet were planted, his thin legs braced, and his face set in hard, unyielding lines. To Dell's amazement, Lloyd B. seemed to be daring the younger man to come try to take him again!

"Fight me while I'm on my feet, whitemeat, you vicious damn redneck.'' It was Lloyd's quietly emphatic, familiar rumble, as commanding as of old.

"Or take your crazy little honky whore and get the fuck out of my daddy's house!"

"I *ain't* crazy." Kee said, jabbing the point of her paring knife into the broad back before her as a tray of coffee she was carrying from the kitchen clattered on the floor. Steaming fluid splashed her legs and Lloyd's, and neither—for different reasons—flinched. "An' I isn't really a whore neither, not technic'ly. I'm still a good girl, in fack."

Wounded but not gravely, humming a song of pain, Lloyd spun to face the girl. Instinctively, he reached out to grab at her small wrist, tried to wrest the knife away.

But then an object that didn't itself draw a drop of blood jammed against Lloyd's spine and he knew, instantly, what Dell had in his hand.

"—I'm afeerd I'd jest hafta shoot yew." Dell hauled in the thread of his interrupted reply. "Somewheres thet it did not suspend yore existence. Then we'd put yew on the pyre jest like thet. A'course, it could make yore chances for gettin' renewed less en-couragin'."

Kee's eyes got big over the idea of burnin' up someone, but Lloyd Benson's mind simply settled—with something like supernatural dread—on the word *pyre*. Nobody incinerated human bodies on *pyres* any longer, did they?

Keeping one hand on the wound in his back, only dimly wondering how bad he was bleeding, Lloyd turned back to Dell and forced his shoulders into a shrug. "Might I ask something else without her stabbin' me again?"

"Don't cut up my guru no more," Dell told Kee, then nodded amiably at their host. "Yew shore can, Lloyd B.—but let's us start headin to the door whilst Kee rounds up some old newspapers 'n magazines, wooden crap an' all." He glanced commandingly at her. "Whutever might make a real, nice fire."

Next to Dell but one step in front, Lloyd began walking slowly toward his foyer, using his bloodied back for an excuse not to rush. Kee, looking at the bookshelves, called, "I s'pose 'whutever' don't include these. Not even the paperback ones?"

"'*Speshally* not them," Dell said firmly. "If ol' Lloyd don't git renewed, I want t'hunt for a new *Book of Webster's*." They were in the foyer and he let Lloyd B. stop there. "Whut did yew want t'ask, Lloyd?"

"*Why?*" The old man's expression was one of puzzlement. "*Why* a funeral pyre? Do you really want to find out if the legend of the phoenix works? Or do you hate me so much for saving that worthless hide of yours?"

Dell had to chuckle. "I don't like or hate nobuddy. Thet's the pure truth of it, Lloyd. An' I don't need no proof about the phoenix neither, 'cause yew said once faith don't re-quire any."

"Faith? What . . . *faith?*" Lloyd yearned to sit down. He'd checked his palm and found it dripping with blood.

"Well, could be thet's not the right *term*, Lloyd B.," Dell allowed. "It's jest thet I hasn't got any-thang in the world 'cept the bird 'n the words—

'cause I done put all the belief I had in *The Book* an' the phoenix.''

Lloyd said swiftly, ''Dell, it's a *dictionary*, that book. And I told you about the phoenix legend to help you change, to *improve yourself.*''

''An' I did, too, I thanks yew fer thet,'' Dell declared, nodding his long head. ''Yew made me fuckin' invulner'ble t'hurt, an' immortal, too.'' He stuck his face up close to Lloyd's so the girl wouldn't hear his secrets. ''The vicarious sacrifices made me like this, Lloyd. But I don't much *feel* nothin' no more when I gits 'em t'die fer me—and I'm afeerd I might be losin' the magic. Pissin' it away a few drops at a time. An' without magic, why, my whole gawdamn life would be nothin but a waste.''

Nodding, listening intently, Lloyd kept his eyes wide to show interest. Then he remembered Dell's desire to find another dictionary among his own books. ''You—you've failed to *preserve* your copy of . . . *The Book of Webster's*?'' Lloyd asked it with as much incredulity as it was humanly possible to muster.

''Jesus, I didn't *mean* t'let 'er fall apart,'' Dell said defensively. ''I stuck the cover back on *real* often an' used the best damn tape I could find at the drugstore.''

Lloyd Benson spread his arms wide, grinned, did everything except cry ''Excelsior!'' Chuckling with delight, he even blew a kiss to the teenage girl who was gathering a pile of his favorite possessions from all over the house like some warped prehistoric homemaker. ''You don't have to go to all this

trouble, meat—neither do I! You're forgetting a primary tenet of all magic; one that comes in two parts
if I remember it properly—'If you build it'—which
means the magic within the heart of a shaman's
pupil—'he can go. And if he comes again, you can
build it *anew*.' I think that's it.'' Lloyd beamed on
first one and then the other of the murder team,
praying they didn't see many movies. ''And you *did*
go . . . free! Also, you *have* come again—so *I* can
give you another copy of *The Book*—because *I* am
the one who gave you your first copy. I alone!''

Dell saw the disappointment in Kee's expression and the sweaty, sweet hope in Lloyd B.'s. He
almost believed what he was hearing for a minute.
Then Dell sighed. ''Trouble with thet is, like yew
said, yew *are* the shamein. I am purely sorry I can't
jest take another dictionary from yew, but I figgered
everythang out on the long, lonely road. See, yew're
the *other* one who knows 'bout the phoenix—so
yew're the one keepin' me from havin' all the magic
fer myself.'' Dell shook his head and poked Lloyd in
the ribs with the unloaded Magnum, prodding him
forward again to the front door. ''Don't try t'talk me
outta it no more, Lloyd, 'cause this is hard fer me,
too, after seein' yore white beard 'n knowing yew're
who I been dreamin' about. Thet's why I decided
t'let you renew yourself 'steada my wringin' yore
scrawny neck.''

Lloyd had to open the door, step out. ''Well, I
'preciate it, whitemeat. You givin' me one chance
like this.'' It was colder, windier outside than before.
He would have asked for a coat except he'd be a lot

warmer soon unless he stalled them somehow. Dell was close behind, Kee was through the door, too, her arms filled with magazines he'd saved from prison. Thirty *years* of magazines, a complete *file!* "D'you think you should find something to use as a stake?" Lloyd realized the instant he'd asked it they might think of beef steak. "A pole to tie me to, in case I pass out from the smoke and—"

"Yew still think I'm dumb as dirt!" Dell said, cutting him off. "Kee, this wonnerful ol' boy thinks I'm so iggurant I'd burn a cross in his yard with *him* on it!"

Kee glanced around at the other houses in the block, just as Lloyd was doing—nobody was outside on this brisk late afternoon in Black Hawk—and giggled in nervous anticipation.

"Wouldn't thet be somethin'?" Dell said, marveling, moving in lockstep with Lloyd toward the leaves he'd raked before white people had once again changed the course of his life. "Yew 'n me standin' here waitin' for Lloyd t'turn into a phoenix whilst folks from all over this neighborhood come to kill us, 'cause they purely misunnerstood what we's doin'!"

"Yeah, boy," Kee put in, to the shivering Lloyd—"yew'd like *that*, wouldn't yew?"

Lloyd had no idea whether attempting to explain that many people knew of the phoenix, and therefore silencing him was idiotic, would help or hasten his doom. They were closely grouped as a trio on his front lawn, he expected momentarily to be told to stand amid the leaves, and part of Lloyd's mind wanted nearly as much to laugh as to scream.

"My rake," he said on impulse, suddenly pointing to the object on the ground. At least he might succeed in braining one of them with it if he had the chance—or would blows to *their* heads simply produce more giggles and smirks? "I could lean on that, couldn't I, Dell?" He turned his head to peer eagerly at the crazy peckerwood. "It'd steady my body . . . for a while."

For a moment Dell considered that. "Makes sense," he nodded. "Go ahead 'n git it. But don't yew forget I've still got this here gun on yew."

"I'm not apt to," Lloyd grunted, stooping to pick up the rake. Pain from his bleeding back and from the sickness inside of him made him dizzy, caused him to put out the fingers of one hand to balance himself on the ground while he reached with his other hand.

"'Apt,'" Dell chuckled appreciatively, wiping his seeping eye with his sleeve without knowing he did it. "Yew and yore nice words! I'd think them by theirselves would quallerfy yew t'become a new man." He turned his head sideways to catch Kee's eye, nodded for her to get a book of matches from his shirt pocket. Suppressing her delight, she fetched them and peeled the cover back, waiting with sunny readiness and eyes shiny as any angel's.

"Tell yew whut, Lloyd B.," Dell said. "If this magic works fer yew like I knows it will someday for me, I'll leave that hotty-totty BMW in the drive for yore nephew, an' yew kin come along t'California with me 'n Kee. Wouldn't thet be somethin'?"

Lloyd had his hand on the wooden handle of the

rake. He was trying to utilize his frailty as an excuse for working his legs and feet into the right position for one effective swing at them—one good cut of the bat that would either win or lose the World Series of his life. His major problem wasn't the terror of what would happen if he didn't connect; he knew what the penalty was for striking out in *this* contest. His problem was that he felt as if he might faint—pass out like an old woman—before he could either stand or swing.

At the exact instant when his leg and shoulder muscles were tensing and he had a solid grasp on the rake—just as gravity made his cold sweat of illness and fear run into his eyes, further undermining his courage—Lloyd noticed a car turning into the street half a block away. Another white man was at the wheel and, because that was a very good reason to consider following through with his desperate last-ditch idea, Lloyd came within a hair of taking his cut then.

Instead, he shoved himself awkwardly to his feet, using the rake, and switched another part of his mind to a remark Jesus made to God Almighty while the disciples slept—brief minutes before a multitude of high priests, commonfolk, and Judas Iscariot showed up to arrest Him: "Father, if thou be willing, remove this cup from me; nevertheless not my will, but thine, be done." Lloyd had borrowed the prayer for his own often enough. The first time, best as he could remember at the moment, was thirty-some years ago when he was convicted of a crime he did not commit.

"Be much obliged t'yew," said Dell, "t'step right in among them leaves." Speaking very softly, and smilin', Dell looked carefully to the left and then to the right for any indication of intrusion. Neither he, Kee, nor Lloyd Benson saw a neighbor on the street or in any of the front yards within view. "At least yew're going t'get 'em burnt up the old-fashioned way like yew wanted, no matter whut!"

Lloyd couldn't see where the car had gone, the car with the white driver he'd wanted so much to believe was a policeman coming to save him. Honky mother probably had pulled into another driveway, there to harass somebody, interrogate or bust them.

Because he was clearly obliged to die in a way Lloyd supposed would be extremely agonizing, he had to get immediately used to the weird notion that God's will was about to be exerted through the evil agency of . . . them.

Of course they *might* get near enough for him to whack away with the rake, Lloyd reminded himself encouragingly. It had a nice reach. But he couldn't cope with either of them now, one on one, regardless of the bluff he'd run inside the house. It had exhausted him after raking the yard—along with the wound, and all the horror. Maybe letting the girl go ahead and strike her matches, toss 'em into the leaves the way she was so obviously aching to do, would be less painful in the long run. Hell, who knew for a fact that a bullet from a Magnum was a better way to go than being burned? For all he knew the smoke might knock him out; then he wouldn't know it when the flames bit in . . .

"Yew have any last words under yore birth name of Lloyd . . . what *is* yore last name, Lloyd B.?" Dell inquired politely.

"B," Lloyd said tiredly. "Just that, meat." He lifted the rake an inch or so from the ground, experimentally. Kee had edged nearer with the matches. "Don't ask me if I want to pray, please. That word on your lips is a notion I find revolting."

Dell, unoffended, smiled and nodded. "But I *will* say some words over yew unless yew turns into a phoenix bird purty fast."

He nodded to Kee that it was okay t'strike a match, then glanced down to shift the Magnum to his other hand and pull the tattered *Book of Webster's* from his hip pocket.

Lloyd got his arms out as far as he could get them, then swung the rake in a gigantic arc. He did it without the slightest conscious thought—just *did* it, *then*.

He got good wood on Kee, sent her sprawling—

And the prongs at the end of the rake clawed at the skin of Dell's face, directly under his bad eye.

Because the rake's teeth weren't sharp enough to sink in, Lloyd instinctively thrust *up* at his end of the garden tool. That sent Dell tumbling backward to the ground, the automatic falling from his hand and bouncing away while Dell still held fanatically to *The Book* for all he was worth.

Flame whooshed up behind Lloyd, but he half-jumped, half-teetered a fast path out of the pyre.

He understood instantly somehow that the crazy
girl had dropped her matches on the leaves at the
instant when the rake struck her.

And now she was pouncing on the Magnum,
catlike. She came to a kneeling position directly in
front of Lloyd, the rest of her small form wobbly but
her aim at Lloyd's head perfectly level. Yet a seg-
ment of his brain sensed that she did not see him
personally—she saw groups of people, real or
imagined—ghosts, maybe. "Yew been jus' *starin'*
straight at me since we come for our visit! Don't
yew try to deny it!"

"Only because you're so—bright, so pretty,"
Lloyd said. She was getting back on her feet; the
resilience of youth was swiftly restoring her vigor.
He thought he heard a door slam somewhere, but he
didn't dare turn his head to find out. "I—I used to
teach other s-sweet young girls, in school." Heat
from the nearby bonfire was becoming overwhelming, dizzying Lloyd. "Kee, Dell is"—he stopped,
searched for words he prayed were the right ones—
"he isn't *for* you, dear. He's gotten you into *so much*
trouble. You see, Dell is—"

"Yew shut yore face!" Furious with loyalty to
her own dreams and visions, Kee tightened her
finger on the trigger. Her eyes seemed ready to pop
out. She was more insanely angry—more committed to her fantasies—than any man Lloyd had ever
seen in prison. Abruptly, unexpectedly, she gave
Lloyd an endearing and youthfully distant smile.
"Dellie's my very own dream man," she said, and
pulled the trigger.

Nothing at all emerged from the Magnum barrel at the same instant a bullet fired from Kirk Douglas's revolver drove Kee to the earth on her back as though she had been hammered onto the spot. Apart from the thump made by her when she hit, Kee didn't make a sound.

Half his face streaming a variety of substances, Dell, his gaze jumping from the twitching girl to an ashen, crouched Lloyd Benson and then to the short and compactly built man whose loaded police revolved was trained on him now. Dell re-entered the tableau with an air of mixed fascination, amusement, determination, and mild irritation showing in his expression. He appeared unhurt except for his ruined face, and quite untroubled by that.

"Stop right there, Dell," Detective Douglas commanded. He'd hoped not to have had to shoot either of the offenders, but he'd thought Kee was about to fire. "Mr. Benson, please get over behind me while I read this . . . man . . . his rights."

"Hey, Lloyd B., thet was real quick thinkin'," Dell called, veering off from the detective as Lloyd responded to Kirk's order. He noticed Kee lying next to the pyre. There were some signs of life in her, Dell thought, but she hadn't got all of the flameables onto the leaves. Well, it was a decent lookin' fire anyhow, Dell decided. He knew the detective was tellin' him what his rights was but he already knew 'em. Whatever else Douglas wanted, shit. "Lloyd B., yew see how purely satisfact'ry vi-carious sacrifice is? Yew didn't put a mark on me anywheres!"

Douglas wasn't actually *reading* Dell's rights to

him because he hadn't been that big a fool in years. He kept his piece centered squarely on the bastard as he recited them from memory, making sure Benson was safely to his rear. He'd have to do something soon for the female he'd shot; meanwhile, he surveyed the weird wreck of a man who had helped Kee McCaulter slaughter nearly one hundred people, wondering who had infected whom with which mad delusions. All Dell had in his hands was the remnant of a paperback book, but Kirk didn't let his gaze on the creep drift an inch, he just started walking toward Dell, eager to cuff him. *This* was a man with the charisma to influence the public? Kirk hoped very much he himself didn't really want Dell to do something foolish, as he had certainly done in coming to Illinois. The media had finally done something right by announcing Lloyd Benson's release, and Dell had his own sins to thank for making him so "glamorous."

The man smiled—the oddest, least humorous smile Kirk had had to suffer. "Yew look even less like thet actor in person. Yew ain't even got no cliff chin." Dell glanced down at Kee, sighed. "Yew ain't that bad a shot, though—better'n me." Dell flexed his fingers, his thumbs. "Kee was a gawdamn *good* shot."

"Dell, I want you to—"

"Just a minute. I ain't armed." The smile widening, Dell opened the book he had, squinted down at it with the eye that still functioned. Smoke was getting in it. "I ain't sure yew had any right t'come in here and interrupt no religious ob-servances. But jest so's yew'll know whut's happenin', I think yew oughter take a gander at this here picture."

The paperback was casually raised in front of Kirk's face. The fact that the man was still a safe twelve feet away only combined with Dell's natural and unthreatening gesture to draw Kirk's briefest attention. He glimpsed the drawing of a large bird, read the word *phoenix* . . .

And Dell was himself rushing onto the flaming pyre with a bizarre noise that sounded like the mixture of a murmur, a discordant hum, and a soulless, snuffling laugh.

Douglas tried to run forward to drag Dell out when he saw what had happened, but sparks were flying, then *continuing* to fly as the fire truly caught hold—and as the man in the middle of the flames energetically pumped both his legs and arms as if to *make the flames grow!*

"Dear Lord," Lloyd Benson said to himself, unable to tear his eyes away. "He's really *tryin'* it!"

"Go, Dellie—*go!*" Kee yelled as she rolled onto her good side. She was wide-eyed with excitement as she stared at the burning man, her own agony forgotten.

Kirk ripped off his suit coat, uprooted himself from where he had stood transfixed. Somewhere fire engines screamed, but they'd be too late to help this crazy son of a bitch. Kirk headed manfully forward.

But within a few scorching feet of the inferno, Kirk saw a sight he knew he would not forget if he survived to become the first immortal real-life police detective.

Inside the walls of flame engulfing and continually searing his flesh, Dell was *flapping his arms*! Skin was starting to come off his face in layers and the rest of it was charring, strips of it beginning to ignite before it could peel away—and *Dell was beating his arms, faster and faster!*

"My God," Kirk whispered, the heat driving him back a hasty pace, "I think he's trying to *fly!*"

Without warning then—unsupported by stake or by rake—Dell's body crumbled into the flames and lay still, smoldering.

Kee saw it happen. Kirk realized that when he finally gave up on Dell and went to try to help the girl.

But he couldn't. Nothing human could have. Douglas imagined for a moment that the teenage child was grimacing with pain. Dropping down beside her, his heart melting, he heard her mumble something strange about "eyes, ghost eyes"—and then something else.

He heard it clearly when he put his ear close to her lips and realized, too late, Kee's message was not meant for him.

"We *did* it, Dellie," she choked the words out on a plume of arterial blood. "Yew 'n me, we did it after all! See, Dellie—*we* makes it *an even hunderd!*"

"A man and woman teamed together for . . . mutual destruction . . . are one of the deadliest combinations known to crime. Between them they have a strike force of physical strength, deceit, resolution, sex appeal, boldness, and amorality."— Colin Wilson, *The Mammoth Book of True Crime* (Carroll and Graf, 1988).